Warmaster 9: Stormwatch Citadel

Melissa McShane

Cover design by Etheric Tales www.etherictales.com

Map by Matt Pivots

CHAPTER ONE

Aderyn huddled into her increasingly threadbare coat and concentrated on not shivering. Finion's Gate on the brink of winter was *cold*, with a wind that cut through the seams of her coat and clothing to seek out and nip at flesh. The contrast to the muggy heat of the southlands was nice for about three seconds, and then it turned into a different kind of misery.

"Slow down, Aderyn, we're not in a hurry," Owen said from close behind her where **[Keep Pace]** hustled him along.

"Of course we're in a hurry. It's freezing out here. I want to reach shelter as fast as possible. Also, walking fast warms me up. I don't know how you're not frozen solid." She glanced eastward at the sun's disk, yellow-white behind a high, thin overcast, and couldn't believe it was the same sun as beat down on the southlands. It was impossible to imagine this sun ever warming anything.

"I like winter," Owen said. "When I was in college, my friends and I used to go to Montana in the winter. Snowmobiling, skiing, sitting by the fire with a hot drink and a hotter girl—um. I'll just stop there. You probably don't want to hear about that."

"Thinking of anything hot warms me," Weston said. He didn't look cold either, with his <**Cloak of Mists**> hanging open over his coat, which was also open at the throat. "You should tell us quickly what snowmobiling is, because we're only a few minutes away from joining the gate queue."

"It—hmm. Remember the self-propelled carts at the Repository? Snowmobiles are like those, except you can drive them freely over the snow instead of on a rail and they go as fast as we did in Akdukhur's shaft in the Enchanterium." Owen came up even with Aderyn and clasped her hand. His skin was almost hot by comparison to hers. "Wow, you really are cold. You're right, we should move faster."

"We will be stuck in the queue for at least twenty minutes," Isold said. His eyes narrowed as he surveyed the line of people and wagons inching toward one of Finion's Gate's many entrances.

"Let's be glad it's not snowing," Livia said. "Though there's something I'm curious about. Do you think Tidecallers gain strength if they're out in the rain, or the snow?"

Aderyn came to a stop. "Are you serious?"

"Why not? I draw strength from the earth, why not drawing strength from a snowstorm? Or Windwardens in a tornado?"

"That is the most whimsical thing I've ever heard out of you," Weston said.

"It's something I think about more the closer we get to level twenty," Livia said. "Like, what could possibly be available to us at higher levels? The idea that it might be refinements on what we already have doesn't seem impossible."

"And *that* verges on optimistic. What have you done with my wife?"

Livia elbowed Weston in the side. "I'm not anticipating

getting there. Just thinking about what might be different. My older sisters liked to speculate about absurd skills that would make someone unstoppable, but I'm not sure that's the answer."

Aderyn shivered. "I agree it's interesting, but can we talk about it as we walk? Quickly? Explain to me again why we couldn't just *world door* into the Alabaster Inn's front yard."

"There's an interdiction on Finion's Gate like the one preventing magical transportation into the high-risk zone. It's why we had to arrive outside Ikharatia's gates, too. I think most cities, maybe even most villages, have it. It's to keep evil people from bypassing the system's protective barrier."

"But Varoun's <**Wand of World Door**> let us go straight to the front of the palace, and that was in the middle of a city."

Livia shrugged. "I think because that was a high-level item belonging to the ruler of the southlander kingdom, it was authorized to bypass the interdiction. It's still a dangerous exception. Imagine if Brigands could teleport past the gates? In a city the size of Ikharatia, or Finion's Gate, they could go anywhere."

"It probably affects trade, too, since the gate guards collect the entry fee." Owen came to a halt near the man and woman at the tail end of the queue. "I'm sure it's a substantial sum."

The man glanced idly over the five of them and did a double take. "Thunderation. You're Owen the Swordsworn!"

Owen blinked. "Um. Yes?"

The man grabbed Owen's hand and pumped it enthusiastically. "I made a bundle betting on you in the Glory Games. A real bundle. Margit, look who this is!"

The woman, Margit, eyed Owen speculatively, though she didn't look like she was Assessing him in any way but the most fundamental. "This is Owen? I guess I should thank you, too. Harus spent most of that money adding a couple of rooms onto our house."

"Well, ah, you're welcome." Owen retrieved his hand from Harus's grip. "You probably know these are the Wildcats, if you were there for the last Glory Games."

"No kidding! Well, of course, since you're married to the Swift." Harus frowned. "What in the blistering thunder are you doing standing in line? Go to the front of the queue!"

"Oh, we couldn't do that," Aderyn protested.

"Don't be silly. You're famous! Everyone will be fine with it." Harus poked the man in front of him. "Hey, recognize these folks? Glory Games champions! You don't mind if they cut ahead, right?"

The man and his three companions stared at Owen and then a little longer at Aderyn. "Of course not. Go on, we'll pass the word. Owen and the Wildcats—never thought we'd meet someone famous!"

Aderyn's cheeks flamed. She hated being stared at, and she hated even more getting preferential treatment, but what she hated most of all, she discovered, was standing around in the cold. So she followed Owen as they made their way up the line, slowly, pausing to receive congratulations or shake hands.

"This is so embarrassing," she whispered to Owen.

"I'll say. 'Owen and the Wildcats'—that sounds like an '80s glam rock band."

"Did you make that up to distract me?"

"No. Though that's why I said it out loud instead of keeping the thought to myself." Owen smiled and gripped her hand more tightly. "We made them happy, Aderyn, and it sounds like we made a few of them rich. We can enjoy this expression of their appreciation."

It took only a few minutes for them to make it past the queue to the gate. As they approached it, Aderyn watched the guards, who were clearly keeping an eye on them as a potentially dangerous anomaly. She could tell the moment the news of their identity reached the guards, because the uniformed men huddled together, talking intently while casting occasional glances at them, and then straightened to attention in a way they hadn't before. They looked so much like a bunch of children trying to impress adults Aderyn's embarrassment vanished. She was just Aderyn of Far Haven, nobody important, but if her fame as the Swift mattered to some people, she could be gracious enough to respect that.

The guards all wore the same uniform, black trousers and maroon shirts under heavy coats Aderyn envied, with metal insignia pins two inches in diameter on the right breast of the coats. The insignia were elaborate versions of the traditional symbols for the classes, almost all of them silver. The guard who wore a golden fireball pin stepped forward as they approached. "Welcome back to Finion's Gate," he said. "I'm Captain Gulan, and may I add my personal welcome. We're always glad to see our champions return. Is there anything we can do for you?"

"Thank you," Owen said, shaking Gulan's hand. "It's good to be back. We're just here for a few days, but we appreciate the welcome." He sounded calm, but **[Read Body Language]** told Aderyn he saw the ridiculousness of them being given special treatment just because they'd fought some duels and defeated a handful of miniature dungeons. On the other hand, until recently the Glory Games had played an integral part in determining who governed Finion's Gate, so it was likely the gate guards saw them differently.

The thought reminded Aderyn of how their last stay in Finion's Gate had ended, with the revelation that Councilor Raynir had manipulated the Games in a bid for power that had succeeded despite their team's unwitting interference. Raynir had paid a lot of money to send them on their way, and he'd implied they should never return. Aderyn had voiced this concern before they left Ikharatia, and Owen had said, "We'll only be there a few days, and we'll keep a low profile. The alternative is resupplying in Branlight or Elkenforest and then taking a chance on using *world door* to get far north, and that's both dangerous and time consuming."

"Not to mention we will gain better-quality information about the northlands in Finion's Gate, because it is the last large city before entering them," Isold had said. "There's no reason we should meet Raynir or even interact with the ruling class. We'll be safe."

Now they were doing the exact opposite of keeping a low profile. But if Raynir had spread the word that his number-one ranked champion and the top-ranked Glory Games team weren't to be allowed back in, it hadn't reached Captain Gulan. The captain shook hands with each of them, said, "No charge for you all, of course—and it looks like the Swift needs warming up, so if you need a recommendation for an inn—no? Well, then, enjoy your stay," and gestured them to pass through the open gate.

The tunnel through the city wall would have made Aderyn feel claustrophobic three months ago. Now, having nearly died from being buried in a tunnel collapse, her earlier fears of close spaces seemed ridiculous—or maybe it was just that she knew how narrow a space could actually get, and the low ceiling of the tunnel didn't come close to qualifying.

She followed Isold through the streets of Foundation, Finion's Gate's lowest level, to the Alabaster Inn, where they'd stayed on their last visit. Despite the name, its walls were made of large granite blocks; Livia had explained that actual alabaster was far too fragile for anything but decorative use, and granite might not be flashy, but it was strong enough to support tall structures. The inn was beautiful nonetheless, with marble sculptures of leaping fish along its eaves. It was also busy, with men and women passing through its oak front door in both directions.

"It didn't occur to me that there might not be room for us," Isold said, his steps slowing. "We did gain Gerant and Arlia notoriety the last time we stayed here. I won't begrudge them success, but I would prefer not to search for another inn."

"Let's go in and ask," Owen suggested.

Weston held the door open for two women exiting the inn, and the team hurried inside. The front room, with its oak-paneled walls, was as small as Aderyn remembered, but more brightly lit, and the five of them made it crowded. She wasn't sure where to go. Previously, they'd been greeted by the innkeepers' son Davith, but apart from a small family with two pre-teen children descending the stairs, no one else was there.

"I guess we could go into—" Owen began.

The door to the taproom swung open, and Davith pushed through. "Sorry, sorry about that, I—*hey!*" His voice squeaked in his excitement. "You're back! I didn't think we'd see you again!"

"It's good to see you, too, Davith," Owen said. "I don't suppose you have rooms to spare?"

Davith's eyes widened. "For you lot? Of course. Always! But —" He bit his lower lip in thought. "It might take a few hours. We're busier than usual these days, not just because of your fame rubbing off on the inn, but there are a lot more adventurers coming through recently. So we'll have rooms ready by this afternoon, if that's all right. I'm really sorry."

"Don't be sorry," Aderyn protested. "It's not like you knew we were coming. If anything, we should apologize for demanding special treatment."

Davith laughed. "You all left us with a reputation Pa says could otherwise take decades to achieve. You get special treatment." He brushed past them. "Just a minute—sorry, sir, madam,

I apologize for my distraction—you all want to wait in the taproom? Drinks on the house." He didn't wait for a reply, but approached the family on the stairs. The father looked irritated. The mother, by her stunned expression, looked as if she'd Assessed the team and knew who they were. The two children were idly hitting each other in a way Aderyn remembered her own siblings doing.

Owen grasped her elbow and steered her away before her idle regard could turn into rude staring. "Let's sit. I'm ready for something hot to drink."

A fire blazed in the taproom fireplace, which was made of smoothly rounded river stones and took up nearly all of one wall. The fire drew Aderyn like a hook pulls a fish from the water, its crackling warmth beckoning to her. She chose the table closest to the fire and sat with her booted feet on the hearth. "I love this fire. Owen, how about we adopt this fire and take it with us?"

"I think Gerant would have something to say about the giant hole in his taproom wall," Owen said. He sat beside her and pulled her to lean against him. "It is welcoming, though."

Isold and Livia sat as well, while Weston had a word with the bartender. The woman behind the bar was unfamiliar, but she had a friendly smile. In moments, the serving lads brought a coffee urn and a couple of teapots and a handful of oversized ceramic mugs. Aderyn drank the delicious, aromatic tea Owen poured for her and sighed in pleasure as heat coursed through her body, warming her insides as well as the fire did her outsides.

"You know something strange?" Livia said as she sipped her coffee. "I don't feel the need for morning coffee anymore. I only gave it up for two weeks, and I've had the habit for years. You'd think two weeks' abstinence wouldn't be enough to break that length of a habit. And it's not like I love it less." She saluted Weston with her mug. "This stuff is really good, too. It's more like there's a need the spell replacement ritual scoured out of me."

"So you got two benefits out of it," Weston said. "But I hope you don't plan to replace any other spells. You were downright cranky at the start."

"I thought about it, once or twice, but I only have so many sacrifices I can make. I think the system makes it hard to change out your spells to impress on spellslingers the need for caution and deliberation in choosing." Livia grinned. "Besides, the next thing I'd have to give up is sex, and I don't think swapping *mud minion* for *shatter* is worth that."

Weston shuddered. "Let's not do that."

Davith came back into the taproom and took a seat at their table. "So, where have you been? Did you do more Fated One things? You didn't break the level cap, people would have said— oh, sorry, I'm letting my tongue flap again."

"We did many amazing things, and were I a composer, I would turn them into songs," Isold said, winking at Aderyn.

"Songs! That would be great!" Davith rocked his chair back so he balanced on only two of its legs. "Greater than breaking the level cap. I know, that's what everyone always talks about, but I'm not going to accept the Call, so it doesn't matter so much to me. It's like what you said before, about how there should be classes for other things than adventuring. If I could choose an Innkeeper class, that would be great! But since it's random what you get— that's too risky for me. I don't want to be a Lightfingers, they're all on the verge of being crooked, and Swordsworns end up fighting monsters—sorry."

Owen's shoulders were tense with suppressed laughter. "Yeah, Davith, that seems a little unfair. Do you think the system only cares about people who adventure?"

Davith's lips pursed as he thought about this. "Maybe? I don't know. I can Assess people to find out their names and if they're married, but wouldn't it make sense if I could figure out what customers wanted through Assessing them?"

"I agree," Aderyn said. "I remember when I got the Call, how the system message said I'd achieved a level of development and could advance my destiny. That sort of implies the system doesn't think highly of those who reject the Call."

She immediately regretted saying this. She was fairly sure now that the system heard what she said and even knew some of her thoughts, and it was always so chatty and friendly what she'd just said verged on ingratitude for everything it had done for her. But this was something she'd thought about, on and off, since setting out on her adventures. There were plenty of non-classed people who did amazing things—why couldn't they have classes that fit their desires?

"Right, Aderyn?" Davith said.

Aderyn jerked out of her fugue. "Sorry, Davith, I was distracted. What did you say?"

"I said, I think the system has a reason for it," Davith said, not sounding offended. "But Pa says the world is what it is, and not everything happens for a reason."

"I... yes, I'm sure the system has a reason," Aderyn stammered.

The taproom door banged open, and the sound of several people laughing and talking at volume filled the room. Davith's eyes widened. "I forgot," he said. "I meant to tell you someone staying here says she knows you."

Aderyn had already recognized one of the voices. She shot out of her chair and had to grab its back to keep from knocking it over. In a voice that carried over the noise, she exclaimed, "*Jessemia!*"

CHAPTER TWO

The woman with chestnut hair at the head of the little group now entering let out a small shriek and flung herself at Aderyn, laughing. "Aderyn! I can't believe it! When did you get here?"

"We walked in about five minutes ago." Aderyn hugged her friend. Jessemia was still a few inches taller than Aderyn, but she'd put on muscle since they'd parted ways over two months before, and her chestnut curls were bound up in a tight braid, giving added definition to her heart-shaped face. "What are the odds?"

"Better than you think," Jessemia said. "How are you all? It's so good to see you again." She clasped Owen's hand as he rose from the table to greet her.

"Sit, and we'll trade stories," Owen said.

"Of course—no, wait a minute." Jessemia turned to the group she'd come in with, who were hanging back the way people do when they're not sure how much part to take in someone else's reunion. "This is Hectoran, Merris, and Pryton. I guided them here from Elkenforest. Everyone, this is the team I told you about.

The ones who swept the most recent Glory Games. Do you mind if I sit with them?"

Hectoran, a burly level eight Stalwart, shook his head ponderously. "Of course not. Not to be abrupt, but we don't expect more from you than we agreed on. Thanks again."

Jessemia shook hands with the trio in a professional way and, when they moved away to find a table, dropped into a chair between Aderyn and Weston. "They're nice people, but it will be good for them to go out on their own," she said in a low voice.

"You guided them here? As a quest?" Aderyn asked.

"It's what I've been doing for the last almost two months. I did some city quests with Ehren, Meladria, and Calista until I reached level nine, and then someone offered me an escort quest to take a couple of families from Guerdon Deep to Branlight. Ehren and Meladria got married, and they all wanted to retire, so I was looking for something new. It's interesting work, plus it turns out some quests are more suited to a person's class than others, and you gain more experience from them than other classes would. Though maybe you know that already." Jessemia showed no sign of self-consciousness at her potential error.

"*I* didn't," Weston said. "You mean, if I took quests that needed stealth, I'd gain experience faster?"

"That's what I understand. Anyway, I've been running all around the central plains, guiding people places. My map skills keep growing—I'm sure your maps look different from mine, Isold, but now I know what it's like for you."

Isold smiled. "Something we have in common."

"But you ended up in Finion's Gate, in the only inn we've ever stayed at here," Aderyn said. "How is that not extremely unlikely?"

"I guess you really do know them," Davith said, with an air of grudging acceptance. "Pa said you knew too many details to be lying, but I say, better skeptical than sorry."

Jessemia laughed. "Thank you for not kicking me out, Davith."

"I would never, not if Pa says not to," Davith protested. He rose from the table. "I have to get back to work, but let me know if you need anything, all right?" He collected the empty teapot and left the taproom.

"I'm sorry, this still seems coincidental," Livia said. "There must be more to the story."

"There is. This is my second visit to Finion's Gate. The first time, all anyone was talking about was Owen the Swordsworn and his team the Wildcats, and I overheard someone say the Alabaster Inn was where you all had stayed before and you'd made it famous. So I stayed here, too, because I thought it would be fun to have that connection. And then, when I arrived in the city two nights ago, I didn't want to hunt for a different good inn. So it's really only a coincidence that we're in Finion's Gate at the same time." Jessemia hugged Aderyn again. "Now, tell me everything. Owen won the Glory Games? And you defeated—I'm not sure I understand what tiny dungeons are."

"It's a long story, so I hope you have time," Aderyn warned.

Jessemia stretched. "I'm between quests and I'm not sure what I want to do next. But I'd make time for this if I had to."

By the time Aderyn, with interjections from the others, had given Jessemia an overview of everything they'd done since parting company in Guerdon Deep, it was time for lunch. They ate wedgers and bowls of thick, creamy tomato soup and washed it down with some of the Alabaster Inn's famous apple juice. Aderyn welcomed how the juice soothed her scratchy throat after how long she'd talked.

She eyed Isold curiously. The Herald had contributed details, but not many, and his uncharacteristic quietness worried her. When he did speak, it was almost never directly to Jessemia. Aderyn thought back to how Jessemia had treated him before her change of heart and complete alteration in behavior. Isold wasn't the type to hold a grudge, she thought, but what if she was wrong? Except—

Aderyn glanced at Jessemia, who ate her wedger in silence. Jessemia didn't behave any differently toward Isold than to any of them. And Isold *had* said, back when they'd separated, that his attitude toward Jessemia had changed enough he'd consider a romantic interlude with her. But that had been before his realization that his approach to sex no longer satisfied him. So he wasn't quiet because he was planning a seduction, and he wasn't quiet because he hated Jessemia, but what did that leave?

Aderyn told herself to stop fretting about it. It was just as likely she was seeing things that weren't there, and nothing was wrong between Isold and Jessemia. Besides, it wasn't as if they could team up, not with them being nine levels higher than the Pathseer, and Isold and Jessemia wouldn't be thrown into each other's company for any tension or awkwardness to be an issue.

"So, just to be perfectly clear," Jessemia said, "you gained six levels since I last saw you. That's astonishing. I was told I leveled fast to gain two in that time."

"That is fast," Owen said. "Do you think it was association with the Fated One, or just hard work?"

"The latter, I think. If I was in your team, that would be different." Jessemia scraped the last of her soup from her bowl.

"But your skill ranks are also higher than normal," Aderyn

said, having Assessed Jessemia earlier. "I don't have an explanation for that, unless it's related to the kinds of quests you've been doing. Maybe using your class skills as part of a related quest improves those ranks like it increases your experience."

"I didn't know that. I really have no idea what's normal, after the way I started." Jessemia took on the glassy-eyed look of someone reading her Codex. "All I know is my **[Improved Map Access]** went from three ranks to twelve over that time period. I'm sure that's high for a level ten Pathseer."

"What does your map show you?" Isold asked. He hadn't spoken abruptly, but he'd been so quiet his entrance into the conversation startled Aderyn.

"You know how you told me your maps populate themselves as you move through cities?" Jessemia said. "It's like that, only for wilderness areas. And the more often I travel a route, the more detailed the map becomes. Also, if I accept a quest to guide someone to a place I've never been, the place appears on my map along with some basic landmarks that let me plot a course. And that's gotten more detailed over time, too."

"Remarkable," Isold said. "Of all the Pathseers we've met in our travels, you're the only one we've known well. I admit to being fascinated by your skill, since it seems parallel to a Herald's."

"I understand. Who knew we would have so much in common, between that and the various Knowledge skills I have?" Jessemia smiled and saluted Isold with her glass. Isold smiled in return, but Aderyn thought he looked uncomfortable. She'd long ago told herself to stop wishing for impossible things, but **[Read Body Language]** was so effective on Owen she couldn't help thinking how nice it would be if it worked on everyone. At the very least, she might understand what was wrong with Isold.

"And you've completed four **[Fated One's Destiny]** quests,"

Jessemia went on. "Do you have any idea how many more there are?"

"No idea at all," Owen said. "I hope we're getting close, though. What would really suck would be to reach level twenty and have to go on fighting and questing for years without leveling any more. That would feel like such a waste."

"I think we are close," Aderyn declared. "The first three—not counting Tarani's memorial—those each tested a different trait. But this newest one is so generic it must represent a turning point in the quest chain."

"You said, cunning, compassion, and strength," Jessemia said. "I can't think what else would be left. Knowledge?"

"It's possible accessing Tarani's memorial meant knowledge," Isold said, "and that makes it more connected than we realized."

"Good point," Weston said. "Not knowledge. Wisdom? Endurance?"

"I don't think we'll know until we learn more about the new quest," Owen said. "We should ask around about it this afternoon. See what we can learn about the Northlands. We also need to see about unloading some of the stuff we've been hauling around. I like the idea of making a clean start if we're traveling into uncharted territory."

"I can sell things," Weston said. "As long as it's something Isold or Livia has identified, I'm the best of us at getting a good deal. Isold and I should go together when it's time to buy."

"I'll clean out the **<Knapsack of Plenty>** before I go out to talk to people," Aderyn said. "Jessemia, you want to come with me? I'm sure you've had more adventures than we've had time to talk about."

"Of course!" Jessemia pushed her chair back and stood. "Do you have rooms? I'm on the third floor."

"Oh." Aderyn had forgotten that little detail. She didn't want to empty her knapsack onto a table in the middle of the taproom. "Davith said nothing's available yet. Do you mind if I do this in your room? Everyone, we'll need to stow the things we're keeping elsewhere, and then Weston can take the **<Knapsack of Plenty>** and just sell whatever's in it."

"We'll wait here," Owen said. "No need to rush. We may need to spend several days in Finion's Gate."

Aderyn scowled. "How sure are you that's a good idea, sweetheart?"

"Why wouldn't it be a good idea?" Jessemia asked. "Isn't getting information the important thing, and not speed?"

They hadn't explained what had happened with Raynir at the end of their amazing Glory Games careers, given that they were sitting in public where anyone could overhear. "Let's go upstairs, and I'll explain."

Jessemia's room wasn't as large or as nice as the one Aderyn remembered having, but it was still a size that allowed for a bed big enough for two, a wardrobe rather than a clothespress, a rocking chair padded with two fat cushions, and a washstand with hot and cold running water. Jessemia closed the door behind them and said, "There's a lot you didn't say, isn't there?"

"Well, yes, but half of that was because so much happened, and the other half shouldn't be made public, not because I didn't want you to know." Aderyn set the **<Knapsack of Plenty>** on the bed and opened it. It never looked full no matter what they shoveled into it, but when it was open, Aderyn could clearly see how much crap, as Owen put it, had accumulated.

"I didn't mean that as prying. Sorry." Jessemia perched on the edge of the rocking chair and used both feet to keep it from moving.

"It's not prying. We're friends. Friends share things with each other." Aderyn extricated one of the **<Everburning Logs>**, then the other, and set them on end on the floor. "We learned Chief Councilor Raynir was manipulating the Games so he could take permanent control. He got Owen killed and he seriously pissed me off. So we might have agreed not to come here again. I doubt he'll know we're in town, and there's not a lot he can do—" She stopped abruptly.

"What? You thought of something?"

"No. Just—nothing. I think." Aderyn sat on the edge of the bed and stared at Jessemia. "I think we shouldn't underestimate Raynir's commitment to his political position. *We* know we're not a threat to him, but scared people do crazy things. I need to remind everyone of that."

Jessemia started the rocking chair moving. "You're different now. You were always strong and capable, but... I don't know. I guess leading an army had an effect on you."

Aderyn laughed. "They never did figure out whether to call me 'sir' or 'ma'am'. It was funny in an awkward way." She dragged the knapsack onto her lap and began pulling things out of it. "Wow, there sure is a lot of—oh. I forgot this was in there." She pulled out the pieces of the broken laboratory minion, the one shaped like a crab, and showed them to Jessemia.

Jessemia gasped. "What is it?"

"A Forged creation that doesn't work. I'm going to give it to my grandfather Marrius. Definitely not selling it."

Jessemia picked it up and examined it. "Is Isold feeling all right?"

Aderyn paused with her hand on the <**Laborer's Staff**>. "What makes you ask that?"

"He was just really quiet. And he wouldn't look at me. I was afraid maybe he still... well, you know. Thinks about how I tried to use him." Jessemia wasn't meeting Aderyn's eyes, and her cheeks were red.

"I'm sure that's not the case," Aderyn said, pretending she hadn't wondered exactly that only a short while ago. "We've all been through a lot, and Isold had some realizations I shouldn't be the one to share. You should talk to him. At the very least, I think you both deserve to see what kind of friendship you have now that you've changed. I mean both of you have changed."

"That makes me so curious I want to run down there and drag Isold into the private parlor immediately for a conversation," Jessemia said wryly. "Seriously, I wish I didn't have those memories, but I use them to keep myself focused on not slipping back into bad habits."

"I understand."

Aderyn finished emptying the knapsack and set about putting things back into it, more neatly this time. The <**Knapsack of Plenty**> worked like she remembered her father's kitchen pantry: it started out organized, and then things got taken out or added, not always in an orderly way, and before you knew it, everything was a cluttered mess. "Hmm. Most of these things we got from the Enchanterium, we can sell, if Weston can find a buyer who appreciates them. Not the broken minion, and not the <**Laborer's Staff**>."

"It doesn't look like a powerful weapon. What does it do?" Jessemia picked the staff up and ran her fingers over the crook.

"Transforms into several useful tools, like an axe or a shovel." The <**Draftsman's Pen**> should stay, and if they were heading into the Northlands, they ought to keep at least one of the <**Everburning Logs**>. No, better make it both of them.

Satisfied, she closed the knapsack and set it on the floor. "Is it all right if I leave the rest of this here for now?"

"Sure. Davith was very clear on how they prize their reputation for security." Jessemia propped the staff in a corner. "I should probably search for new quests, because I finished that escort quest a couple of days ago and I get antsy if I'm not questing." She laughed. "A year ago I would have laughed myself silly to know I'd feel that way now."

"Have you considered going back to Obsidian?" Aderyn asked.

Jessemia sobered. "Not really. The thought of home—I mean, it isn't really home anymore, now that Papa lost everything—anyway, the thought of it feels uncomfortable. Embarrassing, even. I'm not that awful person anymore, but no one in Obsidian knows that. There really isn't anything there for me. I sent a message to Papa so he knows I'm alive, of course. But I'd rather stay in the east. I know it's different for you."

"Yes. I look forward to settling in Far Haven eventually, having my children grow up with their cousins." It was Aderyn's turn to laugh. "Look at me, making far-future plans when we don't even know what the next quest entails."

"It's natural, isn't it? Thinking about the future? I know when exciting or scary things happen to me, I tell myself 'this will make a great story for my grandchildren,' even though I'm not planning to marry any time soon. I'd have to meet someone first."

"I guess it's not so unexpected." Aderyn made neat piles of the belongings they were keeping and shouldered the <**Knapsack of Plenty**>. "You could come with me this afternoon if you want. We can look for information about our separate quests together."

Jessemia smiled. "I'd love that."

CHAPTER THREE

That evening, Aderyn and Jessemia joined the others in the private dining room reserved for paying guests. Half-paneled in maple below and painted a pale eggshell blue above, it was smaller and more intimate than the taproom, with heavy floor-length drapes in rose and silver patterned damask that muffled the sounds of conversation. Though it had four oblong tables that each seated six, only theirs was occupied. "Gerant insisted on giving us privacy," Weston said. "I almost had to force him to accept payment for our rooms. He must be doing *really* well."

"That would have been welcome last time, before we stumbled into a fortune," Owen said. He lifted the domed silver cover off an enormous roast goose and drew his belt knife to carve. "You all want to pass around the rest of these dishes?"

Aderyn loaded her plate with potatoes mashed in their ruddy skins, a pile of roasted root vegetables with honey glaze, soft white rolls the size of Weston's fist, and most decadent of all, fresh green peas that must have come from someone's greenhouse and were so out of season they were probably grown by magic. Owen set a slice of breast meat on her plate, and she fell to eating happily. "Nobody talk," she said through a mouthful of goose and potatoes. "Appreciate Arlia's genius."

Everyone followed Aderyn's advice, speaking only to request someone to pass a particular dish. Aderyn had never felt so content. She idly considered what she and Owen would do about cooking when they retired from adventuring. She could handle the basics, but she wasn't an inspired cook like her father, and she'd never asked Owen if he knew how.

She remembered her conversation with Jessemia that afternoon. That was two times now she'd fallen into daydreaming about a future she couldn't guarantee would ever happen. That was fine as long as they were in civilization, but she needed to control herself when they headed north. Being distracted by what might happen could only be a disaster.

Weston mopped up the last of his gravy with a soft roll. "I'm full. Call me picky, but much as I liked southern cuisine, I'm glad to be back where I recognize all the food on my plate. Though, I wonder if Arlia could learn to fry parotta. I'll miss that most."

"If Weston is full, it's time to talk," Owen said. "I have some information, and Aderyn, you said you didn't have much luck, but Jessemia did."

"There were a lot of people wanting to be guided north," Jessemia said. "None of them had specific destinations in mind, and most of them hoped *I* knew where they should go. They all talked about locating abandoned settlements, which makes no sense. I didn't think humans had ever lived north of Finion's Gate."

"I learned nothing," Livia groused. "Everyone wanted to buy Livia Stonefist a drink, but they all only wanted me to talk about our dungeon victories. Isold, I'm going to guess you learned the most. What can you tell us about the Northlands?"

"Getting information was easy," Isold said, "requiring almost no reliance on my Herald's skills or even on my reputation as a member of the Wildcats. It seems Finion's Gate is crawling with adventurers keen on restoring human settlements so they can stake their claim to the land in advance of the new kingdom forming there."

"The *what?*" Livia and Aderyn said in unison.

Isold smiled. "Possibly a lesson is in order, if you'll indulge me. My ranks in **[Knowledge: World Lore]** told me very little about the Northlands. About one-third of the land is a high-risk zone, rumored to be home to a number of dangerous monsters, including dragons."

"Just like every other high-risk zone," Weston said. "Which means it's likely worse than anyone can imagine, if the Blighted Range is representative."

Isold nodded. "The rest of it used to be inhabited by humans, but those settlements were abandoned several hundred years ago. The implication is that the level cap made the area too dangerous for non-adventurers, even with the system's protection over settlements, but I'm not sure that's true. Humans live in many places with higher-level monsters roaming the area, and they thrive there."

"The level cap gets blamed for a lot of things, I see," Owen said. "Sorry. Go on."

"As I said, the Northlands settlements were abandoned, and the land became a hunting ground for adventurers looking to level up through killing monsters. This is as much as I knew before this afternoon. Today I learned that while this is all true, hunting the Northlands wilderness is considered a desperate gamble, not because of danger but because prey is relatively scarce and the weather is cold and rainy even at the height of summer and stormy and snowy the other three-quarters of the year. Grinding for experience up north is, I'm told, the sort of thing adventurers do because they think their luck is superior to everyone else who tells them it's a bad idea." Isold leaned forward. "But now we have this supposed new kingdom being established."

"I heard those rumors, too, but I thought the idea of a new kingdom was made up," Owen said. "You're saying it's real?"

"I don't know what to believe," Isold said. "Certainly almost every adventurer here believes it enough to make the journey. I spoke to a few people who said they weren't sure it was true, but they didn't want to miss out if it was. Hence their willingness to head north at the beginning of winter, which to me sounds potentially suicidal."

"That explains why I got such good prices on some of our stuff," Weston said. "The shopkeepers I spoke to were all eager to replace their stock. And the shelves did look bare. We might have trouble resupplying."

"But this could be good news," Aderyn said. "If it's these adventurers who are making the land less peaceful, and we're supposed to resolve their issues, that might be what it takes to fulfill the [Eye of the Storm] quest. Where did these rumors about a new kingdom come from? And why is the idea so appealing to so many?"

"As far as I can tell, no one knows where the stories started," Isold said. "Everyone cited information that boiled down to 'some fellow at a tavern told me his brother's cousin heard it.' Which is what makes me most suspicious, frankly. If no one claims responsibility for founding this supposed kingdom, where did knowledge of its proposed existence come from?"

"You mean you couldn't find patient zero," Owen said. "Sorry. I mean, the person who started the rumors."

"What an evocative phrase. No, I did not, and I didn't try to. Finion's Gate is big enough, and the stories have been going on long enough, that identifying a source would be impossible without some very specialized magic or skills." Isold glanced briefly at Jessemia. "A Pathseer could do it, but not, I'm afraid, at level ten."

"I understand," Jessemia said. "The idea of having such skills eventually excites me. I know you don't mean anything derogatory by it."

"Of course not." Isold inclined his head politely. "As to the fundamental question, humans are always pushing the boundaries of civilization. It wasn't so long ago that the plains between Obsidian and Guerdon Deep were uninhabited, and we've seen how many villages and towns are there now. Granted, I hadn't realized the pressure to own land was so great as to make the Northlands appealing, but possibly the promise of a kingdom—an organized governing entity to provide greater protection against monsters and environmental threats—is what increases the appeal."

"But if the thing about a kingdom is a lie, those people are going to come into conflict with each other," Livia said, "which brings us back to *our* quest. I don't like it. The Northlands are a big place even if a third of them are off limits. We might be striking out at random."

"I agree, but it's too early to worry about that. We still don't know enough." Aderyn turned to Isold. "Any ideas?"

Isold nodded. "Tomorrow I will dig deeper into the history of the Northlands. One of my informants told me the Orelaine Library on Terrace One has the largest collection of books and scrolls in the world, bigger even than the library at the University of Ikharatia. It's open to the public, free of charge, though the person also said the librarians accept payment for their services if someone wants to hire a researcher. I anticipate learning a great deal."

"We'll do some searching on our own, then," Owen said.

"Owen, is that safe?" Aderyn asked.

"Aderyn, I'm sure Raynir isn't in a position to know about every person who enters Finion's Gate." Owen clasped her hand in reassurance. "I don't think we need to hole up here. We'll be careful. No drinking at other taverns, no spreading word of our presence. We won't make contact with any of the people we met during the Games. That should be enough."

His recitation didn't comfort Aderyn as much as she'd hoped. She smiled anyway. "We won't be here long, right? So that will be fine."

As she spoke, someone knocked twice on the door, and Gerant pushed it open. "Sorry to intrude, but you have visitors."

"Visitors? You don't mean strangers, do you?" Owen sounded calm, but **[Read Body Language]** told Aderyn he suspected Gerant of revealing their presence at the Alabaster Inn.

"They're not strangers, and I promise you I wouldn't capitalize on your fame," Gerant said. He didn't sound offended, but Aderyn suspected he was good at concealing his emotions from accusatory or irritated guests. "It's Raewyn and Gabryl."

Aderyn shot Owen an annoyed glare. "What was that about not making contact?"

"Hey, I didn't send them an engraved invitation!" Owen exclaimed. "I don't know why they're here. It's not like they're close friends."

"Would you prefer I tell them you're not staying here?" Gerant asked, still distant and polite.

"No. No, it's fine." Owen ran his hands through his hair in a typically frustrated gesture. "Will you show them in, Gerant? And I'm sorry I implied anything bad about your confidentiality."

Gerant nodded and shut the door.

"Who are Gabryl and Raewyn?" Jessemia asked.

"They were Glory Games champions also sponsored by Raynir," Aderyn said. "They were secretly in love, and the Beguiler Damaris forced Gabryl to reveal their affair in front of an entire stadium of people, which ruined their careers. But now Gabryl is retired, and Raewyn has a new sponsor and will be competing in the next Games. Oh, I hope their coming here together means they're, well, together!"

"You're an unabashed romantic," Livia drawled.

The door opened, and Raewyn entered, followed by Gabryl. The two didn't look any different than they had the last time Aderyn saw them. Raewyn the Swifthands still moved as gracefully as if she was only lightly connected to the earth, more lithe than a Windwarden. Gabryl, tall and muscular, had the same grim expression Aderyn was familiar with. Before anyone could speak, Aderyn Assessed Raewyn, looking for only one thing.

"You're married!" she exclaimed. "I'm so glad!"

That made Gabryl's grimness disappear and Raewyn's cheeks redden. Raewyn clasped Gabryl's hand and smiled. "You were right," she said to Aderyn. "About everything. Making amends gave us the chance to really evaluate our relationship, what it would look like once we no longer had to conceal it, and this is the agreement we came to."

"I'm teaching swordplay to those who come to the city wanting to be Glory Games challengers," Gabryl said, "and Raewyn is training hard to regain her position as a champion."

"Better than regain," Raewyn said. She nodded at Owen. "Now that it's been proven that Kendria can be beaten, I'm even more determined to show I'm the best."

"Good luck," Owen said. "I love the sound of that."

"Yes. Too bad you bowed out. You and I never did fight." She winked. "I'd like to say I could take you, but all I'm sure of is it would be spectacular."

"But we're not here to chat." Gabryl frowned. "We came here to warn you, once we learned you were back. You may be in danger."

Owen stilled. "Are you talking about Raynir?"

Aderyn refrained from elbowing her husband in the ribs. **[Read Body Language]** would convey her "I told you so" more clearly than any gesture.

"We don't know why he's got it in for you," Gabryl said, "but I pay attention to the councilors these days. They haven't announced a new form of government, which makes sense because that's the sort of thing that should be hashed out over time and it's only been a few weeks. But that means anything might happen, and I don't like uncertainty. No idea how he learned you're in town, but he's got people secretly searching for you."

"But he must know we're at the Alabaster Inn," Aderyn said. "He knows it's where we stayed before."

"That's why you're worried, though," Weston said. "If his people are looking for us on the sly, that means they want to find us when we're at a disadvantage. Otherwise he'd send a messenger here. And it means whatever he wants from us, it can't be linked to him."

"Right." Gabryl nodded. "It seemed suspicious. You helped me and Raewyn before, and I wanted to return the favor. Don't go anywhere alone, and stay off Terrace Two—it's where Raynir's presence is strongest."

"We'll keep that in mind. Thanks." Owen extended a hand to Gabryl, who shook it firmly.

"We can't stay long, or I'd ask about where you've been that you all look like you've gotten some sun," Raewyn said with a grin. "It's good to see you again."

"You, too," Aderyn said. "Thanks—and congratulations."

When Gabryl and Raewyn were gone, Owen said, "So, tomorrow Isold is going to that library. I was going to suggest the rest of us spread out and see what we can learn based on this information, but it sounds like we're better off staying indoors."

"It's going to snow tomorrow, anyway," Jessemia said. She grinned when they all stared at her. "I have ten ranks in **[Improved Survival]**. That gives me a good sense of the weather for the next twenty-four hours."

"That's astonishing," Aderyn exclaimed. "And how useful to a Pathseer. To anyone, really."

"And I didn't even have to be wounded to get it. One of the stable hands at my—at Papa's house could tell when a storm was coming because his right knee was a mass of scar tissue and it twinged." Jessemia stretched. "If you want, I can ask around tomorrow. This Raynir person isn't looking for me."

"We don't want you to put yourself out," Isold said.

"It's no trouble. If I can confirm there's really someone founding a kingdom somewhere, I might take an escort quest guiding a team there, and I'll need that information for myself. But if you don't want me to—"

"No, it's a good idea," Aderyn said, glaring at Isold, who ignored her. Her earlier assumption that he didn't resent Jessemia was looking less likely by the minute. "And if you can locate shops selling winter clothing, that's something we need, too. My old coat isn't good for anything but rags, Livia says. But now I'm ready for bed. Owen?"

They trudged upstairs as a group, saying good night to Jessemia at the third-floor landing. Jessemia didn't look hurt by Isold's rather chilly words, but her "good night" wasn't enthusiastic. Aderyn mulled that over all the way to her room. She knew she was closer to Jessemia than the others were, but they'd all become friends, at least, during the journey to Guerdon Deep, and Isold was normally the politest and kindest of all of them.

The moment their bedroom door shut behind them, Owen said, "All right. Let's have it."

"Have what?" Aderyn was still thinking about Jessemia and Isold. "Do you think Isold is still angry?"

"What? What does Isold have to do with it?"

Aderyn shook her head, trying to focus. "What are you talking about?"

"You were right about Raynir. Go ahead and say it. Say 'I told you so.'" Owen sounded weary rather than hostile, but his abruptness put Aderyn's back up.

"I wasn't going to say that," she lied.

"You already said it with your body language. You're entitled to the actual words."

Aderyn closed her eyes and silently counted to five. "I did think it at first, that's true, but I don't think I should look for ways to lord my being right over you. Besides, if Raynir has people out looking to beat us up or something, this is not the time to worry about who should have listened to who."

Owen winced. "All right. I deserved that. But—yeah. I'm sorry, and I'd like us to move past this. Do you have any ideas? This is a kind of war, after all, and we need a winning strategy."

Aderyn sat on the edge of the bed and pulled her boots off. They were looking worn, too. Maybe she needed a whole new wardrobe. "If all we intend to do is stay here long enough to learn what we need for this quest, the strategy is to stay hidden and not give Raynir any openings. If we have to fight him more directly, I'll need more information. My preference is to stick with keeping ourselves out of his reach."

"That's a plan I can get behind," Owen said. He pulled off his own boots, standing like a stork with one leg raised and then the other. Then, to her surprise, he knelt before her and took her hands gently in his. "How can I help *you*?"

Aderyn smiled. "I didn't think I needed help."

Owen didn't return her smile. "You're still having nightmares. It breaks my heart to wake to you clinging to me and sobbing like you're terrified you're still buried alive. Aderyn, I love you. I want to be the one who protects you from the things you can't fight. But I can't challenge a dream to a duel."

Aderyn's heart swelled. She leaned forward and kissed him, a long, lingering kiss that stirred her body's desires. "I think it takes time. It hasn't even been a week since it happened. I need you to do exactly what you've been doing, comforting me and holding me. Oh. And I need one more thing."

"What's that?"

She kissed him again, caressing the side of his face. "I need you," she said, "to tear all my clothes off and have your way with me."

Owen's eyebrows raised. "Is that all? And here was me thinking you wanted something challenging."

She slid her hand inside his shirt. "The challenge is that it might take more than once to satisfy me."

Owen smiled. "Challenge accepted."

CHAPTER FOUR

They cuddled together afterward, not speaking, Owen's warm breath stirring the hair falling over Aderyn's forehead. For once, the memories that always lurked at the back of her awareness were gone. "I needed that," she said.

"Me too," Owen replied. "It's been a while. Not that I was counting days or anything."

"I was. Two weeks."

Owen laughed and drew her closer. "An eternity, then."

Aderyn kissed him lightly. "Oh, Owen. I feel so much better. I wish—" She stopped herself, unsure if she should share her concerns about Isold with Owen. It wasn't as if she had anything concrete to go on.

"What do you wish? Because I'm afraid I'm going to need some time." Owen waggled his eyebrows suggestively.

She slapped him lightly on the shoulder. "Not that." She recalled Jessemia's downhearted expression when they'd said good night and made a decision. "Did you think Isold behaved strangely to Jessemia?"

"Strangely? No. Well, not strangely for the average person who's trying to decide how attracted he is to someone. Since it's Isold, it's strange that he wasn't forthright about it. If that makes sense."

Aderyn sat up, breaking the gentle hold Owen had on her shoulder. "Attracted to Jessemia? But he barely looked at her, and he was almost curt when he spoke. That's the opposite of attraction."

Owen's smile became an amused, rueful expression. "Sweetheart, you're the one who told me men in this world have to approach the women they're interested in. Haven't you ever seen a man who finds a woman attractive and is afraid he'll be shot down?"

Aderyn decided to ignore the nonsense phrase "shot down." "Of course! Well, maybe. Hmm. I guess I never thought about it. All the men who ever approached me were direct and fearless about it. But that can't be right. Isold and Jessemia are friends. He knows she wouldn't be cruel."

"At the risk of lecturing you, it's not that simple. My guess is Isold doesn't know how to approach a woman now that he understands his own desires better, and the fact that the one he's interested in is a friend complicates matters because she isn't someone he'll spend a night with and never see again." Owen pulled Aderyn down to lie with him again. "It's fine, Aderyn. Isold and Jessemia will work things out. Don't feel like it's your responsibility to make them happy."

He'd spoken kindly, but Aderyn felt the secret sting in his words. "I don't try to save everyone."

"I didn't mean that, love. I just know that you care very much about your friends' happiness, and you don't like to sit by and watch them suffering. That's a wonderful trait. But you shouldn't let it make *you* unhappy. They wouldn't want that."

Aderyn hadn't ever thought about it that way. "You're right. That's a better way to look at it."

Owen pulled her close. "You know," he said, "you are the best thing that's ever happened to me. I remember, sometimes, my life in my world, and it feels like a dream, with all the pointless things I used to do being hazy and tangled together. And then I remember the moment I knew I was in love with you, and that moment is so clear by comparison it feels like nothing else was real."

"What moment was that?"

Owen chuckled. "It wasn't anything extraordinary. We were on the caravan route from Guerdon Deep to Ashenfell, the two of us walking point, and you saw an unusual bird and pointed it out to me. And you were so excited—I guess it was a rare bird—and you looked at me with this amazing smile, and it hit me like a brick to the chest. I knew then I wanted to wake up next to that smile every day for the rest of my life."

Unexpected tears came to Aderyn's eyes. She blinked them away. "That's so beautiful. Nothing like that happened to me— just realizing gradually that you were more than a friend. And now, here we are."

"Here we are." Owen ran his fingers over her bare shoulder and down her arm. "Sometimes I think about what we'll do when we're done adventuring. Settle down in Far Haven, have kids. The weird thing is those thoughts aren't... I don't know the right word. What we're doing now is so extraordinary, so full of adventure, you'd think anything that simple and peaceful would be dull. But to me it feels like a different kind of adventure."

Aderyn nodded. "That's a good way to put it. It's how I feel, too. I try not to dwell on that future too much, because it could be a distraction from our quest, but I can't help wondering what kind of world we will give our children."

"Something amazing," Owen said. "Limitless possibilities. Or they'll choose not to accept the Call and be amazing some other way."

The idea was uncomfortable, and Aderyn didn't know why. She took a moment to think about it. "I hope our children become adventurers, though. Wouldn't it be, I don't know, a waste of our efforts if they didn't want to level as high as possible?"

"I understand what you mean, but it has to be their choice—you know that. So, I agree with you that I hope they'll follow in our path, but—" He laughed. "We don't even have kids yet and we're planning their futures. We should probably stop here."

Aderyn giggled. "Yes, because that path leads to supposing we raise our kids alongside Weston and Livia's, and they fall in love, and..."

Owen groaned. "Matchmaking for nonexistent children. Maybe we need to head north sooner than I thought. Do something real and present rather than daydreaming."

"A few days, and we'll be on our way," Aderyn said.

AT BREAKFAST THE NEXT MORNING, ISOLD WAS talkative and alert and sounded just like himself. He even included Jessemia in his remarks and met her eyes without hesitation. "I will be fine going to the Orelaine Library on my own," he told Owen. "I'm not without ranks in [Awareness], and with my map being as detailed as it is, I defy any denizen of Finion's Gate to find his way more easily than I can."

"I'm not saying you can't," Owen said. "I'm saying I'm certain Raynir has his people watching this place, and they'll be on your tail the instant you step out the door. If they have more in mind than just following you, they'll be in a position to lay an ambush."

"Which is why I think I should *transport* Isold somewhere closer to the library that they won't be watching," Livia said. "They can watch this inn all they want if we're not limited to using the front door."

"Even *transporting* to the nearest lift would be an advantage," Isold persisted. "Raynir isn't stupid, and even he isn't so paranoid as to have someone watching every single lift on every terrace. We can't let ourselves be trapped by what might not be real fears. We have to gain more knowledge if we're going to succeed in our quest."

"Isold is right," Aderyn said. "We have three choices. We can hole up in the inn and wait for Raynir to get bored and leave us alone. We can leave for the Northlands now, or for some other city where we can resupply, and take our chances on an extended journey. Or we can be cautious, get what we need here, and get out."

Owen regarded her suspiciously. "You're not just talking about Isold, are you."

"It makes sense for me to be the one who goes shopping, if Isold can't." Aderyn gripped his hand tightly. "I can't be ambushed, and if I'm alert, which I always am, I can't be targeted by anything short of a Deadeye of my level or higher. And we already know Raynir doesn't have anyone like that on tap. If I go with Jessemia, I'll be back before noon."

Owen's gaze slid to Jessemia. Jessemia nodded. "There are shops selling what you need very near here. I know where they are and I know the shortest route between them. We really won't be out in the open for long."

"I hate this plan," Owen said. "But you make sense, all of you. Isold, how far away is the library?"

Isold got the faraway look of someone consulting his system

map. "It's several miles north of where we are, but on Terrace One, so another quarter-mile up. Not far at all."

"Too far for *transport*," Livia said, shaking her head. "I know that's what you were going to ask, Owen. Because it would be ideal for both me and Isold to go so I could *transport* us back."

"Well, crap. Another plan busted." Owen's lips thinned in frustration.

"The alternative is that one of us goes with Isold," Weston said, "but we wouldn't have anything to do while he's in there, and if they don't let non-patrons hang out inside—"

"They don't," Isold said.

"Then that person would be very conspicuous, hanging around in the open, and we'd have the problem we're trying to avoid," Weston continued. "I think this is the best we can do, if we're not just going to *world door* to Branlight instead. *Transport* sends Isold somewhere on Terrace One—*not* to a lift, because, I'm sorry, Isold, but I'm inclined to paranoia about Raynir's resources and willingness to use them—and Isold arranges to meet Livia at that place later today. And Aderyn and Jessemia do the shopping this morning."

Owen nodded. "I agree. This is our best option. I just hate any plan where I have to sit on the sidelines and cheer."

"I don't know what sidelines are, but cheering is optional," Aderyn said. She kissed him on the cheek. "Jessemia, are you ready? I want to get this over with."

She and Jessemia, bundled up against the cold, ventured out into the streets of Foundation. Jessemia's prediction of snow had come true, but contrary to Aderyn's fears, it was a light powdering that dusted the rooftops and the heads of pedestrians and melted when it contacted the paving stones and the raised walkways flanking them. Aderyn knew this wasn't the first snowfall of the season, but it was the first one she'd seen, and she delighted in the feathery touch of snowflakes on her face. It was cold, true, but the wind that had tormented her the day before was gone, and she could almost convince herself her battered coat was enough protection.

"It's too bad we have to be quick. I like shopping," Jessemia said. "It's much nicer now that I'm spending my own money and not Papa's, which is strange because I had so much more money in Obsidian."

"It feels good when you've earned it yourself," Aderyn said. "Or looted it from a keep built by orcs. Or, I guess, not orcs. The system said Charnel Keep was built by another monstrous race."

"I didn't know there were any monstrous races with enough intelligence to build structures like we do."

"Neither did I. The kobolds in the Lonely Tor made use of the Enchanterium instead of building their own structures. But whoever built Charnel Keep was much bigger than humans or orcs. The ceilings were much too high."

Jessemia frowned. "You mean, giants? I thought those were mythical like trolls."

"I don't know. I'm suspicious these days of calling any monster 'mythical,' because of the kobolds. Maybe there were giants once in the Blighted Range and they all died out, or were destroyed." Aderyn reflected briefly on the idea of trolls being real and suppressed a shudder. That was a nasty monster she hoped didn't exist outside the pages of books.

"Ew, not trolls," Jessemia said as if she'd heard Aderyn's thoughts. "Oh, here, this is the clothier's shop. They sell ready-made—do you know what that is? I haven't seen it anywhere but in Finion's Gate. They make clothes that fit imaginary people and you pick the one that's closest to your height and weight."

Aderyn stopped in front of the store. "Imaginary people? How does that work?"

"Not *exactly* imaginary people. I'm not explaining it well. Let's go in and you can ask the shopkeeper to clear things up."

The seamstress Mariet, back in Far Haven, made clothes she then altered to fit the buyer, so the shopkeeper's explanation about ready-made clothes didn't confuse Aderyn much. But Mariet's clothing came in only two sizes, and what the shopkeeper said about multiple size categories didn't make a lot of sense to Aderyn —how could they know what the size categories ought to be, given how different human bodies were?

But between her list of necessities and the shopkeeper's quick understanding, Aderyn came away with assorted clothing to replace the items Livia had said were at the end of their lifespan, beyond the reach of *mending* or *repair*. Knowing that they wouldn't have to wait on a tailor or a spellslinger with the right spells to alter clothes to fit eased her mind.

The second shop was also a clothier, but this one sold cold-weather gear, coats and cloaks and knitted caps that reminded Aderyn of the Swifthands Revelin whom they'd encountered in the Lonely Tor. She stuffed everything into the <**Knapsack of Plenty**> except the warm, heavy leather coat with the fur lining she bought for herself. That, she wore out of the shop. It was almost too warm for comfort even on that chilly day, but Aderyn told herself how much she would love it when they traveled north and encountered real storms.

She wasn't equipped with the right skills to negotiate for unique or magical items. That would have to wait for Isold, though it was possible they didn't need any upgrades to what they had. But their last stop was a lucky one. The shopkeeper, a burly man named Caldan with a kind smile and graying black hair, recognized the Swift and took time to guide her through selecting gear for traveling and camping in the frozen North. With his help, Aderyn ended up with more than she'd anticipated, all of it essential, plus instructions on how to use the more unusual items.

She turned down the offer of tents, explaining about the <**Soldier's Friend**>, and Caldan's eyes widened. "Only ever saw one of those before," he said. "Is it true it can make a thousand tents at once?"

"Yes, and they're all the best-made tents you can imagine." Aderyn hoped he didn't take that as a slight on his wares.

Caldan nodded. "What about ground cloths?"

"They have those too. Though they're not very thick."

"Then you'll want those, at least. I have some heavy canvas ones I can let you have at a discount, on account of how they're discolored. It's not as if color matters, right? But some customers are picky." Caldan's frown made him look even more like a Stalwart, though he was non-classed.

"Have you had a lot of adventurers in here, buying supplies?" Aderyn asked, feeling inspired.

"Have I had adventurers in here? More like, who haven't I had?" Caldan laughed, a big-bellied sound that drew laughter out of Aderyn and Jessemia. "They tend not to stay because my wares are high-quality and therefore costly, which puts them outside the reach of most adventurers' purses. But enough buy from me that I have a sense for the type. Lots of mid-level adventurers, I believe, thinking they'll make their fortunes and their names settling this new kingdom. I just nod and agree with whatever they say. Never argue yourself out of a sale, I always say."

"That's wise," Jessemia said. "My Papa said something similar, but he always said it after some shopkeeper had offended him."

"I'd say he sounds wise, but maybe he was the easily offended sort—you never know." Caldan retreated into the back room and returned with a pile of folded tan canvases streaked with brown.

Aderyn awkwardly folded them one at a time into the **<Knapsack of Plenty>**, making Caldan's eyes bulge again.

"A **<Soldier's Friend>**, a **<Knapsack of Plenty>**," he said in awe. "What level are you, anyway?"

"Nineteen." Aderyn felt unexpectedly awkward at saying this, like there was something shameful about being level nineteen with powerful magical items.

Caldan whistled. "You weren't that level when the Wildcats were competing, I'm sure of it. How did you manage that trick? Oh, I remember. Your husband is the Fated One. Came back from the dead, right? Well, I'd believe anything of you lot. Is there anything else I can get for you?"

Aderyn willed her reddened cheeks to cool. "I think that's all. Thank you. You've been so helpful."

"It's no trouble, no trouble at all. Though—wait a moment." Caldan went into the back room again. When he returned, he was carrying a couple of flat, narrow boxes. He handed one each to Aderyn and Jessemia. "It's a trinket, really, but you never know when you might need light. It's called a **<Firefly>**, and when you activate it, it provides a small light for about four hours. Shake it hard for thirty seconds to make it work."

Aderyn opened the box. The magic item was a clear glass bug about two inches from front to back. It looked more like a cicada than a firefly, with transparent wings that glimmered with a faint rainbow effect folded over its carapace. A leather thong long enough to be a necklace tied around the bug's midsection.

"This is really generous," Jessemia said. "Thank you."

"It's my pleasure. Good luck, ladies, and wish your husband the best from me." Caldan opened the door for them and waved them goodbye.

"That was so sweet," Aderyn said. "I'm glad we didn't send

Weston. He'd have wanted to haggle, and I think Caldan deserves full price for his goods."

Jessemia nodded. "Are you done? Let's hurry back. I'm hungry."

None of their friends were in the taproom when they returned, and when Aderyn went upstairs to leave the <**Knapsack of Plenty**>, she found the bedroom empty. She and Jessemia finally found Owen, Weston, and Livia in one of the private salons. Weston and Livia were reading the same book at the same time, something that always astonished Aderyn. Owen had a pile of flat wooden shapes in front of him that he was moving around like they were a puzzle. "I am so bored I think I might actually go crazy," he said without looking up. "Did you get everything?"

"Yes, but Isold really needs to do the rest tomorrow. I don't know anything about magic items." Aderyn sat next to her husband and kissed him.

"I want to see if he can recharge the <**Wand of Epic Bounty**>," Livia said. "And he said the <**Healing Stone**> needs recharging, too. But most of all I want to see what his luck turns up. He has the most amazing knack for stumbling on weird and wonderful items."

"Like my <**Fire Dancer's Knives**>," Weston said, turning a page without making Livia protest. "I'm still mad I lost one of them in the caverns under Charnel Keep. Stupid skitterlings."

"When will Isold come back?" Jessemia asked.

"I arranged to meet him where I left him on Terrace One at five o'clock. Right at sunset." Livia put a hand over the book's page. "I hope he's all right. I have a bad feeling about this."

"You suggested it, dearest," Weston said.

"That doesn't mean I can't have forebodings." Livia shook her head. "It's nothing. Just me being pessimistic. Let's have lunch."

They ate, and afterward Jessemia told stories of the funnier parts of her quests. She had a knack for storytelling and a keen eye for the ridiculous, and Aderyn laughed so hard it was a surprise when Livia stood and said, "It's nearly five. I'm going to go. Aderyn, you should come with me."

"Me? Why?"

"So if anything goes wrong, we have **<Bonded Mind>** to communicate with everyone here." Livia spoke lightly, but her expression was serious.

"That's a great idea." Owen hugged Aderyn. "Be careful, you two."

Aderyn put her arms around Livia's shoulders, and Livia chanted the long syllables of *transport*. With a tug and an enormous thunderclap, they were elsewhere. The temperature dropped instantly as they went from the comfortable warmth of the parlor to the near-freezing chill of the outdoors at sunset. Aderyn didn't recognize their location, but it wasn't as if she knew many places on Terrace One.

"Over here," Livia said, leading the way to a sheltered nook between two tall stone buildings with large, well-lit glass windows displaying the shops' wares. "It shouldn't be long. Isold knows the danger as well as any of us, and he won't take unnecessary risks."

Aderyn nodded. She stood with Livia and watched the passersby. As with the last time she'd been on Terrace One, most of them appeared to be servants on errands for their masters. None of them were as warmly dressed as she was. This coat was her new favorite possession.

A few minutes passed. Livia checked her pocket watch, holding it close to her eyes in the dimness. "Time to start worrying. It's six minutes after the hour."

"Isold might have gotten caught up in research," Aderyn offered, but her heart wasn't in the reassurance.

Abruptly, Owen's voice sounded in her head. *You need to get back here now. Right now. You might be in danger.*

Why? Owen's immaterial voice had never sounded so urgent.

We just got a message. Isold's been kidnapped.

CHAPTER FIVE

When the tug and shatteringly loud clap of *transport* brought Aderyn and Livia back to the Alabaster Inn, Owen said, "Good. I had this vision of Raynir's goons picking you up off the street."

"They'd have had a thundering good fight if they'd tried," Livia said. "What happened to Isold?"

Weston handed Livia a folded sheet of white paper, tinged blue like fresh snowfall. "Someone delivered this just a few minutes ago. Davith didn't bring it right away because people have been leaving and arriving in droves for the last hour, but he said it was no more than ten minutes. He was devastated when he found out what it said."

Livia unfolded the paper and read aloud. "'Leave Finion's Gate now or you'll never see your Herald friend again.' Leave? Why no demands for ransom? Isn't that what kidnappers always want?"

"It's a ploy to get us to come charging to the rescue," Owen said. "If Raynir's been watching the inn, he knows we've hunkered down and aren't likely to go where he can snatch all of us. He doesn't want us to leave, he wants us neutralized, but if he says that, we'll be even more on the defensive. So he lets us know he has Isold, pretends he wants us gone, and hopes we'll make a rescue attempt so he can capture the rest of us. But wherever Isold is, it will be a trap."

"That's convoluted even for a Finion's Gate councilor," Livia said. "So, what do we do? We can't abandon Isold."

"We do what Raynir least wants us to do," Owen said. "We break into his mansion and remind him why he doesn't want to make us angry."

"*Yes,*" Livia said, punching the air. "I love this plan."

"I agree, but shouldn't we be concerned about the political repercussions? We didn't want to be involved in Finion's Gate politics a few months back, and that hasn't changed." Aderyn took the paper from Livia and absently folded it. "We can't kill Raynir, and he knows it, which means any physical threats we make lack the proper force."

"I'm sure we can think of something that doesn't involve death," Weston said. "Because Owen's right. Raynir needs to learn a lesson."

"The important thing right now is to come down hard on Raynir before he's expecting us," Owen said. "He knows how long it will take his messenger to get from here to his mansion—"

"We also don't know if that's where he's got Isold," Weston said. "Raynir's wealthy, and wealthy people in Finion's Gate own multiple properties all over the city."

Owen let out a frustrated sigh. "Aderyn, what's our move? This has become a war game."

Aderyn thought for a moment. "At least we know Isold's still alive. And he's unwounded, according to the team roster. Livia, can you find out where he is with *scry*? Or is there a way Raynir can block *scrying* magic?"

"He could block *scry*, but not *greater scry*. Thunderation, but I'm glad I exchanged *acid ray* for it." Livia pulled out her scrying mirror and said a few nonsense words, waving her hand across the mirror's surface. It flashed bright silver and then darkened. Everyone crowded around to look. "Just a minute," Livia said, tilting the mirror one way and then the other. "There."

Aderyn gasped. The little oval now showed Isold, lying on the wooden floor of an empty room. He was bound hand and foot and gagged, and he lay so still a flash of fear made Aderyn check the team roster to confirm he was alive. The view shifted as if rotating around him, and his face came into view. His eyes were closed, but his face was unmarked, and in all it didn't look like he'd been beaten.

"He's not asleep or unconscious," Weston said.

"How can you be sure?" Livia asked.

"Unconscious bodies aren't tense like that. He's awake, and I think he's trying to use a skill." Weston leaned back so Owen could get a look.

"See if you can identify the location," Owen said.

Livia nodded and turned her attention back to the mirror. The view shifted as if backing away from Isold, expanding so it showed the rest of the room. It was unfurnished, and nothing hung on the walls, which were plaster that needed a fresh coat of whitewash. The view also revealed two armed men seated near Isold, watching him closely. Then the view became one of stones and beams of wood that flashed past and were gone. In seconds, the oval mirror showed rooftops, and then the entire house was visible.

Weston groaned. "It's Raynir's mansion."

"That's good," Aderyn said. "It's a location I've already

Assessed for weak points, and it means we don't have to go racing across the city to some unknown place. That more than makes up for how it will be fortified."

"All right," Livia said. "Should I *transport* us in? He's within range."

"That might trigger whatever trap Raynir's set," Aderyn said. "And even if there's no trap, and we *transport* in, grab Isold, and *transport* out, we still have to deal with Raynir and any other attacks he might make. I refuse to flee this city when we haven't achieved our goal."

"Then, what do you propose?" Owen asked.

"We'll have to do this the hard way. We need an indirect approach. The <**Wayfinder**> is no help, because it takes us the most direct route to my heart's desire."

"I can do it," Jessemia said.

Aderyn had almost forgotten Jessemia was there, she was so quiet. "I thought you weren't a high enough level to locate a person."

"I'm not. But [**Improved Map Access**] shows me locations on my system map when I become aware of them." Jessemia gazed into the middle distance the way Isold always did when consulting his map. "It won't plot a course to the mansion, because it's not in the wilderness, but I've run around Finion's Gate enough that my map is well detailed, and I can figure out a course myself. One that will take us a roundabout way."

"Not to be insulting, Jessemia, but should you come with us?" Livia asked. "This could be dangerous, and you're a lot lower level than we are."

"Not to mention this will put you on the chief councilor's shit list," Weston said.

"I know. But level ten is still high enough to defend myself against the average fighter, and I have skills that protect me during infiltration. **[Hide]**, for one, and **[Camouflage]** works as long as there are plants around." Jessemia sounded more serious than Aderyn had ever heard her. "And Isold's my friend, too. I can wait outside if you think it's necessary, but it sounds like my skill is the only one that will make Aderyn's plan work."

"I agree," Aderyn said. "Livia, I want you to *transport* us out of here. We can't walk out the front door without being followed by whoever Raynir set to watch the inn. Take us somewhere close to Raynir's mansion, but not too close."

"I can do that, but that person will hear it and might guess we've left," Livia warned.

"That's all right. The important thing is that we put ourselves outside the possibility of anyone seeing our approach to the mansion." Aderyn met Owen's gaze. "Then we follow Jessemia to an unobserved entrance. That's as far as we can plan. From there, we find Isold and Raynir and make a decision."

"Understood," Owen said. "Everybody huddle up."

Aderyn barely felt the tug of *transport* or the disconcerting moment of arrival. Despite her words about not being able to plan, she couldn't help going over possibilities. It was true Raynir couldn't be allowed to get away with manipulating them, because he'd go on doing it, and then they really wouldn't be able to return to Finion's Gate, ever. But it was also true Aderyn had no idea what else was possible. That went from being tactics to the realm of politics, something Aderyn wasn't good at. Punish Raynir, convince him not to try this again... killing him would accomplish that, but even Aderyn's poor grasp of political maneuvering knew that would have all of Finion's Gate coming after them.

She removed her arms from around Owen and Jessemia's shoulders and straightened. Tall buildings of granite and marble made a stony gray canyon down which the paved street unrolled like a frozen river. Short flights of stairs led up from street level to doors, all of them painted black, all of them lit by clear glass lanterns affixed to the doorposts. The busy street teemed with carriages shaped like pumpkins and a handful of pedestrians. All the pedestrians had stopped to stare, and the carriage drivers shouted and jerked on their horses' reins to stop them panicking over the loud noise of *transport*. Aderyn couldn't believe no one was screaming about explosions or lightning strikes.

Owen grabbed her hand. "We need to move before they figure out who we are," he said. "Jessemia?"

"Follow me." Jessemia took off running.

They all ran, sometimes slipping on the cobblestones, which were slick with melted snow starting to freeze now that the sun had set, down wide streets and around corners until Jessemia came to a stop. "We're well away from where we arrived. Give me a moment to decide on a route."

"I thought we were following the route already," Weston said.

Jessemia shook her head. "That was just getting us out of sight, in case anyone recognized you all and spread rumors that Raynir might hear. Probably those rumors wouldn't reach him before we do, but no sense not taking precautions." Her eyes shifted rapidly as she examined her invisible map.

"I'm so proud," Weston said, pretending to wipe a tear from his eye.

Livia elbowed him lightly in the ribs. "Get the levity out of your system before things get dangerous."

"That's what I'm doing. I tried to think of a joke about Raynir's house not being impenetrable, but everything that came to mind was the sort of thing you'd slap me for."

Aderyn giggled and shut herself up before it could sound hysterical. Still, the laugh eased some of her tension. She didn't need to be wound tight just before a fight—that was how mistakes happened.

"There are two possibilities," Jessemia finally said. "Both of them lead around back of the mansion."

Aderyn recalled her Assessment. "The best entrance for this situation is through the coal cellar, which is near the servants' entrance. Is there anything special to distinguish one route from the other?"

"One is shorter, but more public."

"Then let's take the longer route. We don't want to be observed."

They followed Jessemia through the streets of Terrace Two. They'd left the residential area behind for a business district, its streets wider and paved with large, rectangular stones rather than cobbles. Three- and four-story buildings, all of them with wide windows displaying goods for sale, still glowed with light despite the hour. Aderyn had noticed that in Foundation, the shops that sold merchandise and the offices for business owners who sold services closed before six o'clock. She wasn't sure what time it was, but it had to be nearing that time, and yet these shops showed no sign of closing.

She realized in the next moment the genius of Jessemia's plan. With the streets thronged with shoppers, some of them armed adventurers, Aderyn and her friends blended right in despite not being dressed as finely as almost everyone else. So long as they kept moving and didn't make eye contact, they were unlikely to be recognized as Glory Games champions.

After making a few turns, Jessemia led them into quieter neighborhoods of tall, narrow houses, where the streets were almost empty except for a few carriages. They were now the only pedestrians, but none of the carriages stopped to harass them. The houses shared walls and appeared to be only two rooms wide, but unlike similar houses Aderyn had seen elsewhere in Finion's Gate, they were built of fine white bricks with decorative stone along the eaves and the small porticos guarding each door. Aderyn sensed the influence of wealth, though not as much as Raynir had.

With that thought, she followed Jessemia around another corner and realized they were on the street behind Raynir's mansion, three houses down. She'd observed on their last visit that the streets in this part of Terrace Two were laid out like a grid, with wide thoroughfares alternating with narrower streets. All the mansions faced the thoroughfares, and their backs opened on the narrow streets. Owen had said it meant nobody had to look at someone else's back door and their trash. It made sense, but at the moment Aderyn was grateful that it meant their entrance would be mostly concealed.

She put a hand on Jessemia's shoulder to stop her moving forward. "This is close enough. Thanks."

Jessemia nodded. "Do you see the guards?"

Aderyn blinked. "Where?"

"At the back door, and there's one who walks a pattern from the front of the house to the rear. Then two on the roof." Jessemia's nose wrinkled. "I can smell the walking one from here. He chews aniseed."

"You can *smell* that? From here?"

Jessemia smiled wryly. "It's called **[Keen Senses]**. All my senses are heightened, not just sight and hearing."

"I don't know if that's a blessing or a curse."

"Neither do I, yet. I only just got it at level ten." Jessemia sobered. "I think I should come in with you. I'm good at concealing myself, but if they find me—"

"That can't lead to anything good, I agree. All right." Aderyn turned to Weston, who was right behind her. "Four guards. We need to get into the coal cellar—it's those wooden doors lying nearly flat on the ground, between us and the servants' door."

Weston's gaze flicked from the roof to the door. "Give me a

minute." He put up the hood of the <**Cloak of Mists**> and crept silently toward the aniseed-chewing guard, who had paused at the corner of the mansion. Aderyn held her breath. If he'd heard something, and was looking for them—but no, he just spat on the ground, spraying tiny particles of aniseed husk, and put another pinch of the stuff into his mouth. When he turned his back, Weston pounced, getting his powerful arm around the guard's neck and sending him unconscious.

Weston lowered him to the ground and gestured, not to Aderyn, but to Jessemia. Jessemia darted to his side. To Aderyn, she looked like a moving shadow thanks to **[Hide]**. Aderyn hadn't realized the skill worked while someone was moving. Jessemia wasn't as invisible as if she'd stood still, but it impressed Aderyn that it had even that much effect on a moving person.

Together, Weston and Jessemia bound the guard and gagged him, triggering a system defeat notice that surprised Aderyn. She hadn't thought of this adventure in terms of gaining experience from subduing low-level guards. Then Weston led Jessemia a roundabout way to subdue the guard standing at the servants' entrance, earning the team a second system defeat message. The second guard, Weston carried struggling over his shoulder as they returned. "We'll stash them in the coal cellar," he said. "Here, hold this fellow while I unlock the doors."

"Aren't you worried about the guards on the roof?" Livia said.

"They're watching the approaches, not the house," Weston said. "Looking for anyone attacking the house from the obvious streets. Raynir didn't get his money's worth out of them. Stay here, and run when I beckon." He hurried across the open space again and knelt by the coal cellar door.

Jessemia took a step and winced. She lifted her right leg and rotated her ankle. "I twisted it when I tackled the guard. I'm not injured, but it does hurt some." She gingerly put her weight on her leg and grimaced again. "I need to walk it off."

"Are you sure you don't want to stay here?" Aderyn asked.

"I won't slow us down, I promise. If I'm wrong about that, I'll stay behind and keep an eye on the captured guards." Jessemia's face was set and resolute in the light from the nearby streetlamps.

Weston sat back on his haunches and put back the hood of his cloak so his wave was visible. Aderyn ran with Jessemia, who hobbled a little but kept up with the others. Weston hauled open one of the big wooden doors and hurried away, returning moments later with the other guard. Together, they got their captives through the doorway and into the darkness of the coal cellar.

When the door was safely shut, Livia made *orbs of light* that illuminated the small room, though not by much. Raynir's coal cellar was well stocked for the winter, filled with overflowing sacks of coal. Aderyn had never heard of heating a house with coal until coming to Finion's Gate, and she couldn't believe, looking around, how much coal was needed for just one house. The coal seemed to absorb the light and make the room feel almost claustrophobic. Again, Aderyn wasn't afraid of the small quarters. Maybe she was cured of her fear.

Weston had a hand on the door leading out of the room. "Livia, what's beyond this?"

Livia's eyes flashed blue. "It's a little room filled with tools for gardening and shelves containing I don't know what. It's not too dark for *clairvoyance*, obviously. There are two doors, both—" She stopped speaking and held up a hand. "Everyone be quiet!"

Aderyn froze. Beside her, Jessemia balanced without putting weight on her injured ankle. She appeared to be listening to something. After a few seconds, Livia relaxed. "Someone came in from the kitchen, which is beyond one of the doors. The other one must go deeper into the house."

"That's our route." Aderyn pulled out the <**Wayfinder**>. "Let's see about reaching Isold first, and then we'll deal with Raynir."

The room Livia had described as "little" was larger than Aderyn expected, but she didn't pause to examine it. Now she could hear what Jessemia had been listening to, the faint noise of people clattering dishes and banging pots and calling out requests for some ingredient or other. The other door was unlocked, and Aderyn eased it open quietly and checked for observers. The hall was empty.

Swiftly, she followed the <**Wayfinder**> down the hall to narrow stairs going up and down. The <**Wayfinder**> pointed upward, so she climbed the next flight of steps to a swinging door with no latch. These were clearly passages for the servants, so they didn't intrude on their master or do anything so gauche as carry a broom where a guest might see. The swinging door opened on a room containing cleaning supplies, mops, buckets, piles of rags, and the brooms Aderyn had imagined. Another door, this one sturdier, was locked. Aderyn gave way to Weston. The <**Wayfinder**> was almost hot to the touch now, and glowed a nice bright cherry red.

Weston grunted as the lock clicked open. Aderyn opened the door and gasped. Two armed men stood there, barring the way. She closed her hand on the <**Wayfinder**> as one of them laid the blade of his sword along her throat. "Don't try any attacks," the man said. "You will come with us. Chief Councilor Raynir wants a word with you."

CHAPTER SIX

Aderyn swiftly Assessed the two men. One was Swordsworn, one a Swifthands, and both were level thirteen. In the moment before anyone acted, Aderyn said in a clear, carrying voice, "All right. We won't fight you. Take us to Raynir." She hoped Owen was watching her to see her body language convey the message *It's where we want to go.*

The Swordsworn pushed forward, and with his sword's edge pressed against her skin, Aderyn had to back up or have her throat slit. She reviewed her options and came up blank. It was impossible. Raynir shouldn't have been able to track them. The plan was perfect—except that clearly wasn't true, so where had she failed? Jessemia's **[Tracking]**, *transport,* locating Isold using *scry*—

Oh. Aderyn wanted to kick herself. Raynir had had someone find them using *scry* after they left the Alabaster Inn, and then that spellslinger had gone on watching them while Raynir put his mercenaries in place so the team could walk right into them. Livia had even mentioned the possibility of blocking *scry* and it still hadn't occurred to Aderyn that someone might use the spell against them. It was small comfort that Livia didn't have a spell to defend against it; Aderyn still should have come up with the possibility. She told herself not to fret over it now. Later would be soon enough for self-castigation. Assuming they had a later. Aderyn couldn't help considering all the other ways her plan might have betrayed them.

One by one, her friends emerged from the stairs into the storage room, and the Swifthands relieved them of their obvious weapons. This made Aderyn feel slightly better. Competent hired fighters would have thought to pat them down for the unobvious weapons, and they certainly would have taken the <**Sunsword**>, which at the moment was deactivated and looked like a hilt with no blade. Two against five was ridiculous by any measure, and yet these men acted like they had the upper hand. They clearly hadn't been in Finion's Gate for the Glory Games. She reminded herself not to be overconfident. She didn't know what awaited them.

The Swordsworn removed his blade from Aderyn's throat and prodded her with its tip. "Up the stairs. Move."

Owen growled. The Swordsworn smiled, a nasty, smug expression. "You don't like it? I can do whatever I like, and you can't do a thing to stop me. *Anything* I like."

"A mercenary with a death wish," Owen said. "How unexpected."

The Swordsworn's smile faded slightly in the face of Owen's steely calm. He said nothing more, just prodded Aderyn harder. "That way. Follow him."

Aderyn obediently followed the Swifthands up the stairs to the next landing, where the man pushed the door open and indicated she should exit and follow him. She covertly examined her surroundings as they walked. The lower walls to hip height were paneled with grooved slats of wood painted white, with flocked red velvet as stiff and bristly as five o'clock shadow covering the walls above. Aderyn recognized the décor; it would have told her she was in Raynir's manor if she hadn't already known. The hall was wide enough for three people to walk abreast, which made it plenty wide enough for a fight, or for her to dodge the Swifthands and make a break for freedom, which she didn't want to do. At least it was an option.

Widely-spaced doors, also painted white, flanked pedestals bearing spidery plants in colorful enameled urns. The plants' long, thin leaves were striped dark green and a lighter green that was almost yellow, and they waved in the wind of the Swifthands' rapid passage. Aderyn contemplated using [**Improvised Distraction**], throwing an urn at the Swifthands' head, but it would be self-indulgent. Fun, but self-indulgent, and they still needed to meet Raynir.

The hall turned a corner, and now Aderyn recognized where in the mansion she was: the hall outside Raynir's private study. She and Owen had come here the night of the Glory Games gala to confront Raynir about his role in the plot to destroy the Games. From here, she could find the front door. She quickened her pace briefly, then reminded herself to slow down. She didn't intend to leave, and running ahead didn't benefit her. It might help her and her friends if their escorts believed they still had control.

The Swifthands stopped at the door to the study and appeared nonplussed when he realized his hands were too full to open it. Aderyn avoided catching his eye in case he could tell she was laughing at him on the inside. Instead, she waited for the Swordsworn to open the door for her. He brushed past her, close enough for an intimate touch, and Owen growled again. Aderyn thought about using [**Reposition**] to shove the man into Owen so Owen could throttle him, decided that was another self-indulgent wish, and pretended not to notice the man's unsubtle groping.

The Swordsworn smirked as if he'd done something clever. "Inside," he snapped. "Show some respect to the chief councilor."

"Don't worry, Emmon, Aderyn knows her place," Raynir said from within the room. "Please, all of you, come in."

Aderyn walked through the doorway, noting that the furnishings looked the same as before except there was a new drinks cabinet opposite the fireplace, where the fire currently burned low. She kept going, scuffing her boots over the fine woven carpet and wishing her feet were muddy, until she stood in front of the enormous mahogany desk, within arm's reach of the fat silken bell rope hanging above it.

Raynir sat behind the desk, his hands with the fingers interlaced resting on its smooth green blotter covering most of the top. He looked almost exactly as Aderyn remembered, heavyset with a fleshy face, but well-dressed in clothes that made his weight look suited to him. His brown hair had more silver in it, and it was cut short now. His dark-eyed gaze swept over Aderyn and then settled on Owen, who had moved to stand next to her.

"Leave us," he told Emmon the Swordsworn. "Both of you, out. Watch the door to see that we're not interrupted."

"Sir, they're dangerous," the Swifthands said.

"Not to me," Raynir said. "Do as I command."

Both the Swifthands and Emmon bowed and closed the door after them.

No one spoke for a moment. Aderyn hoped Owen had a plan, because she had counted on having more time to assess the situation. They were in political territory now. Owen's back and shoulders were tense, and his hand gripped the <Sunsword's> hilt tightly enough his knuckles were white. To Aderyn, that meant he was waiting for Raynir to make the first move.

Finally, Raynir spoke. "I thought we had an agreement that you were never to return to Finion's Gate."

"We didn't," Owen said. "The agreement was that we wouldn't reveal what we knew about your plot to take over the city's government. Though I'll grant you, never returning was implied. But we didn't break an agreement in coming here."

"Don't mince words with an old politician, young man," Raynir said, still calm. He tapped his forefingers on the desk. "You knew what I meant. You wouldn't have agreed to leave if you hadn't."

"The point is that you aggressed on us for no reason." Owen sounded as calm as Raynir, but the tension in the room was thick as superdense steel and as unyielding. "We had no intention of breaking what we *did* agree to. Kidnapping Isold was stupid."

"You don't expect me to believe your innocence, do you?" Raynir raised one eyebrow. "You mean to say you just happened to visit Finion's Gate practically on the eve of the announcement of our first election? At a perfect time to spread slanders about me to ruin my chances?"

"We didn't know any of that," Owen said, his voice rising. "We've been in the southlands for weeks. What makes you think we give a damn about Finion's Gate politics?"

Raynir rose explosively from his seat. "You want revenge," he shouted. "You said it yourself—my way of gaining power repulses you. You weren't in a position to stop me then, but you are now. Lie all you want. I know the truth."

Owen threw up his arms and turned away. "You're delusional. And we're leaving. Release Isold. We'll finish our business here and get out of your hair."

"That's not good enough."

"It had damn well better be, because we're not offering terms."

Owen turned back to face Raynir. "You ought to be afraid for your life. We're all level nineteen now, and any one of us can turn you into a corpse. With or without weapons."

"But you won't dare." Raynir slowly resumed his seat. "I've signed and deposited an affidavit with the magistrates, swearing to your avowed animosity. If anything happens to me, the magistrates will have you taken into custody and tried for murder. If you fight them, you'll be doubly guilty. Kill me if you want, but I'll have my revenge one way or another."

"Owen," Aderyn said.

Owen shook his head, telling her not to say anything more. Aderyn hoped even more deeply that he had a plan, because she didn't see a way out of this.

"Here is what I require," Raynir said. "You'll gather your things from the Alabaster Inn. Right now. You'll go to Gate Five —I've arranged for them to open the gate for you even though it's after sunset. Once you're there, and my contact assures me none of you have stayed behind, I'll send your companion to join you."

"And if we refuse?" Owen said.

Raynir smiled. "I pull that bell rope, and Isold dies."

Jessemia gasped. Raynir's gaze fixed on her. "Who's this?"

"No one," Owen said. "Just a guide who led us to your mansion. What's stopping us from coming back later and killing you in your sleep?"

"I can make it look like five different kinds of accident," Weston said in his deepest, most menacing voice.

Raynir shrugged. "I was *very* clear in my affidavit. They'll arrest you no matter what my death looks like, and *truthspeak* will establish your guilt. You've got five seconds to decide." He grasped the bell rope. "Five. Four."

"Stop!" Aderyn exclaimed.

Outside the room, something hit the door with a thud. A second thud sounded like someone falling. Raynir stood. "What—"

Faster than thought, Weston flung a knife at the rope, held taut by Raynir's grip. The knife's blade slashed partway through it but didn't completely sever it. Raynir snarled and jerked on the rope, once, twice before it snapped. Aderyn screamed and dove at the chief councilor with no idea what she meant to do.

The door slammed open, revealing Isold. His hair was disordered, and a bruise darkened his left temple, but he was definitely alive.

Jessemia gasped again. Raynir fought off Aderyn's attack and backed away, his eyes narrowed. "Right," he snarled. "Who am I going to have to execute for—"

Isold strode to the desk and raised a hand palm-out. "*Sit.*"

Raynir sat, missed the chair, and landed on the floor behind the desk. He gasped, "You dare raise a hand to me? I'll see all of you—"

"*Silence,*" Isold commanded. Raynir's mouth closed with an audible click of teeth snapping together. His jaw moved as if he was fighting an invisible hand clamping his mouth shut.

Isold hauled Raynir to his feet by the collar, holding the man inches from his face. "You dared make me a pawn," he snarled, with a fury that stunned Aderyn. "You used me to threaten my friends. You thought you could get away with it because we can't murder you. You're right. Your death solves nothing."

Then Isold smiled, and Aderyn felt sick, because he looked nothing like himself. "But you did not consider," he said, biting off his words with precision, "that there is such a thing as a fate worse than death. I can make you do anything I want. I can force you to reveal your crimes in front of the entire city. I can turn you into a thief and a murderer. I can compel you to perform acts of deviance, *in public,* that will turn every citizen of this city against you in disgust. And you will do it all believing it's your heart's desire. You will rejoice in your ruination until you come to your senses and discover you've destroyed your life. That's if you don't decide suicide is a better option. Have I made myself clear?"

Raynir, his eyes so wide the whites showed all around, struggled to speak. Isold slapped him. "Nod if you understand. I don't want to hear your voice."

Raynir nodded vigorously.

"Isold," Jessemia said.

Isold didn't turn around. "He deserves it. No one makes me a pawn."

"Yes," Jessemia said, "he deserves it. But you don't."

Isold jerked and released Raynir, who scrambled backward out of the Herald's reach. Isold's heavy breathing made his shoulders tremble. "You don't understand."

"I understand regret," Jessemia said, "and I understand living with memories that burn. Don't, Isold. Nothing is worth that."

For a moment, Isold was motionless. Then his shoulders slumped, and he drew in a deep breath and let it out slowly. "Raynir," he said, "you attacked us because if our positions were reversed, you would have wanted to ruin us. You have no concept of loyalty or honor, because those things don't benefit a Finion's Gate councilor. So to you it seems reasonable that we would come back only to hurt you. I assure you, we have no interest in politics either in general or in specific."

Raynir got to his feet with the help of the wall. He rubbed his jaw and worked his mouth a few times, establishing that it wasn't locked shut. "This has all been a terrible misunderstanding. I accept that you meant no harm."

"I'm not finished." Isold straightened and looked Raynir in the eye. "We will be leaving Finion's Gate in a few days. We may or may not return in future. At any time we are in the city, you will leave us alone. You won't send your men to harass us, you won't try kidnapping any of us again, and in return we will never involve ourselves in this city's politics." He paused, and to Aderyn's eye he was sorting through options. "If you so much as think about violating our agreement, you and I will have a conversation, and then you will have a conversation with the other councilors. It will not be voluntary. Do you understand?"

Raynir opened his mouth to speak. Isold's eyes narrowed. Raynir shut his mouth and nodded.

"We're leaving now," Isold said. "Don't worry, your staff will wake naturally in a couple of hours." He turned on his heel, and put a hand on Jessemia's arm to steady himself when he nearly walked into her. Jessemia's stunned expression mirrored how Aderyn felt she looked herself. Isold released Jessemia and strode to the door, which still hung open. Owen glanced from Raynir, who had fallen into his chair and was shaking, to Aderyn, and then gestured to everyone to follow.

Isold waited outside the door. Emmon and the Swifthands lay in boneless, sleeping heaps to either side. The team's confiscated weapons were scattered on the floor where the Swifthands had dropped them. Aderyn picked up her sword and said, "Isold?"

"I'll explain everything when we're out of here," Isold said, not looking at her. "Let's go."

This time, they went out the front door. They passed more than a few servants, all sleeping as deeply as the mercenaries. Aderyn's embarrassment at having assumed Isold needed rescuing grew every time they stepped over a fallen maidservant or butler.

When they reached the steps leading to the street, Livia said,

"Wait. What are we doing? Let's use *transport* and get ourselves where it's warm."

Isold laughed, somewhat ruefully, but he sounded so much like himself it eased Aderyn's heart. "That didn't occur to me. I was too preoccupied with making a dramatic exit."

"Understandable," Owen said, clapping Isold on the shoulder. "But it's cold as hell out here and I want a hot fire and a hot drink."

They huddled together for *transport*. Aderyn ended up opposite Isold in their huddle. When she caught his eye, he looked away quickly and didn't look back. It felt like a kick to the stomach, harsher even than the tug of *transport*. She knew Isold didn't hate her, and she hadn't done anything wrong, so she feared Isold's humiliation over having so nearly given in to his darkest impulses meant he was going to feel awkward around his friends for a while. She hoped he'd eventually be able to talk about it.

They arrived in the private parlor just as the bell rang for the first supper service. Aderyn stepped away from Jessemia and Owen and said, "Should I see if Davith will serve us in here? I don't want to eat in the taproom, and I hate how they turn others away from the dining room to give us privacy."

"One moment, Aderyn," Isold said. "I need—well, you know I need to ask your forgiveness, all of you. I hate being used, probably because I still fear being made to use my skills against people I care about, and I hate even more when someone uses me to manipulate my friends. Thank you for bringing me to my senses."

"We understand about losing control," Owen said. "And it wasn't as if you were completely wrong. You just went a little overboard."

Isold shook his head. "I never knew I had that in me. And now I feel I have better control than before, if only because I've seen what the alternative could be." He smiled. "But I think I would enjoy a quiet dinner with friends, because I learned much at the Orelaine Library I need to share."

"Then I'll see what Arlia has for dinner tonight, if the rest of you will rearrange the furniture and clear that table." Aderyn smiled at Isold and was heartened by the smile he gave her, normal and unshadowed by anger.

CHAPTER SEVEN

"I can grudgingly admit it was a neat little kidnapping," Isold said as they ate. "I was preoccupied with my studies and failed to guess Raynir would order his men to take me from inside the library. They caught me off guard, knocked me unconscious, and I awoke to find myself bound and gagged with two guards standing over me."

"We saw that much with *scry*," Livia said. "How did you escape?"

Isold smiled. "Raynir's paranoia was his downfall. He had those guards there to ensure I couldn't get free and use my Herald's tricks on anyone. What he didn't know is that I have several skills that require no speech or song, and that as of level nineteen, I can **[Hypnotize]** up to three people at once. He essentially provided me with the tools for my escape. I hypnotized them to release me, then I put them to sleep and went in search of Raynir."

"And we know the rest," Aderyn said, not wanting to revisit

the story. "If he took you at the end of the day, does that mean you learned enough?"

"I learned a great deal, and I hope most of it is useful." Isold laid his knife and fork across his empty plate and pushed it away so he could rest his elbows on the table. "The Orelaine Library has a surprising number of books and scrolls about the Northlands, but more than two-thirds of what I found was fictional. I didn't realize how popular a subject it is."

"What kind of stories?" Owen asked. "Maybe there's a kernel of truth in them, if they all talk about the same thing."

"That occurred to me as well. I didn't have time to read them, of course, but I hired a researcher named Bellina to help me, and she was familiar with almost all the fiction available. I chose her because the Northlands are her research specialty, but I got the feeling this was a longstanding passion of hers beyond the intellectual."

"A reader of adventure stories," Weston said. "Woman after my own heart."

Isold nodded. "Indeed. According to Bellina, most of the stories are centered on surviving the Northlands—not just the monsters, but the weather. Many of them are pure fantasy—non-classed men or women who end up in the wilderness after some absurd twist or other and have to learn survival skills such as fire lighting or shelter building."

"That could have influenced some of these adventurers looking to settle," Weston said. "It's a romantic notion, braving the elements. Not something I find appealing, but I see why someone would."

"That hadn't occurred to me, but you're right," Isold said. "There are also stories about raiding dungeons, but all those dungeons were completely invented by the authors. Almost none of the fictional books were written by people who have extensive experience in traveling the Northlands, Bellina told me. More usually the authors spend a winter north of Finion's Gate, within reach of the city in case of emergencies, to gain enough real-life experience to flavor their stories."

"That means those books don't have much more to offer than details about survival," Owen said. "Valuable, but not what we need."

"I asked Bellina to provide me with a list of books containing facts, and while I studied those, I had her create two lists from the fiction material. One was a list of monsters mentioned. The other was a list of supplies. I don't know what Aderyn bought today, but I thought, if there was some unusual survival need, we might want to know what item to buy to meet it."

"I had some help from a shopkeeper who was thorough," Aderyn said, "but I like the idea of—what is it you say, Owen? Covering the bases? Making sure we aren't missing anything."

Isold removed a sheaf of folded paper from inside his vest. "This is the supplies list," he said, handing a page to Aderyn, "and this is the list of monsters. I cross-referenced it with one of the tomes Bellina recommended, which was an enormous book listing monsters by name, by usual terrain, by power level, and by type, with an exhaustive index. I think it should have been four books, given how much information there was, but as it seems to have been added to since its creation, possibly that was too much work for the author or authors."

"How do you know it was added to?" Livia asked.

"Three-quarters of it was neatly divided into those four sections I mentioned. The rest of it was a disorganized clutter of pages stitched into the binding, as if when people discover a new monster or realize there's an omission, they simply add it in at random." Isold scowled. "So annoying."

"Yes, I'm sure your inner librarian was frothing at the mouth,"

Owen said with a grin. "That sounds like an amazing resource regardless."

"It was. For one thing, each entry has to be vouched for, either by one person who can prove they defeated the monster, or by three people who encountered it but didn't engage in combat. So every monster listed in the book exists. It's what you would get if every adventurer in the world could pour the contents of their Monster Folios into a physical book."

"I get it," Aderyn said. "You checked the list of monsters from fiction against the facts."

"I did." Isold sorted through the papers and removed two more. "These are monsters with verified existence that those authors claimed roamed the Northlands. It saved me having to read the whole tome."

"But you can't assume the monsters they wrote about that *aren't* in the tome don't exist," Weston said. "Or that there aren't some no one knows about to mention."

"That's right." Isold handed a fourth sheet to Weston. "These are the ones that might or might not be real. I marked the ones I found evidence for in the other books, the non-fictional ones. Those didn't have the kind of detail the tome did, but at least we know what to be alert for."

Weston scanned the sheet. "Snow spears, frost naiads, and the snow fiend. What's a snow fiend?"

"It's a bipedal monster covered with thick white fur, taller than the tallest ape. The books I studied were unclear about its territory, because few people have ever encountered it and survived," Isold said. "I also found many, many hints at unnamed dungeons, real ones, and a handful of stories about ice dragons living in the high-risk zone and their enormous piles of treasure. There were also stories of abandoned cities, as I mentioned earlier.

Cities from the time before the level cap. Those, too, are supposedly full of treasure."

"Which makes no sense," Owen said. "If they abandoned their cities, they had enough time to pack up what they cared about, like with the Enchanterium. But people are people."

"So true." Isold flipped through the papers. "I took many notes from the books Bellina provided, but my most useful find—or, rather, Bellina's find—was the journal of a Pathseer who traveled a short distance into the Northlands some seventy years ago. According to my system map, the Northlands are separated from us by an isthmus of land that terminates in a mountain range. The Pathseer, Toren, traveled as far as the foothills of that mountain range, which is the farthest anyone has traveled north in living memory. His journal confirmed many of the details, and I was tempted to steal it." He smiled. "Bellina was intrigued enough by my research quest she might have given it to me if I'd asked. Sadly, my respect for library integrity outweighed my thirst for knowledge."

"She sounds really helpful," Weston said.

"She was. I told her when I hired her what my interest was—I didn't think it was a secret, and researchers don't do as well when they don't know what the point of a search is—and she threw herself into the search. She was more excited at finding Toren's journal than I was."

Aderyn stopped herself before she could tease Isold about charming the librarian. She was sure he hadn't used any of his Herald's charm, but he might not be in a mood to appreciate a joke, not so soon after what Raynir had tried. Instead, she said, "That was nice of her."

"Bellina asked me many questions about the Fated One quests. It seems her brother was a Fated One, one of the serious ones, but he was killed by a cat-hawk outside Elkenforest before he could make any progress. She hopes we succeed, of course, but it felt as if it was personal for her." Isold stacked the pile of papers neatly together.

"This sounds like a lot," Owen said. "Can you sum up what we need to know?"

Isold nodded. "We're going into the Northlands at almost the worst possible time, five weeks before the turn of the year. It's small comfort that most of the big storms don't hit until a few weeks later, because even the small winter storms are serious by our standards. However, food and water won't be a problem. Even without Livia's *drench* spell and the <**Forager's Belt**>, there are herds of deer and elk, and any number of other prey animals to survive on."

"Because there haven't been hunters to thin the herds in centuries," Owen said.

"We can't count on that being the case anymore, if all those adventurers are headed north," Aderyn said. "Still, it's a good point. Even twice that many adventurers won't make a dent in those herds. And Caldan was so helpful in supplying us, I think we will be all right for staying warm."

"That's right," Isold said. "So, that's survival. As to what we'll find there, I have been giving the quest a lot of thought, and my conclusion is that there must be more to it than resolving the clashes of groups of human settlers. They will be too busy surviving the winter. No, I think something or someone else living in the Northlands is in need of settling a conflict, either among themselves or between them and the new settlers. My instinct is that it's a lost settlement of humans—that perhaps not all of them moved south when the level cap affected the area. But it's not impossible that we're talking about an intelligent nonhuman race such as the kobolds or the orcs."

"You don't mean aggressive and antagonistic like the orcs, do you?" Livia said. "Because I'm not sure I can be committed to bringing peace to a bunch of monsters who either don't want it or will use it to attack humans."

"I don't have any idea what it might be. I do think, if the system gave us this quest, there will be a solution. The system doesn't give quests we can't complete." Isold's eyes grew distant, as if he was reading his Codex. "I now know of two cities north of here that may have more concrete advice about survival. My system map isn't completely updated beyond that, since it's wilderness area, but it will fill in as we go."

"Does that mean we can leave tomorrow?" Aderyn asked.

Everyone looked at Owen. Owen chewed his lower lip in thought. "If Aderyn is sure we have everything we need, and Isold doesn't want to search for magic items—"

"I have to recharge the <**Healing Stone**>, and there are a few items I want to try to locate," Isold said. "But I doubt that will take more than an hour or two."

"I'll read through this list and see if there's anything else we want," Aderyn said. "But I can take care of that while Isold is busy."

Owen nodded. "How far are those cities?"

Isold again got the faraway, distant look in his eyes. "Not too far. If we leave here by eleven o'clock tomorrow, we should reach the first of them before sunset."

Owen nodded. "I think that's settled, then. Everyone be ready to head out before noon."

Everyone rose from the table. Jessemia took a step and grabbed Aderyn's shoulder to keep from falling. "My ankle," she said. "It stopped hurting while I was sitting, and I forgot about it."

"Jessemia was injured getting us into Raynir's mansion," Aderyn told Isold.

"Sit here, and I'll get the <**Wand of Healing**>," Isold said.

"Oh, I'm sure it will be fine," Jessemia protested.

Isold gave her a look of pretend reprimand. "Just sit, Jessemia."

Weston and Livia followed Isold out the door. Owen said, "I'm going to have a drink, Aderyn, do you want to join me?"

"I'll wait with Jessemia first," Aderyn said.

When they were alone in the parlor, Aderyn said, "What's wrong? You've been really quiet. Are you in more pain than you implied?"

"No, I was serious about it not hurting until I put weight on it," Jessemia said. "It's the aftereffects of all the tension and excitement. I thought Isold was dead when Raynir pulled the bell rope."

"So did I." Aderyn hesitated. "I think you should have a talk with him."

"Me? Why?"

"I did say Isold's changed in ways you should know about, if you're friends, and you were the one who talked him down from the metaphorical ledge when he was going to destroy Raynir. I didn't have any idea what to say to stop him. That might be important."

Jessemia lowered her head. "I think you may have a point. I would like to stop feeling so awkward around him."

"If we're leaving tomorrow, now's your chance." Aderyn squeezed Jessemia's hand and rose from her seat. "Come have a drink with us afterward. And ask Isold to sing. I think he could use the release."

"I'll do that." Jessemia smiled, and if it was weak, at least it was a smile. Aderyn told herself to stop worrying about her friend and left the room.

CHAPTER EIGHT

Aderyn sat close beside Owen with a glass of wine near at hand and closed her eyes. Isold's merry song mingled with the heat of the fire until it felt the music was made of flames that caressed her skin and soothed her heart. Owen's hand closed on hers, his thumb gently rubbing her knuckles. "Hey," he murmured in her ear. "I love you."

The unexpected endearment shivered through her, as welcome as the music and the fire. "I love you, too. What brought that on?"

"Just thinking about that idiot Swordsworn who thought he could abuse you. You know I'll never let anything happen to you if I can stop it, right?"

Aderyn opened her eyes. Owen's eyes were intent on her, his expression serious. "I know. I love that you want to protect me, and that you never let that desire lead you to overprotecting me."

"Yeah. I'm glad you're able to fight for yourself. I can't be with you every second." Owen drained his mug and set it down. "You want another glass of wine?"

"I'm still working on this one. Thanks, though."

Owen got up and walked over to the bar. Aderyn closed her eyes again and let the music wash over her. Isold had picked a funny song about a young woman courting a man who couldn't make up his mind. It was a popular song, Aderyn thought because it turned expectations on their heads by having the woman make the advances.

The song came to an end, and Isold waved to acknowledge the applause. "Something different now, I think," he said, and drew out his shining silver flute. When the first notes of "Come Tumbling Down" sounded, a cry of appreciation went up from the listeners, and people shoved chairs and tables out of the way to make space for an impromptu dance floor.

Aderyn swept up her wine glass and hurried to one side, near where Weston and Livia and Jessemia had gathered. As men and women leaped and swayed in the figures of the traditional dance, she looked for Owen, but she couldn't see him past the crowd. This wasn't a dance he knew, and it was too complex for her to teach it to him on the spot, but the rhythm was infectious and she wanted to move, even if it wasn't the right dance.

"I know," Weston said to Livia. "You don't dance. That's all right, this isn't a partnered dance, anyway. And I'm not sure I know it well enough."

Livia gave him a long, considering look. Then she pressed her pint mug into Weston's hands and approached the dancers. When Isold trilled through the notes leading from the chorus to the verse, she took two sliding steps and leaped with the others on the upbeat, putting herself solidly in the center of the floor.

And Livia danced.

Aderyn watched with her mouth open in astonishment. Livia's movements were graceful and perfectly timed, flowing and lithe when the music sailed in a crescendo like a waterfall. Gradually, all the other dancers slowed to a halt until Livia danced alone. Aderyn had never seen anything like it. The music didn't move Livia; she *was* the music, as if Isold's flute had brought her to life.

The flute's voice rose higher and higher until it was almost inaudible, then trilled sweetly to its conclusion. With the final note, Livia held her pose, not moving until the crowd's shouts and applause freed her. Breathing heavily, she returned to Weston's side and took her mug from his unresisting hand. In one gulp, she drained its contents.

"And *that*," she said, "is why I don't dance. Seventeen years of instruction and performance, including ten years with Asylum's premier dance troupe. It took me that long to realize that dance shouldn't just be performative—it ought to be a celebration. But people tend to stare."

Weston grabbed his wife around the waist and twirled her around, making her squawk indignantly. "I don't care who stares," he said, and kissed her soundly. "I want you to dance with me, every chance we get, and you can learn to forget all those lessons and let the music carry you away."

Livia blushed. "You've got a deal."

Owen joined them, holding a mug foaming over with suds. "Did I really just see Livia dance? I thought she didn't know how."

"It turns out she was concealing her talents from the world," Weston said, kissing Livia again, "which none of us ought to do, right? Anybody else have skills they've been hiding?"

"All my skills are useless because you don't have electricity, computer games, or Frisbees in this world," Owen said, not speaking loudly, though the noise of people pulling chairs and tables back into their original positions meant it was unlikely anyone could hear them. "But if someone invents discus golf, I'm your man."

"You already know I'm a master of Wall," Aderyn said. "What about you, Jessemia?"

"What?" Jessemia turned from where she'd been watching Isold, who was singing something slow and melodic. "Oh. I guess I'm good at horseback riding. Why isn't that a system skill?"

Weston opened his mouth, frowned, and said, "It's not, is it? I wonder why that is."

"Well, adventurers don't usually ride horses in the wilderness," Livia said. "That's just inviting a monster to have a nice snack."

"Yes, but—hmm." Aderyn considered it. "It's not a system skill, which means anyone can learn it, classed or non-classed. And it might be a useful skill to someone who is traveling cross-country and doesn't intend to get into fights with monsters. I wonder."

"Wonder what?" Livia asked.

"Whether the skills people can learn and improve at through practice rather than through advancement are that way on purpose. Maybe the system *doesn't* discriminate against the people who reject the Call."

"Did we think it did?" Weston asked.

"It was something Jessemia and I were talking about earlier, about why there aren't non-adventuring classes. Like Davith growing up to become an Innkeeper class. We were wondering, if the system tells us we're ready to advance our destiny when we get the Call, does it not like the people who reject it? Like they're spurning its offer of a destiny?"

"That," said Owen, "sounds like late night philosophizing, and I'm not drunk enough for that. Come on, Isold's singing, let's appreciate him."

Aderyn found a new seat, her old one having been appropriated by a burly Stalwart whose petite Deadeye companion sat on his enormous knee, and let herself be captivated by the music. It was a song she recognized, a melancholy song Isold often sang around the campfire about lost loves, and it made her heart ache for the story of the man and woman who loved each other and could never be together. Why sad songs felt so much more powerful when she was happy and content, she didn't know.

She glanced at Jessemia and was dismayed to see tears in her friend's eyes. It wasn't *that* sad a song. Jessemia and Isold had entered the taproom together, smiling and talking cheerfully, so Aderyn had thought they were back on course to being friends. But something else was clearly bothering Jessemia, and Aderyn wished she knew how to help.

She and Owen stayed another hour, listening to Isold singing and playing, until a yawn triggered Aderyn's sleepiness. "I'm ready for bed," she told Owen.

"Me too. But I need antitoxin first if I don't want to wake up hung over."

Aderyn hadn't drunk heavily, but she tipped back the shot glass of vile green liquid, and her head cleared immediately. Strangely, that made her even more tired. With Owen, she climbed the stairs to their room, which was chillier than she remembered. She undressed rapidly and dove under the heavy featherbed.

Owen joined her moments later, putting his arms around her and pulling her close. "Are you very sleepy?"

"I'm actually not in the mood for sex, sorry."

"I didn't mean that. No, there was something I wanted to discuss. But not if you're too tired. It can wait for morning."

Aderyn groaned. "Suspense will keep me awake, thanks. What is it?"

Owen chuckled. "Sorry. It's just that I'm considering asking Jessemia to join us on the northward journey."

That woke Aderyn like ice down her shift. "What? Owen, Jessemia's too low a level to be on our team. She can't join us."

"I didn't say join our party, I said come on the journey with us. As our guide. The more Isold said about what he learned, the more convinced I became that we need a Pathseer to help us find our goal. Jessemia said quest objectives appear on her map when she knows what they are. That could keep us from wandering aimlessly. Not to mention that she has weather sense and [Tracking] and [Improved Survival] and I don't know how many other wilderness-oriented skills. And she's a friend, so we wouldn't have the awkwardness of getting to know a stranger. I don't know about you, but I don't want to team up with someone we don't know just as we're on the verge of completing the [Fated One's Destiny] quest."

Aderyn sat up. [Darkvision] made Owen a clearly-outlined gray figure next to her. He didn't look like he was joking. "Owen, she's only level ten. Yes, her skills would help us even at that level, but we might be going into dangerous territory. What if we can't keep her safe?"

"That would be her decision, Aderyn. I think we should make the offer and see what she wants. She already said it was possible she'd be hired to guide questers hoping to settle, so she must not be too troubled by worries about the dangers of the Northlands." Owen fumbled to clasp Aderyn's hand. "I thought you'd like the idea of having her along."

"She's a wonderful companion, you know that. And she knows you're from another world, so we wouldn't have to guard our speech. I just—" Aderyn sighed. "You're right. She should be the one to choose. And I agree with you on both counts—needing a Pathseer and not wanting to bring in a stranger. But we should discuss this with the others first."

"In the morning." Owen yawned and tugged on Aderyn's hand to make her lie down. "We have plenty of time for once."

"Jinx," Aderyn said muzzily, and drifted off to sleep.

THE NEXT MORNING, ADERYN WAS ONLY BARELY dressed when Owen said, "I want to decide about Jessemia before we go down to breakfast. We shouldn't mention the possibility to her before we're all agreed."

"You don't think anyone will be opposed to it?"

"No. But it's still awkward if we talk around her like she's not there."

Owen left the room, and Aderyn sat on the edge of the bed and pulled her boots on. That was what she'd forgotten, new boots. Something to take care of after they ate.

Owen returned with Isold trailing him, and Livia and Weston entered a few minutes later. "This seems ominous," Livia said. "Is something wrong?"

"No. But I want to ask Jessemia to guide us into the Northlands, and we should all agree. Thoughts?" Owen asked.

"Jessemia's only level ten," Weston said. "That's outside the allowed range to join our team. But—you said, ask her to guide us. So you mean she wouldn't be on the roster."

"I like it," Livia said. "It beats hiring a stranger."

"That's what I said," Aderyn said. "What do you think, Isold?"

Isold focused on Aderyn, and she got the feeling he had mentally been elsewhere. "Do we need a Pathseer?" he said. "We never have before."

"Before, we weren't going into completely unknown territory," Owen replied. "Jessemia has skills that will benefit us, and her map will be more thorough than yours—you know what an advantage your map is in a city, and hers is like that but for the wilderness. I'm in favor of anything that keeps us from wandering, given how nebulous the **[Eye of the Storm]** quest is."

"You don't have anything against Jessemia, right?" Aderyn asked Isold.

"Of course not. But we could be putting her in danger, given her low level. My question is, if we need a Pathseer, is it more important to find one of high level and greater skills?"

"I agree with Livia about not wanting to include a stranger," Owen said. "And I told Aderyn last night that the choice would be Jessemia's. We don't know that she'll even want to do it. But, to answer your question, I don't think we need a Pathseer so desperately that we should hunt for a more level-appropriate option. I see Jessemia meeting us here as an opportunity we ought to explore."

"I admit my reservations are about the likelihood that we will be drawn into dangers Jessemia can't face at her level," Isold said. "You make a good point. She may not want to join us."

"Then I'll ask her, and we'll see what she says," Owen said. "Then, after breakfast, Isold and Aderyn will handle some last business, and we'll be out of Finion's Gate before lunch."

Weston made an exaggeratedly pained face and grinned when Livia nudged him.

Guests occupied two of the tables in the private dining room when the friends entered, but Jessemia wasn't there. "I'll see if she's in her room," Aderyn said. "Tell Davith I want sausages, all right? I'll be back."

Jessemia didn't answer her door immediately when Aderyn knocked. When she finally did, she was tying the lace binding her braid and was barefoot. "I had a late night and I'm just getting started," she explained. "I hope you didn't come all the way up here just to get me."

"Of course I did. I was afraid you wouldn't think you had a

standing invitation to dine with us." Aderyn waited for Jessemia to finish dressing, and the two descended the stairs.

"I thought I did, but then I didn't want to presume, and then I told myself I was being silly," Jessemia said with a laugh. "Are you leaving today? I wanted to say goodbye. I should have found a quest yesterday, but things were so chaotic, it slipped my mind."

"Well, we have an idea about that." Aderyn pushed open the dining room door.

A plate with three steaming, glistening sausages and a pile of hashed potatoes with flecks of ham waited at Aderyn's place. She seated herself and dug in happily. Who knew when they'd eat like this again?

Jessemia accepted a serving of eggs scrambled with cheese. "What idea is that? Did someone mention a quest I could take?"

"Sort of," Owen said. "We want you to come with us as a guide to the Northlands."

Jessemia dropped her fork onto her plate, scattering bits of egg across her lap. "You want *what?*"

"Sorry," Owen said with a grin. "I didn't think it was that outrageous a suggestion."

"Well, no, but it was a surprise. I can't team with you." Jessemia picked up her fork. "So I assumed you were leaving this morning without me."

"Only if it's what you want. We could use a guide, and we want that guide to be you. So we'd issue you the quest, possibly more than one quest, and you'd gain experience from completing that."

Jessemia's gaze flicked to Isold, then to Weston and Livia. "And you're all in agreement?"

"Of course," Livia said. "I like the idea of knowing what weather to expect. And you've got to be better than us at hunting."

Jessemia shook her head. "I'm sorry, I just had a flashback to someone threatening to drag me by my ankles to Guerdon Deep—doesn't this strike you as at all surreal that you *want* me with you now?"

Everyone laughed. "We're well past that, Jessemia," Owen said.

"But be sure before you accept," Isold said. "We will be going into dangers well above what a level ten Pathseer would normally face. We can only do so much to protect you."

"Isold! Don't be so discouraging," Aderyn said.

"It's not wrong to be cautious, Aderyn," Isold said. "It has to be Jessemia's choice what risks she wants to take."

Jessemia eyed Isold again. "What would you do, in my place?" she asked.

Isold didn't answer. He drained his glass of fresh apple juice and set it down so it made barely any noise against the tabletop. "Are you asking me to make the decision for you?"

"I want to know your opinion, that's all." Jessemia tapped her fork against the edge of her plate, but her attention was all on Isold.

Isold nodded. "It's a dangerous challenge, true, but I see no reason it shouldn't be a successful one. Why not accompany us instead of strangers, if you intend to take on another escort quest?"

"All right." Jessemia's smile widened. "I admit I was feeling a little down about parting ways so soon after meeting again. I'll do it."

"Great!" Owen's enthusiasm faded. "I don't know how to issue a quest."

"Varoun showed me how to issue battle quests, and this isn't much different," Aderyn said. "Open your Codex and focus on the space below your quest list, then say 'Issue quest' and when the silver dot blinks, say what the quest is."

"Hmm. I hadn't thought that far." Owen fell silent for a few seconds, then said, "Issue quest. Guide our team to the place in the Northlands where the [**Fated One's Destiny: Eye of the Storm**] quest begins."

"That might be too specific—" Aderyn began.

Jessemia blinked and lifted her hand to press an invisible letter. "I guess it wasn't. And—wow. That is *really* far north."

"You know where we're going?" Livia exclaimed.

"There's a destination marked on my map now. No label, just a point somewhere north of the Eretai Mountains. And that's the first I've ever seen them named, too." Jessemia blinked again, more rapidly as if clearing her vision.

"Too bad I can't see what you see, or I could use *scry* and get us there tonight," Livia said.

"I could draw a map," Jessemia offered. "It would be pretty accurate. Would that work?"

"Not unless we knew of a unique structure in the area for *scry* to latch onto, like we did with Ikharatia." Livia tapped her fingers against her stone forearm in thought. "If we—no. I could still *scry* our destination and get us closer, but it's possible I would drop us in the middle of something dangerous. It's safer to take the slow overland route."

Jessemia nodded. "I understand. And either way, this is going to be exciting!"

"Let's hang onto that," Owen said. "And, at the risk of incurring Arlia's wrath at our bad manners, eat quickly. Now that we have a destination, I'm increasingly eager to be on the road."

"Not before I recharge the <**Healing Stone**>," Isold said. "Though if Jessemia were to help me, my purchases would go faster."

"Really?" Aderyn began. She caught Isold's eye and was quelled by the intensity of his glare. She'd been about to say that

Isold's map was better than Jessemia's in a city, and Jessemia didn't know Finion's Gate much better than they did, but she realized in time that Isold had a purpose in getting Jessemia alone. More excitement welled up inside her. Maybe Isold had decided he wanted a romantic relationship, after all, and he needed to be alone with Jessemia to declare himself. "Well, that's good, faster is better," she said, hoping she didn't sound awkward. How wonderful if they were all paired neatly off!

CHAPTER NINE

By ten o'clock, the Alabaster Inn's private parlor looked like a shop itself with the team's gear spread out over the floor and chairs and table. Aderyn finished checking the contents of the <**Knapsack of Plenty**> and began loading in the larger items, starting with the ground canvases. "Remember when we were heading away from Dungeon Spiteful and we had to sleep on the bare ground? We've come so far."

"We've had a lot of good fortune," Livia said. "But we shouldn't take it for granted."

"No, but we can be glad of it." Aderyn stretched her feet in their new boots. They had a minor magic of rejuvenation on them that kept blisters from forming as her feet adjusted to them, as well as self-repairing scuffs and tears. That was another thing she was grateful for, the resources to buy nice boots and not have to worry about things like blisters.

Owen was examining the edges of his <**Deadly Blade**>, though to Aderyn's knowledge the knife never lost its keenness. "I sometimes think about the adventurers whose possessions came to us. Like, I don't know the name of the guy who had the <Sunsword> before me, but I like to imagine he's cheering us on."

"I'm not sure that's true of Aurelon," Weston said. "If he was level fifty, he might think Aderyn is presumptuous, daring to wield his sword at such a low level."

"Well, Aurelon doesn't get a say," Aderyn said, patting the hilt of her short sword. "Though if he was responsible for the level cap in some way, maybe he *is* cheering us on as we aim to break it."

"I still say he was a thundering loser," Livia said. "Destroying a city and not caring—yes, I know, that Repository witness might not have been accurate, but that's not the sort of thing you forget or misinterpret. If that's what happens to people at higher levels, I'm not interested."

"I'm sure we're still able to choose how we use our skills and magic," Aderyn protested. "It can't be that *everyone* of level fifty behaved badly, or our civilization wouldn't exist."

The door to the private parlor opened, and Isold and Jessemia entered. They weren't holding hands or behaving in other affectionate ways, and Aderyn, who'd hoped they had used their shopping expedition to resolve more personal issues, concealed her disappointment. "I wish now I'd bought potions in Ikharatia," Isold said. "I'm sorry to say many of the magic items I hoped for had either been sold already or were otherwise unavailable, and even Jessemia's skills combined with my own weren't enough to locate any items of epic bounty, wands or otherwise."

"Damn," Owen said. "I was hoping for those. Are you saying there were enough adventurers of high level passing through Finion's Gate to clean out the vendors?"

"Not quite. The <**Wand of Epic Bounty**> is highly specialized, and we found no Spellcrafters capable of creating or reimbuing it. Which, to me, is less disappointing than if someone else had bought the last one." Isold set his knapsack on the table and opened it. "That's probably not a very honorable attitude."

"It's reasonable," Weston said. "But you did find something, right?"

"Yes, and I need to remember that five levels ago I would have been thrilled at what I acquired and the low prices I paid. Another benefit of being the top-ranked Glory Games team is that people scrambled to give me a bargain so they could say we bought from them."

Jessemia giggled. "It was funny. The Spiritsmith Tryanna who owned the shop where we found the <**Potions of Life**> wanted Isold to sign her wall. Her actual wall. It had all these signatures of famous Glory Games participants."

"That's a small price to pay for a large discount," Livia said.

Isold smiled. "Indeed. I bought all three <**Potions of Life**> she had in stock, plus two magic energy rejuvenation potions—here you are, Livia—and another three weapon enhancement solutions. She did not have <**Potions of Alacrity**>, so I picked up speed enhancers instead. And, in a partial replacement for the <**Wand of Epic Bounty**>, I chose these." Isold held up a tube filled with a glittering pink liquid, as thick as the weapon enhancers. "A <**Potion of Boldness**> gives the drinker the effects of an [**Inspire Courage**] song combined with a <**Potion of Strength**>, as well as resistance to damage for one hour."

Owen took the tube and held it up to the light from the nearest window. "That's not bad, even if it does look like glitter glue."

"I'm not going to ask why your world needs sparkling glue," Isold said. "But, speaking of glue, Tryanna gave us four vials of

<Sovereign Solvent>. It dissolves any adhesive it's applied to. My guess is she gives these away to everyone, but I'm willing to accept her generosity."

"That's not the best part," Jessemia said. "Tell them about the <Twinsword>."

Aderyn gasped. "You didn't sell the <Twinsword>?"

"I hope that's an expression of surprise and not dismay, because I did, in fact, find a buyer for that weapon." Isold's smile became smug. "Not to a weapons seller, but to a collector who has been searching for years for a companion to the <Twinsword> he already has. We made Rafatorus a very happy man today, and I put all of that money into... this."

He removed something that clinked from his knapsack and displayed it. Aderyn expected something made of crystal or glass, but it was a set of copper windchimes, six slender tubes green with verdigris. Isold held it up by the wires so the tubes moved freely and tapped against the central copper disc, chiming softly. The sounds reminded Aderyn of spring days in Far Haven, when the soft breezes blew and every windchime in the village harmonized to sound like a symphony of bells.

"This is a <Wayfarer's Windchimes>," Isold said. "The feather, which is this dish-shaped part that hangs down and catches the wind, is imbued with a Spellcrafter's memory of the perfect spring day. When hung properly, the windchimes generate a bubble of peaceful spring weather regardless of ambient weather conditions. It will deflect the most violent winds and maintain a constant temperature of seventy degrees within the bubble. It's missing the stand from which it is supposed to hang, but so long as it is hung on anything that allows it to move freely, that won't interfere with its performance."

Owen tapped one of the copper tubes so it struck the center

and rang out more loudly. "This could make a huge difference. Where did you find it?"

"It was hanging in the window of a shop we passed," Jessemia said. "Isold bargained the shop owner down to three-quarters the asking price. It was amazing."

"I swear you have better luck at finding random things than anyone should," Weston said, "but since you use it on our behalf, I'm not going to complain too loudly in case the system gets ideas about shutting down whatever exploit that is."

"I enjoy the pleasure of the serendipitous find." Isold handed the <**Wayfarer's Windchimes**> to Aderyn. "Of course, they aren't a perfect solution. The bubble only lasts for twenty-four hours, after which the item must be exposed to still, clear weather for four consecutive hours to recharge. I learned from my research that blizzards in the Northlands can last for days, so we may discover it's less useful than we hoped. And if it's used in very cold weather, the chimes will crack and the item becomes useless. So, we should be cautious with it."

"My [**Improved Survival**] tells me what the ambient temperature is, so we won't be caught by surprise," Jessemia said.

"I'll take what we can get." Owen resumed his seat. "None of you have any experience with snowstorms, do you?"

"Not like the ones you keep warning us about," Livia said. "Are they really that devastating?"

"They can be. They don't get that bad where I come from, but I've seen video of storms you wouldn't believe. I hope the <**Soldier's Friend**> knows how to anchor tents deep."

"Based on what I learned, I don't anticipate many very bad storms this time of year, but we should be prepared. There are always years that are outliers as far as weather goes." Isold closed his knapsack. "And I feel I am as prepared as it's possible to be."

As he spoke, the clock on the mantel chimed the quarter hour. "10:45," Livia said. "We should get moving."

"Are we sure we don't have time for lunch?" Weston pleaded.

"Arlia made us a basket of wedgers for the road," Aderyn said. "And bottles of new beer and peeled hardboiled eggs. Owen says it's picnic food."

"I don't know what a picnic is, but it gets my stamp of approval," Weston said.

THE CLEAR, WINDLESS DAY, THOUGH CHILLY, FELT LIKE a good omen on their journey. For once, the sun warmed Aderyn so she left her leather coat open. She ate her wedger and licked spurts of mustard off her finger and felt wonderfully content. A good meal, the companionship of friends... she couldn't think of a better way to begin a journey.

The road north from Finion's Gate was well trodden, if unpaved, and they had plenty of company as they walked. Other groups that were clearly adventuring teams were visible ahead, and when Aderyn looked back, she saw another two or three groups coming up from behind. She didn't Assess any of them, not seeing the point when it wasn't as if they'd have anything to do with them.

Around three in the afternoon, one of those teams passed them, walking rapidly northward. The team politely didn't shove past, but split to walk on either side of Aderyn and her friends, and in a few minutes they were well ahead.

"I wonder why they're in a hurry," Aderyn said.

"Maybe they want to be sure to get rooms at whatever inn Ravenhearst has," Livia said.

"Crap," Weston said. "I didn't think about that. Ravenhearst isn't all that big, is it?"

"I've never been there, so my information is spotty," Jessemia replied. "I know it's bigger than a village, big enough to have more than one inn, but based on all these people, I'm not sure there will be enough rooms."

"Maybe we should quicken our pace," Isold said.

"We can do that, but our tents are comfortable enough we won't suffer if we have to sleep outdoors." Owen shielded his eyes against the late-afternoon sun. He now wore a knit cap striped in green and white, beneath which his blond hair stuck out in tufts, that he claimed made him look like a mountain man. Aderyn thought it looked odd combined with the dark blue cloak he wore over his armor. "Still, I do like sleeping in a real bed."

"We're another two and a half hours' walk away at our current pace," Jessemia said. "We'll get there just after sunset."

"Did you have to calculate that, or do you just know?" Aderyn asked, curious.

"If I examine my map after I've walked a steady pace for fifteen minutes, some numbers appear that show me how long it will take to reach a destination, assuming I keep that pace the whole way. Convenient, right?"

"That's almost like the system talking to you!"

Jessemia's smile faded. "Is it? I didn't think about it, but I suppose, if I get information others don't, that is like a special communication. I'm not sure how I feel about that. I'd rather not have the system's attention if I can help it."

"Why not?" Aderyn asked.

"I suppose because I spent a lot of time thinking I was special without giving any consideration to what that meant, and the system never did anything to tell me otherwise. That left me feeling like if I *did* have the system's attention, it might not be a positive thing."

Since Jessemia didn't sound self-derogatory, Aderyn didn't reassure her that she was wrong. "That's possible, I guess. Suveer said the system was usually critical of him in its communications. I still don't know why that was."

"I'm amazed the system talks to you in your Assessments at all," Jessemia said. "Or to anyone. It's the system, not a person. Unless that's wrong, too."

"I have no idea." Aderyn still had no answer for this question. The few times she tried communicating with the system other than for an Assessment, she always got a response, but there wasn't anything in those responses to confirm that it was a person she was talking to. And yet, what else was there? "It seems wrong, because how could a person have that much power?"

"Aurelon at level fifty had enough power to level cities," Isold said.

"Yes, but isn't destructive power simple? It's far more difficult to create. At least, I think so."

"So do I," Livia said. "My resource cost for things like [Elemental Blast] or *launch* is lower than for, say, *greater polymorph*. Or *summon earth elemental*. I think the system can't possibly be a person, not with all the complexity it has to manage."

"I used to think it was a computer," Owen said, "back when I first arrived here. But it would have to be AI, and... well, I guess this world might be more advanced in that way, but if the system is an AI, why aren't there other computers here?"

"What's AI?" Weston asked.

"It means artificial intelligence. My world was developing it when I left. It's when you have enough of the right kind of computing power for a machine to think or respond like a human.

Sort of. I never really paid attention—it seemed like more hype than reality."

"Computers are like the Spellcrafted devices in the Enchanterium, right?" Aderyn said. "With those scrying screens and the buttons?"

"Right." Owen hesitated. "Right. So I guess you *do* have something like computers, and an AI running the world might not be so odd."

"You don't sound like it's a good thing."

Owen laughed. "It's just that my world has hundreds, maybe thousands of stories about rogue computers or AIs taking over the world and turning humans into slaves. Not so many about the good AI that protects the world and gives it classes and adventuring and the Codex. So the odds feel stacked against us, if the system is a computer."

Aderyn wasn't sure she followed all of that, but what she did understand left her feeling tense. The pleasure of the day and of walking with friends disappeared. "I guess we're not likely to find out the truth, unless the system decides to reveal itself." She waited, hoping and fearing for a response, but no silver letters appeared.

Weston cleared his throat. "In the spirit of not talking about potentially discouraging things, how about we walk faster? Just in case we need to arm-wrestle someone for the last rooms in the inn."

They picked up the pace for fifteen minutes, at which point Jessemia declared they would now reach Ravenhearst in an hour and twenty-two minutes. It was an easily maintainable speed, but between that and the sun and her heavy coat, Aderyn had worked up a light sweat by the time she saw Ravenhearst in the distance. The city was large to be visible from more than a mile away, with a stone wall that looked like someone had painted a black line at the base of the tall buildings. Smoke rose from its many chimneys, drawing charcoal streaks across the pale blue sky.

On a whim, she Assessed the city. They weren't planning to spend more than one night there, and they didn't need to buy supplies, but it was always a good idea to gain information.

Name: Ravenhearst

Status: City

Government: Dukedom

Civilization level: 12

Resources: Spiritsmith x8, Spellcrafter x10, Tidecaller x7, Windwarden x15, Flamecrafter x13, Earthbreaker x19, Bonemender x8; Crafters level 13; Hospitality level 13; Food supply level 13

Ravenhearst is the last city before the northern frontier. It's close enough to Finion's Gate that citizens of Ravenhearst speak casually of "going to the city" to take advantage of the metropolis's greater resources. Many people from Ravenhearst take pride in their proximity to Finion's Gate as if Ravenhearst were an adjunct. You can ask your husband what a suburb is sometime.

Aside from this, and despite what its citizens believe, Ravenhearst is nothing special. It's unlikely you'll remember it when you're gone.

Aderyn choked back a laugh at how dismissive the system's words were. She pictured a city full of snooty people who weren't as great as they thought they were. Hopefully they weren't arrogant to travelers, because she didn't think she could keep from laughing if they patronized her or her friends to their faces.

Though the road wasn't thronged with adventurers, the closer the team drew to Ravenhearst, the more men and women they passed. Aderyn noted in passing that there weren't any non-classed among them, no families traveling north. That brought home more clearly than anything else the fact that they were traveling into uncharted lands. No one, even potential settlers, would endanger their family that way.

The Ravenhearst gate rose a good twenty feet high, much higher than the wall, but aside from this it looked just the way a typical city gate did, two solid slabs of oak banded with iron pitted with age. The short queue in front of the gate reassured Aderyn that walking faster had been a good idea. Now she Assessed the adventurers in line ahead of them and determined there were three teams, two with an average level of around twelve and the other averaging fourteen. Only the team at the end of the queue glanced their way, and Aderyn avoided meeting anyone's eyes, in case they found her regard intimidating.

Slowly, the queue advanced. The higher-level team entered, and then, to Aderyn's surprise, the next group in line, after some inaudible argument, walked away from the gate. The five adventurers in that group stomped angrily past Aderyn, none of them speaking, and headed back toward Finion's Gate. "They didn't like the entrance fee," Weston whispered.

Owen raised his eyebrows. "That's unexpected. Too high for them to afford, or just unreasonable?"

Weston shook his head. "Couldn't tell. I doubt it will be a problem for us."

The team immediately ahead paused at the gate while the Stalwart in the front negotiated for entrance. After a minute, that team filed through the gate with a few final words with the guards, and it was their turn at the gate.

Aderyn moved forward behind Owen. There were four guards, two male Swordsworn and a male and a female Swifthands, all of them level fifteen, and none of them looked friendly. Aderyn had the sense that they had been on duty for a while and were tired of interacting with strangers. If the team that had walked away wasn't the only one to argue over the price of admission, no wonder the guards were weary.

A Swordsworn and the male Swifthands stepped forward to block Owen's progress, as abruptly as if he'd tried to run them down instead of stopping ten feet from the gate. "That's far enough," the Swordsworn said. A copper disc pin secured his dark green cloak at the throat, but unlike the guards at Finion's Gate, it was beaten copper without class insignia. "Your business in Ravenhearst?"

"Just looking to spend a night here before traveling on," Owen said. He was doing the thing where he pretended not to notice someone's animosity. The genuine sound of his responses impressed Aderyn every time.

"We'll see." The Swordsworn, who was taller than Owen, looked him up and down. "Jacob Owen Lindberg. That's a weird name."

"It's the only one I have," Owen said cheerfully. "I go by Owen. And you are?"

The Swordsworn sneered. "The entry fee is forty gold. Each."

Aderyn, caught by surprise, let out a squeak. The Swordsworn's gaze fixed on her. "Too rich for you, Warmaster?"

"Are you always this hostile, or are you just having a bad day?" Owen asked. He still sounded pleasant, but the stiffness of his shoulders told Aderyn he was losing patience.

"I'm not interested in a chat," the Swordsworn said. "Two hundred forty gold. Or you can take your chances outside tonight."

Irritated, Aderyn sorted through the <**Purse of Great Capacity**> for a handful of coins. Normally she wouldn't reveal just how much the little purse could hold, but the Swordsworn's attitude and the exorbitant fee annoyed her into sorting through the handful where the man could watch. "Here," she said, slapping four large gold coins and four smaller ones into his hand. "Satisfied?"

The Swordsworn snorted derisively. "Your fates don't matter to me. Go on in. No fighting, stealing, vandalism, or defrauding others."

"Or we'll get kicked out?" Owen no longer sounded polite.

"Hah. Or you'll get your asses beaten and *then* we'll kick you out." The Swordsworn turned his attention on the team standing behind Weston. "You've been warned."

Weston stepped forward. He loomed over the Swordsworn, who for the first time looked uncertain. "Excuse me," Weston said in his deepest, most menacing voice. "I want to get a head start on the fighting and vandalism so you and I can see whose ass gets beaten."

The Swordsworn swallowed. "Threatening a guard—"

"Who, me? Threaten?" Weston smiled cheerfully, his whole demeanor changing. "I've never threatened anyone in my life. Have a good evening, all." He strode past, hooking Livia's stone arm by the elbow and towing her along with him. Aderyn hurried to follow.

Past the gate, the street opened up, and businesses with signs that showed they catered to adventurers lined the road: general supply stores, weapons merchants, taverns, clothiers, even a bathhouse. Aderyn barely noticed the buildings in her hurry to leave the guards behind.

"That was unpleasant," she said when they were well away from the gate.

"Yes, and now it's over. We'll have a meal, get some rest, and be on our way in the morning," Owen said. "No need to get into trouble here."

Jessemia, who'd been at the head of their group, slowed her steps. "Are you sure about that?"

She pointed at the bathhouse, which advertised its services with a large wooden sign hanging from two short chains above the door. The sign depicted a burly, hairy-chested man sitting in a tub, wielding a long-handled scrubbing brush. The picture was awkwardly painted, and not at all appealing to Aderyn despite her love of baths, but that wasn't what Jessemia pointed to. Nailed to the door was a sheet of grimy paper, on which was written in blocky, dark letters, FATED ONES NOT WELCOME HERE.

CHAPTER TEN

"What the hell?" Owen exclaimed.

Aderyn shushed him. "Don't draw attention!"

"Aderyn, it's not like anyone can Assess me for my —" Owen shut his mouth and surreptitiously pointed at the sign. "But why would someone care about excluding Fated Ones? The fakers usually spend money like water—you'd think merchants would want them as customers."

"Fakers?" Jessemia said. "But doesn't the system still treat the ones who aren't serious about the Fated One quests like it does you? Back when I thought I was the Fated One, I wasn't pretending."

"That's true. I guess I mean they're unserious, like you say. There are a lot of people who claim the title who never have any intention of pursuing it. That's enough of a difference from me to make me resentful of them for putting themselves on the same level as me after we've put our lives on the line for the Fated One quests." Owen was still staring at the sign. "This is too weird for words."

"It's just the one sign," Weston said, gazing at the nearby businesses. "Maybe a wannabe Fated One tore up the bathhouse. Maybe a Fated One seduced the owner's wife. It's probably personal."

"Still. It's weird." Owen sighed. "Let's see about an inn. We should avoid the first one we come to, because that's where everyone stops. Isold?"

Isold was already reading his system map. "Three inns, all of them along the main network of roads. Ravenhearst is not laid out as neatly as Finion's Gate—it has the look of a small village that grew bigger by adding to the original structures rather than widening and expanding their streets. But there are streets that are clearly larger than others. It's actually quite beautiful, like the veins of a leaf." He blinked rapidly. "This way."

At half an hour before sunset, Ravenhearst's main street teemed with men and women strolling along in pairs or in groups. Aderyn didn't bother Assessing anyone, because no one stood out as interesting or potentially dangerous. Instead, she looked at the signs over the doors as they passed. None of them had lettering, just pictures, but the pictures were surprisingly detailed. She especially liked the one above a bootmaker's shop that depicted a cat wearing very fine boots, chasing a mouse. The mouse's smile said it didn't expect to be caught.

"There's another one," Livia said. "'No Fated Ones allowed.' On the brothel door. The *brothel*. Seriously, how weird is that? Banning Fated Ones from a brothel?"

"And on that Spiritsmith's shop," Isold said. "And the herbalist's next door."

"Now I'm worried," Aderyn said. "Not about Owen being detected as, well, you know. But if there's something going on about Fated Ones, maybe we need to know what it is. In case it affects the real one."

Isold turned down the next side street. "The inn is this way. The Lucky Diamond."

"That sounds more like a casino to me," Owen said. "That's like a tavern just for gambling."

"I never considered anything like that could exist," Weston said. "I wonder..."

Livia lightly slapped his arm. "It would get boring after you fleeced a hundred people."

"Yes, but I'd have a hundred fortunes. Don't say you wouldn't appreciate a hundred fortunes."

"We already have enough to buy a mansion in Asylum if we want!"

"I'm sorry I mentioned it," Owen said with a laugh. "Let's see if this place has rooms available."

The Lucky Diamond Inn showed signs of prosperity in its wide glass windows, big enough to show people seated in the taproom, and in the neat little garden surrounding it. The garden wasn't pretty at this time of year, but in the summer the shrubs would blossom with color and the grass edging the path would be vibrantly green. Owen strode up the three steps to the wide porch circling the building and pushed open the door, letting out warm air that smelled of pork roast and ale. The sounds of a dozen cheerful conversations drifted out on the air, along with the clink of utensils and the *tock* of wooden tankards hitting tabletops.

Aderyn followed Owen to the bar, where a wide-hipped, heavyset woman with powerful arms and a stern expression poured beer from a tap into a pewter pitcher Aderyn didn't think she herself could lift one handed. "You want something to drink?" the woman said, her voice deep and commanding.

"We do, and we were hoping to take rooms for the night." Owen leaned his elbows on the bar. "Do you have anything available?"

The woman eyed their group for so long Aderyn Assessed her. If they were going to have a problem, she wanted to know what kind.

Name: Briallen

Traits: suspicious, generous, tough, unrelenting

Suspicious paired with generous and tough suggested Briallen didn't trust easily, but when she gave her trust, she gave it whole-heartedly. Unrelenting could be good or bad, but Aderyn was willing to give the woman the benefit of the doubt.

"Married couples," Briallen said. She slid the full pitcher across the bar to a serving woman and picked up another pitcher. "What about you two?"

"We're not together," Jessemia said quickly.

"That's right," Isold said almost at the same time. "We're not together."

Briallen again silently sized them up. "Rooms are ten gold per night per person, up to four people per room. Can't say I want to rent a room to just one person, if you're looking to split up. You'd share with whoever else I put in there, no complaining."

"I understand," Isold said. "You'd lose money that way. Suppose we were to pay fifty gold each for two rooms? On the understanding that you won't rent the extra space to anyone else?"

Briallen laughed. "That's pretty poor bargaining. You're not going to make it far with skills like that."

Isold smiled. "I'm a Herald, actually, and my intent is to purchase your good will, given how many people no doubt want your services. We have the coin; you have the lodgings and, to judge by the smell, an extremely fine cook. What do you say?"

"Huh." Briallen's eyes narrowed in thought. "You willing to perform tonight?"

"In exchange for our meal? Certainly."

Briallen let out a hearty laugh. "Now *that* is more like it. Fair enough. One hundred gold for a night's lodgings for the six of you, plus tonight's supper is on the house."

"Excellent." Isold shook the woman's hand. Aderyn grabbed a handful of coin and sorted out ten of the middle-sized gold coins. Briallen's attention focused on the <**Purse of Great Capacity**>.

"That's magic," she said bluntly.

"It is. Is that a problem?" Aderyn asked.

"Not to me, but you'd better keep it close on you. Most adventurers aren't evil, but they are opportunists." Briallen pocketed the coins and shouted, "Kian! Take these folks upstairs to rooms seven and eight. Put you close together."

A skinny boy dressed as a server, in a tan apron over the same white shirt it looked like all the servers wore, dodged a couple of drinkers and nodded to Owen. "Follow me, sir." He didn't look like much, but if he'd identified Owen as the leader, he wasn't someone to be underestimated. Aderyn Assessed him, too, and discovered he was a level one Spiritsmith. Older than he looked, too, if he'd accepted the Call. Why he wasn't in the safe zone killing diseased rats, she didn't know, but she resolved to keep an eye on him.

The upper floor looked like most inns Aderyn had ever seen, one long hall with doors on either side. Rooms seven and eight were halfway down the hall on the right. Kian opened the door with the number 7 painted on it and reeled off instructions in a bored-sounding way. "Two beds guaranteed vermin-free, there's a chest to keep your belongings in but there's no locks so it's your own lookout if you do, washstand has hot and cold running water. You're to leave before noon if you don't want to pay for another night."

"Thank you, Kian," Aderyn said. On a whim, she slipped him a five-silver piece. "Any other advice?"

Kian examined the coin before putting it away in his belt pouch. "None of you are a Fated One, are you?"

"Why does that matter?" Owen asked. "We've seen a lot of signs around town declaring they're not welcome—why is that?"

Kian snorted. "Almost every team that comes through Ravenhearst these days has a Fated One with it, and all of them act like they're entitled to the best treatment no matter how they behave. And then they tear up inns when they don't get their way, or take stuff from stores without paying full price, like it's their due. Ravenhearst is sick of it."

"I don't blame you," Weston said. "It's too bad there's no way to prove someone is really a Fated One."

"As if that matters. Real, fake, they're all the same." Kian narrowed his eyes at Owen. "And you didn't answer the question."

Owen spread his arms wide. "Would a Fated One be married? Everyone knows they're all in it to get laid."

Kian's eyes shifted like he was reading invisible letters off the air. "Huh. Guess you are married. But that's just the four of you. You two might be concealing the truth."

"I assure you, neither Jessemia nor I are Fated Ones," Isold said. His voice throbbed with the subtle harmonics of **[Charm]**. "And none of us have any intention of destroying this fine establishment and being unable to partake of its offerings."

Kian relaxed, and his face lit with a smile. "You sure talk fancy. Never heard a Fated One talk so nice. I guess you're all right. Come on down once you're settled, but I was serious about not leaving anything you care about unattended. Normally we guarantee security, but with all these fire-blasted Fated Ones concealing themselves, breaking into rooms and stealing stuff, Briallen doesn't have the resources."

"We appreciate your consideration, Kian," Isold said. He twitched his head in Aderyn's direction. Aderyn gave Kian another five silver. The young man looked as thrilled as if she'd handed him a diamond. He bowed politely and disappeared down the hall.

"Inside," Owen said.

The room was big enough to fit all of them comfortably if not for the wide beds, which took up most of the space. Aderyn sat on the edge of the one nearest the door and said, "Why would so many Fated Ones be here?"

"That is precisely the question I have," Isold said. "It can't be coincidence. Something has brought them to Ravenhearst."

"No, something has brought them to go northward," Owen said. "All these teams want to settle the Northlands, but why would that have anything to do with the Fated One?"

"I can make guesses, but they'd be completely at random," Aderyn said. "Like, suppose these Fated Ones believe they're destined to rule the new Northland kingdom? That sort of thing."

"That's a compelling story, but you're right, it isn't based in fact because we don't have facts," Jessemia said. "I think we need to find one of these Fated Ones and get some information out of him or her."

"I agree, but it sounds like that might be difficult, given the ban," Isold said.

Weston laughed. "I'm guessing at least a few of these fellows lied about their status the way we did. It's not like Fated One shows up in an Assessment. It's going to take some clever investigation—something I know *you* are good at," he added, pointing at Isold.

"Then let's go back downstairs." Owen made a face. "Carrying all our gear. Maybe we should have camped, after all."

"We wouldn't have learned about the Fated One thing if we'd camped," Livia said. "I'll stay here with our things. I'm terrible at interrogations and even worse when they have to be subtle. Weston can bring me dinner."

"That's a great plan." Owen removed his knapsack and dropped it next to where Aderyn sat. "We'll spread out and see what we can learn. Isold, maybe you can use your Herald's skills while you perform, relax these people into feeling talkative."

"That's simple." Isold removed his flute from its sheath along the side of his knapsack and polished a smear on the shining surface with the tail of his shirt. "But, food first."

The five of them found seats at one of the communal tables. Though the taproom was growing increasingly crowded, most of those present wanted liquor more than they wanted food, based on how many leaned on the bar or sat at the tall stools lining the windowed wall. Aderyn ate roast pork dripping with juices and carrots glazed in honey and mopped her plate with slices of thick, dark brown bread and listened to the conversations around her. A Moonlighter could have picked out details from seven different conversations at once, but Aderyn had to focus on listening to just one at a time.

The man and woman seated to her right spoke in hushed voices, but when Aderyn finally made out their words, it turned out they were just flirting. She had a harder time hearing the trio on the opposite side of the flirters, three men who looked like an illustration for the children's story about the three alley cats, big, bigger, and biggest. All their faces were sharp-featured with long noses, so similar they had to be siblings. She Assessed them and discovered they were a Lightfingers named Stevan, a Staffsworn named Mael, and a Stalwart named Alrick, in order of increasing size. What little she heard from them intrigued her.

She nudged Isold, who was sitting across from her, under the table. When he leaned forward, she whispered, "Those three said something about Fated Ones."

Isold nodded, but didn't move until Weston, seated between him and the three men, rose from his seat and declared loudly, "I'm for a drink, anyone else?" before walking to the bar. Isold slid into Weston's abandoned spot and tapped the nearest man, the Stalwart, on the shoulder.

Aderyn was distracted from his words by a shout from the doorway. A tall, willowy woman wearing much-worn traveler's clothes tussled with a beefy guy Aderyn took for Briallen's bouncer. "Hey, I paid to be here!" the woman shouted. Her words slurred enough to show clearly she was drunk. "I haven't done anything wrong."

"No Fated Ones," the bouncer said in a surprisingly high-pitched voice. "You'll get your money back. Briallen's no cheat. But you're not welcome here." He wrestled the door open with one hand while he contained the woman with the other, then pushed her over the threshold so she fell on her rear end. Briallen came up beside him and tossed a coin at the woman's head. The woman swore in the same slurred voice and groped for the coin that had bounced off her forehead. The bouncer shut the door on her and took up a position that said he wasn't sure the trouble was over, but Briallen waved a hand at the door.

"That's a reminder. No exceptions," she said to the room at large. "This is so you can enjoy your evening free of disruption. Go on with your business." She stumped behind the bar and busied herself with tapping a new cask.

Aderyn and Owen exchanged glances. The tilt of Owen's head told Aderyn he wasn't sure whether to be concerned or amused. Aderyn shrugged. "I'm going to get some wine," she said, loudly enough to be overheard if anyone was suspicious of *them*.

When she returned with her wine glass, Isold and the three adventurers were roaring with laughter. Isold pounded the Stalwart on the back. "'Without his pants!'" he chuckled. "I'll have to remember that one. Something to tell when the mood needs lightening. I can't believe that Fated One thought she could flout the rules."

"They're all full of themselves," the Lightfingers, Stevan, said with a giggle that annoyed Aderyn. "All of them. Think that declaring themselves the Fated One is enough. Everybody knows it takes more than that to fulfil prophecy."

"I heard from some fellows who'd been in Finion's Gate for the Glory Games that the real Fated One was the winner this season," Alrick the Stalwart said. Aderyn controlled a shiver of fear. If anyone here had been to the Glory Games, Owen might be outed.

"Really?" Isold said, putting on an air of nonchalant interest. "Were they anyone here?"

"Nah, it was some fellows we met on the road, going south." Alrick took a long pull on his tankard. He didn't sound drunk, but his eyes were glassy. "I guess this Fated One was a big fellow, by what they said. Came back from the dead and everything. I'd swear they were having us on, but the one fellow was too serious to ever play a prank."

"Even if it would do him some good," Mael the Staffsworn said. "Too stuck up, is my guess."

"This is more Fated Ones in one place than I've ever seen," Isold said. "I heard they're all headed north because of this new kingdom someone's founding."

All three burst out laughing. "Them? Fated Ones don't care about settling down. No, they're in search of an undiscovered dungeon. Winterforge, it's called." Alrick leaned over Isold. "You say you've never heard of it?"

Isold didn't flinch. "No, of course not. The whole thing sounds ridiculous, dungeon or settlement. Heading into the

Northlands at the beginning of winter strikes me as potentially suicidal."

"Back off, Alrick, he's not a bad sort," Mael said. "We're going after Winterforge ourselves, and we wouldn't do that if we thought it was nothing but a story."

"But all these teams with Fated Ones, they say it's part of their quest," Stevan said. "Leaving decent adventurers like us fighting it out to get there first."

"I'll be thunderblasted if I let some Fated One cheat me out of what I've rightfully earned." Alrick still looked like he suspected Isold of running off that instant to beat him to Winterforge.

"That's reasonable." Isold drained his mug. "I wish you luck. I would hate to see those Fated Ones win—especially with them lying about their quest. How could they possibly be given a quest when fellows like you don't have the same benefit?"

"That's what I said," Stevan said, shooting Mael a dirty look. "I think they made it up. Mael says they have inside knowledge, like maybe there's something to this Fated One thing."

"I *said* it's too coincidental otherwise," Mael said. "Maybe the system is winnowing out the fake Fated Ones by sending them into the Northlands where most of them will die. If it's true there's a real Fated One, maybe the system is finally getting rid of the others."

"Yeah, well, that gives them too much credit!"

"You may both be right," Isold interjected. "I don't believe in this nonsense about Fated Ones, but the idea that the system knows who has claimed that title and is winnowing them out, as you say, is not preposterous. But I'm afraid Briallen is giving me the sign that she wants me to perform, so I have to leave you gentlemen. It's been good talking to you." His last words hummed with **[Charm]**. Stevan, Mael, and Alrick beamed happily, as if Isold had given them a wonderful gift.

Someone tapped her arm. "Over here," Owen said in a low voice.

Jessemia had disappeared, and Weston was at the bar chatting with an attractive young woman, so Aderyn followed Owen to a quiet corner. It was quiet, she discovered, because of a strong draft from the door that chilled Aderyn instantly. "Were you listening?" she asked.

"Yes. I think we could be in trouble if anyone who was at the Games comes here."

"That was my thought. What do we do?"

Owen glanced around. "Nothing, for now. We take our chances. If someone outs me, then we leave."

"I hate that idea. Mainly because I think we need to know more about why all these Fated Ones think they have a quest for some mysterious dungeon no one's ever heard of." Aderyn scanned the room. "Where's Jessemia?"

"I don't see her—no, she's sitting with that man by the fire."

Jessemia was leaning close to an attractive man who leaned in as well, putting them close enough for a quiet conversation—or for a flirtation. Then the man put his hand on Jessemia's wrist. Jessemia's smile faltered, and she tried to free herself, but the man's grip tightened.

Aderyn took a few steps in their direction, and Owen brought her to a halt. "What are you doing?"

"Can't you see Jessemia doesn't want that man's attention?"

"Didn't you Assess him? He's a Moonlighter four levels lower than her. She's fine."

Just then, Jessemia broke the Moonlighter's grip and pushed her chair away. "I thought Fated Ones weren't allowed here," she said loudly.

That stopped the conversations cold. Isold, who was only a

few feet from Jessemia, stood still. The Moonlighter looked stunned. "I'm not—"

"You told me you were the Fated One," Jessemia declared. "As if I can be swayed by good looks and a supposed destiny. You'll need to try harder than that if you want to bed me."

Now the Moonlighter was crimson. He pushed his own chair back and stood. "You're lying. The bitch is a liar."

Suddenly Isold was there, pressing a hand to the Moonlighter's chest to back him away from Jessemia. The Moonlighter, despite being well built, was not tall, and Isold towered over him. "My companion is neither of those things," Isold said, "and you should reconsider saying anything else. Get out before you're thrown out."

The Moonlighter snarled at Isold. "You think—"

"You fool," Isold said calmly. "What chance do you have against a level nineteen Herald? Cut your losses and leave. Now."

"Level nineteen?" The Moonlighter's eyes glazed over as he Assessed Isold. Aderyn could tell the moment he discovered Isold was so much higher a level than six the Assessment simply failed, because his jaw slackened and he couldn't stop staring at Isold.

Briallen, from behind the bar, said, "Elkin, give him back his money for tonight's stay, and see him to the door."

The Moonlighter swore viciously at Jessemia, who didn't react. Isold shoved the man hard enough to make him fall. In a voice that shook the room, he said, "*Leave.*"

The force behind **[Compulsion]** was powerful enough Aderyn felt the briefest impulse to run to the door. The Moonlighter scrabbled backward, crawled a few steps, then got to his feet. With a moment's scrabbling at the doorknob, he finally got the door open and ran into the night, not shutting the door behind him.

The room was silent except for the crackling of the fire and the wind blowing across the doorway. Finally, Briallen's bouncer shut the door, and the noise of conversation grew until it was louder than the howl of the wind.

Isold stood in front of the fireplace. "I'm sorry you had to witness that," he said. "I take it personally when my companions are insulted."

The clear warning in his words silenced the crowd. Then Isold smiled and twirled his flute. "Let's have some cheer now, how does that sound?" he exclaimed, and played the first few notes of a merry tune Aderyn didn't recognize.

Aderyn stayed in the corner with Owen, though the chill was becoming unbearable, until the mood relaxed and people were tapping their toes along with Isold's music. "What was that about?" she asked.

"I've never seen him react that way," Owen replied. "You don't think something is going on with them?"

"I doubt it." But now Aderyn wasn't sure. "At any rate—"

She shut her mouth as Jessemia approached. "Are you all right?" she asked her friend. "What are the odds you stumbled on another Fated One after that woman was ejected?"

"Not good at all," Jessemia said. "He wasn't a Fated One. I lied."

Aderyn sputtered. "You did what?"

"I don't like men who assume because I'm friendly, they deserve more than friendship." Jessemia's fierceness silenced Aderyn's next protest. "But that's not the important thing. I know what's going on with the Fated Ones."

CHAPTER ELEVEN

I t was nearly eleven o'clock before Isold waved away requests for just one more song, and the five friends climbed the stairs to their rooms. The long wait to hear what Jessemia had learned keyed Aderyn's nerves to the breaking point. Jessemia had said, rightly, it wasn't something to discuss in public, and none of them had wanted to leave Isold, who was committed to playing for their suppers. So Aderyn waited, impatiently, and drank just enough to feel tipsy, and made herself sing along with the songs she knew.

Jessemia, for her part, seemed perfectly composed. Remembering Owen's question, Aderyn watched her friend closely, but she saw no signs that Jessemia cared for Isold as more than a friend, and Isold was focused on his music and paid no more attention to Jessemia than he did to anyone. That he also ignored the blatant come-ons from a handful of women in his audience didn't prove anything. Aderyn couldn't decide if she should ask Jessemia directly how she felt, or if she should leave things alone, but ultimately she realized it was Jessemia's decision, and Aderyn wouldn't help matters by prying.

They all piled into the women's room, where Livia sat up from where she'd been napping. "Sorry, but you all took forever, and I was bored," she said. "Did we learn things?"

"Jessemia?" Owen said.

"I'm sorry I reacted so dramatically," Isold said.

"Well, I was actually lying," Jessemia began.

"Stop. Stop!" Livia stood up and rubbed sleep out of her eyes. "You'd better start at the beginning. I'm picturing Isold making some poor fellow wet his trousers over Jessemia lying."

"Not quite," Owen said, sounding amused. "Here's the basics."

Owen ran through what had happened, from the female Fated One being kicked out through Isold's conversation with the adventuring trio and to Jessemia declaring she'd been assaulted by a Fated One. "Isold went a long way toward intimidating everyone," he said, "and even I'm afraid to mess with him now."

"I hope that's a joke," Isold said, his smile strained.

"Of course it's a joke. Sorry. I know—anyway. So it turned out Jessemia lied about the man being a Fated One so he'd get kicked out, and now I'm afraid to mess with *her* because that was pretty damn ruthless."

"That's right," Jessemia declared with a wink. "I'm fine with you being afraid of me."

"I thought so. Anyway, that was when Jessemia said she learned something, but we couldn't get away to discuss it until now." Owen swept Jessemia a bow. "Take it away, milady."

"Um, take what away?"

Owen rolled his eyes. "Sorry. I mean, tell us what you learned."

Jessemia sat on the edge of one of the beds. "That Moonlighter, Barcus, seemed innocuous at first. Then I Assessed him and found out he's level six, and that was a warning—men who flirt that aggressively with women of significantly higher level tend to have overinflated opinions of their abilities. So I was looking for a way to gracefully end the conversation when he told me he'd left his team recently because their leader, a Fated One named Kacia, declared she'd had a vision of the Northlands and accepted a quest to find the Winterforge dungeon. A quest, she claimed, that would prove she was the real Fated One."

"A vision?" Aderyn and Livia said simultaneously.

"That's what he said. I couldn't get him to give me many details, which makes sense since he wasn't the one who saw it, but he said Kacia's description was enough to convince their team. They came this far north, he and Kacia fought, and they left him here two days ago."

Owen said, "Did he tell you what she said?"

"In between saying what an evil bitch she was, and how they'd been lovers for a year, and he was never again going to be taken in by someone who lied about being the Fated One to get him to sleep with her." Jessemia's smile was bitter. "I don't regret lying about him. He's a nasty piece of work. Anyway, yes. To sum up what I put together from his ramblings, Kacia had a vision of a mountain. It was blood-red—not literally, Barcus said they all agreed that was the light of sunset—with a tower made of ice nestled into it. At the tower's heart, Kacia saw a forge fire that burned without fuel. She also claimed she saw monsters filling the tower—ordinary monsters, but made of snow or ice, if that makes sense."

"I get it," Owen said. "Like an ice bugbear."

"Right. And she heard someone tell her, 'The Fated One quenches the fire.' Or something along those lines. Barcus said it three times and it was a little different each time, but that was the gist."

"So, that happened here?" Owen asked.

"No. They were in a village south of Finion's Gate. Barcus said he was convinced at first, but then they reached Ravenhearst and found out there were a *lot* of Fated Ones who'd all had the same vision, or close to, and that's when he and Kacia fought. He told me Kacia couldn't go on claiming to be *the* Fated One when she was only one of many." Jessemia chuckled. "He said he spurned her, but my guess is she told him if he couldn't support her, they were over."

"That sounds likely," Weston said. "But what does this mean for us? Owen hasn't had a vision."

"No, but I'm also not a wannabe Fated One," Owen said.

"And none of them are the real thing, so why would they get any special treatment from the system?" Weston persisted.

"Assuming it is the system that gave them this supposed vision," Isold said.

"I don't see what else it could be. If a magic item had that kind of power, the person wielding it wouldn't mess around tricking Fated Ones, they'd rule the world." Weston looked uncharacteristically serious.

"Does it matter? I mean, it's not like we have to defeat this dungeon as part of our quest," Aderyn said.

"Not now, no, but who knows if the **[Fated One's Destiny]** quest will direct us to this Winterforge eventually?" Isold looked pensive. "The name is evocative, but not informative. A forge in winter, heat meeting cold... it's dramatic, certainly, but there's nothing about it that demands we go there."

"I think it's too coincidental that someone discovered this new dungeon just as we're headed north for a different quest," Weston persisted. "We can't ignore Winterforge entirely, if only because it doubles the number of human adventurer teams headed into the Northlands to potentially be entangled with our quest. Those poser Fated Ones are the type to make everything about themselves. It doesn't even have to be about visions."

"That makes sense," Livia said. "Winterforge might have been discovered independently, and the thing about the visions is a lie some fake Fated One spread to give himself, or herself, legitimate claim to it. It wouldn't take much for the rest of them to pick up on it. All those wannabes are in it for money, fame, and sex, and finding and defeating a mysterious unknown dungeon would deliver all three, if you figure money and fame are a good enticement for sex."

"This is a lot of assumptions," Aderyn protested. "We don't know how they got these visions, we don't know what the visions actually mean, and we don't know that it's trickery. I actually buy that the visions really happened. Maybe it's like that Staffsworn Mael said, that the system wants to clear away the fake Fated Ones, and it's testing them all to see if any of them have what it takes to be the real thing." She scowled. "I hate that idea. We've worked our asses off pursuing the **[Fated One's Destiny]** quest, and if I'm right, there are a lot of men and women who are taking a shortcut to what we've achieved."

"I don't think so," Owen said. "We had to find the beginning of the quest chain, and so did Ruan's team, so even if a few new actual Fated Ones pop up because of this Winterforge thing, they'd all have to pursue the path we did."

That made Aderyn feel better. "I can live with that."

"As I see it, it still has nothing to with us," Owen went on. "We have a quest that doesn't involve the Winterforge dungeon, at least not now, and there's no reason we should have to interact with the teams following that vision. We rest, we set out tomorrow morning, and we leave all this nonsense behind."

No one spoke for a few moments. Then Livia said, "I was

waiting for someone to break down the door and accuse Owen of being a Fated One. I guess he's not as jinxed as I thought."

Owen laughed. "Let's sleep. I'm ready for this weird-ass day to be over." He hugged Aderyn and kissed her lightly on the lips. "Even if it means sleeping next to Weston, who snores."

"I'm the big fellow. I get a bed to myself," Weston said smugly.

"Out," Livia said. "We'll see you all in the morning."

When the men were gone, Aderyn wearily pulled her shirt off and stood for a moment holding it in a wad in front of her. "Tiredness just hit me out of nowhere. I didn't think I'd drunk that much."

"You didn't," Jessemia said. She was already in her shift and drawers. "Does anyone care who gets the bed to herself?"

"Livia is a restless sleeper," Aderyn said. "Between her rolling over and Weston's snoring, it's amazing either of them ever gets any sleep."

Livia sneered. "Show me the 'flipping the bird' gesture again so I can use it on you."

"Enough," Jessemia said with a laugh. She lay down and pulled the blanket up to her chin. "Good night."

Aderyn climbed into bed and lay on her back. Across the room, Livia extinguished the *orbs of light* illuminating the room. Almost immediately, Aderyn's **[Darkvision]** adjusted her eyes to the dim, indirect light of the streetlamps, and she stared at the palely glowing square that was the drapes-shrouded window. Despite her words, her mind was too busy for sleep. Fake Fated Ones having visions. A mysterious dungeon. Isold—

"Aderyn, is something wrong?" Jessemia said. Across the room, Livia rolled over in her sleep.

"No, why?"

"You keep sighing, like you're disturbed by something."

"Oh. I didn't realize. It was nothing."

"Uh *huh*," Jessemia said. "Then go to sleep."

Aderyn fell silent again. Jessemia rolled onto her side, Aderyn thought facing away from her, until Jessemia's voice came from the darkness near Aderyn's head. "Isold scared me tonight."

"He scared you? You mean because of how he used [**Compulsion**] on that bastard? You didn't seem upset. And you know he'd never turn his skills on you."

"It's not that. It was that he went for... I don't know what to call it. Like he had a choice of weapons and he picked a magical sword of decapitation instead of the <**Peacemaker's Burden**>." Jessemia's quiet voice trembled slightly, but when she spoke next, she sounded like her usual self. "Barcus was a loser and a complete waste of air, but he didn't deserve that. Or maybe I mean that's not who I thought Isold was."

"It surprised me, too." Aderyn reviewed the evening's events and spoke almost without thinking. "You don't suppose it was because he was defending you?"

"I don't know if it's good for him to be untrue to himself even in defense of his friends."

Aderyn shook her head, realized Jessemia couldn't see her, and said, "I mean that he wouldn't have acted so harshly for any of the rest of us. Just you."

Jessemia pushed herself onto her elbows. Aderyn clearly saw her astonished face. "Why would you say that? He didn't say anything, did he?"

Something clicked in Aderyn's head at Jessemia's near-panic. "Something happened between you, didn't it? You *are* romantically involved!"

"No!" Jessemia put her hands over her face. "I mean, yes. Sort of. But it's nothing really. We slept together, that's all."

"Jessemia! That's not nothing!" Aderyn hugged her. "That's wonderful!"

"*No*, Aderyn. I mean, we slept together, and that's it. Just the one time." Jessemia pulled away from Aderyn. "It was the night before Owen asked me to guide your team. Isold and I... I never did apologize to him, not really, and I went to his room, and things went forward from there. And that's all. Just the one time."

Aderyn, listening to the tone of Jessemia's voice, made another intuitive leap. "But you want there to be more."

"It doesn't matter what I want. Isold knows what he needs, and apparently I'm not the one who can give it to him. And we're friends now, Aderyn. I'm not going to destroy that by imposing on him." Jessemia lay back down. "Please, don't tell anyone. I thought it really would be all, because you were leaving in the morning, and now I feel awkward if I think about it too much."

"But—Jessemia, how sure are you of what he wants? Because I could see his actions tonight as those of someone defending the woman he cares about."

"Or he'd have done it for any of us. You don't know." Jessemia sounded weary rather than upset. "I need you to let it go. I know you want everyone you care about to be happy, and I'm telling you how to achieve that for me. Isold has to work things out for himself."

"I understand," Aderyn said.

She closed her eyes and concentrated on her breathing, in through the nose, out through the mouth, until Jessemia's own breathing showed she was asleep. Then she rolled onto her side, facing the wall. Jessemia and Isold. The idea of her two friends finding happiness together was impossible to push aside. And yet, if it wasn't what they wanted, Aderyn's meddling would make them miserable instead. Unless she could—

Aderyn cut off that line of thought. She didn't know what Isold wanted from a relationship, or even if he wanted a relationship with just one person. He'd always been happy with spending just one night with a woman, or group of women, and there was no reason to think that had changed. And even if she did know what would be good for Isold, it was wrong for Aderyn to interfere, like Isold was a child.

But—Jessemia. Aderyn was sure Jessemia was more deeply attached to Isold than she claimed. Now the memory of asking her to join their team burned. How hard it would be to be near someone she cared about who didn't return her feelings! Aderyn's heart ached in sympathy.

She told herself to stop dwelling on it. Talk about inappropriate sympathy. Aderyn might be putting her own feelings on Jessemia, and maybe she was wrong, and Jessemia had been satisfied with one time. Aderyn should let it go.

But it took her an hour to fall asleep.

THE TAPROOM WAS QUIET WHEN THEY ALL CAME downstairs the next morning. The Lucky Diamond only served one meal a day, so they left without seeing Briallen or anyone else and found a pie vendor selling sweet or savory pies the size of Weston's palm. Aderyn munched her apple pie, which was a little too sweet for her taste this early in the day, and watched Isold. He neither avoided nor singled out Jessemia, and he seemed just like his usual self. She reminded herself not to meddle and turned away.

"Jessemia, how close is that other village?" Owen asked.

Jessemia wiped meat juice from her lips. "It's another five hours from here, six if we go slowly."

"I think we'll bypass it, then," Owen said. "We can make

better progress than that, and you said our quest destination is very far north. Is everyone okay with that?"

Some nods and murmured agreement followed. Aderyn finished her pie and poured water from her waterskin over her sticky fingers to clean them. "I feel like somebody ought to say something as we set out. It feels anticlimactic to begin this journey like any other, if we're close to the end of the quest chain."

"We only hope we are," Owen reminded her. "Even so. How about 'Avengers assemble'?"

"Or 'onward to victory!'" Weston said with a grin.

Aderyn rolled her eyes. "I don't know which of you to smack first."

"That's as good a rallying cry as any," Livia said. "Come on. The open road is calling our names."

Aderyn nodded. "I like that one the best."

CHAPTER TWELVE

Thirteen days later, with the Eretai Mountains looming in the near distance, Aderyn paused at the top of one the low foothills they'd trudged through for the last three days. "I've never seen mountains so tall. Even the Lonely Tor was shorter than those."

"I hope the quest doesn't require us to climb them," Owen said. He stopped beside her and put his arm around her waist. "I don't think we have the right equipment. Those are high enough we might need oxygen."

"I've heard the air thins the higher you get," Isold said, "but not at what point there is too little to support life. I'll join in your hope that it's not an issue for us."

Aderyn hoped so too. It had been an uneventful two weeks for a journey into unexplored, untamed wilderness. They'd fought a handful of monsters, none of them unknown, and had been ambushed only once, by vile sarcocarps—or would have been without Aderyn's skill **[Sense Ambush]**. The only interesting thing was the gradual approach of the mountains. Aderyn thought of it that way even though it was her team getting closer. The Eretai Mountains were enormous enough to feel menacing even from this distance.

Jessemia stopped a short distance from Aderyn. "We should camp early tonight. A storm is coming."

"I'm grateful for **[Improved Survival]**," Aderyn said.

"In this case, I see storm clouds ahead," Jessemia replied with a smile. "North and east, with the wind blowing them this way. But **[Improved Survival]** says we'll have snow by sunset."

"Fair enough." Owen tugged on Aderyn's hand. "Half an hour more, but everyone watch for good camping spots."

They continued onward, Weston and Jessemia in the lead, with Livia behind them, Isold near the middle, and Aderyn and Owen at the rear. The cloud cover darkened gradually, and the wind picked up so Aderyn could see the clouds blown along by it. Dry, dead yellow grass crunched under her feet, and occasionally they passed a bush or a lone tree that clung to its last leaves like a miser hoarding gold. Still, despite the wind and the clouds obscuring the sun, it wasn't all that cold, and Aderyn in her heavy leather coat was comfortably warm.

Weston came to a stop at the top of another hill. This one led into a broad valley with a plain divided in half by a narrow river that from here looked like a dusty blue thread unspooling across the landscape. "That's odd. I don't know what that is." He pointed.

Aderyn shielded her eyes from the scant sunshine and stared into the distance. "It looks like blobs to me. Grayish blobs."

"They're boulders," Weston said. "Not round ones, big elongated stones standing on end in a circle, or maybe a spiral pattern. I've never seen anything like it."

"They're too far away for me to sense," Livia said.

She set off down the hill into the valley where the mysterious stones stood, but Weston grabbed her arm and brought her to a halt. "I don't know if it's safe. Stones don't get like that naturally, you know that. Someone, or something, put them there, and if that person or thing is still around, I want to be cautious."

"I agree," Owen said. "In my world, standing stone rings are associated with religion. Gods and so forth. But you don't have gods, so Weston is right it's probably a person or creature who did it. I don't know how big they are, but if they're at all like the ones I'm familiar with, it would take magic or some damn big monster to set them upright like that."

"So we'll be careful," Livia said. "Come on. I'm curious."

She took the lead, though Weston followed her closely. Aderyn hung back with Owen. Weston's caution had impressed on her the reminder that they were in dangerous, unknown territory. So she stayed alert, her gaze never settling anywhere for long. The cry of a hunting hawk drew her attention, but it was just a bird, not a monster. The rising wind carried with it the scent of snow and dry grass, nothing dangerous.

Despite the peacefulness of their surroundings, the stones unsettled Aderyn the closer she drew to them. From less than a hundred feet away, it became clear their dark, smooth surfaces were polished, not by weather but by hands. No amount of wind or storm could produce that sheen, glossy and almost oily. To her, they stood at random intervals, no pattern, but Weston said, "I was right. It's a spiral."

"Stop," Jessemia said, with such force Livia and Weston turned around. "I smell blood."

"Where?" Owen asked.

"On those stones, or in their direction." Jessemia focused on the stone spiral, then took off running. "There's someone there," she called over her shoulder.

"Jessemia!" Aderyn shouted.

"She's right. I see someone curled up in the shadow of that stone," Weston said.

"Don't let her approach alone," Owen shouted. "Go, go!"

Isold was already in the lead, his long legs pumping hard as he closed the distance between himself and Jessemia. Then Livia surged past him, throwing up a spray of dirt as *earth glide* propelled her faster than a horse could run. Aderyn was only in the rear for a few paces before **[Keep Pace]** grabbed her and brought her to run even with Owen.

By the time she and Owen reached the others, Jessemia was standing beside a large, huddled form that lay in the lee of the biggest stone. "I thought its size was an illusion," she said. "But it's as big as I believed."

Aderyn slowed her steps. "It's a giant."

She understood what Jessemia meant. From a distance, it had looked like a human, and the stones had seemed to be only a few feet tall. Now, with a proper perspective, it was clear the stones ranged from ten to fifteen feet tall. The dead giant lay on his back, staring at the cloudy sky. Blood soaked the ground around him and spattered the gray surface of the polished stone in long arcs of dark red arterial spray. His throat was slit deeply, and dried blood coated his chest and hands and clung to the tips of his blond hair.

"This happened recently," Jessemia said. "Last night, or early this morning." Her calmness, and the certainty in her words, made her seem a different person.

"How can you tell?" Livia asked.

"**[Tracking]** adds new features every other level. I can tell roughly when something or someone died from the body's stiffness and how dry the blood is." Jessemia wiped her fingers on a corner of the giant's cloak, in a spot no blood had landed. "I can also tell what attack dealt damage, specifically what weapon or monster attack it was. For example, I can tell the difference between a short sword and a longsword blow."

"That's incredible," Aderyn said.

"But this—not to disparage your ability—this creature's throat was clearly slit," Owen said.

"Yes," Jessemia said. "Either by a weapon or a very sharp claw. By someone standing behind him. He was fleeing the attack."

"But that makes no sense," Isold said. "This creature's body should have disappeared by now. Monster corpses don't last more than an hour after death."

"Then it's not what we think," Aderyn said. "Giants are supposed to be mythical. Maybe that means, if they exist, that there's something unique about them. Something that makes them different from other monsters."

Jessemia backed away and surveyed the ground around the stone, prowling like a hunting wolf. "There was a terrible fight, and the victor ran north. The scary thing is I don't see footprints other than the ones the giant made. Just the passage of something light over the grass."

"This isn't good," Owen said. "Any ideas what could have happened?"

"Two monsters fighting, but I don't have any idea what killed this creature," Jessemia said. "My **[Knowledge: Monsters]** skill is spotty because I haven't adventured in many different places. It's been filling in since we started this journey, but it's not complete. I don't know why the other monster wouldn't leave footprints."

"But what about the stones?" Aderyn said. "Why here?"

"Coincidence?" Jessemia shrugged. "The stones are weird, granted, but I don't see why they would make a difference."

"Give me a minute, and I'll find out," Livia said.

She walked around the stones, following the spiral. Every time she passed one of the stones, she trailed her fingers across its surface, caressing it like it was a beloved child. When she reached the central stone, she circled it, avoiding the body, then retraced her steps around the spiral until she stopped beside one of the stones that was unmarked by blood. "This one had a good view of the stone where the giant was killed. Now, everyone be quiet while I use **[Speak With Stone]**. Stones' voices aren't very intelligible, and with the wind rising it will be hard to hear."

She pressed both her palms, side by side, against the stone's smooth surface. Slowly, she slid her hands apart and stepped forward until she was almost hugging the stone. She rested her forehead against the stone and closed her eyes. Aderyn, standing to her right, saw her lips move in silent speech.

They all waited as Livia's silent conversation stretched from seconds to minutes. Aderyn controlled a shiver. Movement wouldn't distract Livia, but Aderyn didn't want to intrude in any way. She'd only rarely seen Livia use this skill, and Livia had never explained how it worked aside from saying that stones' memories were longer than trees, and speaking with them meant having tremendous patience and tact.

Finally, after about fifteen minutes during which Aderyn grew increasingly cold from standing still, Livia pushed herself upright and rubbed her hands together. "That was unexpected."

"Did it see anything?" Aderyn asked.

"I asked it about the fight. It was cooperative, but its perceptions aren't like ours, so it didn't see much we can use. And it's mostly asleep right now." Livia rested a hand on the stone, again touching it gently.

"At least the moon is just a few days off from full, and it was a clear night for once," Owen said. "Or does that not matter?"

"Stones have senses the way we do. Not the same as ours, but they do have a sense that's analogous to sight. The problem is that the time we live in is so fast by their standards, they blink and they miss whole years. What this one saw was like watching people who've drunk <**Potions of Alacrity**>, but a dozen potions at a time, if you could do that to multiply the effect and not just kill yourself. But it did see things."

"The killers?" Owen asked.

"Yes. But stones think all organic, sentient life is the same. They can't tell the difference between a human and a goblin, or even a human and a hulking horror. Kind of like how for most people, all rocks are just rocks. So it saw what it called stonekin and swifts, and I had to dig for details. The stonekin, I think, was the giant. The swifts were the killers."

"How did it describe the swifts?" Weston asked.

"Not well. Pale shapes—stones can't see colors—that moved quickly. Four of them. Shorter than the stonekin, but not by much. It didn't understand my question about how many feet they walked on, and I was afraid of sending it spinning off into an irrelevant aside. Stones are distractible." Livia looked at the stone as if Assessing it. "My understanding, and this is me putting its words into something we'd recognize, is that the giant fought the swifts and held his own for a little while before trying to run, which is when the swifts cut him down."

"But the swifts could be anything," Isold said. "Well. Not *anything*. Any creature that's no more than ten feet tall and fights with claws or bladed weapons. And not another giant, or the stone wouldn't have made the distinction."

"That narrows it down quite a bit," Jessemia said. She had the abstracted look of someone reviewing her Monster Folio. "I don't want to make assumptions, though, because like I said, I don't have as complete an understanding of monsters as I'd like."

"I'm glad it's a monster," Owen said. "I'd started to imagine ritual sacrifice."

They all stared at him. "What are you talking about?" Weston said.

"Well, you know, standing stones, an altar... of course you don't know anything about that." Owen shook his head. "It's a thing from my world's history, or rather a combination of things, since I didn't study much European history and it's not like people accuse the druids of human sacrifice at Stonehenge. And now I'm confusing you further. It was just an idle thought, all right? I'm sorry I said anything."

"All right," Aderyn said, though she was even more curious than before about what the difference was between sacrificing a habit and sacrificing a ritual. "It really doesn't matter what it was that killed the giant, since we're alert when we're in the wilderness regardless. It's not necessarily a threat to us."

"Right," Jessemia said. "The bigger question is, are there more giants around? Because *they* might be a threat to us."

"Maybe," Livia said. "It occurred to me to ask where the stone came from. Or, rather, how it got here. There's no other sources of stone of its type for miles around, and of course it didn't stand itself up on its own. It said it was brought here by the stonekin."

"Stonekin? Like the giant?" Owen said. "So maybe the stone is important, after all. Maybe the giant came here on purpose. Could it have been looking for protection?"

Livia shrugged. "No idea. It just repeated 'stonekin' every time I asked for more details. The only specifics I could get out of it was that they're capable of working stone and they show up every few blinks and then are gone again."

"'Blinks' being what time is to a stone," Owen said.

"That's right. So, if giants made this spiral, and one of them was killed here, it's possible more of them will show up. Something to watch out for." Livia yawned. "I'm not tired, it's just that stones are so slow I have the urge to nap in between their responses. We should move on."

"I think we should bury him," Jessemia said.

They all stared at her. "Bury a monster?" Livia said.

"They don't sound like typical monsters. They wear clothes, they build structures—standing stone spirals, sure, not houses, but still." Jessemia blushed. "It feels weird to leave him lying there."

"You're going to displace Aderyn as the champion of inappropriate sympathy for monsters," Owen said, hugging Aderyn to show he was teasing. "But you have a point. This creature looks just like a human except for his size, and we'd show respect to a dead adventurer we stumbled across, right?"

He stepped back as the body floated gently into the air. Livia guided it with *telekinesis* to lie well away from the stone spiral. "I don't know what this thing's purpose is, so I don't want to risk burying him inside it."

"Risk what?" Weston said. "You make it sound like we might be in trouble for disrupting this place."

"That could be true, dearest. And it's not as if it's more difficult for me to bury him in a different place."

Aderyn concealed a smile. She wasn't the only sentimental one in the team.

As the body came to rest, the ground beneath it sagged and folded as if the land were a handkerchief wrapping him up in a final embrace. Livia's *move earth* spell buried him neatly and then smoothed out the surface so it was flat, undisturbed earth marked only by being free of vegetation. She then used *drench* to wash the stones— "again, just in case," she said.

Finally, Owen said, "Jessemia, do you know how much farther we have to go?"

"The quest location marked on my map is another two weeks'

journey." Jessemia examined her map, her lips moving as she silently counted. "We skirt the mountains to the river and go downstream a ways."

"Then we'd better get moving. I want to camp before the storm hits." Owen glanced around as if an ideal campsite would pop up out of nowhere. "And I want to be well away from these stones. The deliberateness of the spiral creeps me out."

"You said it wasn't that sacrifice ritual thing," Aderyn reminded him.

"I know what I said. I've also seen too many horror movies not to imagine robed and hooded cultists descending on our camp in the night." Owen shuddered. "Let's get out of here."

CHAPTER THIRTEEN

They walked another twenty minutes before finding a good campsite, a sheltered space at the base of a steep-sided hill. By then, thick, dark clouds blocked out the sun, creating an unnatural dimness like an early sunset. Aderyn had never been more grateful for the <**Soldier's Friend**> and how quickly it set up their camp. It took a little longer this time because they all spread the heavier ground cloths before Livia activated the item, but when the whirlwind vanished, the magic had placed each tent atop a ground cloth and left a neatly folded stack of the ones it usually used next to the campfire.

Owen and Weston set about using those cloths to build a shelter protecting the fire while Aderyn, Isold, and Livia prepared water for tea and Jessemia vanished into the growing darkness to hunt. The water hadn't yet boiled when Jessemia returned, her shoulders and hair dusted with snowflakes, carrying a load of neatly butchered meat. "Never leave a carcass near the camp unless you want nocturnal visitors," she said when Aderyn protested that they could have helped her skin the deer. "This is faster. And I like using my skills. The feeling of competence hasn't gotten old yet."

They roasted venison over the fire and ate seedless green grapes in silence. Aderyn was still thinking about the dead giant they'd left behind and who he might have been. It was stupid, she knew, because she made up stories and when nothing happened to contradict them she had trouble remembering they weren't true, at least as far as her emotions went.

To distract herself, she said, "Isold, will you sing for us tonight?"

"If you want," Isold said. "I was thinking I wished one of us was a storyteller, frankly. I feel in the mood for more entertainment than I can provide."

"Jessemia tells funny stories," Livia said.

"Only about my own adventures, and you already heard those," Jessemia replied.

"Fair enough. Well, Owen knows all those stories from his world."

"Yes, but I'm hardly a storyteller," Owen protested. "Besides, I've already told all the ones I like that you have context for. I had to stretch to explain *Finding Nemo*."

"That was the fish story, right?" Weston said. "I still think the idea of putting a fish in a glass box just so you can watch it swim is weird. And why don't the humans understand the fish and birds if the fish and birds are capable of speech?"

"This is why I stick to superhero movies. This world is full of adventurers who might as well be superheroes, so it's something you instinctively relate to." Owen finished his blackberry tea and poured himself another cup. "I guess you could call *Die Hard* a dungeon crawl. We've explored buildings that are dungeons, like the Ivory Palace, and that movie takes place in a skyscraper. That means a tall building, taller than anything you have in this world. Dozens of stories tall."

"Ooh, interesting." Aderyn pulled her coat closer around herself. "How does it stay up?"

"Engineering."

"Isn't that the answer you give when you don't understand how something in your world works?" Weston said with a grin.

"It is. I know that skyscrapers need a solid stone foundation and steel girders, and that is the extent of my information." Owen drank more tea. "If I'd known I was going to be dragged into another world, I'd have majored in engineering or gotten a certification as a plumber."

"What you know about your world's history has helped in the past." Struck by an idea, Aderyn said, "What about a story from history? You have those, right?"

"Sure, but I don't..." Owen watched the river amble sluggishly past. "Actually, the river and the cold remind me of a story from my country's history that might not require a lot of explanation. You remember how in the southlands, they told us about how the kingdom of Durga fought the main southlander kingdom for its freedom to rule itself? This story comes from a time when my country was fighting another for the same reason."

Aderyn snuggled closer. She loved hearing about Owen's world. His stories always made her feel closer to him. "So your kingdom wanted to be free of the other kingdom."

"More or less. We didn't have a king—that was mostly the point, that we didn't want to be ruled by a king of a country across the ocean from us. Like if Devendra tried to rule Finion's Gate." Owen drew Aderyn closer. "This happened more than two hundred years before I was born. My country wasn't even a country then, just a bunch of colonies—that means smaller regions settled by men and women from another country. The other country was Great Britain, and it was an empire—not just one country, but many colonies all over the world. Our colonies decided to band together to throw out the British and be their own rulers."

"Did they have trouble agreeing on who would be in charge?" Aderyn asked. "Several governments... it makes me think of what might happen if the cities of the safe zone formed a country like you describe. They'd all fight over who got to make decisions."

"They did, but that's not part of this story. But they agreed enough to choose someone named George Washington as their commander general. He hadn't ever commanded a large army before, but he was naturally gifted, like a Warmaster. He'd also learned a lot about British tactics because he'd been part of their army before the American colonies decided to fight them. This was valuable stuff, because the British Army was considered the best fighting force in the world."

"Nice, an underdog story," Livia said.

"Yes. This story happened near the end of the year, when Washington's army needed a victory to raise morale. Washington decided to secretly move his army across the Delaware River so they'd be in a position to surprise attack the British, specifically their fighting auxiliaries the Hessians. He decided to do it on Christmas Day—that's an important holiday for us. It was a daring move, because it was freezing, the river was full of ice, and a storm rose during that day. But the troops they faced were the best of the best, and Washington needed the element of surprise if he wanted to defeat them. He figured the Hessians would be distracted by the holiday and wouldn't expect an attack."

"They didn't have magic, so how did they get across?" Weston asked.

"Lots of boats brought from the nearby communities. They had artillery—hmm. Really big iron guns, heavier than a horse, that needed sturdy boats to carry them across the river. Washington's army gathered slowly over the course of the day, and a few at a time, they made it across the river in the growing darkness."

Owen leaned forward, lowering his voice. "Everything went wrong from the start. They had to keep track of all those little boats in a darkness so intense the boatmen couldn't see the far shore. Two supporting units didn't make it across the river at all. But despite everything, Washington's army surprised the Hessians and defeated them."

"Was it enough to win the war?" Aderyn asked.

"This was still early in the war, but it made a huge difference to how Washington's army fought later. The amazing thing, to me, is that they crossed the Delaware River twice more before the end of the year. The second time, they returned across the river with supplies and prisoners from the initial attack, and the third time, they positioned themselves to attack the commander general of the British forces. They kicked his ass, too." Owen grinned as if he took personal responsibility for the ass-kicking.

"That's an inspiring story, if only because it makes me grateful we don't have to cross this river in flimsy little boats," Weston said, pointing at the river. Aderyn tried to imagine it filled with chunks of ice. That just made her shiver.

"I have more questions," Livia said. "Why did they keep pushing their luck? That river crossing was dangerous, if some of the army couldn't accomplish it. And if they kicked the ass of the enemy general, why didn't that end the war?"

"Those are enough stories to keep us going all the way to our destination," Owen said. "Maybe later I'll tell you what happened after that, during their winter quarters at Valley Forge."

"I liked it," Aderyn declared, and kissed her husband on the cheek.

Weston shivered. "It's getting cold. Time to get some sleep."

Jessemia rose. "I'll start my watch now. I want to check for nearby animal or monster tracks."

Weston handed her the **<Cat's Eye Goggles>**. "Give a shout if you see anything. I'm off to bed. Waking before dawn is one thing, but waking when dawn is still an hour off unsettles even me."

Aderyn said good night and followed Owen into their tent. She was about to take off her coat when he grabbed her around the waist and kissed her soundly. "I love you," he murmured in her ear. "How much do you think the snow will muffle the sound of us making love?"

"Owen!" Aderyn giggled. She kissed him in return. "What brought this on?"

"No idea. No, that's wrong. It was seeing that dead giant and thinking about how life is short—too short, in his case—and how I don't want to miss out on any of the good stuff. Which includes sex with the most beautiful woman I've ever known." He slipped his hands inside her coat and trailed his fingers along her spine.

"Most beautiful? That's me, right?" Aderyn teased. "I don't know. Aren't you afraid we'll get tired of it if we do it too often?"

Owen pulled back to stare at her. "In the first place, that's crazy. In the second place, we haven't had sex since before we left Finion's Gate. In the third place, if I ever get tired of sex, you can bury me where I lie. In the fourth—"

Aderyn silenced him with a kiss. "That's enough places. I'm convinced."

AFTERWARD, SHE LAY NESTLED IN OWEN'S ARMS AND listened to the wind blow. If Jessemia walked near their tent, Aderyn's hearing wasn't good enough to detect her. She found she didn't mind if her friends knew what she and Owen had been doing, so long as she gave them an excuse not to have to acknowledge it.

"Hey," Owen whispered. "What's going on with Isold and Jessemia?"

"What?" Surprise made Aderyn's voice shrill, and Owen hushed her. "I don't know what you mean," she said in a calmer voice. "What have you noticed?"

"They're both really formal with each other, and Isold goes out of his way not to touch her. Even when she needs healing."

"Oh." Aderyn had noticed this, too, but since she knew what had passed between her two friends, she had assumed it was lingering embarrassment at being pushed into each other's company after believing they were parting ways. "I... I'm not sure," she said. She never lied to Owen, but she was sure she shouldn't share Jessemia's confidences with anyone, including her husband.

"Huh." Owen lay back and looked up at the tent ceiling. "It looked to me like maybe they'd kissed or something and now they're conflicted about how they feel."

Owen was smart, but she'd never guessed he was this perceptive. "Do you think that's possible? Isold is never awkward about sex, or kissing, or relationships."

"He's changed. I said before he might not know how he feels about sex anymore, what he wants for himself. Maybe Jessemia turned him down, and he hasn't come to terms with it."

"Why would Jessemia turn him down?" Aderyn felt unexpectedly defensive of her friend, given that she knew Jessemia *hadn't* turned Isold down.

"Just because Isold is a stud doesn't mean every woman in the world is going to fall at his feet. Besides, Jessemia already made a pass at him and they both know that was a disaster. She might not be willing to try again.”

Aderyn pinched her lips closed. So much of what she wanted to say was off limits. “I don’t want to speculate, because I wish they would give each other a chance, and this conversation is depressing. Wouldn’t it be nice if they fell in love?”

Owen chuckled. “Sweetheart, you are the nicest person I know as well as the most beautiful. You really do want all your friends to be happy, don’t you?”

“Of course! And I don’t think it has to be happiness on my terms, in case you were wondering. But there’s no harm in dreaming.”

“None at all,” Owen said.

They fell silent. Aderyn had almost drifted off to sleep when Jessemia’s distant shout woke her. “We’re under attack!”

Aderyn scooted out of her bedroll, flung her <**Gossamer Mail**> over her head, shoved her feet into her boots, and snatched up her sword. Beside her, Owen was fumbling rapidly with the buckles of his cuirass. “Go!” he urged. “I’m right behind you.”

When Aderyn burst out of her tent, Weston was kicking life into the banked fire, brightening the area. Snow fell heavily, obscuring Aderyn’s vision. Jessemia wasn’t there. Livia had just summoned the shifting stone slabs that served as her armor. A howl shook the night, followed by more howling cries. “That doesn’t sound like wolves. What is it?” Aderyn said.

“The first one was Isold,” Weston said grimly. “Where in thunder did they go?”

As he spoke, Isold and Jessemia lurched between the tents and collapsed by the fire. Isold was supporting Jessemia, whose left leg dragged behind her. “It bludgeoned me,” she said through gritted teeth. “I think my leg is broken. The thing was two-legged, about eight feet tall. Hit me with a tree branch. It was almost invisible in the snow."

As she spoke, the howls cut off. In the eerie silence, Livia said, "They might have decided we're not easy prey."

"Or they're regrouping," Weston said.

Aderyn didn't joke about the two of them taking each other's roles as optimist and pessimist. Instead, she scanned the darkness beyond the tents, Assessing. **[Improved Assess 4]** wasn't affected by her imperfect perceptions. No system messages popped up.

"How many?" Owen asked, joining them.

Jessemia's face was unusually pale. "Three that I saw, one more that I smelled. Might be more outside the range of my senses. This snowfall is messing me up." She hissed as Isold palpated her wounded leg.

"They aren't closing," Aderyn said. "Why not? If this is what killed that giant—"

Out of the darkness flew the ghostly shape of an enormous rock, aimed at her head.

CHAPTER FOURTEEN

Aderyn gasped and ducked. The real rock hurtled out of the darkness a second later and impacted against Jessemia's tent, tearing a gash in the white fabric before collapsing it. More stones hailed down on them, causing the team to scatter. Jessemia lunged to avoid a rock, let out a short scream as her broken leg gave way beneath her, and fell sprawling over the damp ground. Isold threw himself over Jessemia and shouted, "Go after them!"

Owen activated the <**Sunsword**> and ran into the darkness. Aderyn drew her sword and followed him. Even with [**Darkvision**], thanks to the heavy snowfall she could see practically nothing but the curved white line of the <**Sunsword**>. Owen himself was a dim shape just ahead of her, always close thanks to [**Keep Pace**]. More stones flew at them, large enough to be visible. Owen grunted as he failed to dodge one that clipped his shoulder, making a loud metallic crack as it struck his armor.

"Stop!" Aderyn shouted. Running wildly into the storm wasn't doing them any good. "Cover me while I Assess!"

She faced the direction the last stone had come from and Assessed the darkness. Instantly the Codex came to life.

Name: Taavek
Type: Giant, juvenile
Power level: 10
Terrain: mountains, hills, plains
Attack(s): missile attack, bludgeoning weapon
Immune to: none
Resistant to: bludgeoning weapons damage
Vulnerable to: [Charm], sonic damage
You have now encountered three intelligent nonhuman races. Consider what you have learned, Aderyn. Then use your initiative.

"Juvenile?" Aderyn exclaimed. "Juvenile giant?"

"What?" Owen shouted over the rising wind.

"He's a child! We can't kill him!"

Owen turned on her, swearing. "Child or not, he's trying to kill us! What do we do?"

Another stone sailed out of the darkness. Aderyn pushed Owen out of the way just as a bigger shape hurtled toward them. It was well over eight feet tall and horrifically deformed. Aderyn realized the apparent deformation was because the creature wielded most of a tree as a bludgeon just seconds before it roared a challenge and swung the tree at her.

Aderyn dodged easily. "Stop!" she shouted, sheathing her sword. "Stop! We're not your enemies! *Isold!*"

"Aderyn, what the *hell* are you doing?" Owen shouted. He dodged a second swipe of the tree and ducked inside the giant's reach, driving the <**Sunsword**> into the creature's thigh. The giant bellowed in pain. Answering howls from the darkness sounded to the left and right. Aderyn counted. Four.

The wounded giant, Taavek, dropped the tree and staggered

backward, clutching his leg. Owen followed him, raising his sword for another blow. Aderyn grabbed his arm. "Don't! It's a child! This is a misunderstanding."

"Aderyn, you've gone too far. They attacked Jessemia and they threw rocks at the rest of us. Now is not the time to sympathize!"

"It's not about sympathy. This is what the Assessment said— they're juveniles. The system told me to think and to use my initiative. Please, Owen." Aderyn released him and approached the giant, who backed away further, tripped, and fell with a tremendous thud Aderyn felt in her bones.

A roar echoed through the night, and another huge figure emerged from the darkness, pounding toward them like he didn't intend to stop until they were trampled. Aderyn stood her ground, though her heart was pounding and she was sweating despite the cold. "Stop!" she shouted, waving her arms. "Stop! We won't hurt you!"

"Like they're worried about us hurting them," Owen said.

The running figure kept coming. Aderyn didn't budge. "*Isold!* They are vulnerable to **[Charm]**! We have to get them to calm down!"

"Aderyn!" Owen grabbed her by the shoulders and tried to pull her out of the way of the rampaging giant.

Aderyn fought him. "We have to show we're not afraid—"

"I'm not letting you be hurt or killed for the sake of a possibility!" Owen swore again and grabbed her around the waist, lifting her bodily.

The oncoming giant slowed. In seconds, it had come to a halt. "See?" Aderyn exclaimed.

"It wasn't you," Owen said, pointing.

Behind them, Isold stood, his body still with concentration. "That's right, I'm your friend," he murmured. "We're all friends. You don't need to attack us."

The giant blinked. "Friends," it said in a voice that boomed through the snowy air. "But you defiled the stones. You can't be friends."

Aderyn Assessed him and got the name Zalk, along with an Assessment identical to Taavek's. "Zalk, that wasn't us," she said, keeping her voice calm to match Isold's. "What made you think it was?"

"How do you know my name?" Zalk exclaimed. "Did you Assess me? How can humans do that?"

"Who cares about that? They stabbed me!" Taavek exclaimed. "They aren't friends. They attacked me!"

"You attacked first, you idiot," Owen snarled.

"Owen, that's not helping," Aderyn murmured.

"I don't give a damn about helping. If Isold stops using **[Charm]**, they'll go back to being antagonistic. We need to deal with them now, before that happens."

Aderyn groaned. "Just—let me do this, please?"

She walked to where Taavek lay sprawled on the ground, clutching his wounded leg so blood spilled between his fingers. "I'm sorry, but Owen is right, you attacked us first. If we attacked you without provocation, you'd be justified in fighting back, right?"

"You bloodied the stones. We have a right," Taavek said. Despite his fierce words, he sounded weak from pain and blood loss. "Washing the stones can't hide your guilt."

"I promise that wasn't us," Aderyn said. "Look. If we heal you, will you agree to talk?"

Taavek glared at her, but said nothing.

Aderyn returned to Isold's side. "Zalk, Isold is going to heal Taavek now. Will you call your other friends to join us?"

"Don't listen to it, Zalk," Taavek muttered. "It wants us all in one place so they can kill us."

"Zalk, you know that's not true," Aderyn said. She was terrifyingly aware that she didn't know where Weston and Livia were, and if they killed one of these giants there was probably no chance of an agreement. "I promise we won't hurt you."

"Zalk—"

"Shut up, Taavek, I'm the leader and I decide." Zalk whistled a complicated birdsong. Moments later, two more giants emerged from the snowstorm. One of them was cradling his—no, her—arm like it hurt, but neither was bloody.

"Isold?" Aderyn said.

Owen sighed heavily. "I'll go find the others." He was gone before Aderyn could say anything else. Fighting the uneasy feeling that she had made a mistake, she followed Isold to Taavek's side, where Isold used the <**Wand of Healing**> on the giant's leg. The other giants crowded around, not too closely. When the green healing light was gone, they all sighed as if disappointed.

"See?" Aderyn said. "We don't want to hurt you."

"That's a lie. Humans and giants hate each other." Taavek didn't sound convinced.

"Taavek, humans haven't seen giants in centuries. We don't know you to be able to hate you." Aderyn turned to Isold. "Right?"

"That's correct," Isold said. "And we were not the ones who shed blood on those stones. We came upon the body of a giant there after he was killed. We buried him well away from the spiral and washed the blood away. I won't claim we understand what those stones mean to you, but we did our best to be respectful on our terms."

"One of the People?" Zalk said. "Who? What did he look like?"

"Um," Aderyn said. "He was blond, bigger than you, with an old scar cutting across his left eyebrow."

The four young giants recoiled. "Emmil," Taavek said. "He's been out hunting for several days. You couldn't have killed him, not as small as you are."

Aderyn considered all the monsters they'd killed that were considerably larger than the dead Emmil and chose not to respond to this. "Like we said, we didn't kill him. I'm sorry if we made the wrong choice, but we gave him the respect we would have given one of our own."

The female giant slapped Zalk across the back of his head, not lightly. "You made a mistake, Zalk. We shouldn't have voted you leader."

"We *all* agreed it was the most likely possibility, Freta," Zalk said irritably. "Don't go shifting blame. We all made the mistake."

"I don't want to go on about blame," Aderyn said. "What matters is what we do going forward. Why are giant children responsible for the spiral of stones?"

"We're not children," Taavek exclaimed, half a breath ahead of Freta.

"We'll be nine soon, all of us," Zalk said. "That's close enough to being adults that we can fight to defend our home. Don't think we're not capable, because we are."

"Eight years old?" Aderyn said. "But that's not—"

"One moment, Aderyn." Isold turned to Zalk. "You are quite mature, aren't you? Tell me, Zalk, how old is the oldest person in your clan? Or do you call it your family?"

"Yrsa is the oldest in our village. She's fifty-four and too weak to walk, but her mind's still sharp, as she tells everyone at least three times a day."

"Fifty-four is ancient indeed. I imagine most people die at a much earlier age. Is that true?"

"I guess. My gran'pa is forty-four and he complains a lot about his aches and pains. He lies in bed all day complaining. Why do you care?"

Isold nodded. "Early maturity, old age in the mid-forties... Aderyn, I believe their lifespans aren't as long as ours."

"Oh," Aderyn said, feeling stupid for having made assumptions. Why should other intelligent races be like humans just because they shared a world and a language? "I, um, I'm sorry I thought you were children. You're more like young adults, right? But I still don't understand why you're responsible for the stone circle."

None of the young giants spoke. Freta glared at Zalk, who scowled. "We're not officially in charge. But we care about our heritage and we don't want it defiled by humans."

"We shouldn't be here," the fourth giant said. "We ought to go home. You know how Ragna and Oskarl are about nobody wandering far because of the tempests."

"Shut up, Skalt, you're such a baby," Freta said.

"Don't tell me to shut up!"

"I'll say whatever I want to say, you thundering loser!"

"Stop," Zalk shouted. "Both of you let it go. Nobody knows we're gone, and we won't be in trouble unless somebody talks."

"Except we have to tell someone about Emmil," Freta said. "How are we supposed to do that?"

"I'll think of something." Zalk scowled at Skalt. "That means *me*, not you blabbing to your pa about what you think you know."

"It's not blabbing if it's adult business, Zalk," Skalt shot back.

"He's right, Skalt, you'd better not tattle. We can handle this," Taavek said. He rose to his feet, staggered slightly, and said, "Oh, blast and thunder. I'm covered in blood. Mam will want to know what happened."

"Our companion can clean your clothing," Isold said smoothly.

That reminded Aderyn that she still hadn't seen Weston or Livia. She turned in a slow circle, searching through the heavy snowfall for her friends, and startled when it turned out Livia was right behind her, with Weston to one side. Livia drew even with her and said, "What in thunderation is going on? Are we helping these monsters?"

"We're the People," Freta said. "We're not monsters. *You're* the monster, human."

"Shut up, Freta." Zalk sounded more weary than angry. "Humans aren't what we thought they were, all right?"

"You don't know that!" Freta backed away as Livia approached Taavek. "Watch out, it's got a weapon!"

With a twirl of her wrists, Livia made the [Elemental Hammer] disappear. "I'm a she, not an it. And I don't think I should wash your trousers in this weather, giant, or even you might freeze. But I can mend that tear." She gestured, spat out a few curt words, and the gash in Taavek's trousers sealed up.

"Magic," Taavek breathed. "You didn't even need stone to do it."

"What do you mean, stone?" Livia said, perking up. "Your kind do magic with stones? Is that what the stone spiral is for?"

"We can't stand around in the snow comparing magic, Livia," Owen said. "But it sounds like we have things to talk about. Zalk, right? Do you have a place you can shelter that will accommodate us? You won't fit in our tents."

"We can't stay," Skalt said. "We need to be in our beds soon, before our parents check and find us missing. We should go."

"Skalt, I don't know what's gotten into you, but you're acting like the worst excuse for an adventurer there's ever been among the People," Zalk said wearily. "Unfortunately, you're right. If our parents find out we snuck out, they'll keep a closer watch and we won't have the chance to sneak away again."

"But we can't just walk away," Taavek said. "These are the first humans anyone has seen in centuries."

"I agree." Zalk bent so his face was level with Owen's. "We can meet you here tomorrow, after the storm blows itself out."

"Shouldn't we come to your town?" Owen asked.

"That might be a bad idea. People are scared of humans because of all the stories about how you're vicious monsters." Zalk spoke without a trace of irony.

"We're not—" Aderyn began.

"It doesn't matter, Aderyn." Owen nodded to Zalk. "We'll be here. But we do have to show ourselves to the rest of the gi—the People," he amended. "Maybe together we can work out something that won't scare them."

"We'll try." Zalk returned his nod and gestured to his companions. "Do you need food or anything?"

"We have supplies. Besides, you shouldn't carry a load out of your town and risk suspicion. But thank you for the thought."

Aderyn watched in silence until the giants disappeared into the storm. Then she said, "See?"

"Don't gloat, sweetheart, we don't know everything yet." Owen hugged her to take away the sting of his words. "Let's get back to camp. Isold, where's Jessemia?"

"I didn't have time to heal her leg before you called me." Isold hurried away, followed by Weston and Livia. Aderyn and Owen brought up the rear.

"I'm trying not to ignore my own advice," Owen said as they walked.

"What advice?"

"The advice about not getting ahead of ourselves until we know more. If there are giants living in the Northlands, and they have a civilization, doesn't it seem like the obvious conclusion is that they're the ones we need to bring peace to?"

"You're right. That's getting ahead of ourselves. Even I'm not that optimistic. The most I'm willing to hope for is that we can make contact with the adult giants without getting killed."

Owen stopped and put his hands on Aderyn's shoulders, turning her to face him. Snow dusted his blond hair and his shoulders, making him look like the snowman creature he'd called her once. "I'm sorry."

"Sorry? For what?"

"I keep disregarding your instincts about monsters. Which monsters aren't what we think, I mean. I worry about your safety, and I fear what might happen if you're ever wrong in an Assessment. But that's never happened, and if I continue countering you like I did with those giant adolescents, that's like saying I don't trust you. Which I do. So—I'm sorry."

"Oh." Aderyn brushed snow off the top of his head. "I understood you, that you were worried about me. But you're right, I need you to trust me just as I trust you. So, thank you."

Owen touched her cheek with a cold hand. "Let's see how Jessemia is doing, and then get warmed up."

When they reached the campfire, Jessemia was sitting up and looked less on the verge of passing out from pain. "What do you mean, you can't *repair* it?" she was asking Livia in some perplexity.

"I mean it's so blasted magical my *repair* spell slips right off it," Livia grumbled. "More specifically, the nature of its magic means it repairs itself in between summonings, and that makes it impervious to other alteration magic."

"We could pack up and tear down camp and summon it again," Weston said.

"I don't want to inconvenience everyone," Jessemia said. "I

can sleep under the shelter we built for the fire." She shivered, and wrapped her arms around herself.

"That's unnecessary," Isold said. "There's plenty of room in my tent, and I'm about to go on watch. It's just for a few hours."

Jessemia's face stilled, though she still occasionally shivered. "All right," she said, after a pause that wasn't long enough to be awkward. "Thank you."

"It's no trouble," Isold said.

Aderyn helped Jessemia collect her things from within the collapsed tent. "Are you sure it's all right?" she asked.

Jessemia nodded. "It's just for a night. It's not like we're going to leap on each other just because we're sleeping a few feet apart." She wasn't meeting Aderyn's eyes.

"Jessemia—"

"It's *fine*," Jessemia insisted. "Please don't try to protect me. This isn't a big deal." She wadded her bedroll in her arms and ducked into Isold's tent. Aderyn followed more slowly, carrying Jessemia's knapsack, which she handed to her friend without comment. Then she returned to her own tent and pulled her boots off.

"Aderyn, are you sure there's nothing weird going on between —" Owen began.

"I'm not sure," Aderyn said. "But Jessemia doesn't want a fuss, and I'm going to obey her wishes." She lay back in her bedroll, shivering, until Owen joined her, and the warmth of his body eased her shivering so she could finally fall asleep.

She dreamed and woke and slept again, fitfully, until the storm winds died and the absence of noise woke her again. When Owen shook her out of a semi-doze for her turn at watch, she pulled her boots and armor on eagerly, wanting a distraction from her mental turmoil. She walked the perimeter inside the range of the <**Soldier's Friend's**> alarm spell and saw nothing, not even a nocturnal burrowing animal or hunting owl. But the tenseness of being alert exhausted her so when she turned the watch over to Weston, she was able to fall asleep for real.

She woke to dawn's bright sunlight making the tent walls glow golden-white and lay for a moment, enjoying how warm she was. Owen lay beside her, staring at the tent roof as well. "I'm trying to muster the strength to go out into the cold," he murmured.

"Me too."

"I smell porridge. I guess that's good on a cold morning."

"Good enough."

Owen grunted and sat up. "If you do it all at once, it's not—"

"*We're under attack!*" Weston roared. Deep, booming shouts drowned the rest of his words out.

Surprise and fear jolted Aderyn into motion. She scrambled out of the bedroll and grabbed her boots. Owen started to don his armor, then tossed it aside with a curse and flung himself through the tent flap.

"No, Owen!" Aderyn protested. She dragged her mail shirt over her head. The links caught at her hair, sharply tugging the loose strands. Half-blinded by the neck hole being caught on her forehead, she fumbled around until she found the tent flap and staggered outside.

With a final sharp tug that pulled out several strands of hair, she jerked the <**Gossamer Mail**> into place and swiped loose locks out of her face. "Weston!" she shouted, then fell silent, stunned at what she saw.

Half a dozen giant forms, much taller than Zalk and his friends, loomed over Weston and Owen. They wore thin woven shirts and heavy leather vests with pockets stitched to the fronts and baggy trousers, none of which looked warm enough for the weather. But the giants didn't look like they cared. Their pale skin showed no flush of cold, no white of frostbite.

Though Aderyn didn't see weapons, most of the giants held head-sized rocks, bouncing them in their enormous hands like sizing up their options. A shorter figure lurked behind them. Skalt's nervous expression matched how he jigged on the balls of his feet like he was ready to run at the first sign of violence.

The giant in the lead, his longish blond hair framing his clean-shaven face, was unarmed, though Aderyn considered the size of his fists and doubted he needed a weapon to do damage. He stared down at Weston, his jaw set and rigid.

Nobody moved. Aderyn was about to Assess the giants when the one in the lead, in a voice that sounded like boulders clashing, said, "So. Humans invading our lands. Give me one reason why we shouldn't turn you all into paste."

CHAPTER FIFTEEN

Owen stepped forward. "Because you don't kill indiscriminately," he said, tilting his chin so he could look the giant in the eye. "I know it doesn't matter to you that we didn't know you were here, and that we didn't intrude on your lands intentionally, because we could be a threat regardless. But we haven't harmed any of your people, and we intend to deal honorably by you."

None of the giants moved. The dark-haired one on the left behind the original speaker, the one behind whom Skalt lurked, continued to bounce his rock up and down in his massive hand, but the others holding stones gripped them in a throwing position. Aderyn swiftly Assessed the leader. To her surprise, instead of a monster Assessment, the options for a Level Assessment, Skill Assessment, and Full Assessment appeared, just as they would for a human. She chose the quick Level Assessment.

Name: Oskarl
∞ Kaarina
Level: 16

Class: Hunter

**I can see you're going to need some background informa-
tion. Though giants, or the People, as they call themselves,
are one species, they come in two variants: tall, slim, and
dark-haired, and shorter, stocky, and blond. Giants organize
their society around these physical differences. Over the
centuries, the dark-haired giants tended toward farming
and the husbandry skills, and blond giants were usually
hunters and warriors. Now, the groups refer to themselves
as Tillers and Trappers.**

**Oskarl is the leader of this settlement's Trappers. He's
approaching middle age at thirty-one, and you can
congratulate your friend on deducing the giants' lifespan.
Oskarl excels at hunting and related skills and works in
harmony with Ragna, leader of the Tillers. Don't assume
anything about the personalities involved. Only the most
narrow-minded of giants consider one group superior to
the other, and no sensible giants take those people
seriously.**

**However, Oskarl has never raised a hand or weapon in
violence against any person, and he is a terrible fighter. If he
attacks you, you might be in more danger of falling over
laughing than from his fists. Don't take too much advantage
of him. He will be a valuable ally.**

Oskarl took a menacing step forward. "You can deal honorably with us by leaving our territory. Now. We do not have words
with those who defile our stones."

"We weren't the ones who did that. We're here for a purpose.
We would like to come to terms with you. What will it take to
convince you we mean no harm?" Owen sounded more reasonable
than ever, but **[Read Body Language]** revealed his justifiable
tension.

"Shouldn't you be more worried about *us* harming *you*, little fellow?" the dark-haired giant tossing the stone said.

"You chose to speak to us rather than attack, so that tells me you're at least a little curious," Owen replied. "And we intend to be fully open with you. Aderyn?"

Aderyn stepped forward and addressed the leader. "Your name is Oskarl, and your class is Hunter. We didn't know mon—anyone other than humans could have classes, and that alone makes me want to share knowledge with you. You're level sixteen and you're thirty-one years old—"

Oskarl's face had reddened when she mentioned his class, and he worked his jaw several times in agitation before saying, "Stop! How do you know all that? Who betrayed us?"

"No one, sir. My class allows me to learn detailed information about someone through the skill **[Improved Assess 4]**." Aderyn smiled, though Oskarl was very large and loomed over her like a tree about to fall. Her Assessment about his lack of fighting skills didn't reassure her.

"Humans are liars," the dark-haired giant said. "We can't trust them. Maybe it can Assess like a person, maybe not, but either way, they are dangerous. And *something* certainly killed within the spiral."

"Thank you, Jorm," Oskarl said, forcefully enough that Jorm, who'd looked about to go into more detail about lying humans and the danger they posed, shut up. "Prove you weren't the ones who spilled blood on the standing stones."

"I don't know what evidence you'd take as proof," Owen said. "You won't believe it if I swear an oath. When we stumbled on your stone spiral, we found a dead giant who'd been killed by something our Pathseer couldn't identify. We buried his body a respectful distance from the stones and cleaned off the blood as best we could."

"You can't prove that. Maybe you killed Emmil and you're lying now," Jorm said. Oskarl shot him another murderous look.

"At some point, you have to decide to trust," Owen said. "If you have classes, you have skills, and one of those skills should be **[Sense Truth]**. What does that tell you?"

Oskarl frowned at him in silence for a few seconds. Then he said, "You have classes, all of you. How is that possible?"

"I think there's a lot we don't know about each other, and I would really like to learn more about your people." Owen extended a hand. "This is how we show respect. We shake hands as proof that we don't mean harm to one another."

Oskarl didn't move. "I'm not going to swear peace when I don't know if you're lying."

"Consider it a temporary truce," Owen said without hesitation.

"Oskarl, be careful," Jorm said. He finally stopped tossing his stone, but now he gripped it in a throwing position.

"Jorm—" Oskarl visibly controlled an outburst. "A truce, then. For now." He extended his hand, and Owen clasped it. Oskarl's enormous palm swallowed Owen's up. Owen didn't react as if he was intimidated.

"I'm Owen," he said, "and these are my friends Isold, Weston, Livia, and Jessemia. And my wife, Aderyn."

Oskarl's eyes briefly unfocused. "Assessment says your name is Jacob Owen Lindberg. Is multiple names a human trait?"

"None of the others have three names," the other blond giant said.

"My parents had a different naming tradition," Owen said, perfectly honestly. "I go by Owen because it's shorter. Can we sit somewhere? I'm afraid we don't have any seats that will accommodate you."

"I don't think we know you well enough to share mead,"

Oskarl said. "Explain to me how humans can have classes. You're not of the People."

Owen turned to Aderyn, who said, "I don't have all the answers. To me, it's surprising that giants have classes and can Assess things. If I had to guess, I'd say we're both non-monstrous races connected to the system. And that's so amazing I can hardly believe I heard those words come out of my mouth."

"I'm equally astonished." Oskarl's eyes narrowed. "You are married. Which of you is male, and which female?"

Aderyn had observed the previous night that humans and giants shared the same basic anatomy, and that male and female giants had the same secondary sex traits as humans, but Aderyn and all her friends were bundled up so heavily against the cold none of those things were visible. "I'm female, and so are Livia and Jessemia." She pointed. "The others are male."

"Your classes are odd," another blond giant said. "Warmaster? Swordsworn? The only one that's even close to normal is Pathseer."

Aderyn swiftly Assessed the six giants, glancing only at classes. In passing, she noted that none of them had Trapper or Tiller anywhere in their Assessment, but it was a fleeting observation she had no time to pursue. "I see two Hunters, a Fisher, a Gleaner, a Farmer, and a Plover. We don't have classes like yours, either."

"I'm sure this is interesting, but there's no guarantee they aren't trying to catch us off guard so they can attack us like they did Emmil," Jorm said.

Oskarl briefly closed his eyes in a way Aderyn recognized. She made that gesture herself when she grasped for patience with an annoying person. When Oskarl opened his eyes, he was looking directly at Aderyn. She smiled, feeling a moment's kinship with the giant.

Then Oskarl turned his attention on Jorm. "Jorm, I was

unaware that the Tillers had voted Ragna out of leadership in your favor. Should I defer to you now?"

Jorm took a step back. "No. Of course not."

"I appreciate your concern for our village's safety, but I choose to reserve judgment about what happened. As should you." Oskarl nodded politely and returned his attention to Aderyn. "So, if I understand you correctly, humans and People alike have classes and can Assess others. But your classes are not like ours."

"I don't know why that is. Your classes all seem—the ones I saw, that is—they all seem related to living and working and surviving. Ours are meant for adventuring. For going out and killing monsters and defeating dungeons."

"We fight monsters, but no one is made just for killing them." Oskarl looked as if he was still puzzling things out. "And I don't know what a dungeon is."

Aderyn resolved not to embarrass Oskarl by revealing what the system had said about his lack of fighting skills. "So all of you learn to fight monsters? That's interesting. It's almost the reverse of humans. We don't have any classes for growing things or hunting food."

"Then you are not rooted in stone," the same blond giant said.

"I don't know what that means," Aderyn said, just as Livia burst out, "I am, in a way, and I would really like to know what it means that you are stonekin."

All the giants recoiled. Oskarl's pleasant expression disappeared. "That word is closely guarded by adult People," he growled. "Explain how a human knows it."

"The stones called you that. They said the dead giant was stonekin and that you were the ones who set them in that spiral near here." Livia spoke fearlessly, though she'd taken the solid stance that said she was prepared to use magic. "They didn't say it was a secret name, so I'm sorry if I was disrespectful in using it."

"Not disrespectful, but it is one of our secrets." The other blond giant stepped forward. "My name is Joukkon, and I am a Plover, someone who works metal. I am temporarily the custodian of the stones. How do you know what the stones said?"

"I'm an Earthbreaker, which is a kind of magic that works in stone and earth. I'm a high enough level that I can hear stones speak." Livia was twitching with such excitement Aderyn didn't need **[Read Body Language]** to interpret it. "Look, I know you people don't trust us, but you've never seen humans before, have you? Isn't it obvious that neither of us is what the stories say?"

All the giants looked at Oskarl. Oskarl, in turn, watched Joukkon. "What do you say?" he asked.

"I can ask the stones to verify their story," Joukkon said. "But if this one is stonekin herself and had defiled the stones with the blood of the People, the stones would have crushed her. I say they have earned our consideration of their request, at least."

"Then we should—"

"Stop," Jessemia said, interrupting Oskarl. She tipped her head back and inhaled deeply through her nose. "I smell something rank. There are monsters nearby."

"Monsters?" Jorm exclaimed. "The humans betray us!"

"Oh, shut up, Jorm," Oskarl said. "What monsters?"

"I don't know. My skill **[Keen Senses]** isn't that good yet. But whatever they are, they're approaching from behind that hill." Jessemia drew her sword and pointed with it at the steep hill that had sheltered them the night before.

"I hear it," Weston said. "They're light on their feet, whatever they are."

A howl split the air, an eerie sound that was nothing like Isold's **[Cause Fear]** or the cries of Zalk and his friends. The howl broke into many howls that touched a primal sense of fear deep within Aderyn, a child's fear of things that come scratching around the window at midnight. She shook the feeling off and drew her sword.

The howls sounded again, nearer and more terrifying than before. Over the crest of the hill and around its sides poured a dozen pale blue shapes dusted with white like wolves made of snow. They charged the humans and giants, yelping and howling and snarling.

"Form up," Owen shouted. "Aderyn?"

Aderyn Assessed the oncoming horde.

Name: Rimewolf [12]

Type: Abomination

Power level: 14

Terrain: boreal forest, tundra, ice sheets

Attack(s): bite, claw x2, special

Immune to: elemental damage cold, elemental damage water

Resistant to: [Distraction], [Fascination], [Cause Fear], light-based attacks

Vulnerable to: elemental damage fire

Special attacks: ice aura, chilling howl

Rimewolves are a top predator of the Northlands. They are larger than the typical wolf, the smallest standing five feet tall at the shoulder, and have a bite powerful enough to take off your hand if you're incautious enough to let one get that close. They also have retractable claws like a cat, not as large as a cat-hawk's, but big and sharp enough to tear out your throat or liver. There are much larger rimewolves than these in the Northlands—but I'm getting ahead of myself. Don't worry about it. No, really. It's not important now.

It's probably obvious that rimewolves, being creatures of the northern wastes, are immune to cold attacks. In fact, they carry with them a permanent ice aura that does cold

damage to enemies near them. Their howl is a sonic attack that delivers a [Cause Fear] effect that is more effective the greater their power level compared to that of their victim. Because they are immune to vision-hampering effects such as *sunburst* due to their acclimation to sunlight on snow, they are hard to fool with spells and skills that have visual components. A sword made of light won't frighten them. On the other hand, it's still a sword and will do just as much damage as any length of sharpened steel.

The rimewolves' primary tactic involves separating individuals from the group and killing them one at a time. If your team and the giants stay together, you will have a better chance of defeating them. But watch out for Skalt. He's going to bolt in a second.

"Their primary attacks are their claws and bite!" Aderyn shouted, not bothering with [Amplify Voice]. "They're vulnerable to fire, resist any attack with a visual component, and if you have to close with them, be prepared to take cold damage. And everyone stay close together—"

With a whimpering cry, Skalt backed away from the group and ran. Instantly, four rimewolves peeled away from the pack to pursue him. Jorm shouted, "Get back here!" and ran after Skalt, dropping the stone he held.

Aderyn swore a heartfelt curse. "Livia! Stop those wolves! The rest of you, don't let the rimewolves divide us—they'll prey on anyone who gets separated!" She cast a final glance at Skalt and Jorm, wishing they hadn't been stupid, and then ignored them. Their fate was their own. For now, she had monsters to fight.

CHAPTER SIXTEEN

I n the distance, the earth groaned and opened up under the rimewolves chasing Skalt. One of them scrambled out of the *hungry pit*, its paws flying. The other three vanished as the earth closed over them. The surviving rimewolf got its feet under itself and continued to pursue Skalt and Jorm.

Three identical system defeat notices flashed in quick succession.

**Congratulations! You have defeated [Rimewolf].
You have earned [10,000 XP]**

Aderyn took a stance next to Owen, who activated the **[Sunsword]**. Its brilliant light was dim in full daylight, making the blade seem ethereal, but there was nothing ethereal about the way he stood ready to attack. His elemental cold damage wouldn't help them against rimewolves, but that was the least of what he could do with **[Weapon Mastery]** to an enemy.

The rimewolves were almost on them, running silently now. A

huge stone flew past, impacting on a rimewolf at the middle of the pack with such force the monster was knocked off its feet with a pained yelp and struck one of its packmates. More stones flew, and then the rimewolves closed with the team.

Aderyn slashed the rimewolf attacking her, more to give Owen an opportunity for [Outflank] than with any intent to do serious damage. A fierce chill struck Aderyn like a sharp blow to the face, almost identical to the breath of the ice dragon in Winter's Peril dungeon. She immediately regretted not making a stronger attack. Two seconds in and she'd already disregarded the part of the Assessment that warned about the rimewolves' ice aura.

The blue lines of [Discern Weakness] played across the monster's body, revealing weak spots at the base of the rimewolf's throat, all across its thick-furred belly, and beneath each of its legs where they joined its body. The rimewolf reared up, its terrible black claws extended. Aderyn threw herself forward and thrust for its exposed belly. The rimewolf roared, again sending a thrill of terror through her, but the roar turned into a pained yelp as Owen stabbed it through its flank. Aderyn thrust again, disemboweling it and dodging a gush of violet blood.

Congratulations! You have defeated [Rimewolf].
You have earned [10,000 XP]

"Belly and throat and below the legs!" Aderyn shouted. Now [Amplify Voice] was needed, between the roars of the rimewolves and the shouts of the giants. Oskarl bellowed orders to his companions to stay together, but two more of them had cut and run, and a handful of rimewolves chased them. Aderyn groaned inwardly. The rimewolves and the giants were faster than humans, and catching them might be impossible. [Interchange] would bring one of them back, but it would put

Aderyn far from reinforcements. Maybe it wasn't such a great skill after all.

Another system defeat notice appeared as Weston skewered one monster and flung a burning knife at another, bringing it to a halt within range of Oskarl's fists. The giant's attack was wild and undisciplined, but it brought the rimewolf down. Oskarl retrieved one of the flung stones and shouted, "By thunder, I said *stay together*, you fools!" He wound up and hurled the stone at a rimewolf that pursued a fleeing giant, crushing the monster's head.

Aderyn counted. Five—no, six now that Isold had **[Coerced]** two rimewolves to fight each other, plus two killed by the giants. She swiftly scanned the battlefield. The remaining rimewolves were too distant for even Weston's **[Thrown Weapon Proficiency]** to reach. Jessemia stood near Livia, her sword drawn but unbloodied—well, these monsters were too much for anyone of Jessemia's level. Isold's remaining **[Coerced]** rimewolf chased after the others, circling around in an attempt to herd them back to the team.

Oskarl picked up another stone. "Those fools," he muttered, and ran after the three giants who'd fled.

"We should follow him," Aderyn said.

"We'll never catch them," Livia said. "And I'm not just saying that because I'm no runner. But I have another option." She took a fighting stance and chanted a string of words that almost made sense.

In the distance, the earth humped and rose until the three rimewolves not controlled by Isold tumbled down the slopes of a steep-sided basin. Livia let out a heavy breath. "Wolves don't climb. *Now* we can run." The earth beneath her feet rumbled, and she shot away from them, balancing with *earth glide* as it carried her toward the distant fight.

Aderyn raced after the others, **[Keep Pace]** working hard to prevent her falling behind Owen. The steep basin Livia had created was tall enough to block her sight of the rimewolves caught in it, but the giants stood around it, towering over the edges. When Aderyn reached them, breathing heavily, they were having a heated conversation.

"Then go find something we can use to smash their heads in!" a giant said.

"If we leave them, they'll escape," Jorm said. "We need to take them on one at a time."

"That's insanity," Oskarl said. "You there. Warmaster. What do you suggest?"

"Me?" Aderyn's voice came out squeaky in her surprise. "I don't know. Do you have to kill them yourselves?"

"We won't get experience if we don't," the same unknown giant said.

"That's true," Oskarl said, "but if these humans hadn't fought beside us, some or all of us would be dead now. And what matters is that the rimewolves die so they can't prey on our people and our lands. So I ask again, Warmaster. Aderyn. What should we do?" One of the rimewolves made a leap for freedom, and Oskarl punched it in the snout so it fell whimpering back into the basin. He was doing well for someone with no fighting experience.

"Livia?" Aderyn said.

Livia rose on a pillar of stone and earth so she could see over the edge, prompting every giant to step back and exclaim in surprise and consternation. "*Hungry pit* will take care of them."

"One moment," Isold said. He didn't say anything else, but in seconds, the remaining rimewolf trotted through the crowd as calmly as if it was domesticated and leaped into the basin. "There. That is all of them."

Livia nodded. She gestured, and spoke three polysyllabic words. The earth rumbled loudly, and tremors shook the ground.

Aderyn staggered and grabbed Jessemia's shoulder as Jessemia gripped her hand so they both stayed upright. None of the giants moved.

With a roar of shifting earth that drowned out the yelps of the rimewolves, the basin collapsed on itself, burying the monsters. Shortly, four more system defeat notices appeared. The earth smoothed out over the engulfed rimewolves, and Livia descended from her pillar. The giants backed away from her, all but Jorm, who had the struggling Skalt by the arm in a grip that by the young giant's expression was painful.

"None of us are badly injured, mostly just the freezing damage the rimewolves' ice aura inflicted," Isold said into the sudden silence. "I can heal any of you People who are injured, if you wish."

"You move the earth and stone," Joukkon said to Livia. "How is that possible?"

"Human spellslingers, those of us who work magic, have an elemental specialty," Livia said. Her voice was uncharacteristically gentle, as if she recognized and respected Joukkon's awe. "As I said, I'm an Earthbreaker, and manipulating stone and earth is part of my magic. Do you see why I'm so interested in learning more about your affinity for stone? We have much in common."

"You're not listening to this, are you?" Jorm said. He smacked Skalt across the back of the head, not lightly, to still him. "They're *humans*. We have nothing in common with them. They want to invade—"

"Jorm, for the love of rock and sky, would you shut it already?" Oskarl roared. "The People—the stonekin—are rational and open to change. We don't make up reasons to disbelieve the evidence of our eyes just so we can maintain our traditions. If you can't hold to those laws, you're invited to leave." His gaze fell on Skalt. "And I'd be embarrassed if I were you, young Skalt. Don't think I don't know you were looking to curry favor with your elders by bringing us this information. Tattling is unbecoming one of the People."

"You're just saying that because Taavek broke the rules and didn't admit to it," Jorm snarled. "You're going to protect him—"

Oskarl took a swing at Jorm. It was awkward, and most of its force was lost in how it struck Jorm's stomach instead of his chest, where Oskarl had aimed, but it was enough to make Jorm fold up over Oskarl's fist and let out all his breath in a loud *pah*. Jorm released his grip on Skalt's arm, and the boy scrambled out of reach and then fled. Oskarl followed the blow up with another punch to Jorm's face, equally awkward but still effective.

"That's *enough*," he shouted. "Keep this up, and Ragna will have to challenge me to defend you. Again. You think she isn't going to come after you to prevent that? You're not gaining anything by being stubborn. Take your ignorance gracefully, and remember we all were wrong."

He turned his back on Jorm, which Aderyn thought was tremendously brave—Jorm didn't look like someone who took humiliation well, and his fists were just as big as Oskarl's—and said to Livia, "We extend the hospitality of the mead-hall to you and yours for the space of three days, to speak together and come to greater understanding. That means no one will attack you, and if you abuse our generosity to attack us, we will show no mercy. Are we understood?"

Livia glanced at Owen, then nodded. "Yes, but I'm not the leader. Owen is."

"You are stonekin, which makes you one of us." Oskarl surveyed the team. "We will treat fairly with you, whichever of you leads. Now, we invite you to join us. We will wait while you break camp."

"That won't take long," Owen said.

THE GIANTS STEPPED FAR BACK, MUTTERING TO themselves, when Livia used the <**Soldier's Friend**> to break camp, but didn't otherwise show fear. Aderyn only realized Jessemia wasn't with them when Isold said, "Does anyone know where Jessemia went?"

"Over there," Weston said, pointing. Jessemia knelt beside the nearest rimewolf corpse, slicing through its belly with her long belt knife. She'd removed her coat and rolled her shirtsleeves up to avoid getting purple gore on them. Aderyn hurried to join her, followed by Isold.

"Rimewolf kidneys have potent magic," Jessemia said without looking up from her work. "My **[Knowledge: Monsters]** skill woke up, I guess you could say, and told me they are useful in purification potions and antitoxin, more effective than the components Spiritsmiths use regularly. Which makes sense, if no one's been to the Northlands in centuries to harvest them." She plucked a bluish-red hunk of flesh the size of her fist from the corpse and displayed it. "And they turn to crystal when exposed to cold air, so they're easy to store and transport."

"Astonishing," Isold said. "I had no idea. I believe my knowledge skills about valuable monster parts come at it from a different direction. I know about the item, and connect that to the monster, whereas you seem to know about the monster and that leads you to the item."

"I think you're right." Jessemia removed another kidney from the body and dropped it onto a length of cloth spread nearby. "Anyway, they don't take up much space and will be worth a fortune when we get back to civilization. Well, human civilization, anyway."

"If you show me what to look for, I will help harvest," Isold said.

Jessemia nodded. Her attention was on the rimewolf kidneys, not on Isold, but she sounded perfectly normal when she said, "That will help, thanks."

Aderyn watched the two of them walk away, far enough apart from each other they might as well have been two people coincidentally going in the same direction. She wished she knew what they were thinking. It was getting harder to ignore the awkwardness between them any time they had to perform a task together. Maybe confronting Jessemia, at least, was the right thing to do, if it meant restoring team harmony.

She returned to Owen's side and found Livia surrounded by giants, all of them alertly attentive to her explanation about the **<Soldier's Friend>**. Even Jorm, who lurked on the outskirts of the group, was paying attention. Though the giants weren't interested in Aderyn at the moment, she still didn't want to talk about her concerns over Jessemia and Isold where their new friends could hear. Instead, she said, "Jessemia found valuable rimewolf body parts."

"I like the sound of 'valuable,' but I'm always less thrilled about 'body parts.'" Owen idly took her hand in his. "We'll go as soon as she finishes harvesting those."

"Listen to this," Livia exclaimed to her friends. "Joukkon thinks he can replicate the **<Soldier's Friend>**. Apparently a Plover is both a blacksmith and a kind of Spellcrafter. I don't know enough about Spellcrafter skills to know how much they are similar, but from what I gather Plovers are capable of crafting different kinds of magic items."

"I am more certain I can craft items using the same principles. Replicating this **<Soldier's Friend>** is less likely, given that the tents it creates aren't something the People need." Joukkon examined the bronze cube once more before handing it to Livia.

"Yes, but very few Spellcrafters can do it at all," Livia said. "Your skills are remarkable."

"I'd like to see your village, if we're ready to go," Weston said.

"If Jessemia—there she is," Owen said. Jessemia and Isold approached, still looking like strangers to one another. "What is this item you discovered?"

"A valuable Spiritsmith component," Jessemia said. "And I wish I'd thought this through before I dug into rimewolf bellies. I need a wash."

"And *drench* is ice cold," Livia said.

"It's fine. I'll warm up soon." Jessemia extended her arms well away from the others and shivered as a gout of water fell out of the air, rinsing away blood.

Again, the giants all stepped back in astonishment. "I thought you were stonekin," Oskarl said. "You have water magic as well?"

"Human spellslingers have choices about their spells. We usually stick to ones related to our elemental affinity, but that's not required. Creating water is so useful."

Jessemia rubbed the remaining blood and water away with a corner of the cloth she'd wrapped the kidneys in. "Let's walk. It will warm me up."

"Wait," Oskarl said. "Joukkon, give her a warming stone."

"That may not work for someone not of the People," Joukkon said.

"Then we'll discover that now." Oskarl gestured.

Joukkon reached into the deep pocket of the hide vest he wore and removed a flat, elongated river stone half the size of his fist, pale gray and polished as smoothly as the standing stones. He breathed across its surface. The pale gray stone turned black as if coated with soot. Joukkon drew a complicated, squiggly line in the soot. Then he handed it to Jessemia.

Jessemia accepted it tentatively with both hands and juggled it a bit. "It's hot!"

"Warm," Joukkon said, "but your flesh is cold, so it feels hotter by comparison." He repeated the process with a second stone, which he also gave to her. "Do you know what pockets are? We put these in our pockets on very cold nights when we hunt monsters, to keep our hands flexible."

"I have pockets, yes." Jessemia dropped the stones into the pockets of her coat and thrust her hands in after them. "Ohhh. This feels so good. Thank you."

"I was afraid the magic might not respond to you since you are not of the People and have no stone affinity. It's good to know otherwise." Oskarl gestured. "Follow us, and we will go to the village to talk more."

The strange procession, seven giants, six humans, set out across the snowy hills. Aderyn ended up next to Jessemia, but she didn't challenge her friend on her weird behavior. There were still too many people around. So they walked in silence for a dozen steps before Jessemia exclaimed, "Oh! I forgot. I think it was the rimewolves who killed that giant at the stone spiral."

Everyone came to a halt, staring at Jessemia, who blushed. "I'm sorry it slipped my mind, but as I was walking around, I noticed that the rimewolves hadn't left footprints. It was like the snow closed over them, obliterating them. It's similar to what I noticed before, how there weren't any footprints but giant ones— I mean, belonging to Emmil—around the stones. And the rimewolves' claws are sharp enough to mimic a blade cut."

"Does that mean anything to you, Oskarl?" Owen asked.

Oskarl blinked as if Owen had pulled him out of a reverie. "Rimewolves rarely leave the dangerous lands to the east, so rimewolves attacking the People, either a settlement or travelers, is an omen of a bad winter to come. That, along with other portents…" He shook his head. "It's nothing that concerns you."

"I see," Owen said. "Do you mean rimewolves don't usually attack the People?"

"That's right. We never see them travel in packs as large as that one. It's unusual."

Unexpectedly, silver letters filled Aderyn's vision.

A new quest is available: [Pursue the Hunters].
Rimewolf packs have begun hunting giants throughout the Northlands. Discover why this is and put a stop to it. This is a sub-quest in the quest chain [Fated One's Destiny: Eye of the Storm].
Reward: see [Fated One's Destiny: Eye of the Storm]
Accept? Y / N

"What the hell?" Owen muttered.

"We have to accept it, right?" Aderyn said. "If it's part of the **[Eye of the Storm]** quest?"

"If nothing else, I want to see how it's related," Weston said, swiping the air where the Y would be.

Aderyn did the same and watched the new quest shrink into a silver dot at the side of her Codex display, beneath the golden dot of their primary quest. Then the golden dot enlarged into letters:

[Fated One's Destiny: Eye of the Storm]
Bring peace to the Northlands by [see Pursue the Hunters: Reward].
Sub-quest: [Pursue the Hunters]
Rimewolf packs have begun hunting giants throughout the Northlands. Discover why this is and put a stop to it.

Reward: Additional detail to the primary quest becomes available.

"Additional detail. That sounds great," Livia said.

Aderyn caught Oskarl's eye. The giant leader had the look of someone who is involuntarily eavesdropping and doesn't know how to step away. "I'm sorry, Oskarl. We are here following a quest, and new developments just happened. Do giants—I mean the People have quests?"

"As young men and women on the verge of adulthood, yes," Oskarl said. He shook his head ponderously. "The more I learn, the more questions I have."

"I feel the same," Owen said.

CHAPTER SEVENTEEN

It was less than a mile to the giants' village, and with the sun shining brightly and warming the air, the walk was pleasant despite the increasing slushiness of the snow underfoot. Aderyn's gratitude for her well-made boots increased. In the distance, where the hills grew steeper as they crowded the base of the Eretai Mountains, the dark smudges of evergreens marked the beginning of a vast forest spreading out to cover the western horizon. Aderyn imagined how beautiful the forest would smell if she were surrounded by it.

"Are your hands warming up?" she asked Jessemia, who still walked beside her.

"Yes, very," Jessemia said. "And the warmth is spreading through my arms as well. These are marvelous. I wonder if a Spellcrafter could make something similar?"

"Maybe someday more humans will encounter giants, and exchanges can happen." The moment she said this, Aderyn couldn't help imagining those encounters. With so many adventurers entering the Northlands, humans had to run into giants eventually, and the odds of all of those encounters being peaceful wasn't good.

"I hope they're not violent exchanges," Jessemia said as if she'd heard Aderyn's thoughts. "I still can't believe it. A non-monstrous, non-human race that's connected to the system. Doesn't it make you wonder if there are any others?"

"If there are, where are they? We've been all over the continent. Orcs were evil and definitely not connected to the system. Kobolds aren't evil, but they have their own society."

"I don't know. How sure are we that this is the only continent there is?"

Aderyn opened her mouth to contradict Jessemia and then closed it. "That's a really good question. Your map doesn't show others, does it?"

Jessemia shook her head. "But it's not impossible. And now I'm imagining a whole other land filled with humans and monsters we've never heard of and good non-human races." She laughed. "As if we needed more challenges when our land is challenge enough, right?"

"Right. Still, it's fun speculating."

Jessemia sniffed. "I smell wood smoke. I think we must be near the giants' village." She shielded her eyes against the bright sunlight and added, "Yes, I see farms, and stone buildings, lots of them. I pictured a tiny little hamlet, but this is extensive."

Aderyn squinted, but saw only gray and black smears. Even so, those smears extended widely across the near horizon. "They must build really large structures, too. I mean by our standards." Belatedly, she Assessed the distant village.

Name: Jasperton
Status: Town
Government: Elected dyad
Civilization level: unknown

This town's resources are not available to you yet.

Aderyn didn't blink at the oddity of the Assessment. This was a city of the giants, and she and her friends were barely tolerated. A lack of information made sense. She took heart at the final word "yet."

The giant with gray in his hair broke into a run. Aderyn tensed, but none of the other giants reacted as if this was odd or threatening behavior. She heard Oskarl tell Owen, who was walking beside him, "Durg will talk to Ragna and warn the others that humans are coming. No offense, but all our stories call you frightening monsters."

"Our stories say the same about you, so I'm not offended. Thanks again for giving us the benefit of the doubt." Owen's hand brushed the hilt of the <**Sunsword**>, not with any serious intent, but Aderyn saw the casual gesture and remembered that sword stabbing young Taavek. They'd been lucky the giants hadn't come after them seeking blood.

They passed between vast fields plowed under for the winter, with enormous houses dotting the landscape at intervals between them. Aderyn hadn't grown up on a farm, but she recognized the look of land that was tilled as opposed to unclaimed fields. That got her wondering about the crops giants grew. Were their grains and vegetables giant-sized as well? Or did they have regular-sized tomatoes and potatoes and so forth, and just eat a lot of them? She had more questions the closer they got.

Soon the giants' village was visible even to Aderyn, who stared at it in awe. Beyond the low wall—low to a giant; it was still seven or eight feet tall—the houses were built of squared-off stone with half-timbered upper stories, similar to the house she'd grown up in in Far Haven, but the stones were as big as a human and the buildings rose thirty feet to their steeply-angled slate roofs. Smoke curled from the chimneys, which were made of brown brick rather than stone and looked just like chimneys back home. The eaves dripped with melting icicles that looked dainty against the huge stones, as if icicles clinging to giant roofs ought to be giant as well. Houses lined roads of hard-packed earth that were proportionate to the buildings, giving the impression, from a distance, of a tidy human village.

It took Aderyn a moment to figure out what was wrong. Not the size of the village or the enormous houses; that was strange but expected. Then she realized the streets were deserted. An unexpected pang of discouragement struck her. She'd hoped, when Oskarl said Durg was going to warn the village, that it meant the giants would be curious rather than terrified. She hadn't realized how excited she was about talking to non-monstrous rational creatures until it turned out they weren't interested in talking to her.

As they neared the village, Durg returned to Oskarl's side. "They're gathered in the mead-hall, all but those watching the children."

"Fair enough," Oskarl said. "Where is Ragna?"

"Waiting for us. She took the news well, for all it was a surprise." Durg hesitated. "She was angry you took me instead of her, but she knows the necessity of not risking both leaders."

Oskarl smiled and clapped Durg on the shoulder. "I wouldn't want to be you tonight. You're likely to get an earful."

Durg shrugged. "She's like a tempest, all noise until you reach the center. It helps that we'll have another grandchild for her to spoil soon."

Aderyn, astonished, Assessed Durg. Sure enough, he was married to this Ragna who was leader of the Tillers, if Aderyn's guess was right. And Oskarl was leader of the Trappers. Her early excitement began to cool. If giants had the kind of complex society Aderyn was starting to envision, maybe it wasn't such a good idea to get entangled in it when she and her friends didn't know their customs. But it was too late to worry about that now.

Oskarl led them through the village, past houses with heavy oak doors and windows covered in thin, milky glass. Aderyn took a second look at the windows. If giants could make glass, they were definitely more advanced than she'd imagined. The glass reminded her of sections of stained glass windows like the ornate one in Jessemia's father's house, but more translucent and less glossy. She looked more closely. It wasn't glass. It was very thin, translucent sheets of stone. That struck her as even more impressive than sheets of glass.

The windows weren't transparent enough to show the interiors of the houses, but Aderyn was sure they were being watched as they followed Oskarl down the street. She didn't wave or smile. If the giants were afraid of humans, she shouldn't push.

Oskarl led them to the end of the street, which terminated in an enormous building, far bigger than any they'd seen yet in the village. It wasn't as tall as the houses of Finion's Gate, but the height of its doors and its lack of windows made it seem bigger than Raynir's enormous mansion. When Oskarl drew near the great double doors with their gleaming brass hinges and fittings, Aderyn gauged his height against theirs and estimated the doors were at least twelve feet tall. She didn't need to know the exact height to feel intimidated.

Oskarl pushed both doors open in a ponderous gesture, as if they were heavier than stone, and strode through. "We have guests," he announced. "Make them welcome. Bring the mead-horn!"

A rustling mutter rose up from the room beyond. Though lanterns lit the walls, it was dark by comparison to the bright sunlight, and Aderyn's eyes took a moment to adjust. She blinked rapidly to clear her vision and then came to a halt. Her first impression was of men and women seated on both sides of a wide hall, heated by a low-burning fire in a round fireplace at the hall's center. Then her perspective adjusted, and the size of those men and women registered. Not humans, but giants, which made the hall enormous rather than just big and the fireplace vast enough for her to lie down in.

All the giants who'd accompanied Oskarl took seats on either side of the hall, blond giants on one side, dark-haired giants on the other. The air was close and warm, almost hot by comparison to the crisp chill of outdoors, and its mugginess reminded Aderyn of Ikharatia's heat, though that air had smelled of spices and this smelled of wood smoke.

A dark-haired giant, her long hair streaked with gray and bound in a knot at the back of her neck, approached the fireplace. She was the only one standing. She held a horn that curled at the tip and was banded with brass in three places, a horn that had to be as big as everything else since it looked normal-sized in her hands. "Be welcome," she said, in a voice that didn't sound welcoming at all. She took a long drink from the horn and handed it to Oskarl.

Oskarl drank as well. "We offer you the protection of the mead-hall for three days that we may exchange knowledge." He, by contrast, sounded as if he was reciting a well-memorized speech. "The People swear to deal honorably by you for those three days, as you will deal honorably by us."

Those last words were spoken with a curious inflection, like Oskarl was dropping a hint. He handed the drinking horn to Owen, who took it in both hands. To Aderyn, he looked like he had trouble holding it up. But Owen raised the horn in Oskarl's direction. "We accept your hospitality and swear to deal honorably by you for the three days of that protection." Carefully, he lowered the horn to his lips and drank. A few drops spilled over the edge and landed on Owen's coat. Owen handed the horn to Weston and wiped his lips as Weston drank and passed the horn to Aderyn.

It was as heavy as she'd expected, but even knowing what to expect, she nearly dropped it when Weston released it. She adjusted her grip and lifted the horn so she could drink. She'd never tasted mead before and didn't know what to expect, so the slightly sweet, slightly cinnamon-spicy flavor was a pleasant surprise. She drank just a mouthful, enough to taste the alcohol, and handed the horn to Jessemia.

While the others passed the horn around, Aderyn Level Assessed the female giant.

Name: Ragna

∞ Durg

Level: 16

Class: Farmer

Ragna was first voted leader of the Tillers ten years ago. Giants have elections—oh, you don't know what that means, do you? Choosing a leader by election means each member of a settlement or society puts their support, their vote, behind one candidate for leadership, and the candidate with the most votes becomes the leader. Finion's Gate was about to institute this method of governance when you left.

Giants hold elections every year, with the Trappers voting on their leader one year and the Tillers voting the next, so each group's leader has a two-year term and can be chosen again as often as they prove themselves worthy and effective. You probably don't think this is important now, but trust me, you'll want all the information you can get.

The point here is that Ragna has proven herself a good leader for almost half of a giant's adult lifespan, which is remarkable. That gives her tremendous influence over the

Tillers and to a lesser extent the Trappers. You've noticed she's not thrilled about humans being given hospitality. You'll want to get her on your side.

Isold drank and handed the horn back to Oskarl. Oskarl poured the remaining liquid onto the fire, carefully so he didn't extinguish the flames. "We invite you to introduce yourselves, humans. Give us the honor of your names."

"I'm Owen, and this is Aderyn, Livia, Isold, Weston, and Jessemia." Owen gestured to each in turn. The muttering rose again, making Aderyn worry that they'd done something wrong. Maybe they'd each been expected to speak for themselves?

"You speak for all?" Ragna said, sounding even more displeased than before.

Owen's shoulders tensed, telling Aderyn he felt the same as she did. "Among humans, a leader will sometimes be the unified voice of his or her team," he said, not letting his tension touch his voice. "Just as Oskarl offered hospitality on behalf of all of the People gathered here."

It was the right answer, though Ragna didn't relax much. "You show respect by calling us by the correct name," she said.

"I know we'll make mistakes because we don't know anything about you, so I hope to show our good intentions," Owen replied. "May I have your name?"

Ragna eyed him. After a pause, she said, "I am Ragna, voted leader of the Tillers. And I want to know what you humans intend, here in the Northlands."

The muttering rose again. Oskarl shifted his weight uncomfortably. Aderyn guessed Ragna's abruptness was at the edge of what hospitality decreed. Owen pretended not to notice. "We're pursuing a quest. Oskarl said the People know what quests are."

"We do. They are for the young." Ragna paused. "I assume that is not the case for humans."

"That's right. We only receive quests when we're adults. And we were hoping for your help with this one."

Aderyn twitched. This wasn't something they'd discussed. Getting help from the giants?

"Our help?" Oskarl said. "That's outside the reach of the mead-hall oath."

"Maybe. I don't know." Owen gazed up at Oskarl fearlessly. "It may be a matter of information rather than the People joining us. I hoped, if we told you what we're here for, you might understand better whether you want to assist us. Whether you *can* assist us."

Oskarl gazed back at Owen. "Tell us, then."

Owen looked from Ragna back to Oskarl. "Our quest is to bring peace to the Northlands."

The hall erupted in noise as several hundred giants rose to their feet and began shouting. Aderyn resisted the urge to put her hands over her ears. **[Amplify Voice]** wasn't a good idea, not when she was an outsider, but she wished someone would stop the noise that made her ears and her head throb.

"Enough!" Ragna shouted. Her voice, perfectly pitched to carry above the din, quieted the shouting until the hall was silent again. "You dare suggest that humans can achieve what the People have not, as if we were helpless children?"

"Of course not," Owen said. "We don't know what's been going on here. We only know what quest the system gave us. Are you willing to listen to our story? Because maybe that will give us both answers."

"A story." Ragna's bitterness cut through the warm, close air like shards of ice. "You offer us a story, and then you say you don't believe we're children."

"I said that's not what we meant." Owen's voice rose sharply, and he paused. **[Read Body Language]** told Aderyn he was composing himself. "I swear to you that my friends and I mean you no harm, and we're sincere in pursuing this quest. We want understanding between us. So, yes, I'm offering you a story. It might even be something you can use."

"Ragna," Oskarl said. "These humans fought beside us, defending us. The shortest one is stonekin herself. We should listen."

Ragna regarded him closely. "Then you vouch for them?"

More muttering from the crowd rose up. Oskarl replied, "I do."

"Then on your head be it." Ragna retreated to the right side of the room and took the last empty chair. "Speak, human—"

"My name is Owen," Owen said.

"We'll see," Ragna said. "Tell us your story."

CHAPTER EIGHTEEN

Owen didn't tell them everything. He didn't mention being from another world, and he left out most of the details of the Fated One quests they'd fulfilled. But he told them all about what had prompted their journey, how they'd wanted to find out what the Fated One's destiny actually was, and he explained their theories about what the quests were meant to prove. "We think we've demonstrated intelligence, cleverness, compassion, and strength," he concluded, "and although we're not sure about this latest quest, it seems to me that finding a solution for peace requires wisdom. I hope that's something we have. Or can learn."

"Then you didn't come here to take our lands," Ragna said.

"Of course not," Oskarl said before Owen could speak. "Look at them. They're not settlers."

"They might be an advance force, assessing our weaknesses so others can try to conquer us."

"You don't really believe that, do you?" Oskarl sounded weary, as if this was a much older argument than Aderyn thought. "Caution is one thing. Paranoia is something else. And Livia is stonekin. Stonekin won't betray us."

Ragna sniffed disdainfully. "I want proof."

"You don't believe my word?" Oskarl said.

He'd spoken mildly, but Ragna reddened and looked away. "I believe you would not lie to me. But you can hardly expect me not to be curious. A human who is stonekin."

"I don't mind," Livia said. "I'm not sure what I can do that won't tear up this nice hall of yours. Though—actually..." She walked to the stone wall next to the door and rested the flat of her palm against it. Then she stepped forward into the stone and disappeared.

The gasp of hundreds of giants inhaling simultaneously sounded like a wind through a canyon. Seconds later, Livia reappeared. "It's a skill called **[Pass Through Stone]**. The stone recognizes my affinity for its element and lets me slip through it."

All the giants began talking at once again, some of them shouting at Ragna and Oskarl, others arguing between themselves. Ragna shouted, "Quiet! That's enough!" She added, to Livia, "All right. I'm convinced. How is it possible that a human can be stonekin? You aren't like us."

"When the system makes someone a spellslinger, someone who can do magic, it doesn't give them a specialty at first. We're allowed to choose basic spells and show which ones we're most drawn to by how we use them. Then, at level two, the system reveals our elemental affinity based on what we did at level one. Air, fire, life, water, and earth. Other human spellslingers have other affinities." Livia flexed her stone arm. "This didn't kill me because I'm an Earthbreaker and can control the influence earth and stone have on me."

Ragna leaned forward. "I didn't notice your arm before," she said, for once sounding genuinely interested. "Is that usual for your kind?"

"No. It's the result of an attack." Livia extended her stone arm for Ragna to examine. Ragna, after a moment's hesitation, touched it.

"It is granite," she said. "Living granite. Extraordinary."

"You see?" Oskarl said. "I know the legends of what other humans have tried, but you wouldn't blame all People for the acts of a few deviants, would you? It's worth investigating."

"I agree." Ragna settled back into her seat. "Jorm, bring chairs for our guests. I'm afraid we don't have anything your size," she said to Livia.

"We don't mind," Livia replied.

They waited while Jorm brought wooden chairs from deeper within the mead-hall. Jorm looked thunderously angry, but he didn't do more than set the chairs down with more than necessary force. Aderyn pulled herself onto the carved wooden seat. It was wide enough for her and Owen to fit side by side, and tall enough her feet dangled at least a foot off the ground. She resisted the urge to kick idly and clasped her hands in her lap to still them as well.

When they were all settled, Ragna said, "This Fated One quest chain. You say each quest tests a different quality?"

"We don't know that for sure, but it makes sense, given everything else we've learned." Owen did kick his legs gently, one at a time. "We started this journey with the intent of learning what the Fated One is supposed to do to break the level cap, and the quest chain is what the system gave us to that end. So maybe it's meant to prove we're worthy of that knowledge, or that we have the ability to do something with it once we've gotten it."

"Why does it matter that this level cap you talk about is broken? We don't have anything like it," Oskarl said.

"Well," Owen began. He fell silent, regarding the giants.

"You're different from us in some ways," Aderyn said. "Even though you have classes and a link to the system, none of you are retired. Have any of you reached levels higher than twenty?"

"I don't know what it means to be retired." Oskarl leaned forward as if in emphasis. "And among us, only children care about levels. It's skill ranks that matter."

"Still, it's an interesting point," Joukkon said. "I can't think of any of the People who are higher than level nineteen. Or any now deceased who were higher than that."

"I'm level nineteen!" a shrill voice shouted from the back of the room on the left side where the dark-haired giants gathered. "Have been for years!"

"Yes, Yrsa, we honor your age," Ragna said. "You know we do. Please let others speak." She turned back to Owen. "Explain 'retired.'"

"Humans can choose to become adventurers by accepting the Call. They then gain levels as they gain experience through fighting monsters and completing quests. When they decide they're done, they retire, and the system stops granting them levels and experience, though they still gain skill ranks, I think." Owen looked to Aderyn for confirmation.

"That's right," Aderyn said. "But the other way that stops is if someone reaches level twenty. Then it's like they've retired in that they no longer gain experience."

"What of humans who don't accept this Call?" Ragna asked.

"They are still connected to the system, because they can Assess others and they can Unite in marriage. But they don't have levels. They just live their lives."

"That seems unbalanced," Oskarl said, "if I can say so without giving offense. No one among the People lacks a class."

"How do you gain classes, then, if it isn't when you've reached a given level of development?" Aderyn asked, thinking of her own Call.

"It happens when a young person reaches maturity. At anywhere from nine to ten years old. The leader of their clan has authority from the system to give them their adulthood quest, and when they've completed that, their reward is a class." Oskarl looked like he was thinking about something, but he didn't add anything more.

"This is all very interesting," Ragna said, "but I'm more concerned about what brings humans here. Our conflicts aren't yours."

"It wasn't our idea," Livia said. "The system gave us the quest to bring peace to the Northlands. Your young people receive quests—you must realize the system tells people to do things they wouldn't choose for themselves."

Muttering rose up among the giants, scatterings of muffled conversation. Ragna raised a hand asking for silence. "Even if we don't take your presence as arrogant interference, the point remains. How can humans resolve a problem on behalf of the People?"

"We don't know," Owen said, "because we don't know what tensions or conflicts you're experiencing. And you're right, this might look bad, like you People aren't capable of taking care of your own problems. My feeling is that if the system gave us this quest, it must be something we have to accomplish with your help, not us imposing a solution on you. You are thinking, self-governing individuals, so that wouldn't be a permanent solution, not if you didn't believe in it for yourselves."

"If you tell us what's going on, then we can figure out a plan together," Aderyn said.

"You can't tell these humans our secrets," Jorm burst out. "They will use our weaknesses against us."

"Jorm," Ragna said, with the same weary tone Oskarl had used earlier, "have you listened at all to this conversation? Tiller elections aren't for another twenty moons. If you're trying to rally support for yourself, you've chosen the wrong venue. Politics are forbidden within the mead-hall. Here, the People are one."

"It's not politics to want safety for the People," Jorm persisted.

"And it's not fitting for one of us to pretend to altruism to cover his selfish motives," Ragna shot back. "You lost. Don't make me invoke the Sanction."

Jorm, his pale face mottled with anger, sat back in his chair and was silent.

"Our conflict is both simple and difficult to resolve," Ragna said, behaving as if that interaction hadn't happened. "The season of storms is coming, and with it, the tempest moth—do you know what that is?"

The friends all shook their heads.

"The tempest moth is a merciless creature that lives at the center of a permanent system of storms. Its wings block out the sky, and its body is larger than the largest whale. When it moves, it sheds smaller storms that devastate the lands. For generations, it has followed a flight path that takes it from the northern ocean south along our coasts and a short distance inland. We don't settle that far north, and the storms only rarely affect our cities. At least, until last year."

"The tempest moth's pattern changed," Oskarl continued. "It now moves erratically and it comes much farther inland. Many of our settlements have been affected, and some of the smaller towns have been destroyed. Worse, its new path takes it deeper into the dangerous lands to the northeast, driving monsters out of those areas into our lands. We only rarely saw rimewolves before last year, to give one example."

"I see what you mean by simple," Owen said. "It's a monster

that's wreaking havoc on your lands, but just one monster. What's the difficult part?"

"The difficulty lies in how we People can't agree on what to do," Oskarl said. "Attempts to kill or redirect the tempest moth have failed disastrously. No one who has approached it has returned. Some believe we should move south, but that's been resisted by those of us who already live in the south and don't want our lands overrun."

"Rightly so," Ragna said, scowling. "And of course there are others who reject the idea of leaving their homes. But there is also a sizable minority who see this as an opportunity to move even farther south, into more fertile lands. Lands controlled by humans."

"You can't do that," Aderyn exclaimed. "Humans will see you as invaders and monsters and there will be war."

"Enough voices agree with you that it's not a solution anyone has tried to implement yet," Oskarl said. "But that is the crisis we face. Death from storms, death from monsters, death from humans. Disaster on every side."

"I wish I could say I knew an easy solution," Owen said. "But you're right, it's difficult. I'm not sure where we could even start."

Silver letters filled the air in front of Aderyn's face.

A new quest is available: [The Tempest Moth]
Discover the reason for the alteration in the tempest moth's
pattern and correct it. This is a sub-quest in the quest chain
[Fated One's Destiny: Eye of the Storm].
Reward: see [Fated One's Destiny: Eye of the Storm]
WARNING: Accepting [The Tempest Moth] makes the
remaining sub-quests in the quest chain [Fated One's
Destiny: Eye of the Storm] inaccessible. Sub-quests [The

Liege Lord] and [Death From Above] will be removed from the quest chain.
Accept? Y / N

"Um," Aderyn said. "I don't like the sound of that. Removing sub-quests? What if those are the ones we need?"

"I don't think so," Owen said. "It sounds like **[Eye of the Storm]** is actually a quest tree rather than a quest chain." His eyes shifted like he was reading invisible text. "What I mean is, suppose **[Eye of the Storm]** has at least four sub-quests attached, but we only need to complete two of them to succeed? We've got **[Pursue the Hunters]** already. If we choose not to take **[The Tempest Moth]**, we'll eventually be offered one or both of these other ones, and I bet taking one of them invalidates the other two."

"That is a lot of guesswork, Owen," Weston said. "But it's logical."

"But—" Blocking off access to a quest roused all of Aderyn's worries about missing out on an important adventure to their highest. "What if we choose wrong?"

"How could we choose wrong? The system isn't trying to trick us, or make us play 'guess what's in my head.' We'll just have a different adventure choosing this option than we would choosing either of the others." Owen clasped her hand in reassurance. "Okay, maybe I'm feeling a little railroaded—um, I mean, the tempest moth is a serious threat, so I would feel bad about not taking this quest even if I knew one of the others was more our speed. But since we know nothing about **[The Liege Lord]** or **[Death From Above]**—unless **[Improved Assess 4]** tells you anything?"

Aderyn focused on the two sub-quests and Assessed them.

I can't give you information about quests you haven't been

offered. Sorry, but you're on your own. I will tell you that your husband is correct, so you don't need to fret about missing out on anything.

Aderyn glanced at Oskarl and Ragna, who bore the polite but irritated look of people listening to a conversation they had no part in. She didn't feel like revealing her connection to the system to them. "I don't have any more information about them, but I think you're right about the quest tree thing."

"Then I guess this is where we start," Owen said. He touched the air where the Y would be. "And I'm betting the reward is more information."

Aderyn selected Y and focused on the golden dot that was her primary quest.

[Fated One's Destiny: Eye of the Storm]
Bring peace to the Northlands by [see Pursue the Hunters: Reward] and [see The Tempest Moth: Reward].

Sub-quest: [Pursue the Hunters]
Rimewolf packs have begun hunting giants throughout the Northlands. Discover why this is and put a stop to it. Reward: Additional detail to the primary quest becomes available.

Sub-quest: [The Tempest Moth]
Discover the reason for the alteration in the tempest moth's pattern and correct it. Reward: Additional detail to the primary quest becomes available.

Reward: [100,000 XP] plus any experience gained in the course of completing the quest.

"You said the tempest moth was at the center of a storm system," she said to Ragna. "Isn't the center calm? The eye of the storm?"

"I hope you don't take that to mean it's safe," Ragna said. "It's true there's such a thing as the eye of the storm being a calmer location, but it still contains an enormous monster."

"I know. I meant, our primary quest is called [Eye of the Storm]. It seems like too big a thing to be coincidence that we just received another quest to hunt down a creature that lives at the eye of a storm."

"That's an excellent point," Isold said. "Jessemia, what do you know about the tempest moth?"

Jessemia blinked. "I've never heard of it before now." Her eyes unfocused as she read her Monster Folio. "I now know it's immune to mind control and resistant to all forms of elemental damage. It's as enormous as Ragna said. And it seems to move both at random and with a pattern, meaning it doesn't follow the same path twice, but it doesn't—or didn't—range outside given bounds."

"What about attacks?" Weston asked.

Jessemia shook her head. "It causes terrible storms, but this doesn't say if it has more personal attacks. It might be able to do elemental air damage and lightning attacks, if it's a creature of storm. I'm sorry, I don't know more than that."

"What's more important is if your map shows where the tempest moth is," Owen said.

Jessemia started shaking her head before he finished speaking. "I'm not high enough level for the skill [Find Person], even if this was a person we were talking about. I hoped the system considered it a quest location the way your [Eye of the Storm] is, but I guess not. Still, if it's a giant moth causing storms, I doubt we'll have trouble finding it."

"You will have trouble enough from other of the People," Oskarl said. "They're going to assume you're monsters. I don't know how to prevent that."

"I do," Ragna said. "I intend to send some of us with them."

The murmuring grew loud again. Over the din, Oskarl said, "Who can you send? Winter is almost here, Ragna. We need every adult to make sure the town survives."

"Every adult, yes," Ragna said. "But we have four on the brink of maturity who are ready for their adulthood quests. I propose we send Zalk, Freta, Skalt, and Taavek with these humans—"

It was all she managed before the tumult drowned her words out. Beneath the din, Owen leaned close to Aderyn's ear and said, "We can't take a bunch of adolescents with us. If they're killed, their deaths will be on our heads."

"We also can't travel freely through the Northlands," Aderyn replied in the same way. "What worries me is whether adult giants who are strangers to this settlement will listen to a bunch of kids."

"I said *quiet!*" Oskarl roared. When the noise subsided slightly, he said, "Ragna, I'm not sure this is a good idea. It places a tremendous burden on our young ones."

"This is not a time to cavil at danger," Ragna said. "If we People don't resolve this calamity, we will be destroyed, and that includes our youth. We should give them a chance to show their strength on behalf of their community and their fellow People. Oskarl, it frightens me that things have come to this. But I've watched these children grow up and I have faith in their abilities. I say we offer them this quest."

She put a hand on Oskarl's wrist. "Taavek is strong," she murmured, in a voice that carried no farther than Aderyn and her friends. "You don't need to be afraid for him."

"I'd be lying if I said I wasn't," Oskarl replied. "Very well. We will issue the quest."

He raised his voice. "Ragna and I are in agreement. We will send Taavek, Freta, Skalt, and Zalk with these humans on their adulthood quest. Does anyone have anything to add?"

Two dark-haired women rose as one. "My daughter is strong," the first said, just as the second said, "Zalk will obey. And I have no fear of his leaving."

"Thank you, Ulla, Jorga. The People respect your courage." Ragna turned to Jorm. "Any comments?"

"Skalt's not old enough for a quest," Jorm said. "You're doing this to punish me."

"Shut up, Jorm, or did you want to accuse Ragna of punishing us, too?" the female giant, Ulla, said. "Freta's younger than Skalt by a handful of days and you don't hear me complaining."

Ragna silenced Jorm with a fierce glare that ought to have wilted him. "Oskarl and I will issue the quests today, and we will send the youth and our human allies off in the morning. For now, let's make ready to welcome our guests properly, shall we?"

All the giants rose and began carrying chairs out of the hall. Aderyn slid down off her seat and watched an exceptionally tall giant take the chair away. "Thank you for your hospitality," she said.

"It is what makes us the People," Oskarl said.

"Taavek's your son, isn't he?" Weston said.

"He is my second son, and I'm proud of him. Are any of you parents?"

"No," Weston said. "We—it doesn't matter. We're not parents yet."

"Then my mingled dismay and pride over his nighttime wanderings won't make sense to you," Oskarl said with a rueful smile. "I suppose we were all young once. But then I remember those rimewolves, and my heart freezes to imagine him and his friends encountering those instead of you humans."

"That would have been awful," Owen said. "We were all fortunate that Aderyn's skill showed us Taavek wasn't an evil monster."

"Yes, that's astonishing." Oskarl gestured to them to follow him. "We'll get out of the way of the preparations, and you can explain this skill to me. No one among the People has it."

"Very few among humans, too," Aderyn said. "And I'm more grateful for it by the day."

CHAPTER NINETEEN

When Oskarl brought them back to the mead-hall that evening, the fire at the center of the room burned more brightly, and lantern globes illuminated the room enough to make the carvings covering the walls visible. There were still many chairs, but now they were pushed away from the room's center to line the walls. Great casks on stands nearly as tall as Aderyn were grouped in one corner, and tables bowing under the weight of platters and bowls stood in another.

Aderyn, curious, broke away from their group to approach the tables. Most of the food was familiar, if oversized: piles of giant potatoes cooked in their skins, bowls of carrots the length of Aderyn's arm or cooked greens giving off a rich, tangy aroma. Some vegetables, she didn't recognize, and others, like green peas, she hadn't expected this late in the year. In all, the feast looked alien and delicious.

But most astonishing were the fowls. Aderyn had never seen birds this size. "Is that a turkey?" she asked Oskarl. "It's huge."

"It's a turkey, yes, but of average size," Oskarl said. "Are your foods sized to match your smaller stature?"

"I guess they are." Aderyn considered the drumsticks that might come from such a creature and salivated.

"This feast is as much to celebrate the young people's quest as it is to honor our guests," Joukkon said. He held a handful of round river stones that he rolled over and around each other, making a soft grinding sound.

"We're grateful for your hospitality," Owen said. "Is the quest-giving something we shouldn't be present for?"

"It's not secret. The investiture that makes them adults, when they return successful from their quest, is private. But issuing the quest is done in public." Joukkon nodded politely and walked away. Aderyn watched him deposit the stones he held at the edge of the fire, aligned in a neat row.

"You can stand over here," Oskarl said. The room was filling up with giants, even more than there had been before, and the enormous room felt positively crowded. No one sat despite the many available chairs. Oskarl guided them to a spot at the front of the crowd where they could see the fireplace clearly. Now Aderyn realized no log burned there; the fire danced over black stones, jagged and rough, without consuming them.

No more giants entered, and the crowd settled and stilled until even the quiet murmur of speech was silenced. Joukkon stood separately, near the fireplace. After a few moments of silence, he said, "Open the door and let them enter."

Aderyn couldn't see the door from her position, and since no one moved to look, she didn't either. A cool draft from outdoors brushed her cheeks before the door shut again. She heard the shuffling of many people making way for others, and then Zalk, Skalt, Freta, and Taavek pushed through the crowd to stand before Joukkon. Now that Aderyn knew about the difference between Tillers and Trappers, she recognized that only the blond Taavek was a Trapper. Nobody behaved as if the imbalance was weird, but it did increase her curiosity about the clans' respective numbers.

"Younglings, the People summon you to take the first step toward adulthood," Joukkon said. His voice was pleasant, not at all ponderous as would have fit his words. "Normally, you would not be issued quests until after your ninth birthdays, but these are not normal times. Those of you who would accept the weight of the stone, step forward."

Freta and Zalk took long steps forward immediately, with Taavek a breath behind. Skalt hesitated until someone let out a sharp hiss, then he hurried forward as if he'd been poked with a sharp stick. Again they stood in a line, more ragged this time, facing Joukkon. Aderyn's position put her near the end of the line so Freta was closest to her and Skalt was almost invisible at the far end.

Joukkon picked up one of the river stones from the fire. He jiggled it a little as if the heat burned his fingers, then gripped it firmly and blew across the top. As before, a thick layer of black soot built up on the surface.

"Freta, your quest is to accompany these humans northward in search of that which will bring peace to the Northlands, using your eyes on their behalf," he said. "Will you accept?"

"I will," Freta said, her head raised high.

Joukkon traced a curving, intersecting line in the soot and blew across the top of the stone again. The remaining soot puffed away in a black cloud, but when Joukkon lowered the stone, the line he'd traced remained, glimmering faintly like an oil slick. He handed the stone to Freta, who cradled it in both hands like something precious.

Joukkon picked up another stone. "Zalk, your quest is to

speak on behalf of these humans as you travel northward, convincing the People to give them free passage. Will you accept?"

Zalk said, "I will," and Joukkon repeated his gestures and handed him the stone. Aderyn thought the lines he'd drawn were different between the stones, but she was too far away to be sure.

When Joukkon spoke next, his voice was rough as if suppressing an emotion. "Taavek, your quest is to use your fighting skills to defend your companions as you accompany these humans northward. Will you accept?"

"I will." Taavek's voice rang out clearly. He accepted the stone from Joukkon and pocketed it immediately.

"Skalt, your quest is to turn your skills with herbcraft and the understanding of the natural world to supporting your companions as you travel northward with these humans. Will you accept?"

Again, Skalt hesitated, but only for a moment. "I will." He took the stone awkwardly, as if it was still hot.

"The younglings have accepted their quests," Joukkon said to the room at large. "It's time to celebrate new beginnings!"

A thunderous roar of hundreds of voices shook the timbers, and Aderyn resisted the urge to cover her ears. The crowd surged forward to congratulate the young giants, carefully avoiding the human guests so no one was knocked over. Aderyn clasped Owen's hand for steadiness anyway. "It's like a river in flood," she said.

"What?"

"A river—never mind, it's too loud. When do you suppose we can eat? I'm hungry."

"I want to know how they cooked that turkey so fast. Aren't those supposed to roast for hours? They didn't know there would be a celebration."

"It was probably someone's evening meal. Come on, let's

mingle." Aderyn's discomfort at being a stranger vanished when it became clear no one was staring at her anymore.

The plate Aderyn ended up with was the size of the shield she'd used during the war with the orcs, big enough she couldn't circle it with her arms. It was just the right size for one of the enormous drumsticks, which smelled deliciously of sage and other herbs she didn't recognize. With that and a heaping pile of mashed potatoes and a smaller pile of green peas, she retreated to a chair well away from the heat of the unusual fire. She had to put her plate on the chair next to hers to avoid spilling it as she climbed up. "This is the strangest thing that's ever happened to me," she told Jessemia, who sat on her other side.

"I know I never expected giants to be anything but monsters," Jessemia said. She tackled her slice of white breast meat with her own belt knife and a fork big enough to be a garden implement. "But this is delicious."

Aderyn tore into the drumstick, which spurted juice all over her face, and nodded. She ate, and observed their hosts. Only a few of them sat. The others gathered around the four young giants, who didn't have plates and looked as if the attention overwhelmed them. She couldn't help thinking about how strange this might be for them, too. To them, she and her friends were the monsters.

Owen hopped onto the vacant chair beside Aderyn and drew his plate onto his lap. "I still can't believe we're here."

"That's what we were saying."

"My concern about the safety of the younglings hasn't gone away." Owen carved his slab of meat into smaller pieces before taking his first bite. "It's hard to remember they're just adolescents, as big as they are. I don't want that to trick us into assuming more about their capabilities than is true."

"Do you suppose they'll form an adventuring team?" Jessemia asked. "It ought to be possible."

"I don't know. It would make sense, but who knows how giants think?" Owen offered Aderyn an oversized mug. "We should share. I don't want to get drunk on mead, no matter how good it tastes. I haven't seen any antitoxin around."

Aderyn took a swallow. It tasted different from the first, more alcoholic and less spicy. She liked it, though not as much as the other.

The tumult was settling, and the younglings had moved to the far side of the fireplace, away from the crowds. They huddled together as they ate, like they felt security in numbers. More giants took their seats, eating and talking quietly together. Aderyn wished someone would crack open a window, the room was so stuffy, but there weren't windows and none of the giants seemed bothered by the warmth. The fire burned low as if it knew it wasn't needed.

She finished her meal and looked around for somewhere to set her plate. There was a stack of dishes near the inner door, and she hopped down and carried her plate there, but halfway to the door, a blonde giant woman intercepted her and took the plate. "There's singing next, and dancing. Unless you little folk don't dance."

"We do, but probably not the way you do. That would be too much of a coincidence, don't you think?"

The woman smiled. "Maybe you can show us your ways."

The unexpected friendliness surprised Aderyn. So many of the giants steered clear of their guests, like they were afraid of catching something—or possibly just of accidentally crushing them. "I'm Aderyn. What's your name?"

"I thought humans could Assess," the woman replied. "Don't you know my name?"

"Among humans, it's considered polite to let the other person introduce herself even if you both Assessed each other." Aderyn didn't say she felt uncomfortable about Assessing their hosts, like that would be an imposition greater than usual.

"I see. Well, I'm Kaarina. Oskarl is my husband."

Aderyn remembered her name from Assessing Oskarl. "Oh! It's nice to meet you. That means Taavek is your son, right?"

"He is. We have five children, and Taavek is our second son."

"You must be proud that he's been given such a daring task."

"Proud?" Kaarina smiled ruefully. "Worried, more like. Usually the adulthood quests don't take the younglings far from home. But there's a lot of land northward between here and the ocean, and who knows what might happen?"

"Oh. I'm sorry. I didn't think."

"It's fine. In truth, I am also proud of him for not hesitating when my brother Joukkon issued the quest. And it's a mother's prerogative to worry just as it is her duty to send her children away. I don't suppose you have children?"

"No. We can't have children until we retire from adventuring, which will be some time away. But Owen and I look forward to it."

A chord rose up above the noise of the crowd, the sound of fingers on strings, and Aderyn turned around. A giant man, his dark hair nearly all gray, sat on a stool not too near the fireplace. He held a fat-bellied stringed instrument painted all over its shining sides with brightly-colored flowers, red and blue and green, that contrasted with the light wood of its construction. More slowly, he plucked the strings again, sounding another chord in a minor key. Then he broke into song, his fingers flying rapidly over the strings.

Immediately, the giants began stomping their feet in time with the music and clapping to a different but harmonious beat. Aderyn stood still, surrounded by giants, and listened to the song. The lyrics didn't tell a story the way Aderyn was used to; this song was about the flowing of the seasons one into another and how the earth rose and fell as the year passed. Again, she felt out of place, alien. She couldn't imagine giants mingling with humans on a daily basis. And yet, both races had families and raised crops and sang songs. They were both connected to the system. It shouldn't be that farfetched. But it beggared the imagination to consider it.

When the song ended, she made her way back to Owen. Jessemia had disappeared— "went to relieve herself," Owen said— and Owen sat alone on his chair, looking like a toddler as he kicked his legs. Aderyn climbed up beside him. A blonde woman took the musician's place and went into a song about chasing reindeer over the snow that the rest joined in on. She didn't play an instrument, but her voice was strong and melodic, almost as good as Isold's.

"I wonder if the Trappers and the Tillers have different music," Owen mused.

"You mean, songs that reflect their natures?" Aderyn watched another blonde woman join the first, their voices making a fine harmony. "Tillers have farming songs, and Trappers have hunting songs?"

Owen shrugged. "It's a theory."

Aderyn considered his theory through the next three songs, one of which was also a dance, and concluded there might be something to it. The Trappers sang about journeys and hunting, while the Tillers sang about home and farming. That led her to think about whether Trappers and Tillers ever intermarried, and what the resulting children would be like. She had so many questions she was uncomfortable asking when she didn't know if their hosts would see it as prying.

"Perhaps our guests would like to share their music?" Ragna boomed out. She hesitated. "You *do* play music, don't you?"

Aderyn caught Isold's eye just then and had to control a laugh.

Isold said, "We do, and if you'll indulge me, I'll sing for you." With barely a hesitation, he broke into song, one of Aderyn's favorites about a man and a woman courting each other and their hilarious misunderstandings.

The giants listened politely, and when the song was over, they applauded, but it didn't sound enthusiastic. Aderyn, feeling insulted on Isold's behalf, said, "Don't you have songs about courtship?"

"Of course," Joukkon said. "But why didn't their parents arrange their marriage? It seemed so precarious, them not knowing whether they could be together."

"Do you arrange your marriages, then?" Isold asked.

"How else could anyone be certain their union would be successful?" Ragna sounded genuinely bewildered, as if the song had made even less sense to her than to Joukkon. "Parents observe the younglings and choose who will make their children good spouses."

"That—" Aderyn began.

"It's not how we do things," Owen interjected. "We make that decision for ourselves."

"And... that works?" Ragna now sounded as if she was concealing her horror.

"Most of the time, yes," Weston said. "The system allows us methods for dissolving a marriage if someone makes a mistake. But mostly humans' marriages are happy."

"That's fascinating," Oskarl said in a tone of voice that sounded more like *that's appalling*. "I didn't realize our customs were so different. What other songs do you have?"

"I, well." Isold smiled. "Very few of them will make sense to you, I fear. Let's try this one."

His next song was another familiar one, of love lost and love remembered, and Aderyn had never heard him in better voice.

The crowd fell silent as Isold sang, not even moving. When the song came to an end, Aderyn wiped tears from her eyes. In that moment, she resented the giants for disdaining Isold's gift, for not being able to look beyond their own stupid customs to hear something another culture found valuable.

Then she realized the giants' eyes were reddened, and some were weeping silently. Jorm, standing near the back of the crowd, had the look of someone turned to stone by trying to control a powerful emotion. He abruptly turned and left the mead-hall, letting the door slam shut behind him.

"I suppose we have more in common than we realized," Oskarl said quietly. "That reminded me of my first wife, Martta. She died before we'd been married a year, and I thought my heart would never recover."

"And yet life, and love, goes on," Isold said in the same quiet voice.

"It does." Oskarl clasped Kaarina's hand. "Thank you."

Ragna cleared her throat. "Let's take a moment for the second course, and then I think we should dance."

Murmurs of assent turned gradually into cheerful speech, as if everyone was grateful to Ragna for breaking the beautiful but somber mood. Aderyn turned to Owen. "*Second* course? I ate my fill with the first one!"

"Let's hope politeness lets us get away with nibbling," Owen said.

CHAPTER TWENTY

Aderyn and Owen stayed in Oskarl and Kaarina's house that night, in a room usually occupied by their two youngest daughters. "They'll sleep in the loft and be thrilled about the adventure," Oskarl said. The bed was the size of a kitchen garden, easily big enough for two giant younglings, which meant two humans could get lost in it. Aderyn admired the quilt covering the bed, with patches as big as a lap blanket in bright colors and cheerful patterns. "I wonder if weaving is a Trapper or a Tiller class," she said, "or if it's just a skill."

"An anthropologist would love this place. Someone who studies cultures," Owen amended. "The differences are far greater than there were between our lands and the south."

Aderyn jumped on the soft mattress a couple of times before deciding that was juvenile. She lay beside Owen and stared up at the distant ceiling, barely visible in the low light from the lamp. Kaarina had said it was the smallest lamp they owned, but it was half as tall as Aderyn and had a knob bigger than her hand. "I don't know what to expect next."

"Something unusual, I'm sure." Owen took her in his arms and kissed her lightly on the cheek. "Sleep. We need to get an early start, Oskarl said. Apparently it's traditional to see youngling questers off at dawn."

"I'm not sure I can sleep," Aderyn said, but the warmth of the quilt and the softness of the mattress soon took care of that.

She and her friends all gathered outside the mead-hall in the pre-dawn light and waited for their giant companions to join them. Other giants, not as many as had been present for the feast, milled around, wearing knee-length light coats that were open at the front instead of buttoned. Aderyn, huddled into her lovely fur-lined coat, couldn't imagine how they weren't frozen solid. On the other hand, if this represented fair weather, it was going to get a lot colder as they traveled.

Soon, Freta and Taavek appeared, escorted by their parents. Zalk arrived shortly thereafter. No one spoke. Freta fidgeted from one foot to the other, but by the way she clutched her coat around her chest, Aderyn judged she was colder than the others.

Finally, Oskarl said, "Where is Skalt?"

"Where is Jorm?" Freta's mother Ulla said irritably. "He wouldn't break with tradition, not even as reluctant about this as he is."

"Is it a problem that they're late?" Owen asked.

"It's a bad omen to see these younglings off after the sun rises," Kaarina said. "If Jorm and Skalt ruin it for the rest of us—"

"I think that's them," Jessemia said, pointing.

Two dark-haired figures, one shorter than the other, slouched toward the waiting group. "We're here," Jorm said. "Let's get this farce over with."

"If Skalt is afraid," Oskarl began, his voice calm.

"I'm not afraid!" Skalt exclaimed. His voice shook.

"I'm sure you'd like to make their failure my fault," Jorm said. "These quests are ridiculous. We owe these humans no favors."

"They're doing us favors, too, Jorm," Kaarina said. "Please don't mark this special occasion with bitterness. Our children are embarking on quests more dangerous than any of the People have experienced in a generation."

Jorm muttered something and gave Skalt a little shove in the direction of the other younglings. Skalt stumbled forward and caught himself awkwardly.

The crowd parted for Ragna, who breathed heavily as if she'd been running. "I overslept," she said. "Don't see it as a bad sign. I don't sleep like I did when I was young."

She and Oskarl stood side by side in front of the younglings. "Take the goodwill and best wishes of the People with you as you journey into dark places," Oskarl said. Ragna scooped a handful of white pebbles from her pocket and handed one to each of the younglings. Aderyn caught only a glimpse of them before the four slung them around their necks and tucked them beneath their clothes—she hadn't noticed the fine leather thongs each was strung on.

"Make your goodbyes," Ragna said. Her voice still sounded ragged, but this time Aderyn saw tears in her eyes.

Zalk, Taavek, and Freta embraced their parents. Skalt ducked away from Jorm's heavy hand on his shoulder. So, was Skalt's mother gone, or had she not wanted to show up for this ceremony? Aderyn suppressed a pang of sympathy. Skalt's customs weren't hers, and she couldn't make him change. And for once, she wasn't sure she wanted to, between his timidity and the fact that he'd ratted on them to the adult giants. If Oskarl hadn't been honorable, at least a few people, maybe even some of her friends, might have been injured or killed yesterday morning.

She avoided staring out of a sense that this was something private she shouldn't have witnessed, not because it was a foreign custom but because leave-takings were personal. Eventually, Owen cleared his throat and said, "Thank you for your hospitality, and for the honor you do us in sending your children with us. I promise we'll fight together to keep them safe."

"I hope you succeed in your quest. All the People will benefit, not just us." Oskarl saluted them with one huge fist clapped to his chest.

Aderyn and the others followed Owen in returning Oskarl's salute, and as the sun's disc peeked over the horizon, sending brilliant light flowing over the town, the humans and the giant younglings headed north. Taavek glanced back once, but Aderyn could see his face and he looked resolute, even happy, rather than afraid. Even Skalt kept his eyes on the hills and fields ahead.

"So," Weston said, "what's the plan?"

"We have a quest and two sub-quests," Owen said. "That suggests resolving the sub-quests has to happen either before the main quest or as part of finishing the main quest. My feeling is that we'll have better luck with [The Tempest Moth] than with [Pursue the Hunters], since rimewolves could be anywhere and the tempest moth is enormous and roughly north of here, if it's even made landfall. Does everyone agree?"

"That makes sense," Aderyn said. "Though I was also thinking we have a destination already. Jessemia's map shows where the [Eye of the Storm] quest begins. Maybe we need to look there first. It's northward, so we'd be going in the right direction to find the tempest moth."

"What should we do?" Zalk asked.

Owen stopped. "That's a good point. We need to establish some things before we go much farther. Zalk, are you the leader of your friends?"

Zalk reddened. "Sometimes."

"We voted," Freta said. "Zalk is good at talking to people. We figured, if we got in trouble for our adventures, he could argue us out of it with the adults."

"I'm not sure I understand," Isold said. "What adventures? Does this have something to do with your defense of the stone spiral?"

"We're all the same age, and we grew up playing together," Taavek said. "That never went away as we got older. Now we're the last four who haven't turned nine yet, and the older ones are all adults and don't think we're worth anything. Guess they feel pretty stupid now that we're on an important quest."

"Anyway, Zalk makes decisions, but we all vote if it's something big," Freta said.

"Even Skalt?" Aderyn asked, eyeing the young giant who'd stayed out of the discussion.

Skalt grimaced. "It's not wrong to want adults to make decisions. We're just kids. We can pretend we know what we're doing, but it's just pretend. When things get bad—"

"Skalt, you're more of a baby every day," Freta said. "I'm glad my parents don't want me to marry you. You'd be a terrible father."

"Don't say that," Aderyn exclaimed despite herself. The humiliation on Skalt's face was too much for her to bear. "He's not wrong. Among humans, there are things parents take responsibility for because their children aren't ready to do them themselves, and the children watch and learn so when they're adults, they can follow their parents' example. It doesn't make you a baby to be conscious of your limitations."

"I don't need a human to speak for me," Skalt muttered.

"And you don't need to be ungracious when Aderyn chooses to intervene," Owen said sharply. "Okay. Here's how it's going to go. I am the leader of my team, and from now until we return to Jasperton, I consider you members of that team. That means you take orders from me. This is not because I think you're incapable. It's because I am experienced when it comes to killing monsters and tackling dangers and you are not."

"I don't know," Taavek said. "We didn't vote on this."

"And we're not going to. Some things, voting can't solve. Don't be offended, but you four lack the information to make good decisions out here." Owen fixed each of them in turn with his gaze. "For what it's worth, I intend to see that you each learn what it takes to be adventurers. Real adventurers. And real adults. The goal is not to lecture you or control you. It's to make sure you live to fulfil your quests and return home. Got it?"

Zalk nodded. "I understand. But you'll let us do things, right? You won't tell us to stay back or hide just because we're not nine yet?"

"I won't lie to you, Zalk, sometimes you will have to stay back. But I promise that if I or one of the others tell you to stay where it's safe, it's because we're sure a danger is too much for you at your level."

"He's right," Jessemia said. "Owen and Aderyn helped me when I was leveling up. Sometimes that meant staying out of a fight, and sometimes it meant taking on a monster by myself because it was the right level for me. I promise no one is going to treat you like incompetents."

"And I'm sure none of you are stupid," Aderyn added. "You know you have abilities others don't, and you know when you lack abilities. It doesn't make you weak not to be able to do things. That's teamwork, supporting each other's inabilities with our strengths."

Taavek frowned like he was thinking this over. "I think I

understand. You mean, I know how to hunt, and Freta knows how to cook, and together, we can make dinner."

"That's exactly it." Aderyn turned to Skalt. "Joukkon said you have herbcraft. What can you do with that, Skalt?"

Skalt didn't say anything at first. As Aderyn was about to repeat herself, he said, "I know which plants are good for medicine and which ones are good for food. And which are poison. I don't think that's very important. It's not like I'm a Healer."

"Maybe not yet," Isold said, "but those are important skills that will grow over time. And you and I can work together. I have some knowledge about plants, but I am always interested in learning more."

"And all of you can teach me about stone magic," Livia said.

"I'm just glad not to be the biggest member of the team anymore," Weston said. "I'm sure the four of you can haul more firewood than I can manage. Division of labor, right?"

Freta giggled. "We thought you were a child when we saw you, except you have that weird hair all over your face. The People don't grow hair anywhere but on their heads."

Weston felt all over his face with comic dismay. "No wonder everyone looked at me funny! Quick, somebody shave me!"

"Not a chance, dearest. I like your beard," Livia said, hooking her arm around his. "Is that all settled? You younglings understand what we expect?"

"That makes me wonder what they expect of us," Jessemia said.

Zalk, who'd laughed at Weston's antics, sobered. "I guess... just what we said. That you'll treat us like, maybe not adults, but not like babies."

"Then I think we have an agreement," Owen said. "Let's move. Jessemia, is it still two weeks to our quest destination?"

"Less than that," Jessemia said. "Though there's another

storm coming this afternoon. Not a big one, but we might want to camp early tonight."

"It's a good thing we got an early start, then." Owen tugged his striped cap over his ears. "And I have a feeling we'll need to stretch to keep up with our friends."

They walked across the hills for an hour before reaching the plains where the river flowed. Only a few trees grew along its banks, offering no shelter, but it was a pleasant, sunny day and they didn't want to lose any of the sun's warm rays. Aderyn, looking into the northern distance, couldn't see storm clouds. She'd never been so grateful for Jessemia's **[Improved Survival]** feature that let her sense the coming weather. If it had been up to Aderyn's ignorance, they'd all have marched cheerfully into the unpredicted storm.

The river was wide and ran swiftly northward, merrily burbling over the stones that filled its bed. Sometimes it pooled in calm eddies carved out of the banks, revealing that there, at least, the water wasn't more than two feet deep. But mostly its current was rapid, fast enough that Aderyn was glad not to need to cross it. And it looked ice-cold, too, though that could have been the chill in the air.

Weston said, "There are creatures ahead, playing in the water."

Aderyn shaded her eyes, but saw nothing.

Jessemia added, "They aren't very big. Are they dangerous?"

"Let's see," Aderyn said, and Assessed the river ahead.

Name: Dire Otter [13]
Type: Magical beast
Power level: 11
Terrain: lowland water, ocean
Attack(s): claws x4, bite, special
Immune to: elemental water damage
Resistant to: elemental cold damage

Vulnerable to: none

Special attacks: tail slap

Normal otters are so cute and playful people forget they're predators. Dire otters aren't aggressive, but they're bigger than their ordinary cousins, they're just as cute and playful, and they're even better and more efficient predators than a regular otter. That means if you rouse them, you're on the menu.

Watch out for their tail slap, which is painful enough when it strikes flesh but also does a disorienting sonic attack when it hits water. You might also keep in mind that dire otters are social creatures who fight as a pack, and if you can disperse them, you might get away with your life. Don't let this be an embarrassment like the gopheroons.

"Dire otters," she said.

"Look how adorable they are!" Jessemia exclaimed. "We don't want to kill them, right?"

"[Improved Assess 4] says they aren't aggressive." Aderyn squinted, but she didn't see anything but a darker mass on the distant riverbank. "They'll fight if we attack them."

"We don't need experience that badly," Owen said. "We'll walk around."

Jessemia diverted their path, and they continued forward and to the east. Aderyn kept her eyes on the dire otters, not out of fear but out of curiosity. She didn't know what an otter was, but the idea of there being a monstrous version of the creature that wasn't aggressive intrigued her. Gradually, the dire otters came into view. Jessemia was right; they were adorable, with sleek wet fur and broad snouts. These had either made or were taking advantage of a slippery, grass-free section of the bank that sloped down to the water, climbing to the top of the slope and sliding down it on their bellies or backs to splash into the river.

"I almost wish I could have one for a pet," Jessemia said. "**[Knowledge: Dire Animals]** tells me dire otters are as intelligent as dogs."

"It's still a monster," Livia objected. "How would you keep it from chewing your face off?"

"Some of my knowledge skills let me tame magical beasts or non-aggressive monsters. I've never tried it." Jessemia sounded like trying it was at the top of her mind.

"That would be amazing, if you could train a monster to go into battle with you," Weston said. "Like how the system said adventurers tame those chattering pakshi birds."

"Dangerous to make the attempt, though," Isold said. "I hope you're not considering it seriously."

"Only half-seriously. But not a dire otter. They're semi-aquatic, and we can't guarantee we'd stay near their element." Jessemia cast a glance at the dire otters splashing in the river.

"Zalk, Taavek, you're slowing down," Owen said. "Something wrong?"

"We've never seen dire otters before," Taavek said. "Are you sure they're not dangerous?"

"As long as we don't attack them, yes," Aderyn said.

Just then, one of the dire otters sat up on its hind legs and looked directly at Aderyn. Aderyn, startled, held its gaze until the creature flopped down on all fours and loped toward her. "It's approaching," she said. "Now what?"

"It's fine," Jessemia said. "It's just curious." She broke away from the group and took a few steps toward the dire otter.

"Jessemia!" Owen and Isold said in unison.

"Don't worry," Jessemia crooned, half to the otter and half in response to the others. "We won't hurt you. Go on back to your friends."

The dire otter picked up speed. Three other otters watched it with what to Aderyn looked like keen interest. "Jessemia, maybe you should—"

"It's attacking!" Taavek shouted. "Watch out!"

"It's not attacking," Jessemia said.

As she spoke, a stone whizzed past her and struck the dire otter a glancing blow on its shoulder. The creature recoiled. It let out a high-pitched chittering noise and sprang at Jessemia.

CHAPTER TWENTY-ONE

Jessemia leaped backward, barely avoiding the swipe of the dire otter's claws. "No, stop!" she shouted. "Don't attack!"

"They're all coming!" Taavek said. "We need to fight!"

Isold stepped in front of Jessemia and held up a hand in the dire otter's face. "We're friends," he murmured.

The dire otter, caught mid-leap, dropped flat to the ground and then rolled onto its back, chittering happily. Jessemia knelt beside it and touched the underside of its chin. "We won't hurt you," she said, her voice as soft and compelling as Isold's.

The dire otters who'd been watching broke away from the pack and loped in their direction, chittering rapidly. Owen activated the <**Sunsword**> and took a defensive stance. "We're not going to be able to avoid conflict if they decide they're under attack. Everyone, be ready—"

Movement on her left alerted Aderyn just in time for her to grab Taavek's sling before it released another stone. "Stop it!" she demanded. "Didn't you hear me? You're going to get someone hurt!"

Isold stepped in front of Owen and raised his hand again. The advancing dire otters slowed. One of them turned a slow somersault that ended with it pointed in another direction. The others watched it as if it was a performer in a roadside carnival.

"[Fascination]," Isold said. He didn't sound as if he was under any stress from using the skill. "Are the others following them?"

"Doesn't look like it," Weston said.

"Then I think these three should return to their friends." His voice took on the subtle harmonics of [Suggestion]. The dire otters scrambled to their feet and ran back the way they'd come.

Three identical system messages popped up.

Congratulations! You have defeated [Dire Otter].
You have earned [6775 XP]

Isold let out a long breath. "Jessemia, do you need help?"

"Yes, and no." Jessemia sounded amused and exasperated all at once. "I'm afraid this one has imprinted on me."

Everyone gathered around, even the giants. Jessemia knelt in the tall grasses with her hand on the dire otter's chin, gently scratching it. The creature's head was tilted far back, exposing its throat. It made a crooning sound that intensified whenever Jessemia stopped scratching its chin.

"Well, that's just great," Owen said. "Now what?"

"I was serious about not making a pet out of a dire otter," Jessemia said. "But I've never used my skills to befriend a monster or animal, and I didn't realize it happened so easily. Though I think that was because Isold had to [Charm] it to stop it coming after me. That must have made it extra pliable to my skill."

"I won't apologize," Isold said with a smile.

"Of course not. But it leaves me not knowing what to do."

The crooning increased, and the dire otter butted its head against Jessemia's unmoving hand.

"Can't Isold use **[Suggestion]** to make it leave?" Livia asked.

"I will try. I don't know how Jessemia's skill works, either. But we can't have it following us. Jessemia, stand back." Isold took Jessemia's place beside the dire otter and gripped its chin so its eyes met his. Quietly, he said, "Return to your friends, and forget us."

The dire otter stilled. Its head moved as it examined the humans and giants gathered around. Then it rolled to its feet and ran with that curious loping gait back to the riverbank. Again, the system message appeared.

Jessemia let out a relieved sigh. "Thank you. I had visions of it following us into battle and getting killed by a rimewolf or a scimitar tree."

"That was lucky," Aderyn said.

"Yes, it was," Owen said grimly. "Taavek, what the hell were you thinking?"

Taavek backed up. "It was attacking. I'm supposed to help defend us."

"It wasn't attacking, and you overreacted. That could have been a serious fight in which you or your friends might have been injured." Owen's voice was level, but he stood as if he loomed over the young giant two feet taller than he. "This is exactly what I was talking about. You obey orders, or I'll send you back to Jasperton."

Taavek's mouth fell open. "You can't!"

"He'll fail at his quest," Freta exclaimed. "You can't make him go!"

"I think maybe you People haven't grasped the seriousness of this situation," Owen said. "We are on a difficult, possibly life-threatening journey, with plenty of real dangers that are far worse than a pack of dire otters. I'm guessing you're used to adulthood quests being difficult but not too dangerous, right? How many People of your age fail to come back from them?"

The four giants wouldn't meet his eyes. "People always come back," Zalk muttered.

"Well, in the quest we've undertaken, each of us have come close to dying at least once. Sometimes really close." Owen stepped closer and made Taavek look at him. "You have *got* to start taking this seriously, and by that I mean you will listen to us when it comes to combat. Taavek, you started a fight you couldn't have finished. What do you have to say for yourself?"

Taavek ducked his head. "I'm sorry. I was stupid."

"You were scared and impulsive, not stupid," Owen corrected him. "There's nothing wrong with your instincts. You're right that you should help to defend the others—you're the only one of you four with fighting skills, right? Your mistake was in not listening to Aderyn and Jessemia. Both of them have knowledge about monsters that we all depend on."

"But you weren't sure, either," Freta objected. "You were all acting like Jessemia might be in danger. Taavek didn't know."

Owen regarded her with a level gaze. Then he held the basket hilt of the <**Sunsword**> in front of him and activated the blade. Its light was faded in full daylight, but it still looked impressive. Freta and Taavek, who were closest, took a step back. "It's true we were concerned," Owen said. "But if we'd really believed there was a threat, we would have attacked. The point is that until you gain some life experience, you need to listen to us about monsters. That will keep everyone safe."

He deactivated the blade. "It's good that this happened now. Remember what I said about you learning to be real adventurers? Everyone makes mistakes. The real adventurers learn from them.

You are all going to do just fine if you remember what happened here today and let it affect you going forward. Okay?"

The giants nodded. Aderyn, watching Taavek, thought he looked a little less humiliated than before.

"Let's keep moving," Owen said. "We still may have to camp early. Taavek, did any of you bring shelters?"

"We have tents," Taavek said. It was curt, but Owen didn't react.

"That's good. I'd hate for any of us to sleep rough. Jessemia, you want to lead out?"

Jessemia nodded and strode forward. Everyone fell into their usual marching order, with Weston near Jessemia in the lead, Livia and Isold in the middle, and Aderyn and Owen bringing up the rear. This time, Aderyn was conscious of the four giants slouching along behind. "I guess it's good they're back there, because I for one don't have the legs to keep up with their stride," she murmured to Owen. "You handled that well."

"I feel like a crotchety old man yelling at the kids to stay off my lawn," Owen replied. "You really think I did all right? I felt a little like a hypocrite, given that I ignore your instincts far too often when I'm afraid you'll be hurt."

"That is true. But those four need to wake up to the reality that this journey is dangerous, and I think you struck a good balance between strictness and encouragement." Aderyn glanced over her shoulder, but the giants didn't seem to be listening.

"I have this terrible fear of having to explain to their parents why I didn't keep them safe." Owen, too, glanced back. "But I was serious about them learning to be adventurers. They're doing something remarkable, and that's deserving of respect."

"And that's one of the many reasons I love you," Aderyn said.

THEY STOPPED BRIEFLY AT NOON TO EAT LEFTOVER turkey meat and soft rolls from the previous night's feast, then continued on until Jessemia said, "That storm is rolling in fast. We need to make camp before it hits."

Aderyn Assessed the terrain. Bright green lines making squares five feet across sprang up over the ground, sinking as if into a deep hole when they reached the river. She pointed at a spot near the riverbank, but not too close to the water. "That's a good, flat spot with visibility in every direction. We should camp there."

That was the signal for everyone to remove their knapsacks and stretch, even Aderyn, whose <**Knapsack of Plenty**> weighed almost nothing. Livia dug out the bronze cube <**Soldier's Friend**> and stood in the middle of the spot Aderyn identified. When the whirlwind of tiny figures surrounded her, the giants huddled together, their eyes wide. "What is it?" Freta asked.

"It's magic that sets up our camp," Aderyn explained. "It makes a few tents if there are only a handful of people, or you can choose to make a thousand tents for an army. It lights a magic fire and sets an alarm spell that goes off if anything malevolent crosses it. Which reminds me that we'll need to show you the limit of that spell, so you can pitch your own tents inside it."

Zalk relaxed. "That's impressive magic. We have something similar—the alarm, I mean, not the tents. But it uses stone."

"Livia will want you to show her." Nearby, four elegant white tents appeared, surrounding a tidy little fire ringed by stones.

"She's a lot more powerful than we are, and she's... you know. *Stonekin*." Zalk whispered the word like it was something dangerous.

"Oskarl said stonekin is a word your adults hold close," Aderyn said. "Does that mean you're not supposed to know it?"

Freta elbowed Zalk. "We're not supposed to say it. It's reserved for the adults. But we can't help overhearing. And we're nearly nine, so it's not as if we're that far from adulthood."

"I heard 'stonekin' and I'm curious," Livia said, approaching their group. "It's a secret, right?"

"Sort of," Zalk said, just as Freta said, "Yes." They glared at each other a moment before bursting into laughter.

"Zalk says he has stone magic that works like *alarm*," Aderyn said. "I told him you'd want to see."

"Of course. What is it, Zalk?"

Zalk fished the white stone out of his clothes and dangled it in front of Livia. "This is a warding stone. It's not very strong, and it won't stop a monster from attacking. But—here."

He walked a short distance away, scanning the ground, until he stooped and picked up something small. "You need another stone for this to work. Like this." He returned and displayed a larger, flattish river stone, smoothed from centuries of water flowing over it. Awkwardly, he grasped the white stone on its thong and tapped it against the river stone, which he held several inches from his chin instead of bringing it to meet the white stone.

Light flashed like a tiny star, and the river stone pulsed once with a deep red glow like the <**Wayfinder**> when it reached Aderyn's heart's desire. Aderyn thought at first the stone had returned to its original state, but after a few seconds' observation, she realized it was radiating waves like heat haze, though she felt no warmth from it.

"You put these in a circle, and when something dangerous crosses between them, they shriek a warning," Zalk explained. "The effect only lasts for about ten hours, and a warding stone can't create more than three of these in a day, not enough to make a big circle. But if you're with friends, that's enough."

"That could come in handy," Aderyn said.

Livia touched the stone with her granite forefinger. "I can feel it's changed. It's more... alert, I guess is the best word."

"Why is your hand made of stone?" Taavek asked.

"It's a long story," Livia said. "But we've got a long night ahead, so maybe I'll tell it."

Snow started falling when dinner was almost over. Livia used *repair* to turn the extra ground cloths into an enormous tarpaulin — "Don't ask why that works when these things were never a single piece to begin with," she said—and with some clever use of ropes they made a shelter big and tall enough to protect even Skalt, who was the tallest of the giants. Aderyn settled beside Owen with a mug of hot tea and listened to Livia tell the story of the evil dungeon Sorrowvale. It ended up being a group effort as all of them added details.

"And it's thanks to Jessemia that we made it out in the end," Weston said. "She was the one who knew which path was the one out and which was a lie."

"I'd forgotten that," Jessemia said. "I was so scared and overwhelmed, all I knew was if I didn't see real daylight soon, I would go mad."

"And then Livia destroyed it," Owen said. "I think that was the first time I realized we'd all gotten strong enough to face real challenges."

"It was almost too much for me," Livia said. "In fact... well. At the time, I thought I was imagining things, but now I'm not sure. It felt as if something gave my *move earth* spell a boost. Like I was lifting beyond my capacity."

"Do you think the system helped us, after all?" Aderyn said. "It did thank us for destroying the dungeon."

"The system thanked you?" Taavek exclaimed. "How is that possible? It's the system. It's not a person."

Aderyn's friends all looked at her. Aderyn shook her head. "I'm not sure about that anymore. My skill **[Improved Assess 4]** includes information that I know others don't get, and those Assessments sound as if someone is behind them. Someone with enough awareness to call itself 'I.' But I don't understand how it's possible. A single person couldn't possibly have the knowledge and power to run our world."

"Unless it's many people," Owen said. "Gamboling Coil and Winter's Peril and even Sorrowvale weren't like your system Assessments. They had distinct personalities."

"I guess." In her heart, Aderyn felt that wasn't the answer, but what else could it be?

A whooping cry shattered the stillness. The humans all shot to their feet. "That's the perimeter alarm," Owen told the giants. "Anyone see anything?"

"It came from the river side," Weston said. He and Jessemia were already gazing into the gray dimness of the heavily falling snow. "I don't see anything."

Aderyn hurried to Jessemia's side. "I'll Assess—"

Something big and dark hurtled out of the dimness, knocking Jessemia down. Aderyn shrieked and drew her sword. Jessemia let out a short, pained gasp as if the wind had been knocked out of her. Then, to Aderyn's astonishment, she began to laugh. "I guess **[Suggestion]** wasn't enough," she said, somewhat breathily.

Aderyn lowered her sword and Assessed the dark, sleek shape of the creature pinning Jessemia down.

Name: Dire Otter
Type: Magical beast, companion
Power level: 11
Terrain: lowland water, ocean

Attack(s): claws x4, bite, special
Immune to: elemental water damage
Resistant to: elemental cold damage
Vulnerable to: none
Special attacks: tail slap
He followed your friend home. How much of a problem this is is up to you.

CHAPTER TWENTY-TWO

"*Companion?*" Aderyn exclaimed. "What does that mean?"

Jessemia gently shoved the dire otter aside and got to her feet. "It means it considers me its person, and it isn't going to leave. Crap. I really don't think this is a good idea for so many reasons."

"What, like how we'll go into battle against horrifying high-level monsters it might feel obligated to attack, to defend you?" Weston bent and scratched the creature under its chin. "You're such a handsome fellow."

"Don't encourage it, dearest." Livia stood back as if she feared the dire otter's cuteness was infectious. "Jessemia's right. We can't take it with us."

"Even if all we did was stroll to meet the tempest moth and return, it would be a bad idea. It needs to live near water. We can't guarantee that." Jessemia stepped back involuntarily as the dire otter leaned into her. Rearing up on its short hind legs with its paws on her shoulders, its true size was evident in a way it hadn't been during their first nerve-wracking encounter. Its slick dark brown fur shone in the firelight.

"It likes you," Owen said. "It might as well be a giant dog for all it's acting like a pet."

"I feel I should apologize for making it vulnerable to this effect," Isold said.

"Don't apologize. Without **[Charm]**, it would have bitten my face off. And I didn't need to use my **[Knowledge: Dire Animals]** on it. **[Charm]** would have been enough. So it's really nobody's fault." Jessemia gave up fending the dire otter off and stroked its sleek head.

"So, do you have any idea how to break the companion bond?" Aderyn asked.

"I was hoping you did," Jessemia replied. "All I know is that the companion bond is breakable only by death or betrayal, and look at this fellow. I can't imagine betraying it, and killing it would be evil."

"Definitely," Owen said. "Taavek, you're a hunter. Any ideas? You said you all hadn't ever seen one of these before."

"That's right," Taavek said. "I've never heard of a companion bond before, either. We can't just take it back to its pack?"

"It would follow me again," Jessemia said. "Let me try Assessing it once more. Maybe there are more details."

They all waited as Jessemia took its face in her hands and stared into the dire otter's eyes. It stared back at her, its beady black eyes unblinking, its sides heaving. Finally, Jessemia released it, and it dropped back to the ground and sat on its haunches. "There's some good news. Dire otters aren't like their animal cousins. Though they function best in a semi-aquatic environment, they don't require frequent contact with water the way ordinary otters do. And his breed are northern river otters, which means they thrive in cold climates and freezing water. So we wouldn't condemn him to death just taking him with us."

"That sounds like you've already made up your mind," Owen said. "Isn't there a way to, I don't know, discourage it from following us?"

"I didn't learn anything new about breaking the companion bond. Worse, it grows stronger over time, gradually developing into a two-way empathic bond. Not very high level, but I'll be aware of how it feels and where it is, and vice versa." Jessemia looked as if she wasn't sure whether to laugh or cry. "The only thing I can see breaking it is [Compulsion], and my guess is we've only got a fifty percent chance of that working."

"That is fifty percent worth trying, if it's what you want," Isold said.

"If it's what I want? What do you mean?"

"I mean," Isold said gently, "that to me it seems this creature isn't the only one that's formed a bond. You're already attached."

Jessemia's eyes widened. Then she laughed. "You're right. I am. But it's still not safe for this fellow to stay with us. So I'd like you to try, if you don't mind."

"Of course not." Isold crouched to put himself on the dire otter's level. No one spoke. Isold stared at the creature like he was memorizing its features. Seconds passed. The wind had stopped, and the softly falling snow cast a hush deeper than their silence. Finally, Isold said, *"Leave, and do not return."*

The dire otter jerked. It turned a look on Jessemia that Aderyn couldn't help seeing as a plea. Then it turned and ran into the darkness, its lithe shape disappearing immediately.

"Oh," Jessemia said, her hands covering her mouth. "That felt awful. Even though it was necessary. I felt exactly as if I'd actually betrayed it." She wiped her eyes and laughed weakly. "Which is good, since betrayal is a way to break the companion bond."

No one else said anything. Finally, Jessemia cleared her throat. "That wasn't how I thought this evening would end, but I think it's time for me to go on watch."

Her words felt like a release from **[Charm]**. Aderyn hugged Jessemia and whispered, "That was brave."

"It's not as if we had an actual bond built over time," Jessemia whispered back. "It was much harder leaving Stormy behind. My favorite horse."

"Even so." Aderyn released her. "Good night."

She snuggled up with Owen in their tent and listened to the soft sound of snow striking the roof. "I didn't think snow made a sound if there wasn't wind," she said. "But this feels like an absence of sound. Like the snow muffles everything else."

"I'm not looking forward to our first blizzard," Owen said. "Even with the <**Wayfarer's Windchimes**>, it could be nasty."

"True. But there's no sense worrying about something that hasn't happened yet." Aderyn yawned. "Good night. I love you."

She heard his response in a fog of tiredness, and then she slept.

When Owen woke her much later for her turn at watch, she felt more alert than usual. The snow had stopped falling and drifted a few inches high against the tents, but left only about an inch in the open spaces. She amused herself by following Owen's footsteps once around the camp and then settled in for a real watch.

The giants had camped a short distance away, well within the alarm perimeter. Aderyn already knew she and her friends could pass back and forth across it without setting off the alarm, but she wasn't sure the <**Soldier's Friend**> knew the giants were part of the team. She walked past, making sure they were all safely asleep. Taavek and Freta had wanted to take a turn on watch, but Owen had told them their time would come and not to worry about it yet.

She returned to the tents and did her nightly routine of checking to be sure everyone was still there. She no longer peeked inside, not after one night where she'd disturbed Weston and Livia in nocturnal activities, but she checked the tent flaps and wished she had Weston's hearing to detect breathing.

When she neared Isold's tent, she heard the murmur of voices. She stopped before they became intelligible, but she was still able to make out that it was Isold and Jessemia speaking. A deep curiosity struck her. Isold and Jessemia, alone in Isold's tent late at night? Surely that meant something intimate. But the rhythm of their voices didn't suggest they were having sex or even having the conversation that leads up to sex. Aderyn controlled the urge to listen in. This was none of her business. But she hoped, if there was something going on between her friends, that Jessemia would confide in her eventually.

She backed away from Isold's tent, grateful for the snow, and continued in her path. When she was behind Weston and Livia's tent, she heard a rustling like canvas moving, and peeked around to see a dark shape enter Jessemia's tent. More confidently, she continued walking.

When her uneventful watch ended, she went to wake Weston and tripped over something lying in front of Jessemia's closed tent flap. The thing let out a low chittering and settled back down. Aderyn regarded the dire otter for a few seconds. Then she petted its smooth head. "You're in for more than you imagine," she whispered.

"I'M GOING TO CALL HIM WHISKERS," JESSEMIA SAID.

She sat beside the fire, toasting cheese on a stick, with the dire otter's chin resting on her knee.

"Whiskers?" Aderyn said.

Jessemia blushed. "I know, it's sort of a childish name, but it's what I would have called him back when I was a spoiled fake Fated One, and it feels like... I don't know. Like acknowledging there were good things about that version of me. Including whimsy."

Aderyn stroked the sleek head. "It's not a terrible name. And it's descriptive. Look at those whiskers." The newly-named companion did have a fine set of whiskers bristling across his face.

"I think a dire otter named Whiskers is the weirdest thing we've ever encountered," Owen said. He handed Aderyn a hunk of bread, then gave one to Jessemia. "You're sure he won't be harmed by being away from water?"

"I'm sure. At worst, Livia casts *drench* on him or creates a pool for him to swim in. His diet is more of an issue. Normally he eats fish and crustaceans, but my **[Knowledge: Dire Animals]** tells me he'll eat any kind of meat if he's hungry, raw or cooked. Rats, chickens, even insects."

As if Whiskers understood speech, he pulled away from Jessemia and bounded off toward the river, where he dove in and disappeared beneath the surface. "See, he's hunting now," Jessemia said. She folded her bread around her cheese and took a large bite.

Owen shook his head. "Weirdest thing ever."

"We're close to Marble Hill," Zalk said. "Did you want to go there?"

"What's Marble Hill?" Owen asked.

"It's the closest town to Jasperton. We were talking about it, and we weren't sure if you wanted to try to talk to more of the People on purpose, or only when we can't avoid encountering them." Zalk gestured to himself and his friends.

"We don't want to go out of our way, no. We should focus on

finding the tempest moth. But if we run into People from Marble Hill, I'll want you to explain about our presence here."

Zalk straightened as if he felt honored by Owen's acknowledgment of his skills. "I can do that."

"Then let's finish eating and break camp. What's the weather looking like, Jessemia?"

"More snow this afternoon, but just a light snowfall, and only for an hour. It's going to be clear weather otherwise."

"I love the sound of that," Owen said.

They walked, resting occasionally, through the bright morning and the flurries of afternoon. Whiskers ran with an odd loping gait, occasionally running ahead to splash into the water but always returning to Jessemia's side. He did look a lot like an oversized dog, bigger than Aderyn's parents' neighbor's dog Antarus, which had scared her as a child because it had knocked her down in its enthusiasm more than once. Antarus had died years before, but he remained Aderyn's standard for large dog size. Until now.

The sun was low in the sky when Jessemia came to an abrupt halt. Her chin was raised and her eyes were closed. She inhaled deeply through her nose, once, twice. "There's a storm coming. A big one."

"Did you not notice it before?" Owen asked.

"No. That's what worries me. I don't know much about the Northlands, whether freak storms come out of nowhere like they do on the plains, but it's like one minute my weather sense said everything was clear, and the next it told me we need to take shelter." She looked around. "There isn't anywhere. Maybe it's time for those <**Wayfarer's Windchimes**>."

Owen whistled. "That bad, huh? All right. Do you People have anything to add? Anything you can recommend?"

"Sudden storms come through Jasperton all the time," Skalt

said. "Just not this early in the season. I don't know if our tents will survive."

"You leave that to us," Isold said. "I'll help you pitch your tents. They will need to be closer to ours than usual."

Aderyn stood beside Jessemia as the others made camp. With the fanfare of the <**Soldier's Friend**> resounding in her ears, she said, "Can you see it?"

Jessemia continued to stand still, her head tilted as if the unseen storm was audible. "Not yet. I'm sure it's there."

"Of course you are. Nobody doubts that."

"I mean my awareness of the storm feels like an itch beneath the skin. I'm still not used to everything I can do." She turned to Aderyn. "Let's see if we can help. I need to not think about this. It feels wrong."

"Your weather sense feels wrong, or the storm does?"

"The storm. I wonder—" She shook her head. "It isn't the tempest moth, right? Not this far south?"

The idea chilled Aderyn more than the air. "The giants said it roams the coast and a little inland. If it came this far south already, someone would have told the People in Jasperton."

"You're right." Jessemia still looked concerned. "There's nothing we can do about it either way."

When they returned to the others, the tents were all erected, the fire flickered cheerfully in the rising wind, and Isold was walking around the fire, examining the ground. "May I have the <**Laborer's Staff**>, Aderyn? There are no trees near here to provide support for the chimes."

"Sure." Aderyn rooted in the <**Knapsack of Plenty**> until she found the <**Laborer's Staff**>. The curve of its upper end terminated in a hook that now looked perfect for hanging something from. Isold drove its other end deep into the ground so it stood upright near the fire. Aderyn carefully handed the <**Way-

farer's Windchimes> to Isold, feeling superstitiously that she shouldn't let the item chime until it was properly hung. But Isold took it with less care, making the copper tubes *tink* against each other dully.

"How long does the effect last, again?" Weston asked.

"Twenty-four hours." Isold turned to Jessemia. "I don't suppose you know how long this storm will last?"

"Less than that. I hope. I'm not sure." Jessemia's voice was tight with tension.

"It will be all right. Don't worry about it. But I'll wait to hang it until the storm is nearly on us, just in case."

They waited, listening for the howl of storm winds. Aderyn didn't want to talk, because everything she thought of was hopelessly inane in the face of the unnatural storm. So when Freta said, "What kinds of things do you do as adventurers?" Aderyn welcomed the question as something normal they could discuss.

"We do things that gain us experience," Weston said. "Fighting monsters, accomplishing quests, defeating dungeons."

"Yes, but you said you have that Fated One thing," Zalk said. "It's not like ordinary adventuring, right?"

"That's true," Owen said, "but the Fated One quests still have us doing ordinary adventuring tasks. The difference is we have an unusual goal, and we gain unusual rewards sometimes."

"I always hoped I could be a real adventurer," Freta said. "But our adulthood quests are boring. My sister had to collect five types of berry for hers. Yes, they were berries no one had ever seen before, but... *berries.* That's hardly exciting."

"We have done quests of that type before," Isold said. "Beginning adventurers receive many simple tasks so they can gain experience while they are still low level enough that the more exciting, as you put it, quests and monsters may kill them."

"And exciting isn't always great," Aderyn said. "I remember

when we fought cat-hawks at level six. Isold and I nearly died. That was exciting in a terrible way."

"That's so brave," Taavek said.

"It's not brave to be attacked," Skalt said. "You didn't go after those cat-hawks on purpose, right?"

"That's right," Owen said, "and you're both right about bravery. Being attacked by a powerful enemy isn't brave. It's what you do in response that shows bravery."

"See?" Skalt said, without malice.

"Don't gloat," Taavek said.

"I wasn't gloating! You just never think I'm right."

"Hey, enough with the arguing," Weston said. "The winds are rising."

They all fell silent again. The sky was the color of pewter, and the air smelled, not of snow, but of freezing rain. Aderyn realized the temperature had, against reason, risen enough that her warm coat was too warm. She unbuttoned it and let it hang open.

"Now, I think," Isold said. He hung the **<Wayfarer's Windchimes>** from the stick and flicked the dangling feather. The central disc chimed softly against the copper tubes, a bright ringing barely audible over the wind. The winds moved the disc again, and the ringing grew louder. Then the sound rose swiftly to drown out all other noise, a bell-like ringing in six voices ranging from a tone almost too deep to hear to the sound of a fingernail on crystal.

A puff of air struck Aderyn's body, like someone blowing in her face. She felt suddenly warmer than before, and the winds that had whipped around her body, making her coat flap, were gone. She stood within a bubble of stillness outside which the winds howled and beat against a wall of what seemed like unbreakable glass. The effect spread outward from the magic item until it encompassed all the tents and a space about twenty feet beyond in all directions.

Aderyn stared through the bubble at the oncoming storm. Distantly, she heard birds chirping. "What is that?"

"I believe it's part of the memory this effect is based on," Isold said. "There aren't any birds here."

Whiskers abruptly broke from Jessemia's side and ran for the river some fifty feet away, outside the bubble. "Whiskers, no!" Jessemia exclaimed.

"He'll come back," Livia said. "Watch."

They watched as Whiskers came to a halt just outside the bubble. Rain had begun to fall, probably an icy rain, and the dire otter tilted his head back and let the rain pelt his face. Then he shook himself all over and romped back through the bubble. Aderyn had half expected him to pop it, but he passed through with ease and returned to Jessemia, rearing up to put his muddy paws on her shoulders.

"Ugh, Whiskers, no!" Jessemia said, laughing. She made her companion sit and brushed at the mud. "That was—"

The full force of the storm came upon them. Rain poured down like icy pellets, rattling against the bubble. The sound was distant, but it was loud enough Aderyn was grateful they weren't exposed to the rain. She took Owen's hand and squeezed it. "Such a lucky find."

She took off her coat and marveled at how comfortable she felt, like this really was a perfect spring day. Even the light was brighter inside the bubble, though still dim as if the storm's effect muted it. She sat beside the fire and watched as the icy rain turned into slush that ran down the outside of the bubble and then to snow that whipped through the air, making everything outside invisible in a curtain of pale gray.

Again, no one spoke, though this time Aderyn felt superstitious about speaking, as if noise or laughter would pop the bubble and send the snow pouring down on them. She watched the snow, not thinking of anything much, until the winds died down and the snow stopped flinging itself around. "That wasn't too long," she said.

"It's not stopping," Jessemia said. She stood close to the edge of the bubble, facing northward, the direction they'd been traveling. "It's not stopping. *Look*."

Aderyn joined her. She couldn't see anything but the snow, which was falling lightly enough that the world was again visible. "I don't get it."

Jessemia grabbed Aderyn's hand and crushed it. "It's out there. It's watching us."

Fear stabbed Aderyn's heart. She still saw nothing, but the terror in Jessemia's voice struck her to her core. She stared into the dimness, straining.

"Oh, shit," she heard Weston say. "It's *gigantic*."

The world outside moved, and the shifting motion of the snowstorm came into focus. An elongated body, big and gray with indistinct edges, drifted closer, filling the sky. Aderyn's head tilted back, then farther back, to take in long, drooping antennae and wings patterned like storm clouds and a pair of black, implacable eyes too big for her to comprehend. The tempest moth hung in the sky above them, barely twenty feet away. Then it rose out of sight, taking the calm with it.

CHAPTER TWENTY-THREE

The storm returned with greater force than before, the winds shrieking in three-part discordance like a trio of giant harpies intent on tearing them apart. Aderyn clung to Jessemia's hand. Snow beat against the protective bubble with such a ferocity she feared against all reason that it was alive and wanted to rip through the bubble to destroy her and her friends. The snow flew in every direction, giving shape to the violent winds that seemed to come from everywhere at once. Aderyn thought of her father's whisk, whipping egg whites to froth. This was like a dozen whisks in a single bowl.

She searched the sky. Surely any minute now the tempest moth would return to destroy them. She hadn't had the wits to Assess the thing before, but she wouldn't let that happen a second time. She would Assess it, and learn its weaknesses, and they would defeat it. Again, she scanned the sky, but saw nothing but the storm, so she Assessed the air. **[Improved Assess 4]** wasn't limited by her human perceptions. No system message appeared.

Beside her, Jessemia's breathing slowed, and her grip on

Aderyn's hand loosened. "I think it's gone. The storm is dying. For real this time, not the calm where that monster was."

Owen let out a *whoosh* of breath. "That was unbelievable. When the People talked about it, I know they said bigger than a whale, but that was... I couldn't comprehend how big it was. Bigger than our whole camp, at least. I guess I've never been close to a whale to make the comparison."

"What I didn't like was how indifferent it was," Livia said. "Like we were the bugs, and it couldn't be bothered to squish us. Those eyes were as cold as a snake's."

"Aderyn, did you have time to Assess it?" Isold asked.

"I was too freaked out to think of it," Aderyn said. "Sorry. I hope we don't regret that later."

"The next time we encounter it, we'll be better prepared. We'll know what to look for, at any rate." Isold touched the <**Wayfarer's Windchimes**>, making them ring again. "I won't take these down until the storm blows itself out."

"Everybody sit and try to relax," Owen said. "That was terrifying. I don't think I've ever felt that close to death."

"Did you feel it, too?" Aderyn asked. "That sense of being close to destruction? I didn't even think it was because the tempest moth hated us. Just that its existence alone isn't something humans, or any living creatures, are meant to withstand."

"That's how it felt to me. Maybe that's a fear effect or something," Livia said.

Aderyn's regret at not Assessing the tempest moth redoubled. "I really am sorry—"

"Don't worry about it," Owen said, putting his arm around her. "We'll have our chance. And this means we've made contact with it. Maybe the sub-quest information has changed."

Aderyn brought up the Codex and focused on the little gold dot with two dots below it and to its right.

Sub-quest: [The Tempest Moth]
The tempest moth now ranges much farther south than
usual, encompassing all of the Northlands in its flight path.
Discover the reason for the alteration in the tempest moth's
pattern and correct it. Reward: Additional detail to the
primary quest becomes available.

"Well, that's frightening," Aderyn said. "If it might go anywhere in the Northlands, nowhere is safe."

"Um," Taavek said. "The tempest moth came from the direction of Marble Hill."

"Did it?" Owen said absently. Then he focused on Taavek. "You mean from that direction, or actually from Marble Hill?"

"I don't know. I mean, yes, from that direction, but if it passed through Marble Hill, it might have torn up the town." Taavek straightened. "I think we should make sure they're all right."

He stood as if he expected Owen to criticize or tell him to stay out of adults' business. Instead, Owen said, "You're right."

Taavek blinked. "You mean you agree?"

"I think, setting aside how we should try to help if we can, if the tempest moth went through that town, the People might be able to give us information." Owen glanced around. "And we shouldn't wait much longer. It looks like the storm has mostly passed, or at least the snow has turned to rain. Let's go before it gets cold enough to snow again."

Isold detached the **<Wayfarer's Windchimes>** from the **<Laborer's Staff>**. Again, Aderyn felt the puff of air, this time from the other direction. The temperature immediately dropped several degrees, enough that she gratefully put on her leather coat again, with the collar turned up against the rain. Isold uprooted the staff and handed it back to Aderyn, who stowed it in her knapsack. It really was the most useful item.

Having broken camp, they continued northward and a little to the west, following Taavek this time. The young giant strode confidently, but Aderyn felt a slight discomfort at letting him be their guide. It didn't make sense, because he was a hunter and had been to Marble Hill before. Maybe it was knowing he was still an adolescent that did it. She thought about the kids back in Far Haven, all of them excitable and foolish, none of them the sort of person she'd trust to lead her through the wilderness.

The sun was low on the horizon and shining into Aderyn's eyes when Taavek slowed to a halt. "We're on the outskirts of Marble Hill now. Maybe we should go ahead without you humans."

"Why? Are you afraid the People here won't react well?" Owen asked.

"Yes. Exactly. Everyone thinks humans are monsters." Taavek turned to Zalk. "What do you think? You're the one who's supposed to do the talking."

"I—" Zalk looked at the other giants. "I think we should stay together. If we leave, and some of the Marble Hill People come upon the humans without us there, there will be a fight, and someone will get hurt. At least if we're together, we can explain what's happened. Besides, you know how the People feel about young questers."

"How do they feel about young questers?" Livia asked.

Zalk shrugged. "Like we're set apart to a higher purpose, I guess. Adults respect young questers because theoretically the quest could kill us, even though it never does."

"Let's take advantage of that if we can," Owen said. "Can we reach the town before sunset?"

"We'll have to hurry," Taavek said.

They jogged now, not quite running, across fields that soon became tilled ones, the soil plowed under for winter or the broken stalks of the last harvest showing low against the earth. Giant houses, their single stories as tall as a human two-story house, appeared in the distance, none of them lit, none of them showing movement. Their still darkness was eerie after the tumult of the tempest moth's storm, as if the winds had swept the inhabitants away. Zalk and Taavek, in the lead, didn't slow or deviate. Either they didn't see the silent houses as a problem, or they feared something worse ahead.

When the low wall surrounding Marble Hill became visible, Aderyn at first didn't see anything wrong. It wasn't until they came within a hundred feet that the damage became obvious. Something had battered the wall, taking down broad sections of it in places, leaving the top ragged from missing stones in others. Giant figures moved around it, setting stones back in place. Aderyn instinctively slowed. They moved like people in mourning, and disturbing them felt wrong.

The youngling giants didn't feel the same, by how eagerly they advanced. They walked to the one gap in the wall that looked as if it was meant to be there. Aderyn, trailing behind, heard snatches of conversation carried on the light wind: "...questers from... come to help..." Zalk was saying.

The adult giant he spoke to, a female with dark hair, hadn't yet noticed Zalk's human companions. "This can't be your quest," she said, louder and more forcefully than Zalk. "We appreciate your concern, though. I'm afraid we're not in a position to offer hospitality."

"We wouldn't demand it," Zalk said. "But it's not just us. We have companions who hoped to learn more about the creature who did this."

"Companions?" The giant's gaze fell on Weston. "You brought children on your quest?"

"They're not of the People. They're humans," Zalk said.

The giant recoiled, hit the wall, and slid sideways along it. In that pose, it was clear she was pregnant. "You bring *monsters* to our town?"

"They're not monsters!" Zalk waved a hand at Owen. "They're just like us, only smaller. They have a connection to the system, they have classes and everything. Please, just listen!"

"It's true," Owen said. "We don't want to hurt you. We're here to find out why the tempest moth has changed course and stop it."

The giant didn't respond. Aderyn took a moment to Level Assess her and discovered she was a level sixteen Gleaner named Olva. "Olva, please don't be afraid," Aderyn said, walking to Zalk's side. "I know you have stories about evil humans, just as we have stories about terrible giants. But neither of our people have seen each other in centuries. Couldn't those stories be wrong?"

"You know my name," Olva said. "Did you Assess me? Monsters can't Assess."

"That's right."

Slowly Olva stood upright. "Come here," she said.

Owen twitched. Aderyn gripped his hand once in reassurance and walked confidently to face Olva. "See?"

Olva leaned down to examine Aderyn's face. "How strange. You look perfectly normal, just small, like one of us shrunken."

"And you look like one of us, only bigger." Aderyn held out her hand. "Can you—"

"*Olva!* Get away from it!"

Olva took a step back as Aderyn jerked her hand away. A male giant, blond-haired and bigger than any giant she'd yet seen, pounded toward them along the line of the wall. "Get back! It's a human!"

"I know, Koivok, don't—"

Taavek stepped in front of the oncoming behemoth. "Sir, it's not what you think. We're from—"

Koivok shoved Taavek aside and aimed an enormous fist at Aderyn. Aderyn easily dodged the blow, darting backward. Then Owen was in front of her, the <**Sunsword**> blazing in the evening dimness. "We don't want to hurt you," he said, "but I won't stand by if you try that again."

Koivok readied another blow. Owen stood firm. Olva grabbed Koivok's arm. "That's enough," she said. "They haven't hurt us, Koivok. We need to learn more. Please, go get Linnea. She needs to know."

Koivok slowly lowered his hand. "You're not hurt?"

"No. Ask Linnea to come here. I'm sorry, but I'm not going to allow humans into Marble Hill until we have more answers."

Owen deactivated the <**Sunsword**>. "That's understandable. We can wait here. But—was there much destruction? We don't want to be a burden on you."

Olva's eyes filled with tears. "Many were killed, many more were injured. Not just from the storm. Brother turned on brother in the depths of their despair. It was more than we could withstand."

"Olva, please sit. You've been through enough," Koivok said, his voice suddenly gentle.

"Let me," Livia said. She gestured, said a few words, and the earth next to Olva humped and rose into a short hillock with a curved, flattened top perfect for sitting on. Both Koivok and Olva exclaimed in surprise, and Koivok put an arm around Olva to support her.

"Sorry," Livia said. "I wanted to show you that I am stonekin, like you. I speak to the stone, and it answers. Stonekin won't betray you, right? You don't need to fear us."

Olva ran a hand over the soft earth covering the hillock. "Just a few words," she said. "No stone. I don't understand, but I want to." She lowered herself to sit and breathed out a deep sigh.

Koivok's mouth opened and shut a few times. Finally, he said, "I'll get Linnea," and ran through the gate opening into the town.

"Your baby is all right?" Jessemia asked.

Olva nodded, but her eyes reddened again with tears. "My first. My husband was injured badly during the storm. He's with the Healers now. They don't know—" She swallowed hard. "I have to do something or I will go mad with worry."

"I understand," Jessemia said. "Thank you for being willing to listen. I promise it's worth it."

Heavy, running footsteps sounded, and Koivok returned, followed by a beautiful giant woman whose blonde hair fell in tangled curls around her face as Jessemia's sometimes did. The woman exclaimed, "Olva, are you well?"

"Well enough. Linnea, these youngling questers have brought humans to Marble Hill. Humans that aren't monsters. What should we do?"

Linnea removed an enormous pair of spectacles from a pocket sewn to her loose shirt. She held them before her eyes without putting them on and regarded each of the humans closely. "Koivok said they weren't normal. They really are human, aren't they? How can humans have classes and levels?"

The constant repetition of this startling reality was starting to annoy Aderyn. Sure, every new giant they met was going to have this reaction, but it would be nice if they could convey the information ahead of time so they didn't have to keep going through this. "We said the same about you," she said, cutting off Zalk and not feeling bad about it. "We're both non-monstrous races connected to the system. And we're on a quest to find out what the tempest moth is doing so far from home and make it stop."

"The tempest moth?" Linnea sounded so startled Aderyn at first had the mad thought that the giant woman didn't know what the tempest moth was. Then Linnea went on, "But you're not

Northlanders. Why would the tempest moth's destruction matter to you?"

"That's a long story, and it doesn't sound like you're in a position to listen to stories, not if you're recovering from the disaster," Owen said. "Let's just say it does matter, and we were hoping, if it's not an imposition, to learn anything you discovered from its attack. It will help everyone in the Northlands."

"The tempest moth," Linnea said. "Thanks to its attack, this isn't the craziest thing I've experienced all day."

"We're not in a position to provide hospitality," Koivok said.

"That's nonsense," Linnea said. "The day the People have to turn away strangers just because our homes have been devastated is the day the stones will turn on us. You are welcome here."

"Speaking of the stones," Olva said, "this human is stonekin."

Linnea blinked. "I was wrong. *That* is the craziest thing I've heard all day. And I won't ask how it's possible, because night is falling and we all need to get inside in case that thing comes back." She extended a hand to Olva to help her stand. "Come. Krag survived the healing and he's asleep. You should be there when he wakes."

Olva drew in a shuddering breath. "The stones are generous today."

"Don't say that where anyone else can hear," Linnea warned. "Too many didn't survive for us to see today as a blessing."

"If you have injured, I can help," Isold said.

Linnea eyed him. "Are you a Healer?"

"I am not, but I have a magic item that heals. I would be pleased to share it with you."

Aderyn said, "But—" and shut her mouth when Isold glared at her. He couldn't possibly be thinking of using the <**Healing Stone**> on the giants, could he? Not that she begrudged them healing because they weren't human, but the stone had limited charges, and they weren't anywhere that it could be recharged. If he used it up on the People of Marble Hill, and her team needed it later... no, he had to have something else in mind.

"Koivok, will you show our guests to the mead-hall?" Linnea said. "I'll arrange for food. And—Isold, is it? If you truly can heal, go with Olva to the Healers' house."

"You're so trusting," Koivok said, but he sounded resigned rather than angry.

Linnea, to Aderyn's complete surprise, kissed Koivok and touched his cheek lightly. "With you to defend me, how could I be otherwise?" She hurried away along the wall, waving at a couple of giants who labored farther away.

"Come with me, then," Koivok said. He waved at the gap in the wall. "Four youngling questers, six humans, and—what the stones is *that?*" He pointed at Whiskers with a shaking hand.

"He's my companion, and he's perfectly safe," Jessemia said. She rested a hand on Whiskers's head. "I'm really sorry. We've dumped a lot of strange knowledge on you, just after you've experienced a terrible loss."

Koivok shrugged. "After the day we've had, I can believe anything. Good thing Linnea is the leader of the Trappers, not me."

"You're married, though," Aderyn guessed, not wanting to be distracted by an Assessment just then.

"We are." Koivok smiled. "Best thing that ever happened to me, being matched with her. And here was me thinking my parents didn't know anything."

He led them to a mead-hall that was identical to the one in Jasperton, down to the carvings on the walls. "There's nowhere to sleep, no beds, I mean, and I know what Linnea said, but it's not a slight on you. Most of us will be sleeping cold tonight."

"We really don't expect you to put yourselves out," Owen said. "I mean, take care of our needs at the expense of your own."

"Thank you. These younglings will tell you how it grates on us to be temporarily incapable." Koivok nodded at Zalk and the others. "Excuse me. Someone will return with food soon."

When he was gone, Aderyn rubbed her arms and said, "It's cold in here. Can someone start that fire?"

"We're not stonekin yet," Freta said. "We don't know how."

"It's fine. We can wait for the others." Owen put his arms around Aderyn. "Here, let me warm you up."

The mead-hall door slammed open. A giant with bushy white hair staggered in, one hand outstretched, the other brushing the wall. In his outstretched hand he held a cane he used to feel his way, but not tentatively—he swept the cane back and forth as aggressively as if it was a weapon, smacking its tip on the stone floor.

"Strangers asking about the tempest moth!" he exclaimed, in a voice that creaked like an old hinge. "Strangers from beyond the lands we know! The stones said you would come."

"'Beyond the lands we know,'" Owen repeated. "That's a prophecy of the Fated One."

"Fated One, Fated One, what nonsense!" the old giant said. He turned his head and spat, narrowly missing Skalt's toes. "I'm talking about the stones, because the stones talk about you. Come closer."

Aderyn, almost against her will, drew closer to the old giant as her friends did the same. He looked as if he intended to whisper a secret. This close, she could see his eyes were filmed over with white, and he tilted his head as if listening for their position by their breathing.

"It's the end times!" the giant roared, startling Aderyn into jerking away. "The tempest moth marks the death of the Northlands, unless the strangers intervene. Nobody wants to hear that we can't save ourselves, but who can tell the system why it's wrong?"

"I don't understand you," Owen said.

The old giant cackled. "You will. Because I have the answer to your quest. I have the key to Stormwatch Citadel."

CHAPTER TWENTY-FOUR

"To *what*, now?" Weston said.

Instinctively, Aderyn said, "Check the quest information. I bet it's changed."

She brought up the Codex and focused on the gleaming golden dots until they enlarged.

[Fated One's Destiny: Eye of the Storm]
Bring peace to the Northlands by [see Pursue the Hunters: Reward] and [see The Tempest Moth: Reward].

Sub-quest: [Pursue the Hunters]
Rimewolf packs have begun hunting giants throughout the Northlands. Discover why this is and put a stop to it.
Reward: Additional detail to the primary quest becomes available.

Sub-quest: [The Tempest Moth]
The tempest moth now ranges much farther south than

usual, encompassing all of the Northlands in its flight path. Defeat Stormwatch Citadel to discover the reason for the alteration in the tempest moth's pattern and correct it. Reward: Additional detail to the primary quest becomes available.

Reward: [100,000 XP] plus any experience gained in the course of completing the quest.

"'Defeat Stormwatch Citadel'?" Owen said. "What the hell?"

Still feeling stunned, Aderyn Assessed the old giant with a Skill Assess. Whoever this was, she wanted everything the system could tell her about him.

Name: Vorn

Class: Scribbler

Level: 17

Class Skills: Knowledge: Lore (34); Knowledge: History (32); Extended Memory (40); Recitation (31); Tremorsense (42); Create Wardstone (27); Write Magic (28); Speak With Stone (25)

Vorn is the oldest of the People at Marble Hill. He's considered mad by most standards, but he also remembers lucidly the history of the People, so his fellows treat him with indulgent respect. Don't disregard his words, Aderyn. He rants, but there is wisdom in it.

"Vorn," Aderyn said.

She'd just been repeating the Assessment, but the old giant turned as if she'd addressed him. "You're Aderyn. I know that name. And Weston, and Livia, and Jacob Owen Lindberg. You're missing someone."

"Isold—" Aderyn began.

Vorn waved an impatient hand in her direction and nearly

clipped the side of her head. "It doesn't matter. You're here, and the stones have words for you."

"Go ahead," Owen said.

"Not here. The stones, the stones!" Vorn cackled in delight. "They think I'm mad because I see what can't be seen by eye. But the stones cry out against the destruction that flies on silent wings, and you will know their wisdom and use it."

Zalk cleared his throat. "Um. Venerable one—"

"Hah! The Mouth," Vorn shouted, turning on Zalk with his arms waving wildly. This time, he did connect, hitting Zalk's shoulder a glancing blow. "The speaking one. You're not alone, you know. The Mouth, the Hand, the Eye, the Mind. Three of you are meant for greatness. Don't ask which. The stones keep silence when it comes to destinies, because what would be the point of a quest if you knew how it would turn out?" He patted Zalk's arm as if feeling his way to the youngling's shoulder. "Don't fear. Fear gives you warts."

Zalk met Aderyn's eyes. He looked utterly bewildered. Aderyn took his arm and guided him away from Vorn. "Vorn, we want to know what the stones say," she said, wishing Isold were there to have this conversation. "Is there a place we need to go?"

The door banged open, and Koivok entered, followed by a couple of women bearing baskets. "It's all—Vorn, what are you doing here? You're not pestering these people, are you?"

"He's not," Owen said. "He told us he is the key to defeating the tempest moth. To Stormwatch Citadel. At the risk of being ungracious, why didn't you mention this in the first place?"

Koivok scowled. "Vorn, you should be in bed," he said, more gently than his expression suggested he felt. "Let's leave our guests to their rest, and you can talk to them tomorrow. Maija?"

The blonde giant set her basket on the floor and took Vorn's arm. "Come along, venerable one," she said in the same gentle tone, and led a suddenly docile Vorn out the door.

The other woman shut the door. "Koivok, he's getting worse."

"I can see that," Koivok said. "I'm sorry you had to witness Vorn's madness. He's harmless, but he gets these ideas in his head and then he babbles."

"He seemed fairly lucid to us," Weston said.

"And he said things that fit with what we already know," Owen added. "Things about our quest. I don't think he's as mad as you believe. Or do the stones not speak?"

"He said that?" Koivok exclaimed.

The woman came forward with her basket. "That's forbidden to speak of before non-stonekin. His blindness must have confused him."

"I'm stonekin, so it can't be totally wrong," Livia said.

"*You*, stonekin? Impossible." The woman recoiled like she'd learned Livia had a disease.

"Is he Marble Hill's only Scribbler?" Zalk asked.

"He is." Koivok looked like he wanted to know what business a youngling had interfering in adult business. "He was doing all right for a fifty year old until a week or so ago, when he started telling the People about some distant citadel and the end times and strangers coming to save us. All nonsense."

"Until the tempest moth showed up," Owen said.

"That was coincidence. It's hardly the end times just because of a monster."

"You don't believe that." Owen faced Koivok fearlessly. "You just don't want to think this disaster could mean the end for your People."

"Would you?" the woman interjected. "How does a citadel no one's heard of have anything to do with us?"

"I don't know, but I bet Vorn does," Owen said. "We need to talk to him."

Koivok didn't say anything.

"What harm can it do?" Aderyn said. "If he's mad, then it's harmless babbling, and if he isn't, his knowledge could save everyone in the Northlands."

"You know Scribblers speak with the stones," Zalk said. "Ours always said the stones' wisdom was hard to understand. It could sound like madness, right?"

"I don't want our first interaction with humans in centuries to be one old man who's probably senile," Koivok said. "But... all right. In the morning. Vorn falls asleep fast after he's taken by one of his spells. Here, we brought food, and you're welcome to sleep here tonight—oh, let me light the fire, the mead-hall is a little chilly." He picked up two of the jagged stones from the hearth and cracked them together, sending up sparks that fell on the rest. Flames ignited and spread across the stones, quickly building to a nice heat.

Koivok dropped the two stones into the pile and rubbed his hands on his trousers. "Is there anything else we can do for you? I'm sorry it's not more. We should welcome youngling questers with song, but with all the death and destruction, no one feels up to that."

"It's fine," Taavek said.

"Really, we understand," Freta said.

"Thank you. Sleep well." Koivok nodded in farewell.

After the door shut on the giants, Owen said, "Did any of you younglings know about this? How is it possible we stumbled on the one person in the Northlands who knows details about our quest?"

"I don't think we did," Zalk said. He glanced swiftly at Skalt. "Koivok said Vorn only started talking about this stuff a little more than a week ago. If Vorn learned it from the stones... well, the stones will be silent for months and then communicate from out of nowhere. And they talk to all Scribblers everywhere at the same time when they do."

"But nobody in Jasperton said anything about it," Aderyn said. "Wouldn't your Scribblers have known?"

Again, Zalk gave Skalt a quick, furtive look. "Our Scribbler died three months ago," Zalk said. "She, um—"

"She was sick and she didn't get better," Skalt burst out. "You can say it, Zalk. My mother is dead. She was the only Scribbler in Jasperton, and the system hasn't chosen a new one."

No one spoke. Skalt wasn't meeting anyone's eyes, and his breathing was as heavy as if he'd run a difficult race. After a few seconds, Owen said, "Okay. Then any village we came to would have given us this information."

"It wouldn't have mattered," Jessemia said. "That quest location we've been traveling toward? Thanks to Vorn, it now has a name. That's Stormwatch Citadel. So even if we hadn't encountered any giants—any People—we would have gotten there eventually, and I imagine your quest information would update then."

"But this means we might learn much more," Aderyn said. "If Stormwatch Citadel is a dungeon, anything Vorn can tell us about its secrets is a benefit."

The door opened, letting in a gust of cold air and Isold. His steps slowed as he approached. "You all have the look of people bearing bad news."

"There's an old giant who told us he knows something about us and defeating the tempest moth, and that we have to defeat a dungeon called Stormwatch Citadel," Weston said. "That's as much as I remember. Vorn might not be crazy, but he sure left my thoughts in a muddle."

Isold blinked. "Astonishing."

"Yes, and we're going to talk to him in the morning and see what else he knows," Aderyn said. "Um. Did you, ah, heal People?"

"I know what you're not saying," Isold said. "I did not use up the <**Healing Stone**>. Much of the injuries were relatively minor, though that's small comfort as it means most of those with greater injuries did not survive. But when I bought magic supplies for this trip, I bought a second <**Wand of Healing**> in case the worst happened and we found ourselves far from where our healing items could be recharged. And I only needed half of that wand's charges tonight." He patted his hip where the wand hung. "It surprised me that a single charge was sufficient to heal, say, a broken bone despite that bone being twice the size of a human one. That suggests something about how the system feels about its creations."

Owen let out a deep breath. "Let's eat, and get some rest. I feel overwhelmed after everything that's happened."

The oversized baskets contained two neatly sectioned turkeys, bags of dried fruit, a loaf of bread almost as long as Aderyn was tall, and three giant jugs of mead, big enough Aderyn needed both hands to lift a half-empty one. She drank more than she ordinarily would. She felt as overwhelmed as Owen. The tempest moth, meeting more giants, Vorn's words, even the way Whiskers had adopted Jessemia all made for a long and challenging day.

The stone floor of the mead-hall wasn't comfortable, but Livia separated the extra ground cloths she'd united with *repair* and the humans folded them beneath their bedrolls. It was enough to let them sleep. The fire burned low, sending flickering shadows across the walls. Aderyn watched them until she was drowsy. "I hope tomorrow is better," she whispered.

"*I* hope Vorn doesn't die in his sleep," Owen replied.

He sounded so grumpy Aderyn giggled. "You mean, we arrive just in time for him to fail to pass on his vital information?"

"Yes. That's a tradition of some mystery novels in my world. I hate it. The guy grabs the main character and mutters 'Meet me behind the mill at midnight and I will reveal everything' and then the main character gets there and the guy has been murdered. It's a cheap way to raise tension, I think." He put his arms around Aderyn and snuggled close. "It doesn't matter. Even without Vorn, we now know where we're headed."

"I know." She kissed him. "And we can handle anything."

"Jinx," Owen murmured.

A LOUD POUNDING LIKE STONE SLAMMING AGAINST stone woke Aderyn out of a confused dream about swimming like a river otter. She shot upright, disoriented by the lack of light. "The stones wake soon!" an elderly voice shrieked from outside the mead-hall. "Come, come, you don't want to miss it!"

Beside her, Owen groaned and sat up. "I didn't get nearly enough sleep for this."

"I can tell it's before dawn," Weston said. "It feels early."

Weston's internal clock was unusually good. Aderyn didn't challenge his words. "We'd better go. Livia, do you know what he's talking about? The stones waking?"

"No clue," Livia said. Though she'd shed her coffee addiction weeks ago, she still wasn't a morning person, and right now she sounded like getting out of bed was going to take all her willpower.

"Scribblers see the world in funny ways," Zalk said. "Probably

Vorn doesn't know it's too early for most People. Let's talk to him before he forgets we're here."

"Zalk is right. If this Vorn has something to tell us, we shouldn't delay," Isold said.

"But let's not leave anything here," Owen said. "If we learn something important, we'll want to be able to leave immediately."

Groaning and yawning, they all staggered to their feet, gathered their belongings, and exited the mead-hall. It was still full dark, not even close to sunrise, but the nearly-full moon glowed in the western sky, lighting the ground well enough to see by. The elderly Vorn waited outside, tapping the tip of his cane against the wall. Aderyn was close enough this time to see that the cane was made of stone rather than wood. Its tip was much paler than the rest of it, gleaming white in the moonlight. Marble, maybe?

"Come this way. The stones call me." Vorn jabbed his cane at Livia, who jumped back to avoid being hit. "Do you hear it?"

"I only have five ranks in **[Speak With Stone]**," Livia said. "That's not enough to hear them anywhere but right up close."

"Give it time," Vorn said. He waved his cane wildly before planting it firmly in the ground in front of him. "It's this way. Hurry! You're all slower than mud in winter."

Without another word, Vorn strode away from the mead-hall, deeper into the village. Immediately, they were surrounded by stone houses that towered over them despite being only single-story buildings. It was clear the tempest moth had been here too by how so many of the houses were missing great pieces of their roofs or chunks of wall. Heavy shutters blocked most of the remaining windows, but no light leaked between their cracks. Aderyn was sure they were the only ones awake in Marble Hill.

Rubble filled some of the streets, but Vorn moved confidently, avoiding obstacles with no hesitation. Even with the moonlight, Aderyn struggled to keep up. She couldn't understand how a blind man was capable of such a thing. Even Serria back in Far Haven, whose eyes were only partially impaired, didn't move this rapidly with her staff.

"It's **[Tremorsense]**," Livia murmured, as if Aderyn had spoken her curiosity aloud. "The tip of his walking stick sends out vibrations that connect to the stone and tell him where he is. He must have ranks in that skill I can't even imagine."

Aderyn remembered Vorn had the skill, but she couldn't remember the number of ranks. "So it compensates for his blindness?"

"My hearing works just fine, human!" Vorn exclaimed with a high-pitched tittering laugh. "Never regretted losing my sight. I see what the stones say now, clearer than anything."

Blushing, Aderyn said, "How long have you been blind?"

"Seven years. Long enough for memory. The People don't live as long as humans do, so you won't understand why we keep our records in stone. Generations pass and their knowledge is lost in time."

"I see," Isold said. "You mean that your short lifespans mean you can't count on memory."

"Indeed." Vorn tittered again. "You who keep secrets of your own are wise to the secrets of others, aren't you?"

"I don't know what you mean," Isold said, in a stiff manner that told Aderyn he absolutely knew what Vorn meant.

"No fear, I won't tell, but you really should." Vorn rounded a corner and used his stick to clamber over a pile of fallen masonry. Aderyn picked her way across the street, scrambling to keep up. Ahead of her, Isold was moving faster like he wanted not to be close enough to anyone for conversation, not even Jessemia, who was right behind him helping Whiskers climb over rubble. Aderyn would never pry, but—Isold, carrying a secret? Not prying didn't extend to not feeling curious.

Soon, they approached the city wall, this one not as destroyed as on the other side. Vorn strode through the gap and accelerated enough that the humans had to run to keep up with him. Even the younglings stretched their legs.

The land on this side of Marble Hill was rougher, the ground untilled, the fields bumpy in a series of short rises not big enough to be called hills. In the other direction, the land rose high enough to make it clear where the village had gotten its name. Vorn led their group downhill, across the bumpy ground where winter-dead grass gave the earth a spiky, threatening appearance.

Ahead, a spiral of standing stones stood, frosted silver with moonlight and frozen dew. In the pre-dawn silence, they seemed to be waiting for the humans' and giants' approach. Aderyn slowed despite her need to keep up with Vorn. She didn't like how the stones looked at her. Her sensible, logical mind told her that was ridiculous, that stones couldn't look at people, but her instincts said otherwise.

Prompted by those same instincts, she Assessed the stones.

Name: Stone Spiral

Type: Exceeds authority limit

She hadn't really expected anything more from the system, and she already knew the stones were, if not creatures, objects of power, so this non-answer didn't disappoint her. She was almost grateful not to know more. The stones frightened her in a different way from the tempest moth. That creature had been utterly indifferent to any living creature; the stones felt as if they cared about people, humans or giants, a little too much. Why that was the conclusion she came to, she didn't know, but in her heart it felt right.

She hurried to catch up to the others. Vorn had reached the standing stones and thwacked the nearest one with his stick, prompting Livia to gasp. Vorn ignored her. "Speak, stone!" he shouted. "The ones you saw are here. Give them wisdom!"

Aderyn came to a halt beside Livia, panting. "Can you hear anything now?" she asked.

Livia was silent.

"Livia?" Aderyn asked, nudging her friend.

Livia blinked. The moonlight reflected off her eyes, painting them with a silver glow. Then Aderyn realized Livia's eyes actually were glowing silver.

Frightened, she grabbed Livia's shoulder and shook her. "Wake up!"

A shudder ran through Livia's body. "*We are awake,*" she said, in a voice lower and more gravelly than her own. "*Destruction flies on silent wings. Listen, or be doomed.*"

CHAPTER TWENTY-FIVE

"You see?" Vorn exclaimed. "You see? The stones know you and your purpose. Ask, ask!"

"What did they do to Livia?" Weston demanded. Beside him, Whiskers chirruped and reared up, slapping his front paws together like he had the same question.

"She gives them voice. Stop wasting time." Vorn batted at Weston's shoulder, knocking him off balance. "Ask the question."

Owen stepped forward. "How do we defeat the tempest moth?"

Livia turned her silver eyes on him. "*Stormwatch Citadel holds the key. Its stones cry out for justice. The Mouth, the Hand, the Eye, the Mind. They bring an end and a beginning. You are their instrument.*"

Aderyn didn't waste time protesting that she didn't understand. "Is Stormwatch Citadel a dungeon? How do we defeat it?"

"*Stormwatch Citadel will yield its secrets to you, Warmaster. Look for the impossible answer.*" Livia licked her lips, which were now dry and cracked.

"We are those things you said," Zalk said, cutting off whatever Isold might have asked. "Who is which, and what does it mean?"

"*You know the answer. The one who speaks. The one who fights. The one who sees. The one who knows. Your quests tie to—*" Livia coughed, spraying a fine mist of blood. "*They reveal who you are. Heed the quest-giver's words.*"

Weston grabbed Livia. "Her health is dropping. Vorn, free her!"

"You free her," Vorn said, unexpectedly sulky. "It's not my business."

Whiskers's chittering yelps became frantic as Weston slapped Livia hard across the face. Livia smiled. "*Not everything responds to violence. Take the secret route.*"

"Let go of her!" Weston shouted.

"*Give us a reason.*"

"No," Weston breathed. Then he kissed Livia, a hard, bruising kiss as he crushed her to him. Livia shuddered. Weston kissed her again, more gently. He whispered something in her ear, his hand cradling her head.

Livia shuddered again and blinked rapidly. Her eyes cleared of the silver radiance. In a raspy voice, she said, "Those bastards. Taking advantage of a defenseless woman."

"You, defenseless?" Isold said.

"Against the promise of an eternity in stone? You'd better believe it." She smiled at Weston and caressed his cheek. "Fortunately, I was given the compelling promise of something much better."

She disentangled herself from Weston's embrace and rounded on Vorn. The giant, despite his bent and wizened condition, was nearly twice Livia's height, but Livia stood as if she could batter him into paste. "You knew that would happen, huh? You have enough ranks in [**Speak With Stone**] you're immune to being taken like that, and when the stones identified me to you, you took advantage of that."

"You're the ones who wanted the knowledge," Vorn said, again sounding sulky. "It's not my fault you couldn't take it."

"I survived, so it doesn't matter." Livia approached him closely. "But you get no consideration from me anymore." She grabbed his walking stick and twisted, yanking it out of his hand.

Vorn gasped and flung his hands out for balance. "Give it back!"

"Not yet." Livia tossed the walking stick far behind her. Whiskers loped after it. "Explain why the tempest moth marks the end of times."

Vorn swung a trembling fist in Livia's direction that Livia dodged. "I don't have to talk to humans."

"You do if you want that stick back. Zalk, don't you dare." Zalk, who'd been about to pick up the walking stick, flinched as the earth folded around it, burying it completely. Whiskers whined at being deprived of his toy.

"Fine! Fine! The tempest moth brings destruction. Not just physical. It breeds malice and despair in its wake, and People will fight against People in their fear." Vorn groped across the ground and then sat back, apparently giving up.

"Is that what it means to bring peace to the Northlands?" Owen asked. "Stop the People from reacting to the tempest moth?"

"Yes. Maybe. Who knows? Give me back my stick!"

"What do humans have to do with it?" Skalt asked. "They aren't the People. Why did they get involved?"

Vorn shrugged. "You are the ones who matter. They will get you there. I'm done talking." He pressed his lips together in a hard white line and folded his arms across his chest.

"I think he's serious," Owen said.

Livia nodded. The earth humped and bulged and spat out Vorn's walking stick at her feet. Livia kicked it toward Vorn, who didn't pick it up. "We should go. I don't want to spend time here explaining things to the giants when we already know enough."

"This way," Jessemia said, pointing north.

They made good enough progress that Vorn's huddled shape was a dark blotch against the hills by the time the sun came up. "Should we go back to the river?" Aderyn asked.

"I've been headed that way, yes. There are advantages to being close to the water." Jessemia nodded at Whiskers, who loped beside her. "Not just for Whiskers, though he can hunt for us. I like fresh fish. But the river also leads directly to Stormwatch Citadel, which makes sense if it was once a real castle. They'd need a water supply."

"Enough walking," Owen said. "Let's eat. And we need to talk."

Aderyn sat on the damp ground and dug food out of the **<Knapsack of Plenty>**. "There's not much. We left most of what Koivok gave us in the mead-hall. But it's enough for now." She passed a long, not yet stale loaf to Weston, who broke it in half to share with Livia.

"What did it mean that we bring an end and a beginning?" Taavek demanded. "I don't understand."

Aderyn hadn't wanted to be the first to mention that part of the stones' cryptic words. "It also said we are your instruments. That seems backwards."

"Meaning that Stormwatch Citadel is our quest, not theirs?" Owen bit into an oversized apple. "I don't understand it either. We need to consider the possibility that whatever that thing was that spoke through Livia, it wanted to deceive us."

"It didn't," Livia said. "I felt it. The stones lured me in, true—"

"Would they really have... I don't know. Absorbed you?" Aderyn exclaimed.

"They take living creatures when they can. The giants, the adults, they know this and they're careful to keep away from the stones when they're awake." Livia sounded so grim Aderyn feared for her. "I think Vorn saw an opportunity to spare one of the People."

"That's a lie," Skalt said. "We don't sacrifice living, thinking beings. My mother would never have done that."

"Usually it's an animal, Skalt." Livia's tone became unexpectedly gentle. "But that's irrelevant. The point is that the stones get chatty when they're taking a life, which was what Vorn wanted. I don't know why he cared about giving us information, but he wasn't all there, so who knows what his madness demanded. Maybe he liked feeling powerful. Again, irrelevant."

"But you think they didn't lie," Owen said.

"The stones can't lie. They see what happens differently than we do, true, but lying would make them not-stone. I can't explain it better than that." Livia raised the bread to her lips, but paused before biting into it. "That all means they are completely truthful and completely obscure. We're lucky they were as coherent as they were. That might have been because I'm an Earthbreaker and not easily overwhelmed by stone."

"But you four," Jessemia said. "Your quests didn't involve Stormwatch Citadel."

The four younglings shifted uncomfortably. "We're taught to pay attention to how our quests unfold," Freta said. "The quest-giver sets us on the path, but that path can change."

"But this is crazy," Skalt said. "The path changing means you have to collect five kinds of berry instead of three, or you have to provide for the bear cub whose mother you were tasked to hunt and kill. It doesn't mean getting a completely different quest from the stones!"

"Yes, but it doesn't *not* mean that," Zalk said. "And it was the stones, Skalt. Nobody has a higher authority than that."

"And think about it," Taavek said, his eyes distant. "This is a quest that the People will sing about forever."

"I don't want to be sung about! This is always how it goes, Taavek, you get these mad ideas about glory and then you drag the rest of us into your madness. It was your idea to attack these humans, remember?" Skalt was breathing heavily again. To Aderyn, he looked ready to fight.

"That's enough," Owen said. "Taavek, Skalt, fighting isn't going to resolve this. And we don't know enough to make conclusions. All we know is that you four younglings have more of a role to play than we realized. Our quest hasn't been invalidated—we're still supposed to defeat Stormwatch Citadel. So don't freak out—I mean, don't let this overwhelm you."

Skalt glared at Taavek, but said, "You're right. We don't know enough. I'm sorry."

Taavek looked surprised, like he hadn't expected an apology. "Um. I'm sorry, too. And you're not wrong about how maybe I get a little carried away. I want us to be famous, don't you? With how everyone thinks we're just younglings?"

"I was hoping for the kind of famous that doesn't leave us dead in a mysterious castle far from home," Skalt said with a weak smile.

"That's better." Owen tossed an apple at Skalt. In his hands, it looked normal sized. "Let's eat. And then I think we need to consider a faster route to our destination. If the tempest moth roams freely through the Northlands, we can't afford to take—how long, Jessemia?"

"Twelve days. Eleven if we push ourselves."

"That's way too much time for potential destruction. Livia?"

"I can get us there, but just barely. I'd need to be fully refreshed, and unless we want me to be nearly helpless afterward, I'd have to use one of the magic energy rejuvenation potions." Livia rested her chin on her knees. "If we walk today, and I *scry* out the location tonight, it's possible."

"What's *scry*?" Freta asked.

"It's a spell that lets me see a distant location or person. Very distant, sometimes."

"How come you didn't use it before?"

"Because I didn't know what I was looking for. I would have just used up all my energy searching the wilderness. But what little the stones revealed will make it easier." Livia accepted a handful of green grapes from Isold.

"I don't know why the People don't have magic," Freta said. "It's so useful. We just have stone, and you have to be an adult to use that."

"Technically, you have to be an adult human to use magic," Weston said. "Only humans who have accepted the Call can use magic, and that happens after adolescence. I don't know anyone who got the Call before they were eighteen."

A chittering sound announced Whiskers's return from the river, dripping wet and gripping a small fish in his jaws. He dropped the fish on Jessemia's lap and chittered again.

"Um, thank you, Whiskers," Jessemia said, picking up the fish by its tail with two fingers. "I'm sorry, but much as I like fresh fish, they are icky before they're cleaned. Scales and slime. And we don't want to stop to cook it, do we?"

"We can be grateful Whiskers wants to hunt for you," Isold said. "It will keep until evening."

Jessemia handed him the fish, which he wrapped thoroughly

in a white handkerchief and stowed at the top of his knapsack. "Then let's walk, shall we?" he said cheerfully.

"Isold," Owen said.

"I see no reason not to take the best perspective, which is that at this time tomorrow we will see Stormwatch Citadel for ourselves." Isold rose and stretched.

Aderyn and Owen exchanged glances. Aderyn saw clearly that Owen wanted to press Isold on whatever secrets he was keeping. She shared that feeling. Keeping secrets from your team could be deadly. But Isold was also a grown man who deserved privacy. And Aderyn still hoped that any secrets he kept were related to the romantic feelings for Jessemia Aderyn couldn't prove he had. She shook her head minutely, telling Owen not to push.

"Good point," Owen said. "Okay, time to move out. But take it easy, right? Livia's health is still low after that incident with the stones—can that be healed?"

"I believe so," Isold said, drawing out the <**Wand of Healing**>. He activated it, and the bubbling green flow of magical energy wreathed Livia's throat and chest.

Aderyn watched Livia's health bar rise and then stop well before full. "It didn't work."

"I believe that's because some of the damage she took was not injury," Isold said. "It will take time for her to recover fully."

Owen nodded like he'd expected that. "Well, between that and the fact that any progress we make today won't make a difference to *world door*, I don't see why we should strain ourselves." He chuckled. "A nice stroll through the wastelands."

The day was overcast and chilly, not nearly pleasant enough for a stroll. Wind gusted occasionally, tossing Aderyn's ponytail before disappearing into the distance. She ended up walking next to Isold, whose longer stride forced her to speed up slightly, keeping her warm. Neither of them spoke, but Aderyn's curiosity filled her with impatience over all the words she couldn't say. Finally, she said, "Would you sing?"

"Because the silence is getting to you, you mean?" Isold said with a smile. "Maybe we should all sing. It would pass the time."

"I'm only passable," Aderyn said, "you know that."

"Singing is like dancing, Aderyn. The performance is only part of the joy." Isold broke into a funny song about two young lovers courting. Aderyn knew it well; it had parts for the boy and the girl as they teased each other about their mutual feelings. Isold paused just before the woman's part should begin, and Aderyn was about to join in when someone else started singing. Jessemia, in the lead, didn't turn around, but her soprano voice soared above the wind, beautiful and merry.

Aderyn came to a stop. So, after a moment, did everyone else. Jessemia kept walking for a few steps, looked back, and saw everyone staring at her. She blushed, but didn't stop singing. When she came to the end of her part, there was momentary silence. Then Isold took up the melody again for the chorus, and this time Jessemia sang the harmony.

After the final notes, Weston said, "Speaking of hidden skills. Where did that come from?"

"It's not like I'm a professional. I just like to sing," Jessemia protested.

"You like to sing the way I like to dance," Livia teased.

"It's really not a big deal."

"Of course it is! You should be proud of your skills," Aderyn exclaimed.

"And now I feel like I'm showing off," Jessemia said, blushing harder.

"It's not showing off to embrace something you love," Isold said. He was watching Jessemia closely as if he and not Aderyn had **[Read Body Language]**. "I thought it was beautiful."

Jessemia smiled. "Coming from you, that's a marvelous compliment. Considering that I'm sure you were singing in your cradle."

"Not quite." Isold smiled back at her. "But we ought to sing more duets, now that we've heard what you can do."

"I love duets," Jessemia said.

Aderyn had the sudden feeling that this conversation was happening on more than one level. She held her breath. Now would be an excellent time for Isold to declare his feelings for Jessemia.

Isold began walking, prompting the others to follow. "And now I really would like everyone to sing. Let's give our youngling friends a taste of our music."

Aderyn caught a glimpse of Jessemia's face. Just for a moment, her friend looked as if Isold had slapped her. Then she smiled, and the moment was gone so quickly Aderyn almost doubted her perceptions. But—no. That had been the look of someone whose heart was breaking. She had to talk to Jessemia. But later, privately.

"Your songs are confusing," Taavek said. "Why did the man and the woman pretend not to care for each other? If they were betrothed, that would be ridiculous."

"Didn't you hear? They weren't betrothed," Freta said, thwacking Taavek lightly on the head. "I overheard my mother say humans fall in love first and then get married."

Zalk made a face. "That could be terrible if they fell in love with someone and their parents matched them with someone else."

"It could happen," Skalt said. "For all you know, they convinced their parents to approve their match. And besides, we all grow up together, so it's surprising we don't have *more* younglings making love matches."

"I was going to ask about that," Weston said. "Is it really so uncommon for giants—I mean, for the People to fall in love before they're married?"

"Of course. Imagine if you fell in love and that led you to marry someone who wasn't a good match?" Taavek said. "You'd be so miserable."

"It's better if parents decide," Freta said. "They know their children's personalities and needs. All the People have strong marriages because of that."

"I'm thundering grateful we don't have that tradition," Livia muttered. "My parents would never have picked Weston."

"I wonder if it would work for humans, though." Aderyn considered her parents, then the many young men of her age in Far Haven. Since she loved Owen, she couldn't imagine being happy with any of them, no matter how decent or attractive they were. On the other hand, though, if she was paired with someone who shared her interests and her dreams for the future, didn't that suggest she could have a successful marriage with him? It was what her parents always said about their own marriage, that they were united in more than just the system's awareness.

"It certainly couldn't be worse than some people's own choices," Isold said. "My parents dissolved their union when I was thirteen, citing a change in desires and attraction."

"Isold! You've never said anything about that!" Aderyn exclaimed.

"It's not as if our friendships revolve around knowing every tragic detail of our pasts." Isold shook his head. "I was torn between sorrow at seeing my family dissolved and gratitude that my parents would no longer shout at each other and use me and my brother as weapons in those fights. In my opinion, my parents should never have married, and I say that knowing that means I would not have been born."

"Oh, Isold."

"Don't let your empathy overcome you, Aderyn. It's not a thing I dwell on. Be happy for me that I have learned from their example. I won't marry casually or for superficial reasons."

Aderyn fell silent. It was true, she couldn't help picturing Isold as a boy torn between feuding parents, but he was right that she shouldn't treat him differently as a result.

Isold started singing again, a country song meant to be sung as a round, and Aderyn joined in on the countermelody. The wind picked up the song and carried it across the plains to the river and beyond. Part of her knew this could be dangerous if it alerted monsters to their presence, but the rest of her didn't care. Between the revelations of the stones, Jessemia's unexpected skill, and Isold's tale of his past, she wanted something uncomplicated to clear her head and her heart. Too bad monsters didn't leap at them when she needed it.

CHAPTER TWENTY-SIX

They walked until an hour before sunset, then made camp near the river. The day's journey had been uneventful, with Jessemia's command of Whiskers's obedience the only dramatic moments. They'd all become accustomed to Jessemia shouting "Hunt!" or "Fetch!" and Whiskers diving into the river or loping gracelessly after a thrown stick. Whiskers seemed to consider it great fun no matter what she asked him to do.

Despite the peacefulness of the day, no one spoke much, as if they were too weary for conversation. Aderyn helped Isold chop vegetables for soup without considering ways to get him to spill his secrets. That seemed like too much work. Besides, after the things he'd revealed, she felt guilty about pestering him for more. Far more important was finding a way to get Jessemia alone. There, Aderyn felt herself on steadier ground. Jessemia should know Aderyn was there to listen if she needed to talk.

With dinner finished, they sat around the campfire, even the giant younglings, in silence. The sky was clear for once, and

Aderyn looked up at the stars and thought about what Owen had told her once about people in his world seeing pictures in the stars, or foretelling the future based on the stars' movement and position. That still struck her as odd, but the only foretelling her world had was the Fated One prophecies, so maybe she was the odd one.

"I should *scry* the Stormwatch Citadel," Livia said, but she didn't move to pull out her mirror.

Distantly, a wolf howled.

Everyone sat up. The howl came again, louder, or possibly that of a second wolf. Owen's hand closed on Aderyn's. "That's far away. I doubt it's anything to worry about."

Another howl drowned out his final words. Then a whole chorus of howls shattered the stillness. Jessemia shot to her feet. "Those are rimewolves."

Nobody asked if she was sure. Owen got up and activated the <Sunsword>. "How many?"

"Thirteen, I think." Jessemia stood stiffly, her body angled toward the sound. "Might be fourteen."

"That's fine. We can take them." Owen gestured. "Let's move away from camp to meet them. Better not give ourselves obstacles."

The moon hadn't yet risen, and Owen's <Sunsword> and the small fire were the only sources of light, but Aderyn's [Darkvision] made the vista clear as day, if a day drawn in shades of charcoal. She didn't see the rimewolves, and when she tried Assessing the distance, nothing appeared.

"Over that way," Jessemia said, pointing.

Aderyn faced that direction, northwestward, and Assessed again. This time, [Improved Assess 4] showed her information about the rimewolves approaching them. "It's fourteen. Don't forget about their cold aura damage."

"Got it," Owen said. "Spread out."

They waited. The rimewolves didn't howl again, and they didn't come within sight. Then, terrifyingly, the terrible howl came—from behind the camp.

Owen cursed. "Go—"

"No, it's a feint!" Aderyn shouted. "'Ware the rear, but they're still attacking from this side!"

As she spoke, more howls split the night, and a dozen pale blue bodies rushed the team. Weston, in the front, met the first one's attack with a dagger to its throat. Owen's <Sunsword> blazed as he rushed to meet the other monsters. Aderyn drew Aurelon's sword and joined him. Owen vaulted past his chosen opponent, and [Outflank] tugged at Aderyn's body. Slashing and thrusting, she drove the rimewolf onto Owen's blade.

Congratulations! You have defeated [Rimewolf]. You have earned [10,000 XP]

Two more rimewolves pressed Aderyn from either side, and a third snapped at her from the rear. She searched for a way out and found nothing. Owen was screaming her name from much too far away. "Owen, [Interchange]!" she boomed out with [Amplify Voice].

As she said it, she knew it was a mistake. She'd never tried this newest skill before and had no idea how to activate it. She parried an attack from one of the rimewolves and cast about frantically for a solution, willing the system to be on her side.

A red circle appeared around her feet. As she focused on it, it rose up into a translucent cylinder that completely enclosed her. The rimewolves continued to attack, apparently unmoved by the red veil that didn't conceal her. Aderyn parried again, struck hard enough to make the first rimewolf whimper, and turned her attention on Owen. She couldn't see his feet past their enemies, but in just a second, a blue cylinder rose around him, identical to hers except for the color. Aderyn didn't waste time being amazed. She parried another blow.

Just as she expected rimewolf jaws to tear out her throat, cool air that smelled of roses rushed over her face. Now the cylinder surrounding her was blue, and it was retracting into the ground. No rimewolves threatened her. She turned around and saw Owen standing where she had been, fiercely attacking her opponents.

She got herself back into position for **[Outflank]** just as Owen skewered one of the rimewolves. Between them, they killed all three rapidly. The system defeat notices popped up too rapidly to read.

Distantly, she heard Zalk call her name. Then, more loudly, Freta's terrified scream of "Aderyn! *Watch your rear!*" spun her around and into a rank wind that smelled of corpses.

Before her stood the biggest wolf she'd ever seen, bigger than the rimewolves, bigger than anything her nightmares could conjure. Its mouth hung open in a snarl, and another gust of stinking, chill wind blew over her.

Aderyn realized she'd lowered her sword. She tried to bring it to the ready, but her muscles wouldn't obey her. Someone nearby was shouting at her, but her mind was too numb for anything but **[Improved Assess 4]**.

Name: Bloodmaw

Type: Abomination

Power level: 20

Terrain: boreal forest, tundra, ice sheets

Attack(s): bite, claw x2, special

Immune to: elemental damage cold, elemental damage water

Resistant to: [Distraction], [Fascination], [Cause Fear], light-based attacks

Vulnerable to: elemental damage fire
Special attacks: ice aura, chilling howl, freezing breath
Rimewolves fear their greater counterparts, and greater rimewolves fear Bloodmaw. Part leader of the pack, part master of beasts, Bloodmaw has one desire: to sweep the Northlands clean of giants and humans alike.

Despite this, Bloodmaw has the same resistances and vulnerabilities as an ordinary rimewolf, if I can call such creatures ordinary. In addition to his ice aura and chilling howl, he also has a breath attack similar to an ice dragon's. Don't stand there like a ninny, Aderyn, or you'll find out about it first hand!

Someone tackled Aderyn, bringing her down just as Bloodmaw breathed out a gale filled with glittering, sharp-edged ice crystals. She caught the edge of his breath attack along her shoulder and hip and the hair at the side of her head. It didn't feel freezing, it felt like fire burning wherever it touched, and she let out a pained cry and struggled away from the person pinning her down. "Aderyn, damn it, wake up!" Owen shouted.

She stared up from the ground at Bloodmaw, who hadn't moved after breathing on her. His large, dark-pupiled eyes gazed at her with frightening intelligence. Then he let out a howl, not a terrifying one but one that sounded like a summoning, and turned his back on Aderyn and Owen. In seconds, he had disappeared into the darkness.

Aderyn sat up and gingerly touched her shoulder. Frost coated her fingers, and the leather of her coat cracked into frozen slivers where she touched it. "Bloodmaw," she said. "Why did he flee?"

"He didn't flee," Owen said, helping her to her feet. "He was taunting us. That was a test. And I'm pretty sure we failed."

Aderyn nodded. "They had us surrounded. Though without Bloodmaw, I think we might have won. Was anyone hurt?"

"Isold took a blow to the chest as he was defending our non-combatants, but the <Robe of Sprockets and Cogs> absorbed most of the damage. Are you all right? Aderyn, I thought for sure you were dead when you just stood there like an idiot with that mouth inches from your head!"

"It was a test," Aderyn said absently. On a whim, she brought up the Codex and focused on the **[Fated One's Destiny: Eye of the Storm]** sub-quests.

[Pursue the Hunters]
Rimewolf packs have begun hunting giants throughout the Northlands. Their leader, Bloodmaw, is taking advantage of the destruction caused by the tempest moth to accomplish his goal, which is to drive all giants and humans out of the territory so he can rule as absolute master. Prevent this from happening.

"Well, crap," she muttered.

"What was that?" Owen asked.

She sighed. "Our task just got a lot more complicated."

"Look," Aderyn said five minutes later, "it's not as complicated as I thought. There's the tempest moth, which has changed its pattern for we don't know why, and there's Bloodmaw, who uses the devastation the tempest moth causes to help him kill giants. And the humans who are in the Northlands trying to settle or hunting for that Winterforge dungeon, I guess. But Bloodmaw was killing giants before the tempest moth happened. So his motives are actually independent of it."

"But the two are both sub-quests of the **[Eye of the Storm]** quest," Owen said. "So they have to be linked in more than coincidental ways."

"I think I see Aderyn's point," Weston said. "You're right, Owen, but we don't have to know why they're linked, because we could complete one of them without completing the other."

Owen nodded. "Okay. I get it. It's just that I want everything tied up with a neat little bow."

"Also understandable," Isold said.

"What should we do?" Zalk asked.

"Um. Nothing, I think," Aderyn said. "Your quest is the citadel."

"Yes, but you said Bloodmaw is killing giants. Shouldn't we do something about it? We're giants, too." Zalk's face was pale in the firelight, but his voice was strong.

"That's admirable, Zalk," Owen said. "But there's no reason you should feel obligated to fight a level twenty monster at your level. At least not directly. If you make the tempest moth return to its old flight pattern, you'll have deprived Bloodmaw of a weapon. That's a way to strike at him without risking yourselves."

"Oh." Zalk's brow furrowed in thought. "That's true."

"Good, because not even Taavek is that crazy," Skalt said.

Taavek gave him a good-natured shove. "I'm not the one who suggested fighting that monster, am I?"

"I'm going to *scry* now, before any more level twenty horrors attack," Livia said. "Everyone else stand watch—no, Aderyn, you stay with me in case level nineteen means you can do **[Improved Assess 4]** through a *scrying* mirror."

Aderyn didn't think much of her chances, but she wanted to see the citadel, so she settled beside Livia where she had a clear view of the mirror. Livia chanted, and the mirror's surface flashed bright silver as if struck by a stray sunbeam. The brightness vanished, and a moonlit vista took its place.

Livia tilted the mirror, which showed the same devastated wasteland they'd walked through all day. It seemed to be the Northlands' default state unless giants had carved settlements out of it. "I wish I'd thought to do this while we still had daylight. The moon is good, but it could be better."

The view shifted as if they were a bird sailing high above the ground. "How do you find things when you've never seen them?" Aderyn said.

"With *greater scry,* I can *scry* a destination easily," Livia said. "That's just choosing a spot and directing the mirror there. Like *clairvoyance,* only it doesn't have to be nearby. Harder is *scrying* out a person, but even that isn't difficult at my level. But if I want to find a building, I have to know that it exists and roughly where it—wait, there's something."

Aderyn looked closer. The ground, which had been irregular and rough, now looked weirdly geometric. It took her vision a moment to register what she was seeing: the mostly-destroyed walls and rubble of a city. She had no idea how old the destruction was or if it had been deliberate or just the result of abandonment, but she guessed it was only recognizable as a former city from the air.

Then the vision was blocked out by something large and dark, like a curtain over their view. Aderyn held her breath. "That's it," Livia murmured, and the curtain fell away as the view backed up. Vast walls of granite blocks rising to parapets and wall-walks and towers filled the *scrying* oval.

"Can you Assess it?" Livia asked.

Aderyn tried. "No."

The view fell apart, and Aderyn saw only her reflection and Livia's in the mirror. "No more?" she said.

"I've seen what I need for *world door* to work," Livia said. "No point staring at the place if there's nothing we can do about it—not to criticize."

"I understood you." Aderyn stretched. "Tomorrow is soon enough. Good night."

Rather than go to her tent, she went in search of Jessemia, who always had first watch. She found her friend walking the perimeter with Whiskers loping at her side and occasionally darting away to investigate the movements of small creatures in the undergrowth. "Jessemia. Is something going on with you and Isold?"

With [Darkvision], Jessemia's expression was clear. Once again, Jessemia looked momentarily as if she'd been struck to the heart. "I don't know what you mean. There's nothing between us."

"Jessemia, I saw how you looked this afternoon, and I'm worried. I don't want you to be miserable. Is it—"

"Aderyn. Listen to me. There is *nothing* between us." Jessemia's voice shook. "You can't fix that. Go to sleep. Please."

Aderyn almost pushed harder. Jessemia sounded like someone near breaking. She realized in time how cruel pushing would be, if Jessemia was in love with Isold and he didn't love her. She had no right to interfere. "I—never mind. You're right. I'm sorry I brought it up."

Jessemia surprised her with a hug. "You're a good friend to care so much. Get to bed, all right? Tomorrow we might face terrible danger. You'll need your rest."

"True. Facing Bloodmaw exhausted me. Good night."

Despite her words, she slept poorly, anticipation making her wakeful. She stood her watch in her mended coat and wished her vision was good enough to see all the way to Stormwatch Citadel. Now that they were so close, she was excited the way she always got when facing a new dungeon. Killing monsters was satisfying, quests were exciting, but dungeons could be anything.

The following morning dawned grey and cold, filling Aderyn with an eagerness to take the next step on their quest. Surely the inside of Stormwatch Citadel had to be warmer than this? They all gathered closely around Livia, who made a face. "*World door* doesn't require us stepping on each other's toes. Back up and let me cast the spell."

"I'll go first, then Aderyn," Owen said. "Then Jessemia, in case her wilderness map expands more on seeing Stormwatch Citadel. Then the younglings, Isold, and Weston. You're sure this won't render you unconscious?"

"Pretty sure. If I'm wrong, I'll drink the rejuvenation potion before casting it for myself—that's really where I'm unsure, whether I'll have enough energy for the last one. But I'll know that before it's an issue." Livia patted the potion bottle filled with red liquid hanging at her side.

"Okay. Then we're set."

Livia gestured, chanting a series of words that were almost intelligible, and the wooden oval of *world door* appeared. Owen stepped through and immediately flattened into a painting of himself from behind.

Aderyn glanced around. The wind had picked up, and Jessemia had said a storm was coming in a few hours. "We'll be long gone by then," she'd said. Aderyn hoped she was right. After the encounter with the tempest moth, storms felt sinister even when they were normal.

Owen's shape disappeared, followed by the *world door* oval. Livia took a deep breath and chanted again. This time, when the oval appeared, Aderyn stepped through it.

Livia's skills were improving; the floor was soft and had only a little give instead of throwing Aderyn off-balance with its bounciness, and the walls were pearlescent and only faintly translucent. Aderyn didn't like the shapes that swam beyond the walls and was just as happy not to see them.

Ahead, the end of the *world door* was a vista of gray skies that looked like a discolored curtain stretched over the opening. It never seemed to get any closer—until she was suddenly out. For once, she didn't stumble upon exiting.

Owen stood only a few steps away, staring into the distance. Aderyn joined him, and clasped his hand without saying anything. Ahead, less than half a mile away, stood Stormwatch Citadel.

At first, its size confused her vision. Then she realized it was much farther away than half a mile. At a casual glance, it looked like a typical ancient castle: low walls sheltering a courtyard, taller keep set to one side. A closer look showed that the lower walls alone had to be sixty feet tall, while the keep itself was so much taller Aderyn didn't have anything to compare it to. Towers at each of the keep's corners rose another fifty feet above the crenellated walls, with more crenellations atop each tower. Their height gave them a true bird's-eye view of the countryside. Aderyn imagined clouds snagging on them on a stormy day. She had never seen anything so obviously meant to withstand a siege, not even in the southlander kingdom, not even Charnel Keep.

The ruins of a great city covered the plains between where they stood and the citadel. The nearest remains, a truncated stone wall in which was framed a doorway twelve feet high, showed this had been a giants' city. None of the wood framework remained, and the wall looked poised to come down at any moment.

Someone came up beside Aderyn, staggering under the weight of a dire otter. "That must be Stormwatch Citadel, because I just received experience for completing the escort quest," Jessemia said, letting Whiskers drop out of her arms. "And I leveled to eleven!"

"Congratulations! I guess you were closer than you thought."

"I guess so." Jessemia drew in a deep breath, sniffing the storm winds. "This place is astonishing. Can you imagine it when it was alive?"

"You think of it as dead?"

"Don't you?" Jessemia inhaled deeply again. "It smells of old stone and decay, not at all like a city filled with people all going about their business. Thriving cities have life. This one—even if the buildings were restored, it would still be dead."

This line of conversation discomfited Aderyn. "What does your map tell you? Anything different?"

"I already had Stormwatch Citadel marked on my map. Now I see the river—all right, of course I see the river, it's right there. I mean it shows on my map. It goes all the way to the coast, which isn't far from here. There are other landscape features, too, but nothing that helps us now."

Aderyn nodded. "All right. Time for me to Assess."

Name: Stormwatch Citadel

Type: Standard, huge, victory condition variant C or D

Power Level: 18

Inhabitants: abominations, formless, magical beasts, monstrosities, plants, vermin

Traps: none

Environmental hazards: occasional

Reward: 5,051 gold equivalent at current rates of exchange AND/OR the defeat of the tempest moth

Stormwatch Citadel was the heart of the capital of the Northlands back in the days when humans shared the land with giants. Though the citadel was built by and for giants, it has quarters sized for humans too, as you'll see once you're inside. The reasons for the giants and humans abandoning the city aren't important. I know, you want to know anyway. Let's just say the level cap created differences of

opinion about how the Northlands should be governed, and leave the rest to your imagination.

Why, you ask, was the city destroyed, but the citadel remains mostly intact? Stormwatch Citadel has at its heart a magical... let's call it a device that controls the tempest moth's pattern, keeping it from destroying the settlements. To protect that device, the builders imbued the citadel with as many magical protections as Spellcrafters and Plovers could devise, rendering the structure unbreakable by normal means and impervious to the effects of weather and time. When it became a dungeon some ten years after its abandonment, it became even more durable. Sure, your Earthbreaker friend could level it with enough time, but that would be pointless. And you're not the type to commit wanton destruction, anyway.

It's that device you're here for. Ordinarily, questers defeat Stormwatch Citadel by achieving victory condition C, which means gaining a threshold amount of experience that varies according to the average party level. Victory condition D, however, requires you to find the device and return it to working order so it can again repel the tempest moth. Don't count on your <Wayfinder> to lead you to it. The nature of the device misleads all finding magic. I can't tell you why, but when you find it, you'll understand.

"What did you see?" Jessemia asked as Aderyn was reading the final paragraph.

Aderyn blinked and let her gaze focus on the distant building. She absently put a hand on Whiskers's head, stopping him romping around her legs. "A mystery," she said. "And one we won't unravel quickly."

CHAPTER TWENTY-SEVEN

"But the level cap had something to do with humans leaving the Northlands," Aderyn said five minutes later when they were all gathered together. "And it meant giants abandoned the citadel, too. Doesn't that sound like something we should care about, if our ultimate goal is breaking the level cap?"

"I agree, Aderyn, but what can we do about it now?" Owen said. "We're not in a position to dig up history. Maybe it's something we'll learn when we're inside, but we shouldn't count on it. Zalk, what can you tell us about this place?"

"Me? Nothing." Zalk couldn't take his eyes off the distant citadel. "Giants don't live in places like this. There aren't even records of it happening before. I assumed Stormwatch Citadel was a human construction."

"That's not what **[Improved Assess 4]** says. Something must have happened to change your civilization, maybe the level cap, maybe something else." Aderyn regarded the ruins around them. "And this is a really big change."

"I agree with Owen. It's not something we can discover," Freta said. "It's better to look to the future, anyway. We aren't going back to whatever giants used to be."

"We don't know that either," Taavek said. "What if it turns out we lost something important?"

"Stop," Owen said. "These are all possibilities, but we have to stay focused. There's a magic item in that castle we have to find and repair. That's the goal. Everything else is—not unimportant, maybe, but not essential to our task. Are we agreed?"

The younglings all nodded.

"Aderyn, have you tried the <**Wayfinder**>?" Owen asked.

"I did. I don't know why the system tried to steer me away from using it, because it points right at the castle, just like always." Aderyn brandished the <**Wayfinder**> at the citadel in defiance. "But I'm not ruling out the possibility that once we're inside, things will change."

"Okay. Let's go. Keep your eyes open—these ruins are the perfect place for monsters to hide. And let's see if the Wayfinder can find us the best entrance to reach the device." Owen gestured to Aderyn to precede him. Aderyn concentrated on the <**Wayfinder**>, which immediately turned a soft pink and began spinning. She took a moment to orient herself and then started walking.

Since the <**Wayfinder**> was pointing directly at the citadel, Aderyn paid less attention to it than usual. Instead, she watched the ruins. Despite Owen's words, she didn't feel a sense of menace from them, just that same feeling of emptiness she'd discussed with Jessemia. The ground underfoot felt hard and springy at the same time, and when she scuffed her toe across the ground, the earth scattered, revealing enormous flagstones only a giant or a skilled Earthbreaker could have placed. Based on that and how widely spaced the remnants of walls were, Aderyn thought they were walking along an ancient thoroughfare.

That filled her with unexpected melancholy. Sure, the ancients who'd lived here weren't human, but they were still people, and they'd had lives and hopes and desires, and something had happened to put an end to all of that. She wished she dared ask the system to tell her, but even if she hadn't been surrounded by her friends and reluctant to speak to the system in front of them, the system's words in the Assessment of Stormwatch Citadel suggested it wasn't likely to give her more information. So she kept her curiosity to herself.

The city gave her plenty to be curious about, too. The toppled walls, most of them half-buried in dirt, weren't tall enough to fit giants, but was that because they'd originally been taller, or because some of these had been buildings sized for humans? She tried imagining the layout as it had been when the city was alive, but the spacing and alignment of the wall fragments didn't suggest any one arrangement. It might as well have been a maze as a city.

The ruins were perfectly silent except for human and giant footsteps rasping across the earth-covered stones and the occasional chittering cry from Whiskers. When Aderyn heard birds cheeping, the sound cheered her more than she expected. "I guess it's not so dead if birds can live here."

"Or they're monstrous birds that eat people's livers," Owen said. "Where are they? I don't see them."

"There," Isold said, pointing, just as Weston said, "They're bright red. So much for camouflage."

A flash of red sped past and disappeared behind a wall fragment six feet tall. Aderyn Assessed it, but got nothing. "I missed it. And [Improved Assess 4] only works if there's no solid barrier between me and the monster."

"They haven't attacked," Isold said, "and at the risk of regretting my words, they seem harmless."

"We'll see." Aderyn waited until she was past the wall fragment, then turned **[Improved Assess 4]** on its far side. She saw a blob of crimson tucked into a crevice made by two cracked stones before silver text appeared.

Name: Quillwing [22]
Type: Magical beast
Power level: 13
Terrain: high-elevation forests, cities
Attack(s): claw x2, special
Immune to: none
Resistant to: none
Vulnerable to: none
Special attacks: spinning dart attack

Quillwings are surprisingly beautiful, if you think pigeons are beautiful. You don't? Well, anyway, they are blood-red birds shaped like pigeons, sort of like bloated cardinals. They don't tend to attack creatures much larger than they are, so you're safe unless you threaten their nests, in which case, good luck.

A quillwing's primary attack is a mid-air spin in which they shoot the barbed feathers from their wings like darts at their victim. The spin gives the little darts some extra momentum, and the attack is surprisingly painful, though generally not lethal. The reason for the quillwings' relatively high power level is that they're incredibly hard to hit when they're on the wing. And, of course, there's always the chance they'll put someone's eye out with a feather.

Now that she knew what to look for, Aderyn saw dozens of red blotches, either nesting or zipping past from one hiding place to another. "They're called quillwings," she said. "They won't aggress on us unless we threaten their nests."

"We can't see their nests," Owen said.

"Well, there are a lot of them, and it's not a fight we—"

Weston ducked as a quillwing swept past his head. "Are you sure about the not aggressing?"

"Of course. Just ignore it." As she spoke, a streak of red shot past inches from her face. She flinched. "Maybe not."

"Who knows what they consider aggression?" Livia said.

"They're just birds, though," Taavek said. "It's not like they're dangerous." He tapped the stone beneath one of the niches, one recently vacated by a quillwing. "See? They run away from us."

"Taavek, please don't interfere with the birds," Aderyn said.

Another quillwing swooped past, but slowly, its flight path curving upward until the bird hovered at the peak of the arc. "Watch out!" Aderyn shouted. "It's going to—"

Gracefully, the quillwing spun in midair, its wings gradually stretching to full extension, until it was a crimson blur. A dozen barb-tipped feathers shot away from its body, striking Taavek and Freta in the face. "Ow!" Freta shrieked. "That hurt!"

"Let's move," Owen said. "We need to get out of their territory."

"Too late," Weston said. Three more quillwings arced into position. Suddenly the air was full of flying barbed feathers and fat red birds swooping down on the friends. Freta screamed again and ran for it, blindly caroming off fallen masonry and ducking away from the missiles. More quillwings chased her, diving on her as well as flinging barbs, and she wildly waved her arms in a futile attempt to shoo them away.

"Crap," Owen said. "Somebody stop her!"

The ground rumbled, and stones rose up around Freta, blocking her path. Freta turned, but the stones kept rising, herding her back toward their group. Aderyn drew her sword and searched for a target. She swung at the nearest quillwing, which swept past rapidly and was gone before Aderyn connected. More birds dove at her. She slashed about with increasing ferocity and never hit once.

A system defeat notice appeared.

Congratulations! You have defeated [Quillwing].
You have earned [9950 XP]

"That was luck," Weston said. "We need a Deadeye. These little bastards are fast."

Whiskers reared up on his hind legs and swatted a quillwing to the ground, where he pounced on it and tore its head off between his jaws. "Good boy, Whiskers!" Jessemia exclaimed. "We both got experience for that kill, I think." She shrieked and dropped to a crouch to avoid a spray of barbed feathers.

"They move too fast for **[Reposition]**, too," Aderyn complained. As if the system heard her, a lucky strike from her weapon sent a quillwing spinning across the road to where Owen sliced it in half with the <**Sunsword**>.

"We can't fight them," Owen said. His face was stippled with blood from the many feather dart attacks. "They'll wear us down, and we can't afford to waste energy on chasing them. Everybody run!"

Aderyn sheathed her sword, clutched the <**Wayfinder**> in her left hand, and ran, tugged along with Owen by **[Keep Pace]**. More darts flew past, some of them striking the back of her head with painful twinges. Tiny thumps marked where the barbs struck the <**Gossamer Mail**> and bounced off. Ahead of her, the three giants caught up to Freta, and Skalt and Taavek grabbed her beneath the arms and dragged her with them.

In the next moment, Isold passed her, his long legs flying. Weston and Jessemia drew even with her. Weston had Whiskers in his arms and looked to be fighting a losing battle against the dire otter's wiggling. Then Livia surged past, surfing a wave of stone and earth, and shouted, "They stopped following us!"

Everyone gathered around, all except Livia breathing heavily. Weston let Whiskers slide free and heaved a deep breath. Owen bent over, gripping his knees, and sucked in air. "That was embarrassing."

"I'm sorry, I think it was my fault," Taavek said.

"You're not the one who panicked," Freta muttered. "It was like being dived on by hostile bees. I hate bees."

"I think we intruded on their territory just by walking along the road," Aderyn said. "Still, this was a good lesson. Never assume a monster is harmless no matter how they look."

"And stay together," Owen added. "If we outrun each other, that leaves us defenseless and without allies."

"I understand," Freta and Taavek said together.

Aderyn once more took the lead, half her attention on the <Wayfinder> and half on her surroundings. The quillwings hadn't been deadly, but it was sheer luck that was the monster they'd come across and not rimewolves or something else equally dangerous. She occasionally Assessed the road ahead, but nothing ever appeared.

The closer they got to the citadel, the more intact the buildings were. "It's like the dungeon has a protective aura or something," Aderyn said to Owen. "I mean, it's probably not that really, but who knows what protections those long-dead giants put on it?"

"I was going to say maybe there's a prevailing wind, and these buildings are in the lee of the citadel, but it would have to be a damn powerful wind," Owen replied.

"You mean, the kind of wind the tempest moth brings?"

"Um. You have a point." He walked past the nearest structure, which was two walls that met at a corner and had window holes in both, looking closely at its base. "I don't know what I'm looking for."

"Something is keeping these walls up," Livia said. "I can feel it. A constant trembling beneath the soil. But I would have said it was the sort of thing that knocks buildings over instead of supporting them. You know, like how if you constantly shake a table eventually everything on it gets vibrated off? This is doing the opposite. I think it might actually be a feature of the dungeon."

"Interesting. Is it anything we can use?" Owen asked.

"Only if we wanted to destroy the dungeon."

"Which we don't. Okay. Does the <**Wayfinder**> point to a way in? We're getting close."

Within another five minutes, they reached the walls of Stormwatch Citadel. Again, Aderyn felt small and inconsequential. The walls were made of stones so massive Aderyn was sure it would take at least two giants to lift one. Unlike the fallen walls of the city, which were covered in earth and crusted with dying moss, Stormwatch Citadel's massive walls were clear of dirt and debris to the point of looking scrubbed clean. Aderyn laid a hand against the stone. It felt unexpectedly warm against her chilled hand.

"Which way?" Owen asked.

Aderyn consulted the <**Wayfinder**>. "Left. I think the entrance is on the north side, based on the castle's profile."

"What does that mean?" Jessemia asked.

"It was something I noticed before we approached. On this side, the walls are low on the left—the north—and then the castle itself rises above the walls to the south. In all the stories I read, the entrance to a traditional castle is opposite the keep. So that makes this entrance on the north." She laughed. "My parents always said I read too many fantasy stories about kings and castles. Bet they never guessed the knowledge would be useful."

The <**Wayfinder's**> glow continued to deepen as they walked around the base of the citadel until it was a warm, dark red and the rings spun fast enough to give off an audible hum. Ahead, the base of the tower rose, round instead of squared off and bulging so they couldn't see past the corner. Owen gestured for Weston to walk ahead. Weston, moving as silently as always, hurried around the curve of the tower. In seconds, he returned and gestured to the rest of them to follow.

The north side of the citadel didn't at first look different from the west side. Then Aderyn realized something big and blocky jutted out from the wall ahead, a structure not as tall as the rest of the castle. Her first impression was of a cat crouched beside the citadel, guarding its front, thanks to how the lower part of what-ever it was jutted out at its base and the higher part curved like the paw of a sleeping cat.

The <**Wayfinder**> bounced, nearly jumping out of her hand. She clutched it more tightly, and the color drained away and the rings spun to a stop. For a moment, it was hot, and then that, too, was gone. Aderyn reflexively looked around, though nothing had changed and she was sure she hadn't reached her heart's desire.

"The <**Wayfinder**> stopped working," she said to Owen.

"What, for good?"

"I don't think so. It must just be that we've reached the entrance, though I don't see it."

"Let me scout ahead, then," Weston said. "I think that's the entrance. It looks like guard posts from here."

Aderyn kept her fancies about sleeping cats to herself.

She put the <**Wayfinder**> in her pocket and rubbed her hands together. Another sharp breeze had risen, driving the temperature lower, and the heavy storm clouds looked like they meant to gang up on the adventurers and teach them a lesson about wandering around in the open. Weston had reached the guard posts and disappeared beyond the nearer one. The breeze grew louder and sharper, keening like a lost soul. Owen always called the sound "the voices of the damned," but he couldn't explain what being damned meant. It didn't matter. Aderyn got the meaning from context. It certainly sounded like desperate, terrified people crying out for help.

Jessemia tilted her head back, sniffing the air. "There's another storm coming."

"I can see that."

Jessemia ignored the gentle sarcasm. "I mean the kind of sudden storm we encountered before. The kind the tempest moth brings."

The wind gusted, carrying her words away. Aderyn searched the sky and saw nothing unusual. "Are you sure?"

Jessemia pointed east. "Very sure. We need to get inside. Now."

In the eastern sky, clouds billowed, blown about by winds so fast they seemed to roil like a bubbling stew pot. Beyond the clouds, something enormous shifted. Lightning flashed, illuminating a vast insect body and wings that thrashed the winds to a fever pitch.

Aderyn drew in a breath and with **[Amplify Voice]** shouted, "The tempest moth is coming! No more time for caution—everybody run!"

The younglings looked up from where they'd been lounging in the shelter of one of the more intact walls. "*Now!*" Aderyn bellowed, and ran after Weston.

She slowed only once, to make sure Whiskers was keeping up, and then she rounded the guard post extension and stopped, overwhelmed by the sight of a gate more than forty feet tall, made of lengths of wood neatly slotted together and lacquered to make a single enormous slab. It didn't look like it was made to open, though if it was like the keeps she'd read about, it would open inward and be solidly barred from inside.

Owen was shouting at the younglings to get a move on. Aderyn got control of her astonishment and ran to join Weston, followed by Jessemia and Isold. Weston knelt in front of a human-sized door set in the base of the massive one. A sally port, Aderyn's prodigal childhood told her. Weston didn't acknowledge her, all his attention on deftly picking the lock. "Gate's closed," he said. "The mechanism is inside."

"We don't have time for subtlety. The tempest moth—"

"Is coming fast, I know, I heard." The lock ground open. "But if we break through the main gate to get inside, which I'm sure Livia could manage, we'll be exposed to the monster's storm." He flung the door open. "Get inside, quick!"

Aderyn didn't wait to be told twice. With Jessemia on her heels, she tumbled through the doorway into darkness.

CHAPTER TWENTY-EIGHT

L ight from the doorway barely illuminated the space, which was an unfurnished chamber forty feet wide whose ceiling rose too high for Aderyn to see clearly. She hurried forward to make room for the others piling in behind her, though the space was big enough that even with the four giant younglings, nobody was crowded.

The sally port slammed shut, and a moment later Livia filled the air with a dozen *orbs of light*. "I need more of these," she grumbled, casting the spell again. "This place is too big for ordinary light sources."

"There are sconces on the walls," Isold said. "For torches, not lanterns. I'd call it old-fashioned if not for my awareness that this citadel is centuries old, and I have no idea what they would consider modern in their time."

Aderyn followed the flight of a handful of orbs as they sailed up, higher and higher until they lit the distant ceiling. "I don't see windows, and the only door is the one we came in by. I don't get it."

"There's another door," Weston said, "at the far end. And I see arrow slits. This must be part of the citadel's defenses against monster attack. Though I'm not sure what monster would be courteous enough to use the front door." He jogged toward the far side, trailed by lights. With that end illuminated, the second door was obvious. It was much larger than the sally port, with two slabs of laminated oak like the front door that weren't quite as big, and there was no visible latch.

"How are we supposed to get out of here?" Aderyn said.

"The door's actually open a crack," Weston said. He leaned against one half of the door and pushed, putting his weight behind it. A tremendous shriek of rusted metal filled the air. Weston winced, but went on pushing. Owen and Isold joined him. Slowly, the door creaked open.

"Hey, we can do that," Taavek exclaimed. He put both hands against the wood, well above the men's heads, and shoved. The door shot open, and to the screech of tortured iron was added the wail of a thousand freezing winds. Aderyn registered the big open area beyond the doors, the snow whipping through the air, and shouted, "Close the door!"

The winds were already abating, but Aderyn knew that didn't mean the storm was over. Her heart racing, she ducked under Weston's arm and grabbed the edge of the door as he and Owen and Isold hauled on it. It closed even more slowly, like something dragged on it from the other side. The light was fading like sunset —a sunset at ten o'clock in the morning. Despair clutched at Aderyn's heart. The tempest moth was coming to destroy them all.

The howl of the winds became distant as a titanic shadow spread over the citadel's courtyard, blotting out what little light remained. Aderyn's fingertips were raw from pulling on the oak. She didn't know why she was still trying, because fighting the tempest moth was pointless. But she couldn't stop pulling. Her fingers felt frozen to the door.

The door thudded back into place, nearly taking Aderyn's fingers with it. She pulled free in time and stood staring blankly at the flat wooden surface. "It almost had us."

"That can't have been normal," Owen said. He was breathing heavily and his hair was disordered from the wind. "All I could think was that it was over, that we had no hope. But now those thoughts are distant, like the memory of a dream."

"I felt that when we first encountered the creature as well," Isold said. "Despair and hopelessness. That must be what Vorn said was an effect of the tempest moth."

"And I forgot to Assess it. Again." Aderyn slammed her fist against the wood. The twinge of pain that shot down her arm made her despair retreat further, replaced by a more normal frustration. "We're never going to be able to fight that thing."

"Was that the plan?" Weston said. "Because I thought we were going to defeat it by activating this device so it flies away and never comes back. I don't think we can fight it no matter what [Improved Assess 4] tells us."

"But we're stuck in here until it goes away, and it might not go away," Freta said. "Doesn't that mean fighting it?"

"No," Livia said. She was walking the length of the chamber, trailing a hand along the wall. "There's open space beyond here."

"You can sense that?" Freta exclaimed.

"Well, the arrow slits are a good clue, but yes. I can make an exit that bypasses whatever is beyond those doors. Courtyard, maybe."

The relief Aderyn felt at this statement embarrassed her. "That's fantastic."

"It will take a little while. I don't want to bring the citadel down on our heads." Livia stopped and leaned against the wall with both hands pressed flat against it. "Let me take a look." She exhaled deeply, then walked through the wall.

Skalt and Taavek drew in identical deep breaths. "I don't know anyone who can do that," Skalt said. "Not even the oldest People would dare."

"Is it forbidden?" Jessemia said.

"Is it forbidden to walk off a cliff?" Taavek said. "Nobody needs to forbid it because everyone knows how dangerous it is."

Livia reappeared, though her stone hand remained inside the wall like she was using it to mark her place in a book. "It's a big, empty room, and there's two doors. One of them probably leads to the courtyard, or at least it's parallel to this one. Not sure about the other, but it can't be worse than staying here."

"Famous last words," Weston said, but he was grinning.

They waited, sitting or standing, while Livia shaped an arched doorway out of the wall. Aderyn balled up a pair of dirty socks and tossed it for Whiskers to fetch. The dire otter didn't seem distressed at being so long away from water. It was hard to imagine him as a predator of anything but fish—but Aderyn remembered him tearing the head off a quillwing, and then it was all too easy.

From where she sat, part of the new room was visible through the doorway thanks to more of Livia's *orbs of light*. It was just as Livia had said, big and empty. Still, it was the first step into a new dungeon, and something exciting might be beyond it.

Finally, Livia said, "That's it." The arched entry was tall and wide enough to admit a youngling giant and glowed with light. Aderyn let Owen go first, containing her impatience. Despite her low expectations, the sight of the empty room disappointed her. She'd hoped for at least a few pieces of furniture that would hint at the room's purpose. But rusty iron sconces were all that said the room had once been occupied.

Weston prowled the room's perimeter as the others gathered

near the door. "I can hear the storm when I'm near that one," he said, pointing at the other door. "No idea about the other. But I'm sure this used to be a guard post."

"How can you tell?" Livia asked.

"The flagstones are worn down in places that aren't at random. Here, and here, near the arrow slits, that suggests decades or even centuries of guards watching the entrance. And over here, there are marks where something scraped across the stones for those same centuries. It was giant sized, but it was a desk."

"And look at how the sconces are closer together here, so they'd provide more light to the person at the desk," Jessemia said.

"You two ought to be a detective team," Owen joked.

"Is that a human thing?" Zalk asked.

Aderyn nudged Owen and glared at him. "Yes, it's a human thing," she said. "I think we should see what's beyond the door."

"Aderyn's Assessment said there weren't traps, but we should be cautious anyway." Weston eyed the latch, which was a knob of tarnished brass at eye level. "I hope none of these are locked, because I don't see the mechanism." He slowly turned the knob one way, then the other, until the latch clicked and the door sprang open.

The door was wide enough for two humans to pass through simultaneously. Aderyn followed Weston, trailed by a cluster of glowing orbs, into a hall whose ceiling was again too tall to see. The hall was as wide as the entrance and extended in both directions, but to the right, it ended only fifty or sixty feet away. The light revealed a few wooden doors, giant sized, on both sides of the hall.

"I feel so tiny," Jessemia said. "Whiskers, stay close."

"What do we do?" Taavek asked.

"You four, stay near the middle for now," Owen commanded the younglings. "Aderyn, what does the <**Wayfinder**> say?"

Aderyn let her heart fill with a desire to find the device that would defeat the tempest moth. As the seconds passed, her desires grew stronger until they made her body tingle with urgency. The <Wayfinder> began spinning. She held it in front of her and turned in a slow arc, willing it to show her her heart's desire. As she turned right, toward the end of the hall, the spinning increased, and the central spike glowed a warm pink. "There—"

The ball gave a little hiccupping bounce. Aderyn clutched it tighter. Immediately, it stilled and darkened. Aderyn loosed her grip, but nothing changed. The <Wayfinder> remained inert.

"That way?" Owen asked.

"I don't know. It pointed that way, and then it deactivated. Just the way it does when I reach my heart's desire." Aderyn inhaled deeply and let out her breath in a long, thin stream. "Let me try again."

This time, the <Wayfinder> pointed the other direction, down the dark hallway. Without waiting for the others, Aderyn took a few steps that way. The magic item continued to glow for a few seconds, then hiccupped again and turned dark and still.

"All right," she said, returning to her friends. "I don't think the <Wayfinder> is broken. The Assessment said there was something about the device that interferes with locator magic. I think it's more basic than that. I think the device is moving around. Maybe *transporting*. That would explain why the <Wayfinder> can latch onto its location and then lose it."

"That could be a problem," Weston said. "We can explore the old-fashioned way, sure, but if the device moves that quickly, and maybe teleports all over the dungeon, getting our hands on it could be difficult."

"But it can't be impossible, or the system wouldn't allow the quest," Owen said. "Exploring the dungeon will give us more information, and if the device is moving, maybe what we need to look for is the means to capture it. Which is going to take time, but we're not on a deadline."

"Except for the tempest moth's destruction," Skalt said.

"Yes, true. I guess it's more accurate to say we don't have a countdown. We still have to move quickly, but it's not like Charnel Keep with its twenty-four-hour timer." Owen checked the hallway like he thought it might have changed while he was talking. "We're at one corner of the citadel. Isold, what does your map say?"

"This is the northwest corner, which means one of these doors leads to the tower on that side." Isold's eyes roved over his invisible map. "That glimpse we had of the big open space was enough to fill in my map with the full courtyard. It is far too large for us to have crossed with the tempest moth attacking, in case you were wondering."

"Then we go... that way." Owen pointed at the door nearest the end of the hall. "Let's find the tower."

The door was unlocked. Weston opened it quietly and peered inside. "Huh. Bedframes."

The others followed him inside. Aderyn had pictured wooden beds without mattresses, but these were made of iron bars as thick as her thigh, bent and in some places fused together to form giant bedframes two beds high. Aderyn recalled her friend Jinty back in Far Haven, who had three sisters and seven brothers. Their house wasn't much bigger than average, and the children had beds stacked atop each other like these to take advantage of all the available space. Aderyn had secretly wished for a bed like those, but this room smelled of rust and damp and killed that wish dead.

"Barracks, I bet," Weston said. "And there's the tower entrance." It was an arched doorway with no door, similar to the one Livia had sculpted, and when Aderyn investigated, she discovered wide, steep stairs going up in a tight corkscrew. It was too big for her to feel claustrophobic even if that fear still tormented her, which it didn't, but she still felt the urge to duck her head.

"We leave it for now. No sense going upstairs when we haven't fully explored this level." Owen peered up the stairs like despite his words he wanted to check out their possibilities. "But this is heartening. So far, these giants had lives like humans, nothing bizarre we can't interpret."

"That's not heartening, it's disturbing," Skalt said. "The People don't build like this. I don't even know what a barracks is. Why would we have changed so much?"

"Humans have changed over time, too," Aderyn said. "Not just the level cap, but the way we govern ourselves. We humans don't have kingdoms anymore, not like they do in the south, and yet we have stories about kings and princesses."

"Skalt's right, though," Taavek said. "All of this is built to fit us, and yet the People who built it might as well have been human for all they have anything in common with us. It's weird."

"Don't let it get to you," Weston said, clapping Taavek on the back, which was all the farther he could reach. "We'll learn more as we go, and I bet eventually it all makes sense."

"You are in a position to bring back great knowledge to the People," Isold said. "Consider this part of your quest."

Taavek nodded. He didn't look convinced, but he didn't say anything else.

They proceeded south along the hallway, passing a door on the left— "That's the courtyard," Isold said—and discovering another barracks room on the right.

"I don't get it," Livia said when they'd determined the room was empty. "Humans and giants coexisted before the level cap, so who were all these soldiers meant to fight? Do you think the Northlands was a kingdom like the Southlands once?"

"If the Northlands had a kingdom and an army, they might

have functioned the way Varoun's army did, issuing quests to pursue monsters and so forth." Isold was examining his map as he spoke. "It's horrifying to think of turning that army on non-monstrous people, but that's also a possibility."

"I can't even imagine going to battle against humans I don't have a personal stake in defeating," Aderyn said. "I guess, fighting Brigands, but Brigands don't form groups large enough to require an army to fight them."

"I can't imagine it at all," Jessemia said. She put two fingers to her lips and whistled to Whiskers. "It sounds so impersonal. Surely there's no way a thousand people could have the same goal of eliminating a thousand other people?"

"You should see how it works in my—I mean, it's possible in other places," Owen said. "Let's keep moving."

"What's that light?" Zalk asked, pointing.

A spot of white light the size of a pinhead bobbed at the far end of the hallway, past the range of Livia's lights. Despite its small size, it glowed so brilliantly it hurt Aderyn's eyes. She squinted, her eyes watering, and tried to bring it into focus without it burning a hole in her eyeballs. She couldn't tell how far away it was.

"It's moving," Jessemia said. "Toward us."

To Aderyn, it seemed to be growing rather than moving closer, but in either case it was ominous. She focused on a point above the brightness and Assessed it.

Name: Ball Lightning [5]
Type: Formless
Power level: 13
Terrain: fields, mountains
Attack(s): whip x3, special
Immune to: precision damage, [Outflank], elemental fire

damage, elemental cold damage, mind control skills and spells

Resistant to: weapons damage

Vulnerable to: elemental water damage

Special attacks: engulf, lightning whip, electric shock

City dwellers consider ball lightning a myth because it never appears there. This is like not believing in sharks because they don't walk on land. You've met weresharks, so you're not that foolish.

But you want to know about ball lightning. The creatures form in areas where violent storms distort the air out of shape, thickening it and providing a framework for ambient electrical fields to collect and intensify. They are structurally not much more than this, and if they were aquatic, they'd float. More on that later.

Ball lightning hunts by pretending indifference to its prey. It's so pretty most prey animals are happy to gaze on it —right up until it strikes with its lightning whip. The whip attack does physical damage in addition to electrical damage, and if it entangles you, the whip can retract into the monster's body, bringing you with it. Being engulfed by ball lightning is usually fatal for low-level adventurers, and it's no picnic for your level, either.

The one thing ball lightning is vulnerable to is elemental water damage, which breaks down its fragile structure and grounds the lightning so it dissipates. It takes a *lot* of water to do this if the creature is large enough, so don't get excited.

I did say ball lightning's terrain is fields and mountains, didn't I? You may well ask why they are here in this abandoned castle. You won't get the answer now, but have patience.

In the time it took for Aderyn to read all this, two more spots of white light had appeared, and the ball lightning in front was close enough to be visible as a sphere trailing tendrils of wispy white light. None of her friends had moved. Jessemia, nearest Aderyn, wore a dreamy expression as she stared at the oncoming monsters.

"They're attacking!" Aderyn shouted. "Wake up! Livia, you need to *drench* them!"

With a loud chittering sound, Whiskers launched himself at the nearest ball lightning with his awkward loping gait. Jessemia shook herself. "No, Whiskers, come back!"

Whiskers ignored her. The chittering had become a long, drawn-out growl. The ball lightning continued to drift, seeming nothing more than a harmless apparition. Then, with a snap, one of its wispy tendrils solidified and lashed out. Whiskers howled as the whip wrapped around his foreleg and dragged him toward the jagged-edged hole in the orb's side that gaped open to engulf him.

CHAPTER TWENTY-NINE

J essemia drew her sword and plunged forward, shouting Whiskers's name. "No!" Aderyn screamed. "Livia, water destroys them! Hurry!"

An enormous gout of water fell out of the air over the ball lightning. The monster let out a high-pitched squeal that felt like an icepick through Aderyn's eardrums. Wincing, she drew Aurelon's sword and rushed after Jessemia as all around her the others shook themselves free of the fugue the ball lighting had put them in.

Livia's *drench* had struck the back half of the ball lightning, disintegrating its surface and revealing a fine network of electrical bolts zipping around, crackling loudly, within the creature's body. It reminded Aderyn of how a snowball looked when you poured a stream of water over it, the insides partially eaten away, the water continuing to creep over the surface as it apparently melted. Despite this, the ball lightning didn't react as if half of it was gone. It continued to drag Whiskers toward it. Whiskers bit and clawed at the electric whip, chittering furiously.

Jessemia skidded on the water covering the floor, converted the skid into a controlled slide, and slashed at the whip, severing it. The severed end turned black and limp. Whiskers shrugged free of the whip's coils and struck the monster with his claws, raking grooves across the weird surface that filled back in almost immediately.

Jessemia shouted a wordless cry of fury and stabbed the ball lightning through its open mouth. Its squeal of pain intensified, but it didn't fall. Aderyn reached Jessemia's side and slashed in the same place Whiskers had clawed it. Her sword bit deep. Aderyn's relief lasted only long enough for the ball lightning to strike back, hitting her across the chest with an electric jolt. White hot pain that stank of ozone coursed through her, forcing her back a step.

More freezing water drenched the thing, splashing Aderyn and Jessemia and Whiskers. More of its body disintegrated, but it continued to attack. Aderyn shuddered with cold and pressed forward cautiously. The electric shock attack was too fast for **[See It Coming]** to react to.

Jessemia cried out in pain as the ball lightning shocked her. Without stepping away, she slashed through what was left of the monster's body, cleaving it in half. With a final scream, the lightning scattered into the floor, grounding itself harmlessly in the pools of water left over from *drench*.

The other balls of white light had drifted closer. Now there were four of them. "Keep using *drench*," Aderyn shouted, "and everyone stay out of reach—"

The ball lightnings shot forward as fast as an electric shock, their tendrils reaching for the humans. Aderyn shrieked as one tendril lashed around her wrist, sending another painful shock through her and dragging her forward. Owen brought the <Sunsword> down on the tendril, cutting Aderyn free. The other end of the tendril recoiled from the blade's bright light.

"[Outflank] won't work," Aderyn shouted. "Take it from in front!"

Together, they raced to meet the creature just as *drench* struck its neighbor. The ball lightning they fought ignored the water drops that spattered it. Belatedly, Aderyn used [Discern Weakness] and discovered the whole thing was covered in the red haze that meant resistance to weapons damage. "No weak spots! Just beat on them until they fall, and try not to get hit!"

Weston let out a shout of pain. "You think?" He swept his rapier across the crackling surface, tearing a slash that gradually began to seal up, and followed the blow with another slash in the same place.

Drench again hit the same monster, and Jessemia took advantage of its disintegration to tear through its remaining structure, collapsing it. "Do that!" Aderyn told Owen. "Cut it in half!"

She timed her next blow to coincide with Owen's, and the two of them swung in different directions, slicing the ball lightning almost completely in half. The monster's scream was so high pitched it was almost inaudible. Fluid trickled from Aderyn's ears, hot and cold at the same time. The ball lightning's tendrils flickered faster than she could follow, gripping the cut edges and dragging the ball back together. Swiftly, Aderyn and Owen hacked at the tendrils, snapping them as fast as they could form, until the monster's body sagged and drained away into the water covering the floor.

Congratulations! You have defeated [Ball Lightning]. You have earned [9900 XP]

Another system defeat notice popped up as Livia's *drench* finally killed one, and in the next moment Weston impaled the monster he was fighting, shuddered as it struck him a final time, and drove it down to where a pool of water had gathered in a depression on the floor. It thrashed as it disintegrated, but he held it down until it completely dissolved.

**Congratulations! You have defeated [Ball Lightning].
You have earned [9900 XP]**

Owen, breathing heavily, deactivated the **<Sunsword>**. "Everyone all right?"

"I discovered immediately that they were immune to my attacks, and kept our youngling friends well back," Isold said. He held the **<Peacemaker's Burden>** like mind magic wasn't the only attack he'd made. "Who was struck?"

"I think all of us were hit at least once." Aderyn examined the team roster and was heartened to discover the electric shocks hadn't done much damage, for all they were painful. She wiped blood out of her ears. "Jessemia?"

Jessemia rubbed her upper arm. "I'm fine. It was startling as much as painful."

"Don't conceal injury," Isold warned. "With you not being on our team, no one will notice if you're severely wounded until it's too late."

"I'm not concealing anything. I'm fine." Jessemia drew in a deep breath. "Sorry. I know you mean well. I don't want to be coddled."

"No one is coddling you," Isold said sharply.

"Why are we arguing?" Livia said. "Can we not fight each other, given that this place is full of monsters who are interested in tearing our faces off?"

"I'm not the one—" Jessemia cut off her sharp retort. "You're right. I'm sorry, Isold. I was terrified Whiskers or I was going to die, and that made me snappish. I couldn't have killed either of those ball lightnings without the help of *drench*."

"I'm afraid I'm overly cautious about those of us whose damage I can't see," Isold admitted. "Especially in combats like this one where I'm helpless."

"That won't always be the case," Owen said. "And now we know how to kill those things, so if we encounter them again, we'll be in a stronger position."

"Oh!" Aderyn exclaimed. "The Assessment said something unexpected. It says ball lightning's usual terrain is fields and mountains, and that it's strange to find it in a building. But it wouldn't say why—just that it was a question to consider moving forward."

"That is weird." Owen hooked the basket hilt to his belt and rubbed his hand down his trousers, leaving a sooty mark. "Does anyone have any ideas? No? Because I'm inclined to accept the system's verdict and let the mystery go for now."

"That's how I feel. Though I think something we *can* learn from this is that there may be other creatures here that technically shouldn't be, if Stormwatch Citadel is the mystery." Aderyn sighed. "And that just opened us up to an infinite set of possible monsters."

"Let's just move forward," Livia said. She pointed at Whiskers, who was rolling in the puddle Weston had drowned the ball lightning in. "He's not worried about the future."

"He also has fish breath," Jessemia said. "But he's so brave! Such a good boy." She scratched Whiskers under the chin, and the dire otter chittered happily at her.

With Weston in the lead, they proceeded down the hall. Surrounded by Livia's *orbs of light*, Aderyn imagined herself walking in the center of a bubble of light that illuminated almost nothing beyond their little group. She recalled the darkness beneath the ocean when they'd explored the Ivory Palace and controlled a shudder. The system had mentioned weresharks—was that a hint?

Isold steered them away from the first door they came to on the left. "I can't tell if it opens on the courtyard or not, and it's not a risk we want to take." Instead, they opened the door opposite, which led to a narrow hallway—narrow by giant standards, but still about twenty feet wide—and a handful of other doors and corridors. Weston opened the first one, and they all peered in.

"Looks like storage," Weston said. Tall shelves made of the same iron bars as the bedframes were bolted to the walls, and a row of flat-topped chests big enough for Aderyn to stretch out in for sleep ran down the center of the floor.

"Do you think they left anything?" Skalt whispered.

"Probably not. Why are you whispering?" Weston replied.

"I don't know. This place is creepy. I feel like monsters might leap out at us when we're not looking."

"Don't be a baby, Skalt," Freta said. Her voice trembled.

"Stop calling me a baby!" Skalt yelled. "You're scared, too. I'm the one brave enough to admit it."

"He's got a point, Freta," Owen said. "And you need to stop with the name-calling. When you're in a dangerous situation, you have to have team unity, or you could end up dead."

Freta ducked her head. "We're not a team. But... fine. I'm sorry."

Aderyn didn't think that was much of an apology, but at least Skalt didn't look upset anymore. "What do you mean, you're not a team? Didn't you all join an adventuring team when you got your quests?"

"I don't know what that means," Taavek said. "We're the first questers I can remember who did their quests together."

"Huh." Aderyn Assessed Taavek and got the same Assessment

she had the first time. "There shouldn't be any reason why you can't form a team. But—Jessemia, you're level eleven. Can you invite them to join a team? I wonder if it works for humans and giants together."

"I can try."

Jessemia faced Taavek. She didn't seem to do anything, but after a few seconds, Taavek jerked and took a step back. "I've been invited to join an adventuring team. What do I do?"

"Touch the Y," Jessemia said.

The other giants reacted as Taavek had, but one by one they gestured as if tapping something. "It looks like a normal adventuring team," Jessemia said. "But I didn't think it through. It might dissolve if I leave."

"So stay with them," Aderyn said, feeling inspired. "You can help each other level up."

"We don't care about levels," Zalk said. "It's skill ranks that matter."

"Your skill ranks will increase faster if you're part of an adventuring team," Weston said. "So you'll end up with both. And this way, you can protect each other better."

The giants looked uncomfortable, but nobody said anything. Aderyn couldn't imagine not wanting to join an adventuring team, but on the other hand, it wasn't as if giants knew anything about adventuring to be excited at the prospect. Maybe for them, it was more intimate. A team certainly could become personal over time. Even for younglings who'd grown up together, that could feel awkward.

The small corridors eventually led to a room as big as the barracks, but lined with tables and counters taller than Weston. "A kitchen," Zalk said. "Finally, something I recognize."

Aderyn examined the two fireplaces, which had not been cleaned before the castle was abandoned and were choked with soot and chunks of scorched, ash-dusted wood. "Now I can't tell if they left in a hurry, or were just lazy."

"They didn't use wood for the ovens, they used coal. Like in Finion's Gate." Jessemia was investigating one of the ovens, which were big enough to hold a human. "Zalk, do the People not use wood for cooking?"

"Not the ones who live far from forests," Zalk said. "There are coal mines in the mountains, and some communities make charcoal. That gives a more even heat, anyway."

"There are more small storage rooms this way, and a big empty room with tower access in the corner," Weston said, returning along another of the small corridors. "So we've reached the southwest corner."

"Don't wander off alone," Owen said.

"I can't hear anything in these rooms but us, and if there are invisible monsters lurking in the walls, we have bigger problems than if one of us goes out of sight," Weston said, but he stayed where he was. "Also, I found the commode."

Livia made a face. "I bet it's enormous, too."

"Don't look like that. It hasn't been used in centuries. Where's Isold?"

"Down this way," Isold said, his voice echoing with distance. "There are stairs."

The others hurried to join him. "Going down?" Owen asked. "Or up?"

"Down." Isold gestured at the door that opened on cold darkness. It was one of the small ones that were all identical, though this one looked more battered than the others, with dozens of broad black marks where giant boots had kicked it over many years.

Jessemia's nose wrinkled. "It smells like fungus."

Livia tossed some lights down the stairwell, revealing a vaulted roof and stone stairs worn down in the middle of each step. "The stairs don't go far. I think this might have been a root cellar. Or a wine cellar."

It turned out to be both, which Livia said was a bad idea. No wine bottles or casks of ale remained, just wall racks for bottles sized for giants. The smell came from a fungus colony growing in a pile of old potato sacks, disgusting but not monstrous. They all trooped back upstairs and gathered in the big, empty room where the tower stairs began.

"Isold?" Owen said.

"There's most of a castle between us and the other towers," Isold said, focusing on his map. "But only one door I can guarantee does not lead into the courtyard. It's back down the hall this way."

It wasn't just a door. It was a pair of doors twenty feet tall, banded with steel that still shone despite centuries of neglect and with a pair of handles shaped like lion heads gripping rings in their fiercely snarling mouths. The smoothly lacquered wooden surface reflected the lights of Livia's orbs like tiny, fuzzy-edged suns.

"That is intimidating," Owen said.

"There must be something amazing beyond," Aderyn said. "You wouldn't put doors like this on the privy."

"I don't hear anything, do you?" Weston asked Jessemia. She shook her head.

"Then I guess we see what those ancient giants cared about," Owen said. He pulled on one steel ring, rolled his eyes when the door didn't move, and pushed instead.

The door opened smoothly, the only sound a tiny scraping of wood against wood that didn't impede its movement. The room beyond was the kind of dark only possible in a room completely shut up against the outside, no windows, no cracks of light from beneath other doors. Jessemia made a face. "That's rank. Like overripe fruit just fermenting."

"Even I can smell it," Owen said. "Livia?"

Weston grabbed Livia's arm before she could summon more *orbs of light.* "I heard something. A footstep. And there's another one."

Something moaned in the darkness.

Everyone froze. The moan came again, louder this time. It sounded like someone at the end of their endurance.

Livia swore under her breath. "This is ridiculous, us standing here." She lobbed half a dozen *orbs of light* into the room.

Men and women, human, not giant, stopped moving as if the orbs had startled them into standing still. Light illuminated dozens of faces turned in the friends' direction, white, staring faces in various stages of decay. Their eyes—the ones that still had eyes —bulged from their sockets, yellowish and bloodshot and seemingly incapable of blinking. Clothing hung off their bodies in tatters, revealing withered flesh beneath. Some of them worked their jaws endlessly, chewing immaterial gristle. Others didn't have jaws to chew with.

"Zombies," Owen said. "That's impossible."

As he spoke, Aderyn Assessed the room, not knowing what to expect. Instead of a monster description revealing how many creatures they were dealing with, she got a single message.

Name: Infected Deadeye

Level: 13

Attacks: projectile attack x2 OR melee weapon attack, bite, special

    Immune to: mind control spells and skills

    Resistant to: none

    Vulnerable to: elemental fire damage

    Special attack: infection

An infected adventurer has all the class skills of a normal adventurer of their class and level, but acts and reacts as if under the influence of a *slow* spell. It's almost like it takes more time for their body to get instructions from their brain. Does that suggest anything to you?

In addition to doing weapons damage according to their class, these creatures can pass on their infection to a victim via a bite or a scratch. You don't want that to happen, I promise.

Aderyn blinked the text away. "I don't understand," she began, drawing her sword.

The men and women lurched back into motion, their steps hesitant but growing gradually more certain until, with a terrible roar that came from dozens of desiccated throats, they were running at the door intent on tearing the friends apart.

CHAPTER THIRTY

"Shut the door!" Owen and Weston shouted together. Zalk, who was closest, grabbed one ring while Owen, Weston, and Isold grabbed the other. They hauled the doors shut in time for the first of the creatures to fling itself against the wood with a dull thump. More thumps sounded afterward, erratic at first, then with a pounding rhythm that sounded like fists beating on the door.

"We have to secure the door," Owen said, leaning back so his weight kept the door closed. "If they think to stop pounding and start pulling—"

"I have an idea," Skalt said. "Taavek, come with me." Ignoring Aderyn's protest that they should stick together, he ran down the hall to the north with Taavek trailing him.

The pounding grew louder. "It's fine," Weston said. "We'll know it's not fine when the pounding stops."

Rapid footsteps preceded Skalt and Taavek's return. They were carrying a couple of lengths of iron that were rusted at both ends. "I saw these were nearly broken off one of the beds," Skalt said. "Hold the rings up." He and Taavek maneuvered an iron bar through the rings, effectively locking the door.

"Good idea, Skalt," Owen said, his breathing heavy. "Let's get out of here. Back to the tower room, the southern one."

When they regrouped, Owen put his arms around Aderyn and murmured, "Zombies. It can't be zombies. You people don't have undead monsters."

"I don't know what a zombie is," Taavek said. "Are you saying those weren't humans?"

"Couldn't you tell the difference between us and them?" Livia demanded. "Some of them were missing body parts!"

"I don't know what's normal for you!" Taavek exclaimed.

"Calm down," Aderyn said, though she didn't feel very calm herself. "This isn't normal, Taavek, and none of us have ever seen anything like it. Whatever they are, it's not a typical monster."

"I'll say," Weston said. "Those people looked dead!"

"I don't know if they're dead or not. The Assessment said 'infected,' and it only Assessed one of them the way it does when we're fighting other humans. Meaning that instead of telling me we're facing some number of infected humans, it singled out one adventurer."

"Which means it will take minutes for you to Assess all of them," Isold said.

"Right. And I'm not sure that would help. I'm guessing they're all adventurers who were infected with some illness, and it made them... I don't know what they are now!"

"I'm telling you, those had to be zombies," Owen said. "I watched *The Walking Dead* and I've seen every Romero film—"

"Owen," Isold said, his voice a warning.

"It's all right. I don't think this is the time for caution," Aderyn said. "Owen, maybe you'd better explain what zombies are."

Owen breathed deeply, calming himself. "In my—where I come from, there are stories about zombies, which are dead bodies that are still animated. They aren't real, but it's popular to write about them. I guess this place is enough different from mine that they're real here."

"What do those stories say about them?"

"There are a lot of different movies—I mean, ideas about what zombies are like, but most everyone agrees their bodies continue to decay after death, and the most common concept of how they're created is through infection. So it sounds exactly like your Assessment, Aderyn. We can be grateful they don't have the intelligence to get out of that room."

"But how can they be dead and still have all their skills?" Aderyn asked. "And many infections don't kill you. Isn't it possible they need to be cured rather than destroyed?"

"Didn't you look at them?" Weston said. "Their bodies were eaten away in places. Sometimes a lot of places. More than someone could endure and still go on living."

Aderyn sighed. "I know. I just can't bear the thought of someone dying and being turned into a monster, forced to kill instead of being absorbed into the system."

"You always hope for the best," Jessemia said. "But at this point I think the only compassionate thing we can do for them is kill them."

"There are a lot of them," Isold said. "Shouldn't we be asking the obvious question? Where did they all come from?"

Aderyn, about to answer Jessemia, stopped mid-sentence. "That didn't occur to me. There haven't been humans in the Northlands in centuries. Where *did* all of them come from? And why here? They couldn't possibly have all been infected in different places, right? Because there would be no reason for them to end up here after that."

"Unless there's something here that drew them," Owen said. "Something that called to the infectious agent—" He shook his head. "Now I'm being stupid. There's no brain monster that attracts people infected by whatever this is."

"I really wish you hadn't said that, because now I'm imagining one," Weston said.

"Okay, let's be reasonable." Livia grabbed Weston's chin and made him look at her. "There are no brain monsters. Human adventurers have been coming north for at least a few weeks, maybe a month, looking for abandoned settlements or that Winterforge dungeon. Some of them stumbled on Stormwatch Citadel instead. They entered the dungeon, they ran into whatever infects people, and it turned them into that zombie thing. It doesn't have to be more complicated than that."

Weston nodded. "I agree, and not just because your explanation rules out brain monsters."

"So does that mean there's a boss monster? What was it you said about rumors, Owen? Patient zero?" Aderyn asked.

Owen said, "Yes. Infections have to begin somewhere, which is why they call the initial case of a disease 'patient zero.' But in this case, it doesn't have to be a monster. It could be an effect, or an environmental problem. Stormwatch Citadel has those. I think we have to act on the assumption that killing the zombies—I mean, the infected adventurers—killing them is the goal until we discover there's a boss monster responsible for them."

"I agree with you, but your analysis may oversimplify matters," Isold said, "as there doesn't seem to be a practical way to destroy them except one at a time."

"The Assessment said they're vulnerable to fire, but I'm guessing we don't have a source of fire big enough to burn that entire room," Aderyn said.

"Sadly, no," Livia said. "And even bringing the roof down on them wouldn't do it, not if they decayed that much and still went on moving and attacking."

"Okay." Owen squeezed his eyes shut for a moment. "Okay. We know where they are. Let's leave them locked in there for now and move on. It's possible we'll come up with a solution as we discover more."

"That means going up the tower stairs," Isold said. "And hoping there's a better way across to the east side of the castle on an upper floor."

"Whatever it takes." Owen shuddered. "Zombies. What next?"

They arranged themselves again, Weston and Aderyn in front, the giant younglings in the middle with Owen and Isold, Livia and Jessemia at the rear. Whiskers kept wanting to run ahead, straining Jessemia's powers of persuasion to their fullest. But finally, they were ready to ascend to the next floor.

Surrounded by *orbs of light*, Weston and Aderyn cautiously climbed the tower stairs, listening for anything abnormal. The black stones reflected the light dully, so watching their steps was easy. Taking those steps was more difficult, because the risers were nearly twice as tall as ordinary human stairs. Aderyn chose not to complain. Now that she wasn't terrified, the coldness of the damp air registered and increased her gratitude for her fur-lined leather coat. She wasn't sure anymore which was worse, muggy heat or freezing cold.

They climbed until Aderyn's legs ached with the unaccustomed exercise. Walking miles across flat ground wasn't like mounting stairs, particularly these ones. Eventually, she and Weston reached a landing, which opened on a bare, empty room. The stairs continued going up, but in silent agreement they stopped and Aderyn Assessed the room. Weston's joke about invisible monsters that lived in the walls didn't seem so funny after seeing the very real monsters trapped in the giant room below. "What do you suppose that room was?" she asked Weston, who was checking for secret doors. "The one the infected adventurers were in?"

"No idea. It was blistering huge, though, wasn't it? Maybe a dining hall? Charnel Keep had one of those that was proportionately as big as that." Weston gestured to Owen as he exited the stairwell. "Nothing but the one door out."

"We haven't been rushing ahead, but now it's especially important we not go barging into new rooms that might be populated," Owen said. "You People, stay close to Jessemia and don't attack unless she tells you to."

"We're not really fighters," Freta said. "How can we help? Shouldn't we be armed?"

Owen looked at Jessemia. "It's all right if you don't fight, if you feel you'd be a liability," Jessemia said. "But Taavek, I know, has some experience, and the rest of you aren't weak. So I think we should look for improvised weapons for you as we go. Like the iron bar."

Taavek hoisted the spare iron bar, only a little awkwardly. "I can use this."

"Right. Whiskers, stay still." Jessemia patted the dire otter's head. "You can see Whiskers is eager to fight, but he's an animal and doesn't always know when a situation is too dangerous for him. You're thinking creatures and you're able to evaluate your actions. I'll warn you if you're not safe, but it's a good idea for you to pay attention so you learn the difference for yourselves."

The younglings nodded. Aderyn thought Freta still looked concerned, but she didn't look frightened, and maybe concerned was the best they were going to get.

Aderyn's first glimpse of the next room showed the same kind of big, empty space they'd found everywhere else, but that impression didn't persist past stepping into the room. The walls were covered with murals in bright colors, red and blue and gold and green. "These look brand new."

"There's no smell of fresh paint, not even traces," Jessemia said, sniffing. "The best I can tell you is that it was painted well over a year ago. I think it's just that the room was sealed off that the murals look that good." She ran a finger over the outline of the abstract shape scrawled on one wall and filled in with a wash of color that ran a gradient from blue through green to yellow.

"Any ideas?" Owen asked the younglings.

They all shook their heads. "I've never seen paint in these colors before," Zalk said. "Chalks, yes, but not paint."

Freta was staring at a different wall, one with blotches of white across a black background and no other colors. "That's strange. I know I've seen this before."

"Somewhere near your home?" Aderyn asked.

Freta nodded absently. "Somewhere... oh, I know! It's the stone spiral. Jasperton's stone spiral."

"That doesn't look anything like the stone spiral," Taavek said.

"I'm not making things up! It looks like the stones right up close. Like if you almost press your eye to them. The stones are dark with those white inclusions." Freta elbowed Taavek lightly in the ribs.

"I think you're right," Skalt said. "I've never seen what you describe, but I can imagine how it would look."

"What are the stones made of? What stone are they?" Owen asked.

"Gabbro," the younglings and Livia answered in unison. "It's not flashy, but it's a sturdy igneous rock," Livia added, "and Freta is right that that's how it looks close up."

"Huh." Owen gave the mural a closer look. "Why would giants paint a close-up image of a stone on their walls?"

"Especially since these other ones don't look like they have anything to do with stones," Aderyn said, pointing at the bright colors of the other walls.

"I like it," Skalt said. "It feels like we finally have something in common with those ancient People."

"Let's remember this room, and come back to it again once we've done more exploring," Weston suggested. "I'm increasingly convinced this place is a puzzle, and it won't make sense until we've found all the pieces."

"Two doors," Livia said. "Which one first?"

"Let's start farthest south," Isold suggested.

CHAPTER THIRTY-ONE

Weston checked the door. "It's not locked." He turned the knob with both hands and pushed the door open. Again, the view was of unrelieved darkness. This time, no sounds of movement emerged. "Livia?"

"I am so glad you have that spell," Aderyn said as Livia conjured more lights.

"Remember back when I could only have one at a time and it had to stay attached to me? That's what I'm glad about, that those days are over." Livia sent the lights shooting into the room and stepped inside, following Weston.

Aderyn, coming after her, ran into her as Livia unexpectedly stopped. "Livia?"

"I don't know what it is, but I love it," Livia said in a low, breathy voice.

Aderyn grabbed her arm. "What's wrong? Snap out of it!"

"I'm fine. I've just never seen anything like it." Livia moved forward, and Aderyn followed her.

Even Livia's lights didn't illuminate the room's far side, if it had one. The idea of an unending room was a fantastical thought, because Stormwatch Citadel had bounds like any castle, and the room had to come to an end eventually. But Aderyn couldn't help imagining an endless tunnel with a ceiling so high birds could mistake it for sky. She'd never seen an enclosed space this big. No pillars held the unseen ceiling up, but that didn't frighten her. She couldn't imagine anything this massive collapsing.

She didn't see anything dangerous, just narrow shelves stacked with pieces of stone of all shapes, from flat ovals to jagged chunks and skinny needles. All of them were large, even the needles, which would put finger-sized holes through any fabric they tried to sew. It was odd, but nothing awe-inspiring aside from how there were so many of them. The shelves, too, extended out of sight into the distance.

Behind her, another wooden door stood in the wall adjacent to their entrance, identical in size to the first. Aderyn realized the younglings hadn't entered when Jessemia did and discovered them huddled outside the room. "What's wrong?"

"We're not allowed," Zalk said. "This is stonekin business."

"You probably shouldn't be in there either," Skalt said. "You'll be in trouble."

"Skalt, nobody's been here in centuries. It can't possibly still be forbidden." Aderyn beckoned to them to enter, but none of them moved. "What is it? Or is that forbidden knowledge, too?"

"It's a Remembering Room," Freta said. "I've never seen one this big. Jasperton's Remembering Room is only the size of those store rooms downstairs."

"How do *you* know that?" Taavek asked.

Freta blushed. "I peeked, all right? I was curious. But I didn't go in or anything disrespectful like that. Just a peek."

"Then tell me what a Remembering Room is so we can be properly respectful," Aderyn said. She felt mildly bad about pushing, since she planned to explore it regardless, but information was important even if it was forbidden.

"Adults put memories into the stones," Zalk said. "Important things that happen in a year, births and deaths, anything unusual. Then any stonekin can touch the stone and experience the memory."

"That sounds like the Repository," Aderyn told Owen, who'd joined her at the door. "Zalk, don't you see how important this room is? It must contain the records of generations of the People. Maybe even the truth about why they abandoned this place!"

"I guess," Zalk said. "But we can't experience them. You have to be an adult. They teach you how to do it after you return from your quest."

"I bet I could," Livia said. She was standing close to the wall with her hands joined behind her back as if preventing them from grabbing every stone in sight. "I can try, at least."

"Do we have time for that?" Isold asked. "There are a lot of stones in here." Despite his words, he looked as if he was ready for Livia to start right then.

"I think I should at least see if it's possible," Livia said. "I'm less sure about what to do afterward. If the younglings are right, this is a special place we shouldn't disrespect, but let's balance that against how this is basically the biggest library of the People in existence. We're not going to make Stormwatch Citadel no longer a dungeon, so bringing the stones out of here might be the only way the giants get the knowledge they contain."

"You're right on both counts." Owen surveyed the shelves. "We have time for you to make the attempt, at least, and..." He sighed. "I'm tired of hearing myself say variations on 'we'll come back to this later when we've learned more,' but it's still true."

"All right, younglings, can you tell me anything about how experiencing the memories is done?" Livia asked.

"We really shouldn't tell you," Skalt said.

"And we don't know, either," Taavek said.

Aderyn caught sight of Zalk's face and made an inspired guess. "Zalk, what do you know?"

Zalk startled. "Me? I don't know anything."

"You do so!" Freta exclaimed. "You're doing that thing where you don't look at the person you're talking to. It always means you're not telling the truth."

"It does not!"

"Zalk, I'm not of the People and even to me you look guilty," Aderyn said. "Nobody's going to get you in trouble. If I'm right, your elders will thank you for your knowledge. Now, what can you tell us about this?"

Zalk sighed. "My father talks a lot when he's drunk. He's never mean, but he'll get going on a subject and just talk and talk. He's clever, so it's funny stuff, like stories of his childhood, but sometimes it's how to do things. And one night when Mam was visiting a friend he went on this rant about the Remembering Room and how he never had a need for it because he lives in the moment. But he went into detail about how it works."

The youngling hesitated, then crossed the room and picked up a bowl-shaped stone with a flattish bottom that resembled a mortar. "He said you have to be united with the stone, but not all the way. There's a balance. If you don't connect deeply enough, you won't experience the memory, but if you go too deep, it will sweep you away and then you go unconscious for a while. Sometimes a long while."

Livia took the bowl from Zalk. "That's simple enough, at least as far as using **[Pass Through Stone]** goes. The tricky part is as he said, balancing, and it's not like I have any idea about that. I'm guessing adult giants teach the new adults how to do it properly."

"I don't like the sound of 'unconscious for a while,'" Weston said. "We're not in a position to wait around for you to sleep it off if you go too far."

"If I go slowly, I doubt that will happen." Livia turned the bowl around in her hands, rubbing its surface. "It's just the one stone, right?"

"We'll have to find out eventually, if we're going to know whether or not to return these to the People," Owen said, "and right now nothing's trying to eat our faces. It's as good a time and place as anything."

Livia settled cross-legged on the floor and cradled the bowl in the crook of her right elbow. "My stone hand will either be ineffective or much too effective, is my guess." She closed her eyes and balanced the flattened part of the bowl on her right palm.

Nobody moved. Silence spread outward from Livia until Aderyn imagined she could feel pressure on her still-sore eardrums. She surveyed the nearest shelves, counting the objects that were similar. Twenty-eight orbs. Thirty-seven flat ovals like stones for skimming the surface of a lake. Forty-nine circular stones with holes in the middle. The children of Far Haven all pretended stones like that were magic, and Aderyn had one in a box of treasures in her old bedroom back home.

Everyone else was watching Livia, who still didn't look like she was doing anything. Boredom overtook Aderyn, but she didn't want to be the disruptive one, so instead of fidgeting she went back to watching the room. Six humans, four giant younglings, one dire otter, and—

Something stood in the doorway—literally in the doorway, because the door was closed and the thing looked cut in half, like its back portion was outside. Lines of bluish-white light defined its shape, which wasn't human or giant or anything that might be able to pay attention to things. And yet Aderyn felt sure it was watching them, its nebulous form shifting constantly, but like a tree in a high wind rather than a bank of clouds.

She controlled her amazement and Assessed it. No text appeared. **[Truesight]** told her it wasn't an illusion. Stunned, she let out a little noise, part gasp, part squeak of astonishment. The thing's attention focused on her. It drifted more fully into the Remembering Room, paused, and shrank in on itself to a pinpoint. With a flash of blue light, it was gone.

The air shifted like invisible jelly, roiling as if the creature's disappearance stirred it up. With a pop, a bright speck of light appeared, white this time, and before Aderyn could shout a warning, it expanded into a brilliantly white sphere that crackled with energy.

The ball lightning hovered in place for a moment. It was smaller than the ones they'd encountered before, and Aderyn had the sudden mad thought that it was a baby version of the monster, one she would have no problem killing. She drew her sword. With a crack, two tendrils lashed out, one at Aderyn, the other at Weston, who was intent on Livia but looked up at the noise.

Weston and Aderyn shouted in unison, and Weston lashed out at the tendril with a knife, severing it close to his wrist. Aderyn yanked on the tendril holding her, pulling it tight before slashing through it. Then an enormous gout of water fell out of the air, soaking the ball lightning entirely. It let out a high-pitched squeal and crumbled in on itself, its lightning-charged energy pouring into the puddle on the ground left by *drench*.

Congratulations! You have defeated [Ball Lightning, Immature].
You have earned [6750 XP]

Aderyn squeaked at the cold water that splashed her and

jumped back, too late. Owen appeared at her side, taking her by the shoulders in a protective grip. "What happened?"

"Ball lightning," Aderyn said. She pressed her lips together to stop them quaking from cold.

"It just appeared out of nowhere," Weston said. He hadn't been splashed as thoroughly as Aderyn, but he still looked cold.

"Not exactly," Aderyn said. "I—oh, thank you." Owen had taken her in his arms and hugged her close, warming her. "It appeared, yes, but there was something else here first. Something that came into the room and then vanished. I think it's the source of the ball lightning. And I've never seen anything like it before."

"Let's examine this," Owen said. "Where exactly did you see it?"

Aderyn stepped away from Owen's hold and fumbled her way past Isold and into the place where the thing had been. The air and the floor felt no different than anywhere else in the room.

"Aderyn, what are you doing?" Isold asked.

"I was wondering if it left behind any evidence of its existence." Aderyn crouched and felt along the square stones the size of her palm that made up the floor. She still saw no evidence that the thing had been real.

"Can you describe it?" Owen put himself between her and the door.

"It might have been made of light. I didn't see a structure to it. It came in through the closed door and then it shrank down to a point and vanished." Aderyn stood upright. "And it was watching us. I'm sure of it."

"It wasn't ball lightning?" Jessemia shook her head dismissively. "Of course not. I didn't smell ozone until just a second ago."

"Yes, and it was more nebulous than that. They were similar in both apparently being made of light, except this thing was bluer and less crackling. It didn't make any sound at all. Then it vanished, and the ball lightning was there instead."

"This place gets weirder by the minute," Owen said. "I would have sworn there were no haunted houses in this wor—I mean, um, never mind. Let's just say we have zombies, and now it sounds like we have ghosts. What did **[Improved Assess 4]** say?"

"It didn't say anything. Not even 'exceeds authority limit.' It might as well have been an illusion, but if it was, **[Truesight]** means I wouldn't have seen anything. So it's not a monster, it's not a disguised human or giant, and it's not an environmental hazard."

"Maybe it was the device we're looking for," Jessemia said.

The others all stared at her. "Well, couldn't it be? It vanished in an instant, which is sort of what happened when you tried to use the <**Wayfinder**>, Aderyn. And it has existence, even if it's immaterial enough to pass through doors." Jessemia ran her fingers across the smoothly lacquered surface of the door.

"I think you're right," Weston said. "What worries me is that none of the rest of us noticed it. I mean, yes, we were all watching Livia, but something that makes so little noise it can sneak up on me is frightening."

"But it didn't attack," Aderyn said. "I didn't get the sense that it cared about us except in an idle way. Like it wasn't doing anything else at the moment, so it might as well watch us."

"We can't count on that staying true," Owen said. "If it is the device, and returning it to working order means altering it, it might not be willing to hold still and be altered. But, again—"

"We'll come back to this later when we've learned more?" Weston said with a grin.

Owen sighed. "At least this time someone else said the dread words."

CHAPTER THIRTY-TWO

"We really need to focus," Owen continued. "Livia, did you learn anything, or were you distracted?"

"Sorry," Aderyn said.

"Don't be sorry. What if that thing had attacked?" Livia got up and brushed off her posterior. "And I did learn things. I was able to access the memory, but only barely. Zalk wasn't kidding about the need for balance. It felt like trying to balance on a taut rope while standing on a greased wooden ball. But that just means I need practice. The bad news is, I think the memory is corrupted."

"More infections?" Isold asked.

Livia shook her head. "Experiencing one of those memories, a normal one, must feel like being in that place as if you're living it again. This one... it was more like being in a painting that's been left out in the rain and snow for a dozen years. Parts of it were cloudy, and some parts were blurred, and some of it felt, well, squishy. Like an overripe tomato. I don't think it was my inexperience or the fact that I'm human. If those were an issue, I would simply have failed to perceive anything."

"But that could mean the other memory stones are all right, couldn't it?" Freta asked.

"It could be just this one, or just a few of them, or it could mean the whole lot," Livia said. "And it's possible someone with more experience than I could restore the memory. But we don't have time to deal with it now. It's enough to know that it would be worth retrieving this library."

"That will have to wait, too," Owen warned when Zalk and Taavek headed for the shelves. "There's a lot of stone in here, and there's no guarantee it will all fit in the <**Knapsack of Plenty**>. We'll come back for it later."

"Isold, where are you going?" Jessemia asked.

Isold was already some distance away, walking toward the far side of the vast room. "Checking a theory."

"Somebody go with him. None of us should be alone here." Owen waved to Jessemia, who ran after Isold. Aderyn, on a whim, followed her.

She caught up with them both about a hundred feet from the far end. Isold had the distant expression of someone reviewing his system map. "I think this part of the citadel is symmetrical," he said. "Look. Two doors adjacent to each other, both in mirror-reversed positions from the other side."

"Don't open the door," Jessemia and Aderyn said in unison.

"I'm not stupid," Isold said. "But I am convinced I'm right, enough that I will assert that the room beyond *this* door is another one of the mural rooms."

Aderyn looked back at the others. The room was so big they were the size of bugs at that distance. "This is going to be exhausting if all the rooms are like this. Wait here."

She ran back to the others and arrived in time to hear Weston say, "It's a hallway," and close the door next to the one they'd come in by.

"Isold says the layout is symmetrical and mirrored," Aderyn said. "So there's another one of the mural rooms on the far side."

"And probably another hallway," Owen said. "Let's go there. We might want to use the stairs to access the far side of the ground floor."

Isold and Jessemia were standing some distance apart, not speaking, when the others arrived. They looked so much like strangers it dismayed Aderyn. "Did you find anything else?" she asked.

"We waited," Isold said. "Jessemia didn't hear anything."

"But the doors are thick enough that might not mean anything," Jessemia said.

"Okay, let's see if your guess is right," Owen said.

"Hallway first," Weston said, carefully opening the door a crack and then all the way. "Got it in one." A long, dark hallway stretched out before them.

"Then this is another mural room," Taavek said, throwing the door open.

"Wait—" the others said.

Taavek shouted and lurched backward as a pale, emaciated female figure lunged for him. Aderyn drew her sword, Assessing as she moved.

Name: Infected Swordsworn

Level: 11

Attacks: bladed weapon attack, claw, bite, special

Immune to: mind control spells and skills

Resistant to: none

Vulnerable to: elemental fire damage

Special attack: infection

Infected adventurers can pass on the infection to others through a bite or scratch, but the higher a level the victim is, the greater their chance of resisting it. I still recommend not being bitten. That's dangerous as well as being gross.

Pay attention to what Owen knows about zombies, Aderyn. It's one hundred percent wrong in the fundamentals, but the effects are the same, and that's really all you care about now.

Owen shoved the off-balance Taavek aside and activated the <Sunsword>. The infected adventurer didn't flinch from the brilliance of the blade. She swung her sword at Owen, faster than she'd moved before. Aderyn, moving into place for [Outflank], noted the infected woman's stance was all wrong and she held her head and shoulders as if they weren't attached to the arms wielding the sword. The sword, too, looked out of place compared to the woman's rotting flesh and loose-fitting clothes stained with dark fluids. The blade shone in the light from Livia's orbs, its edge unnotched and free of tarnish.

Aderyn worked her way around behind the infected Swordsworn and thrust at her back, low and aiming for her kidneys. Her sword skewered the woman, sending up such a strong reek of decay Aderyn gagged and had to tighten her grip on her weapon. The infected Swordsworn didn't at first react. Then she pulled away from the blow as if she hadn't felt it immediately and began to turn to face Aderyn. With a shout of effort, Owen struck the monster's neck. A sharp crack like ice shattering reverberated off the walls, and a blast of air even colder than their surroundings struck Aderyn in the face. The <Sunsword> kept going, cutting off the woman's head. The infected Swordsworn kept moving for a second, then collapsed.

Owen prodded the remains with the tip of his sword, checking for signs of life. "Don't get close to it," he warned the others. "Aderyn's Assessment just said the infection could be transmitted by a bite or a scratch, not that those were the only ways."

"Um," Taavek said. "How much of a scratch?"

Owen stilled completely. "Show me, Taavek."

Taavek extended his left arm. Aderyn hissed in sympathy. A deep scratch ran across the youngling's wrist, narrow at one side and gradually widening until it was a finger's width across. Blood trickled from it across his hand. "It's not bleeding much. That's good, right?"

Isold had already drawn the **<Healing Stone>** from his belt pouch and pressed it to Taavek's wrist. "It will be fine," he assured the youngling as the stone's green glow lit Taavek's flesh from within. Swiftly, the wound knit back together and then disappeared.

The other giants watched this huddled together like they were afraid they were next. "Is he infected?" Freta asked.

"I don't know," Isold replied. "In my opinion, we were in time, but I assume you would prefer I not lie to you, and the truth is I simply don't know. I healed the injury immediately, but we don't know how quickly the infection takes hold. We will watch Taavek closely." He put away the **<Healing Stone>**.

Taavek wrapped his hand around his formerly injured wrist. His heavy breathing and blind stare frightened Aderyn. Before she could say anything, Owen said, "Taavek, look at me. Look at me, please."

Taavek slowly turned his gaze on Owen.

"I know this is frightening," Owen said. "If it happened to me, I'd be as paralyzed as you. You're used to challenging things you can see and touch, and this is intangible and invisible. But Isold is right, we healed you quickly, and there's a good chance you'll be just fine."

"But what if I turn into one of those things?" Taavek whispered.

Owen put a hand over the youngling's where it covered his wrist. "If that happens, Taavek, I swear to you I'll kill you myself before it takes you."

Aderyn's mouth fell open. Horrified, she almost contradicted her husband before she registered the set of his shoulders that said *Don't interfere.*

Taavek relaxed. "Promise?"

"I promise." Owen squeezed Taavek's hand. "You won't end up like them."

Taavek let out a breath. "Thanks. That helps."

"Next time, let someone else open the door, all right?" Owen said with a smile. Taavek laughed weakly.

"At the risk of being anticlimactic, Isold was right," Weston said. "There's another mural room here."

"That means we should be close to the other tower, the southeast one," Isold said.

They passed through the mural room without doing more than noting the murals were different and ended up, as Isold had said, in another room with tower stairs spiraling up and down. In this room, the door to the mural room was open, and it wasn't completely empty; a wooden weapons rack leaned against the wall near the stairs, minus its weapons. Weston pulled on it, and it shifted barely an inch before stopping. "Fastened to the wall. I can see why someone wouldn't have wanted to put effort into removing it."

"Do you think the Remembering Room was important enough to guard?" Aderyn said. "If the People respect it that much, you wouldn't think weapons would be necessary."

"Maybe it was the whole second floor they wanted to guard. We haven't found stairs except for the two tower ones, and if this floor is symmetrical, that other empty room was a guard post, too." Weston jiggled the weapons rack back and forth in a restless, idle gesture.

"More things we don't have enough information about," Isold said. "I think we should go downstairs and explore the rest of the ground floor. It might also be a good idea to determine if the tempest moth is still out there. If the worst happens, and we have to flee, we'll need to know what danger we're fleeing into."

"I hadn't considered that, but it makes sense," Owen said.

The room at the bottom of the southeast stairs had two wooden weapons racks, both fastened securely to the wall. "So they *were* guarding the stairs," Owen mused. "Interesting. Maybe the ground floor is public, and the upper floors belonged to the king and his family?"

"But a Remembering Room doesn't belong to only one person," Zalk said.

"Oh! The dungeon Assessment said the castle had places sized for humans, so we know they came here and even stayed for a time. The People might have wanted to restrict which humans were allowed near their special places." Aderyn imagined what those rooms might look like. The ceilings here were high enough to fit a two-story human house.

"Let's see what else is on this side," Owen said. "Is it symmetrical too, Isold?"

"Not as far as I can tell, though this room specifically is the mirror-reverse of the other tower room. We'll have to see."

They walked some distance before reaching another door, this one on the right. It wasn't as ornate as the door that locked the zombies in, being a single door with an ordinary brass knob instead of the lion's-head rings, but the hinges were ornately decorated with curlicues and brass oak leaves. Weston and Jessemia took turns listening at the door before Livia tried *clairvoyance*. "Too dark," she said.

Weston gingerly turned the knob, then booted the door open so hard it thumped against the wall and rebounded almost in his face. Nothing pale and decaying emerged from the darkness. Livia tossed *orbs of light* into the room, and one by one they entered.

By the warm yellow glow of the orbs, the room felt almost cozy despite its size. Golden stone faced all the walls and outlined a door in the far wall. A desk half the size of Aderyn's bedroom in Far Haven took up most of the other side of the room. With its spindly legs and delicately carved edges, it looked like an ordinary desk some spellslinger had enlarged with magic.

Isold and Weston were already checking it out, examining drawers and cubbies. "Nothing," Weston said. "I'm beginning to think that thing about over five thousand gold worth of treasure was a tease."

"Unless the treasure comes off those infected adventurers," Livia said. "That one we fought had a nice sword."

Weston made a face. "I guess there's a limit to my greed."

"This door doesn't have a latch," Jessemia said from across the room. She pushed on it, and it swung easily. "Whiskers, don't," she added as Whiskers made a move to enter the room.

"Be careful," Aderyn said, coming to join her.

"I am. If there was an infected adventurer in here, it would have come after us already." Jessemia pushed the door open wider.

Blue-white light blazed, casting a glow over Jessemia that made her look like the zombies. Whiskers whimpered and hid behind Jessemia. Aderyn grabbed Jessemia's arm, but Jessemia was already moving back, her sword drawn. "Everyone stay back," she said, raising her sword across her body.

Aderyn Assessed the glowing figure, but as in the Remembering Room, no text appeared. The thing drifted forward a few feet before coming to a halt. Again, Aderyn had the sense of being observed closely.

A tremendous shout shook the room, making Jessemia drop her sword. She backed up again, tripped over Whiskers, and grabbed Aderyn's shoulder to stay upright. The glowing thing shook like a tree in a high wind. Its immaterial substance shredded like mist, and then it was gone.

Chapter Thirty-Three

Aderyn, breathing heavily, discovered Jessemia was doing the same. She stared at the place where the apparition had been. Nothing about the stones of the floor or the gently swinging door showed any sign of its presence.

Jessemia picked up her sword. "That was unsettling. It felt unexpectedly warm on my skin, for all it looked freezing cold."

"It touched you?" Isold crossed the room in a few swift strides and took Jessemia's chin in his hand, staring into her eyes. "You're not injured?"

"I don't feel injured." Jessemia removed his hand from her face. "I don't think it could hurt me."

"You don't know that. That thing could be responsible for the infections," Isold said.

"Then I guess we have to keep an eye on me," Jessemia said wryly.

"This isn't funny. You can't be so cavalier about your safety."

"I was careful, Isold." Jessemia sounded like she was controlling an annoyed outburst. "The room was empty when I moved the door the first time. Whatever that thing is, it can teleport, and there's no sign or sound of its appearance or disappearance except that it's suddenly there, or not. So it's not as if I had any warning."

"And we can't go on the assumption that it will appear every time we find someplace new," Aderyn said. "I'm glad **[Shout]** works on it. It seems to have prevented it from releasing a ball lightning, at least."

"That was **[Greater Shout]**, and it should have destroyed it," Isold said grimly. "I have a feeling that wasn't the case."

"Do we want it destroyed?" Skalt asked. "I thought you said it was what we're looking for. The device."

"It could be," Owen said, "and, Isold, I didn't think you were the type to overreact."

"It's not overreacting to show it we're not helpless," Isold replied. "Nothing else in this place has been harmless. We cannot risk ourselves on the unproven theory that this one thing is."

Owen met Isold's implacable gaze. "If that's all this is, sure," he said. "And you're right. We have to be cautious."

Taavek said, "This other room has shelves and a couple more of those desks. But the shelves are empty." He held the swinging door open and was peering into the room beyond.

"What did I say about being cautious?" Owen said, sounding as if he was suppressing a laugh.

"The creature is gone, and there's nothing else dangerous in here. Besides, if I'm—" Taavek shut up.

Aderyn guessed where his thoughts had taken him. "Don't think like that, Taavek. You shouldn't give up before you even know if you'll have to fight."

Taavek nodded curtly. "I'll try."

Weston passed Taavek and entered the second room. "I'm guessing offices," he said, wandering past the shelves and running a hand along the nearer desk as Aderyn watched from the doorway.

"Like, if the king had a place where he wrote decrees and so forth. Do kings do that kind of thing?"

"I have no idea. All the stories I read were about royalty having adventures, but now that I'm older, I can't imagine anyone having the time for adventures *and* ruling a kingdom." Aderyn turned back to Owen, who was staring at the door they'd entered by. "Is it like that in—I mean, where you come from, Owen?"

Owen gave her a sardonic look and raised an eyebrow in a gesture that clearly said *And you gave* me *crap for forgetting the secret.* "It depends on when in history the king or queen ruled. Usually the ruler had a lot of nobles who had government positions, and they did some of the ruling. And then there were some kings who were figureheads, ones whose families had been powerful centuries before but had dwindled during that time."

"This looks like there was a lot of paperwork involved," Weston said. "I can picture these shelves being filled with boring books on law, back in the day."

"Can we go somewhere else, then?" Taavek said.

"You sound eager," Zalk said. "Everything all right?"

"Just want to see what else is here." Taavek tapped his fingers rhythmically on the door frame.

"Nothing wrong with that," Owen said.

They continued down the hallway more slowly now, all of them watching their surroundings, stepping softly so their footsteps wouldn't obscure other sounds. Aderyn, near the front, couldn't stop remembering that flash of bluish-white light shrinking down to a pinpoint and then vanishing. The memory was so strong she thought she saw the light every time she blinked. By the time they reached the end of the hall, her eyes ached from resisting the urge to blink, and her neck hurt from craning to look over her shoulder in case the thing crept up on them.

Weston opened the last door on the right with a powerful

boot intended to slam the door into any enemy lurking behind it. "Nothing but bedframes," he said, looking inside. "And the tower stairs. I think these last two rooms were for the soldiers, like the ones on the other side."

"Then let's go back upstairs," Owen said.

"I'm going to use *clairvoyance* to see whether the tempest moth is still there," Livia said. "This door leads to the courtyard, right?"

They waited while Livia stood in front of the single plain wooden door and stared at it. She stared for so long Weston said, "Livia, what do you see?"

Livia startled and closed her eyes. "It's there. It's not actually in the courtyard, because it's too big. But even its shadow made me feel like everything is pointless."

Weston gathered her into his arms. "We need to avoid that thing. I haven't forgotten that the folks at Marble Hill started attacking each other as well as falling into despair. We can't afford that kind of distraction, not if there are animated dead people wandering this place."

Livia nodded. She wiped her eyes and said, "Upstairs, then."

This time, Aderyn walked behind Jessemia and Weston, prepared to Assess any threat that appeared. Maybe it was the proximity to the tempest moth, or maybe there really was something different about these stairs, but unease filled her, a sense of foreboding that something was coming that they couldn't fight. The dank, dark walls glistened with moisture that beaded on the stones and ran in little trickles down the grooves between them. Despite the wetness, the tower was cold, almost cold enough to freeze. Aderyn bundled closer into her wonderful coat and wished gloves were practical.

Unlike the other tower staircases, this stair terminated at the second floor. "It's like I saw before," Aderyn said as they all spread out searching for hidden doors or caches. "The castle is shorter at the front than the rear."

"They could have put in windows," Jessemia said. "Or I guess not, if those aren't defensible. Even so, the lack of light would get to me after a while." Whiskers romped around the room as if to show he didn't share Jessemia's feelings. It was hard to stay gloomy with the dire otter playing there.

"Two doors," Isold said. "Leading west and south."

"We'll try west first," Owen said. "See what's over the courtyard."

Weston opened the door on gray, pre-storm daylight. A hall extended to the south, lined on the west side with giant sheets of glass that trembled with the rising wind. Aderyn had never seen glass panes that size before.

"Windows," Weston said. "I guess the system heard Jessemia."

"Oh, don't say that," Jessemia exclaimed.

Taavek drifted forward and leaned against one window. "I wish they were open. I could jump. Do you think a fall from this height would kill me?"

"Taavek!" Aderyn cried out. She hurried to his side.

A shadow swept across the courtyard, and the winds died away, leaving behind an unnatural calm. Aderyn looked down at the gray shadow and then at the ground. Taavek might be right. Falling could kill her. If only the windows were open...

"Quit looking at me that way," Isold said to Owen. "I know you think I'm useless. Let's see how useless I am the next time you demand healing."

"That's it," Owen snarled. "I'm sick of your obnoxious mouth. Let's end this." Rather than draw the <Sunsword>, he took a fighting stance, raising his fists. Isold didn't wait for Owen to strike—he punched Owen in the face. Owen staggered back, wiped blood from his nose, and leapt at Isold.

"Stop them!" Jessemia shouted. She grabbed Whiskers around the neck and pulled him away from the fight. "We have to get out of the tempest moth's field!"

Freta grabbed Isold. Skalt grabbed Owen. Zalk dragged Taavek away from the window. Aderyn watched it all dully. It wasn't as if it mattered. Let them fight. It wouldn't change anything.

Hands gripped her upper arms and steered her down the hallway. "Keep walking," Livia said.

"Don't think about anything else," Jessemia added.

To the sound of shouts and cursing, they made their way down the hall and around a corner, out of sight of the windows. Aderyn became aware of how strange it was that Jessemia and Livia were holding her arms. "I'm fine now," she said, stepping away. "Really. That was awful, feeling like nothing mattered. I think that might actually be worse than the storm destruction that monster brings. At least destruction is something you can fix. Suppose those windows were made to open?"

"Sorry," Owen said, gingerly touching his nose. "I hope you don't think that's what I secretly think of you, Isold."

"Nor I, you," Isold replied. He felt along his jaw, which was turning purple with bruises. "We need to avoid that area going forward. The symmetry means we know there are more windows on the far side, and I imagine there are others on the south side of the courtyard."

"There are," Weston said. "And a lot of little doors. 'Little' as in sized for humans. But they all face on the courtyard windows, so it's not safe for us to explore them unless we come up with a solution to the tempest moth's effect."

"Let's not worry about those for now. The device we're looking for was made by giants, for giants, and it's unlikely we'll locate it in spaces built for humans." Owen's speech slowed as he spoke the last five words. "Taavek, what's wrong?"

"I can't make it stop," Taavek said. His voice was tight and frightened. His left arm, the one the zombie had scratched, swung back and forth so powerfully and rapidly it looked like it was trying to escape his body. The youngling grabbed his left wrist with his other hand and strained, forcing the left arm to be still. That lasted for a few seconds before the arm wrenched itself out of his grasp.

"Should we try the <**Potion of Life**>?" Aderyn asked.

"That doesn't cure disease, which is what an infection is," Isold said. "If the infection were gone, the potion would cure any damage it did. Until then, it would be wasted."

"You have to do something!" Skalt exclaimed.

"Try to relax, Taavek," Owen said.

"I can't relax. I'm too scared."

"I know. But sometimes fear makes it hard to control your body. Remember we won't let this take you, okay?" Owen gripped Taavek's left hand and forced the moving arm to stay still briefly.

"I have an idea," Isold said. "Taavek, look at me. Kneel down, in fact."

With Taavek kneeling, Isold took his face in both hands and crooned a wordless lullaby, dodging when the wildly swinging arm nearly clipped him across the side of the head. The singing never stopped, and gradually Taavek's arm stilled. It continued to move, but only the barest of twitches every minute or so.

Finally, Isold stopped singing and offered Taavek a hand up—a gesture of friendliness only, given how much bigger Taavek was. "[Hypnotism] is a temporary measure, but I can go on doing it as often as necessary. And I choose to believe we'll find a solution."

"Thank you." Taavek rubbed his left wrist as if it still hurt. "It feels like it's happening at a distance. Like the effect is someone knocking on a door several rooms away."

"We need to move more quickly, then," Weston said, "but if

we do that, we could miss something or endanger ourselves. The goal is to find the device and repair it—isn't anyone else worried about how we are going to repair an ancient device? Is one of us secretly a Spellcrafter?"

"Find first, worry later," Owen said. "Where does that door go? Anything important?"

Jessemia was just closing the nearest door. "Only in the most fundamental sense. It's a privy."

Livia sent more lights flying down the crooked hallway. "Hey! Stairs!"

They gathered around the next corner and gazed up the stairwell, which ascended into darkness. Unlike the tower stairs, which were narrow and cramped for giants, these stairs were easily forty feet wide and shallow enough for humans not to have to stretch too much. Handrails on either side bore traces of gilt, and the stairwell had once been painted a rich, dark red that had faded to salmon pink. "These look ceremonial," Isold said.

"This isn't like anything the People do now," Freta said. "We believe in simplicity. Maybe those murals make sense, if they're depicting something to do with the Remembering Room, but this is just... it's gaudy."

"That's right," Skalt said. "Gaudy. Unnecessary. I don't understand it."

"Well, it's something we should bypass for now," Owen said, "but I'm glad we have the four of you to interpret this place. Am I right that we're near the Remembering Room again?"

Isold walked to the end of the short hall, another sixty feet away. "Around this corner," he called back.

When everyone had gathered near Isold, the Herald said, "That's the mural room door, and that is the Remembering Room, which leaves only *this* door unaccounted for." He pointed.

"It's probably too dark to see anything, but I'll give *clairvoy-*

ance a try." Livia's eyes sheened over with an icy blue glow. She stiffened. "There's a light source in there. It's the same bluish-white as that thing we can't identify. It's not very bright, but I see darker figures moving around in there, too."

"More zombies," Owen said.

"Yes, but the light creature," Aderyn exclaimed. "I think we need to go in there."

"We can't afford for more of us to be infected," Isold said. "But we also can't shy away from fights out of fear of what might happen."

"Open the door, let Aderyn Assess the room, and we'll figure out a plan from there," Owen said. "Younglings, you stay back and don't let anything escape the room, okay? Everyone else ready?"

Everyone nodded. Jessemia idly stroked Whiskers's head.

"Weston," Owen said.

Weston squared up to the door. Aderyn took a position behind him and to the right, which she judged would give her the best view of the room. She wiped her nervously sweaty hands on her trousers and nodded.

Weston kicked open the door and caught it when it rebounded. Aderyn steadied herself on the door frame and Assessed the room as she surveyed it with her natural vision. Five shambling human figures and what seemed to be sheets of thick, cloudy ice that glowed blue-white in the darkness.

Assess gave her a different story.

Name: Revenant Blight [1]

Type: Formless

Power level: 17

Terrain: any; thrives in warm, humid environments

Attack(s): special

Immune to: mind control spells and skills

Resistant to: bladed weapon damage, piercing weapon damage

Vulnerable to: elemental fire damage, elemental cold damage

Special attacks: paralysis, dominate

This fungus has only one desire: to dominate other living creatures and turn them into its puppets. It infects victims by inserting itself beneath the skin and maneuvering its way into the warm, humid environment of the brain stem, where it takes control of motor functions and forces the victim, who by the way is still conscious, to attack others so the parasite can take more victims. The revenant blight then begins devouring its host, starting with the parts of the brain responsible for consciousness and spreading through the muscles. Eventually, the host dies, but because this happens before the revenant blight's food source runs out, it can go on making the body do what it wants until it's consumed past the point of being useful.

Don't frighten your youngling giant friend with this, but I have to say his future doesn't look good. Think about what I've told you. There's an answer in there somewhere.

A moan rose up from the stiffly-moving figures, who turned as one to shuffle toward the open door with increasing speed.

"Shut the door!" Aderyn shouted.

Weston slammed it shut. "What's in there?"

"A lot," Aderyn gasped. "But I know what to do—"

With a low cry, Taavek launched himself at her throat.

CHAPTER THIRTY-FOUR

[**S**ee It Coming] dropped her to the floor before her conscious brain registered the attack. Taavek, weeping great strangled tears, swung a fist at her that she again dodged. "I can't stop it," he sobbed. "Owen, kill me now!"

"Hold him," Owen said. "Livia, the wand—"

"I got it," Livia said. She fumbled one of the wands from its sheath on her knapsack and aimed it at Taavek. With a complicated squiggle and flick, she activated it, sending a pulse of purple energy at Taavek's head. The youngling sagged, his eyelids drooping, and fell in a limp, sleeping heap.

Owen stepped back. "Damn."

"We can't kill him in cold blood," Weston said.

"I made a promise," Owen said. "It would be worse to let him fall deeper into the infection."

"No, listen!" Aderyn exclaimed. "I think the system gave me a hint. Listen to what I learned from [**Improved Assess 4**]."

She repeated the words of the Assessment of the revenant blight. "It said the fungus gets inside the victim's brain, right? But there are two things odd about that. First, that it said there's only one of it, even though there are five infected people in that room. And second, I think the fungus is what's covering the walls and giving off light. I think the fungus is a single entity that can splinter, or fragment, or something. Which means if we kill enough of it, the rest might die, too. Including the bits that have infected people."

"That's a big guess," Livia said.

"But not an unreasonable one," Isold said.

"And it's a guess we can prove right now," Owen said. "How do we kill a revenant blight?"

"Fire or ice," Aderyn said. "Failing that, a *lot* of weapon damage. And we'll have to hold off those infected adventurers, too."

"That doesn't sound complicated." Owen stared down at the sleeping Taavek. "How long does *deep slumber* last, Livia?"

"An hour, given his size. *Deep slumber* is less effective the bigger the creature. It's never been an issue for us because we usually kill stuff before it wears off." Livia sheathed the wand decisively.

"That's enough. Warmaster?"

Aderyn recalled what she'd seen of the room. "I'm afraid we pulled all the adventurers to the door. Livia, you'll need to shove them out of the way—in fact, if you can *immobilize* some or all of them, that would help. The idea is to avoid engaging with them, they're a distraction. Owen, Weston, and Isold, you batter the revenant blight, Livia will do crowd control, and Jessemia and I will hold off any enemies Livia can't contain."

"That seems dangerous for Jessemia and you," Isold said.

"It's dangerous for all of us, but with the <**Peacemaker's Burden**>, you will be more effective against the fungus than either of us." Aderyn wished she knew why Isold had suddenly become so risk-averse. Well, it didn't matter so long as he did his part of the plan.

"Understood." Isold drew the heavy mace and hefted it, testing its weight.

"Younglings, keep an eye on Taavek and make sure none of the infected humans leave the room, all right?" Aderyn caught each one's gaze in turn, making sure they took her instructions seriously. Freta looked concerned as always. Zalk and Skalt kept glancing at Taavek like they were afraid he'd wake and throttle them, but they looked otherwise resolute.

"Livia in front, the men behind her, Jessemia and me in the rear," Aderyn said. "Let's do this."

This time, when Weston kicked in the door, it bounced off rotting flesh. Aderyn inwardly groaned. No plan lasted more than three seconds past encountering the enemy, but this one hadn't even made it through the door. "Push forward!" she shouted.

Livia called out a few nonsense words and stomped one boot, sending a blast of force arrowing through the stones. *Thunderstomp* knocked all the looming figures off their feet. "All right, *now* push forward!" Aderyn shouted.

Livia ran along the furrow her attack had left and began chanting another spell. Weston, Owen, and Isold followed her, racing for the wall where hung the glowing sheets of white fungus. As tentacles of earth emerged from the ground to *immobilize* two of the infected adventurers, Aderyn and Jessemia took up defensive positions between the other three and their friends hacking at the wall.

Aderyn swiftly Assessed the three. "A Tidecaller, a Lone Wolf, and a Swordsworn," she said, pointing at the creatures pulling themselves to their feet. "None of them higher than level thirteen —will you be all right, Jessemia?"

"I'll have to be. Whiskers, *fetch!*" Jessemia hurled a dagger at the infected Lone Wolf that Whiskers, with a terrifying growl, bounded after. The dagger struck the Lone Wolf square in the chest, staggering him, and then Whiskers leapt at him, knocking him over as the dire otter gripped the dagger hilt and dragged it free. No blood flowed, but the infected adventurer thrashed as if the attack had done serious damage. Jessemia took advantage of his prone position and stabbed into his chest again, driving her sword deep.

"I forgot!" Owen shouted over his shoulder. "You might need to destroy the head to kill them! The head!"

"Got it!" Aderyn replied. The system had said to listen to Owen's knowledge about zombies, and she intended to take advantage of that hint.

She held her ground as the Tidecaller approached. It seemed unlikely that a spellslinger could go on casting spells after death, or at any rate after losing control of their voice, but she wasn't going to lower her guard. The infected Tidecaller's head tilted to the left like she couldn't hold it erect, and her eyes were filmed over, but she seemed to perceive Aderyn just fine by how directly, if slowly, she approached.

The Tidecaller lifted her hands, and **[See It Coming]** warned Aderyn to dodge in time to avoid a hail of icicles the thickness of her wrist. Behind her, Owen let out a pained cry. She soon around to see Owen clutching his shoulder, from which protruded an icy spear. Hands brushed her hair, and she pulled away from the Tidecaller's clawed grip before the infected adventurer could scratch her.

"It's fine!" she heard Weston shout. "Taunt her some more! Those icicles did more damage than we have!"

Right. Vulnerable to cold damage. Aderyn took a step back and gestured rudely. "You missed me, stupid! Try it again!"

It was probably pointless. If the creature was dead, it didn't know what the taunts meant, but since it was controlled by the fungus, it might know not to do anything to harm the fungus's main body.

Sure enough, the Tidecaller summoned a hammer made of ice rather than spray icicles into the room again. Aderyn ducked the hammer a couple of times and then darted in past the monster's guard, thrusting for the eyes. She scored a lucky hit after the first three blows, ramming her sword blade into the monster's eye socket until it grated against the bone of the skull. Still, the Tidecaller didn't fall. "Owen, what was that you said about destroying the head? It's not working!"

"I'm talking decapitation, or bludgeoning, something that smashes it—what I wouldn't give for a shotgun and about five thousand rounds right now!"

"Livia—"

As if by magic, Livia appeared at Aderyn's side, holding a stone hammer that looked a lot more destructive than the Tidecaller's ice weapon with its delicate traceries of feathery frost covering its sides. "Stand back," she said, and without waiting to see if Aderyn would obey, she wound up and slammed the elemental hammer into the Tidecaller's head.

The Tidecaller's skull caved in with a sickening crunch of bone. Her grip on the ice hammer loosened, and both it and she hit the floor at the same time.

**Congratulations! You have defeated [Infected Tidecaller].
You have earned [7000 XP]**

A moment later, Jessemia yelled, "Killed one!"

Aderyn didn't pause to congratulate her. She swept up the ice hammer and ran with it to where Owen's <**Sunsword**> carved chunks out of the fungus covering the wall. Occasionally, a flash of blue light and a gust of freezing air marked where Owen's **[Weapon Master]** elemental damage took effect, but there was still a lot of fungus left untouched. It looked to Aderyn like it was glued fast to the wall.

"Use this," she said, dropping the ice hammer at his feet. "It does cold damage."

She hurried back to join Jessemia, who was fighting the infected Swordsworn with Whiskers darting in and out to claw the creature just as if the pair had **[Outflank]**. The Swordsworn was level thirteen and much more clever than a dead, puppeted creature ought to be. It blocked every attack aimed at severing its head and managed to give Aderyn a nasty sword wound across the side of her neck that would have decapitated *her* if not for **[See It Coming]**.

From behind her, the sound of a sheet of ice creaking under pressure became a sharp series of cracks, and Owen shouted, "Back up! That dust might be infectious!"

**Congratulations! You have defeated [Revenant Blight].
You have earned [33,500 XP]**

The infected Swordsworn collapsed exactly like a puppet whose strings had been cut, his sword skittering away from his hand. The other two infected adventurers trapped by *immobilize* sagged in their earthen bonds as well.

"Well, crap," Livia said. "I hoped we'd get experience for the others."

"I guess the system doesn't count them as defeats, since the fungus was what kept them moving." Aderyn blotted the line of blood along her neck.

"This really hurts," Owen said, gingerly touching his shoulder where the icicle had impaled him. "Did anyone breathe in the fungus dust?"

"I was farther back, so it didn't come close to me," Weston said.

"I don't think so." Isold wielded the **<Wand of Healing>** over Owen's shoulder. "I think it would have triggered a cough or a sneeze, and my lungs feel clear."

"Because the last thing we need is more people infected now that we've defeated the thing," Owen said. "Let's wake Taavek up and see how he feels."

"I'll search this room," Weston said. "Aderyn, Jessemia, you want to join me?"

Aderyn Assessed the room from several directions while the other two searched. "I bet this was the king's bedroom," she said, pointing at the skeletal bedframe, this one of wood rather than iron. Scatterings of tiny holes showed where worms had eaten into the frame. "This, and how there used to be gilt around the ceiling, tells me it belonged to someone important."

"The next room over is totally empty except for some wardrobes in the same condition as the bed," Weston said. "And another privy. I think you're right. Who else rates a personal privy but the king?"

Aderyn nodded. She strolled around the room, examining the walls. The revenant blight had discolored the stones wherever it touched, leaving them a pasty dark gray rather than smooth and variegated granite. And it had been huge, based on the discoloration, big enough to cover all of the bedchamber's southern wall.

She traced by sight the line of the fungus's pattern, which dipped all the way to the floor in places. To the floor, and below...

She drew in a horrified breath. "We might have a problem."

"We have a problem," Owen said, overriding her. "Taavek's still infected." He stood in the doorway with Freta at his side.

"He's doing better, though," Freta said. "He's not out of control anymore."

"Yes, but the fungus is destroyed, so there isn't anything to turn him into a puppet anymore, right?" Weston said.

"That's what I was trying to say," Aderyn said. "I don't think we got the whole thing. Look."

She led the way to the wall and pointed, drawing lines without touching her finger to the discolored wall. "See the flat gray shapes? That's everywhere the fungus touched. Now look at the base of the wall. It looks like it flows down between the stones. Down to the first level."

Owen regarded the stain closely. "Isold, what's beneath us here?"

"The room with all the zombies," Isold said. "Or a room next to it. I can't be more specific than that."

"Shit," Owen said. "That's just fantastic."

"I'm not totally sure I'm right, Owen," Aderyn said, "but the alternative is that we *did* kill the whole fungus, and its death didn't make a difference to Taavek."

"I can find out, though," Livia said. "The fungus glows brightly enough for *clairvoyance*, so if I look through the floor and it's dark, then we know there's no fungus there."

They all waited as Livia cast her spell. Immediately, her back tensed. "Do you want the good news first, or the bad news?"

"Good news," Owen and Weston said as one.

"There's another revenant blight down there. And a door that I think opens on the zombie room. So... maybe a great hall, or dining chamber, attached to some other important room?" She shook her head impatiently. "It's not important. The point is, there's still another fungus, and that could mean a cure for Taavek."

"I'm afraid to ask about the bad news," Aderyn said.

"The bad news is there is a *lot* of fungus. It's all over two of the walls and something protruding from the floor near them. And I counted thirteen figures wandering around in that room, which doesn't include however many are in the zombie room, if they manage to open the door." Livia sat back on her heels and her eyes returned to their normal color. "We're going to need a better solution than hammering away at the revenant blight until it dies."

Owen nodded slowly. "Okay. I think we need a rest, and some time to figure out a plan. Let's go back to the Remembering Room."

Taavek was on his feet and moving, if stiffly, under his own power when they left the king's bedchamber. "I feel it still," he said when Aderyn asked how he was doing. "It's like a predator watching me all the time, waiting to see if I'll flinch, and then it will pounce." He sounded weary rather than frightened, but to Aderyn, that seemed worse.

"We'll figure it out," she assured him. "We know there's a relationship between the infection and the revenant blight monsters, and killing one already had an effect on you. It's just going to take time."

Taavek nodded politely. It didn't take **[Read Body Language]** to know he was suppressing a rude rebuttal to her inane words. She wasn't sure she would have been that polite.

They settled in a loose group on the floor of the Remembering Room, eating but not talking much. Aderyn leaned against Owen and let her mind wander. The problem of dealing with the revenant blight was too difficult for her to contemplate after the stresses of the morning. Better to relax and let her mind work on the puzzle without involving the rest of her.

Isold put away the **<Forager's Belt>** and started singing, and as the notes of his **[Inspire Courage]** song filled the air, Aderyn's heart lifted. The song didn't fill her with false confidence, and it didn't tell lies about how easy the challenge ahead was. Instead, Isold sang of past victories, past triumphs over hardships, and with each verse Aderyn remembered how they'd always managed to come out ahead, and this time would be no different.

When he finished singing, Jessemia said, "Thank you. I feel better now. Less despairing."

"You're welcome," Isold said. "I only wish there was a skill for gifting someone with inspiration in solving a puzzle. I may not be in despair, but I am certainly discouraged."

"Then sing again. Something you love, not anything magical."

Isold smiled. He broke into song, a tune Aderyn had never heard before. It was melancholy and unexpectedly hopeful, a song about lost loves and not giving up despite heartbreak. She hugged her knees to her chest and closed her eyes, drinking in the music.

Someone gasped. Aderyn's eyes flew open, and she blinked away pained tears from the brightness shining just a foot away. The entity of light completely surrounded Isold, pulsing and shifting like a tree in a high wind. Isold was still singing, but his eyes were wide, and it was clear he feared what might happen if he stopped. Jessemia, who had been nearest Isold, had scooted away, but she remained on her hands and knees and looked like she meant to pull him free of the light.

The shifting light moved again, drifting around the circle in which they sat. It didn't go out of its way to encircle each person; it looked more like it had a path to follow and humans or giants were incidental to that path. It brushed past Freta, who shivered, then nearly encompassed Skalt. Then it paused. With a twitch and a jerk, it bypassed Zalk and centered itself on Taavek.

Taavek bucked like a horse shooing a fly and whimpered. The

light pulsed four times, its immaterial body stretching as if the light was a membrane and something inside pressed against it, wanting out. Then it shrank in on itself to a pinpoint of painfully bright light and vanished.

Isold's song cut off mid-syllable. "Are you all right?" Jessemia asked.

"Fine. It wasn't painful. It didn't even feel as if it noticed me." Isold smiled wryly. "If anything, I was afraid it remembered **[Greater Shout]** and wanted revenge."

"I forgot about that." Jessemia sat back. "But—what did it do to Taavek?"

"I don't know," Taavek said. "It didn't hurt. Not like a blow to the face or breaking a bone. More like prodding a mouth sore with your tongue. It hurts the first couple of times, but then you get used to the sensation, you know?"

"It looked to me like it found something it wanted," Weston said.

"That was what I thought," Aderyn said. "But like it didn't expect to find the thing here."

"I don't want to be special anymore!" Taavek shouted. "I just want to go home. Forget about being famous."

No one spoke. Taavek's heavy breathing filled the air. Finally, Owen said, "It's what we all want, in the end, Taavek. You just learned that truth the very hard way."

Taavek nodded. He swiftly dashed away tears everyone pretended not to notice.

Owen stood up and clapped his hands together once. "All right. Enough rest. Let's look at our equipment and see what we've got. No more forgetting a <**Necklace of Fireballs**>, which would be really useful right now, I realize. Still, there must be something we can use."

Isold unrolled the potions bandolier. "Strength, speed, or

boldness... I don't think the <**Death Cloud**> bulbs will be useful against creatures that are effectively already dead..."

"What's that one?" Livia asked, pointing.

"Oh. I'd forgotten. The <**Sovereign Solvent**> we got for free." Isold worked one of the fat tubes free and held it up. The perfectly clear contents looked like slightly thickened water, just a little sluggish.

"Don't we have *anything* that does fire damage?" Owen said.

"Just the <**Fire Dancer's Knives**>, but flinging them randomly seems like a stupid idea," Weston said.

Aderyn perked up. "What about flinging them intentionally?"

"Well, sure, but I don't have any idea what's effective."

"I will," Aderyn said. "And that and the <**Sovereign Solvent**> gives me an idea. Half of an idea."

"What's the other half?" Owen asked.

Aderyn turned to Livia. "How fast can you sculpt stone?"

CHAPTER THIRTY-FIVE

Twenty minutes later, they gathered outside the eastern tower room on the ground floor, near the southern end of the hall. Aderyn surveyed her little army, as she thought of it—Owen was their leader, but this was work for a Warmaster, and that meant she was in charge of this assault.

Owen, Weston, Jessemia, and Isold had their weapons ready and were grouped loosely around Livia, who stood with her palms pressed flat against the wall between them and the room with the revenant blight. Her lips moved silently as if she was calculating in her head. Aderyn didn't distract her by speaking to her.

The four giant younglings stood in a semicircle surrounding the humans. Each of them held a vial of <**Sovereign Solvent**> that looked tiny in their enormous hands. They all looked nervous except Taavek, who wore the expression of someone determined to force his way through an army of foes. "Taavek, do you feel any different?"

"No," Taavek replied. "It's not going to take me this time. I can feel it wants to, but it won't."

Aderyn wasn't certain about this part of the plan. Given that the revenant blight had influenced him to the point of attacking her before, she'd wanted to put him to sleep before they came in view of this bigger, potentially deadlier fungus. But Owen had taken her aside and said, "He's close to breaking. He needs to feel that he's not helpless. Livia will use the **<Wand of Deep Slumber>** if he shows even the littlest sign of being dominated, all right?" and Aderyn had given in.

Now she ran her fingers down the bandolier of sheathed knives Weston had given her. "You're sure these don't have to be thrown to activate?" she asked again.

"Very sure," Weston said. "The **<Fire Dancer's Knives>** catch fire with a speed proportional to how fast they move. That means if you wield one like a regular knife, it will catch fire after it's embedded in your target instead of lighting up in the air when it's thrown."

"That sounds ideal, given that Aderyn doesn't want to be holding it when it burns," Owen said.

"It's less ideal when you're fighting a creature who can knock the knife away before it burns them, but we're attacking the revenant blight, so yes, this is a good setup." Weston, despite his confident words, looked concerned. "Are you sure there's no way for me to do it? I'm certain I can do more damage than you, what with my experience with the weapon."

"I'm sure. I can't think of a way to convey what I see with **[Discern Weakness]** short of running up and marking the vulnerable places for you to target, and that wastes time." Aderyn did her usual ritual of wiping her palms on her trousers, though with as cold as the air was, she wasn't sweaty. The effect of the **<Potion of Boldness>** kept her from being nervous at all, and between that and the feeling of strength flooding her muscles, she felt more confident than she had since entering Stormwatch Citadel.

"I'm ready," Livia said. She still rested her palms against the stone, but now her eyes were closed.

"Then it's time," Aderyn said. "Livia opens a passage through the stone. The rest of the humans run through, followed by the younglings. I'll use **[Discern Weakness]** to identify the best places for us to target, then wield the <**Fire Dancer's Knives**> to set the revenant blight on fire. The other humans will protect you younglings while you use the solvent at the edges of the fungus, as high as you can reach. From there, we evaluate and strategize again, based on how effective fire and solvent are. Any questions?"

No one answered. Whiskers chittered and bumped his head against Jessemia's chest. "Then—let's do this," Aderyn said.

Livia murmured several nonsense words, her voice growing gradually louder until with a shout she gripped the edges of two stones and dragged her hands apart. The wall flew apart, crumpling like a curtain thrust open against the morning sunlight. It made a hole more than ten feet wide and six feet tall, too short for the giants, but Livia had told them what to expect. "Everybody *go!*" Aderyn shouted, and raced for the gap, outpacing the others.

She didn't waste time examining the room beyond or Assessing the shambling figures who'd stopped as if stunned at the crash of the moving stones. All her attention fixed on the glowing white fungus clinging to the wall opposite and draped over a giant-sized chair, so large she couldn't help seeing it as a throne. She stumbled to a halt and turned **[Discern Weakness]** on the revenant blight.

Lines of blue light sprang up, crisscrossing the white fungus as they shifted back and forth. They'd never looked so much like they were seeking out an advantage. In seconds, they shrank to pinpoints of bright blue scattered apparently at random across the eerie white surface. Aderyn ran to the largest one she could reach, drawing one of the <**Fire Dancer's Knives**> and holding it close to her body in case her movement counted as acceleration for the knife's magic.

She skidded to a halt a foot away and with an overarm swing stabbed the fungus through the blue spot her vision clearly marked. It stuck firmly in the waxy substance. Snatching her hand away, she paused, waiting for the fire. Nothing happened. She was about to grab the knife and stab again, faster this time, when a thin line of smoke curled up from where the knife was embedded nearly to the hilt in revenant blight.

With a sound like a cough, greenish flames erupted from the spot, burning wetly as if the fungus was soggy with water and letting off more damp smoke that smelled of mold. Then, a rush of heat spread over Aderyn's face as the flames turned yellow-white and surged across the revenant blight's surface.

Aderyn didn't stop to retrieve the knife, which was still burning; she raced to the next blue spot and repeated her movements. More greenish flames that turned hotter and yellower, more crackling heat. By the time she used the fourth and final knife, the first one was extinguished, but as she ran to retrieve it, the blackened husk of the revenant blight cracked, and the knife fell to the floor. Aderyn swept it up and took a moment to examine the situation.

She'd been barely aware of tall figures racing around, pouring liquids over the upper edges of the revenant blight. The <**Sovereign Solvent**> gave off a sharp, vinegary odor, not normally something Aderyn found pleasant. Compared to the damp, stinking fumes of burning fungus, it smelled delightful. Now the giants gathered in a corner, cringing away from where Weston and Owen, Isold and Jessemia fought off a wave of infected adventurers. One of the younglings sat on the floor, his blond head bowed.

Taavek's whole body shook like he was experiencing his own personal earthquake.

Aderyn ran to join them. "Taavek," she began.

"I can do this!" Taavek shouted.

All Aderyn's instincts cried out a warning. "You can't—"

Taavek's head came up with a jerk. "I have to get away! I can't hurt anyone if I'm gone!" He struggled to get to his feet, but he seemed to be fighting his own body, all his limbs flailing, his lips gnashing like chewing gristle.

"Livia!" Aderyn boomed out with **[Amplify Voice]**.

"No!" Taavek shrieked. His flailing arms struck Freta across the face. Freta stumbled backward and hit the fungus-covered wall. Skalt and Zalk grabbed Taavek's arms and tried to pin him down, but the dominated youngling thrashed and got one arm free long enough to punch Zalk, who went down.

A flash of purple light zipped past Aderyn's ear, striking Taavek. The youngling's eyes rolled up in his head, and he collapsed atop Zalk. Aderyn caught Skalt's gaze and held it. "Watch them, and *stay here*," she commanded. "Don't leave this room unless all of us are overwhelmed, understand? There are too many other dangers in this castle we don't know about that we do not want you running headlong into." She waited only long enough for Skalt's nod, and then she raced to where Owen fought, stopping a few feet behind him so she could Assess the situation.

There were so many infected adventurers Aderyn couldn't count them all. The only thing that kept her friends from being overwhelmed was how slowly the enemy reacted, sluggish like ice water in a wintry river. And more of them kept coming through the door that led to the other room, the first one they'd looked into. It was another pair of doors twenty feet tall, their surfaces gleaming with lacquer and banded with steel, and another pair of handles shaped like lion heads grimaced at Aderyn as if taunting her. If only they could keep them closed! But there were so many monsters between her and the doors there was no way to reach them.

The floor shook. A cube of solid stone rose up in the center of the doorway, blocking it completely except for a narrow sliver of space between the lintel and the stone. It caught two infected adventurers between its stone and the walls, crushing them, and a couple of system defeat notices popped up.

Aderyn turned, awestruck, to Livia, who was bent over gasping like she'd had to move the stone by hand. "It's *stone prison*. I should have thought of it earlier," she wheezed. "Hope it's not too late."

"It can't be," Aderyn exclaimed. "I won't let it."

She made herself turn her back on the fight and surveyed the damage they'd done to the revenant blight. Her heart sank. The fire damage had been moderate, better than she'd hoped, but the <Sovereign Solvent> hadn't done anything—or at least hadn't done anything on its own except color the fungus pale pink. Maybe someone attacking the places where the younglings had poured it would knock pieces off.

"New plan!" she roared. "Weston, collect the knives and attack the fungus—your rapier won't cut off a head. Isold, you join him —smash the places where the fungus is pink. Everyone else, keep Isold and Weston protected. I'm going to see if these infected adventurers learn from their friends' mistakes."

She darted to the left and dodged a dead Staffsworn, easily ducking his staff's leisurely blow. Her target was a Flamecrafter who'd just missed being crushed by Livia's *stone prison*. She'd never seen a Flamecrafter in battle who didn't have some form of fire kindled on their body. If she hadn't had [Improved Assess 4], she wouldn't have known this was a Flamecrafter, given that lack. Aderyn poked the infected adventurer in the shoulder with

Aurelon's sword, not trying to do damage. Anything short of decapitation would just be an annoyance, which was what Aderyn wanted.

"Hey! You there!" she shouted. "That's right! You can't hit me, you... you infected loser!"

Again, she didn't think the infected Flamecrafter had enough intelligence left to understand the taunts, but she followed each of them with an increasingly hard jab to the shoulder or chest. The Flamecrafter followed her as she backed away, positioning herself between the infected woman and the fungus-covered throne.

Finally, Aderyn jabbed the woman in the throat, and instead of staggering after Aderyn, trying to grab her, the infected Flame-crafter gestured. Aderyn saw the ghostly ball of flame well before the real thing came at her, in plenty of time for her to duck and let the fireball strike the revenant blight. The throne went up in flames.

Aderyn let out a "Hah!" of laughter and resumed poking the Flamecrafter. The infected woman ignored her. Her body trembled, then shook harder until she fell to the floor, convulsing. It had to have something to do with the damage to the revenant blight, but Aderyn had no idea what. She decided not to worry about it. A convulsing enemy was an enemy that wasn't trying to kill her or her friends.

Again, she surveyed the room. Weston and Isold were making progress, Weston throwing knives that lit like tiny stars as they spun and hit their target, Isold smashing chunks of fungus with the <Peacemaker's Burden> that scattered in every direction. It reminded Aderyn of chipping away at the wax in the Enchanterium control chamber, but smellier. Less than half the fungus remained. They needed to focus on destroying it.

Aderyn ran to Livia's side. The Earthbreaker had just entangled four infected adventurers in tentacles of earth and looked weary. "I'm running low," she said. "Does it feel like we're winning? Because I only have one rejuvenation potion left, and I'd rather not use it if I have a choice."

Aderyn swiftly counted heads. "There are nineteen of them left, minus these fellows you *immobilized*. I'd say it's time you see what you can do about the fungus."

Livia nodded, and Aderyn ran to Owen's side. "Keep going!" she exclaimed.

Owen used **[Overrun]** to knock down his opponent, and **[Outflank's]** weird effect tugged at Aderyn. "It doesn't do any good if we can't destroy the head!"

The infected Deadeye Owen had hit with **[Overrun]** struggled to stand, rocking back and forth like a turtle on its back. "We just have to protect the others," Aderyn said. "Concentrate on knocking them over, or drawing them away—we're so close!"

Owen switched targets and tripped the next infected adventurer who approached. "Yes, but they're moving faster. I think they know their 'master' is in danger."

Aderyn darted out of the way of the falling body. "It's going to be close!"

An infected Swordsworn, taller and heavier even in his emaciated condition than Owen, loomed up above him, wielding a greatsword nearly as tall as Aderyn. She worked her way around behind the creature as Owen engaged, trading blows made eerie by the infected Swordsworn's total silence. She stabbed the Swordsworn low in the back, but he ignored her completely. Aderyn realized they were close to the throne where the fungus smoked and crumbled. "Owen!"

Owen slashed across his opponent's face and got no reaction, not even a flinch from the brilliance of the <**Sunsword**>. He deflected the greatsword, then with a move too fast for Aderyn to see, he disarmed the infected Swordsworn. For the first time, the creature paused. Owen took advantage of the pause to sweep his sword through the Swordsworn's decaying neck, decapitating him.

Congratulations! You have defeated [Infected Swordsworn]. You have earned [15,050 XP]

For a moment, Aderyn and Owen stood alone and without opponents. Aderyn, breathing heavily, turned to count the remaining infected adventurers and screamed. An enormous figure staggered toward them, iron bar upraised. Taavek's eyes were unfocused, and his jaw hung slack, but his steps were sure and he was obviously intent on killing Owen.

"Owen!" Aderyn shouted again.

Owen spun to meet the oncoming threat. "I promised," he said. "Wish I hadn't been so cavalier about it. He doesn't deserve this."

Taavek brought the iron bar around in a ponderous swing Owen dodged. The blow left Taavek off balance, and Owen tripped him, sending him to the floor with a great *oof* of breath. Taavek didn't immediately get up, and Owen hurried to his side, his weapon at the ready.

"Owen, you have to," Aderyn urged when he didn't at first strike.

"I don't want him to suffer." Owen held the <**Sunsword**> stiffly, looking for an opening.

Taavek stirred. He rolled to his side and started to rise. Owen kicked the hand supporting Taavek's body so the youngling collapsed again. He stepped closer, raising the blade for a powerful blow to the heart.

A tremendous crack like ice breaking thundered through the room. All around them, infected adventurers sagged and collapsed in lifeless piles. Taavek shuddered and flung one arm over his face to shield his eyes from the light of Owen's sword. Owen stepped back, rapidly lowering his sword as if he feared it might carry through with that final attack on its own.

**Congratulations! You have defeated [Revenant Blight].
You have earned [33,500 XP]**

"What happened to Taavek?" Aderyn exclaimed. "Livia, didn't you say he'd sleep for an hour?"

"He's still asleep," Livia said, approaching them. "The revenant blight was able to take control of his body anyway. That's terrifying. I didn't realize how powerful it is."

"It's dead," Owen said. "Let's wake Taavek up and see how he feels."

It took some effort to wake the youngling, but finally Taavek let out a groan and rubbed a hand over his face. "I don't remember anything after attacking you all," he said. "Did I hurt anyone? Owen, you promised!"

"I haven't given up hope, and neither should you," Owen said. "We killed the fungus. Do you feel different?"

Taavek shook his head. "It's still there," he said. "Not as powerful, but I can feel it watching me. Owen—"

"That means one of two things, Taavek," Owen said. "Either the infection can't be eliminated by killing the main body of the fungus, or there's another one in the citadel somewhere. I'm betting on the latter. One more chance, Taavek, and if I'm wrong, we'll make it quick."

Taavek nodded. His body continued to tremble, and his left arm swung back and forth like it wasn't under his control, but his gaze was clear. "I can't take much more of this."

"We'll stay with you," Skalt said. "You're the strongest of us. You can beat this."

Taavek's weak smile made Aderyn's heart ache. "I think I want that in writing, Skalt."

Skalt punched him lightly on the arm that wasn't moving. "Like you know how to read, mumblebrains."

"That's what I like to hear," Owen said. "Aderyn, I think we need the <**Wayfinder**>." He spoke lightly, but Aderyn saw clearly his concern that they might already be too late for Taavek.

When she focused on the orb, its rings spun up immediately, and the central spike glowed dark pink. "We're closer than I imagined," she said. "There's definitely another revenant blight in Stormwatch Citadel."

"It does make you wonder how long this place has been infected," Weston said. "Like, no infected monsters other than humans?"

"I have just imagined a dragon captured and dominated by this thing," Isold said.

"You had to go and say it, didn't you?" Livia exclaimed.

Aderyn led the way back out of the hole Livia had made in the throne room wall. The <**Wayfinder**> guided her to the nearest tower room and up the stairs, past the guard room on the second floor and farther up. "This makes sense," she said. "Taavek, you were infected by a creature we met well away from the other two revenant blight rooms. If there's a link between a specific fungus and the creatures it infects, then the, um, master affecting you hasn't been destroyed, or you'd be free."

Taavek nodded. Aderyn didn't draw attention to how he went on nodding long after he should have stopped.

The stairs ended at a hallway heading west into darkness. Livia sent dozens of *orbs of light* into the air, filling the hall with a soft glow that raised Aderyn's spirits. High above, the vaulted ceiling was painted with the same kind of bright murals they'd seen below. Freta stopped and tilted her head back. "I feel I almost understand them," she said. "Like they're a Remembering Room all on their own."

"Once this is over—" Skalt shut up. He glanced at Taavek, who seemed turned in on his own thoughts and didn't react.

The <Wayfinder> led them around a couple of corners to another of the huge double doors, this one carved all over with abstract designs and with owl faces instead of lions holding iron rings. Freta stopped Owen from opening it. "I recognize some of these symbols. They're on the walls of the Remembering Room in Jasperton—not inside, outside. I think we should be careful, and not just because there could be another fungus in there."

"Understood." Owen gestured to Weston, who took up a position opposite him. As they both took hold of the rings, Taavek let out a loud moan. Livia snatched the <Wand of Deep Slumber> from its sheath, but before she activated it, Taavek waved a hand in her direction, knocking the wand away.

"Just go!" Owen commanded, and he and Weston shoved the door open. It swung slowly, as if it was caught on something, and a terrible howl of wind filled the air. Aderyn burst past the two men before the door was fully open, Assessing the room.

Steps led up from where she stood, rising to a dais ten feet above her head. Snow blanketed the steps because there was no roof, only a square hole with unlit braziers fixed at each corner. Night had fallen while they were inside, and the stormy sky was the gray of charcoal. [Darkvision] showed her the hole wasn't quite as large as the room, and the eaves provided a little shelter, not enough to matter. Aderyn saw no revenant blight anywhere, and [Improved Assess 4] gave her no clues.

Behind her, Taavek's moaning turned into a shriek, and a scuffle broke out, but Aderyn didn't stop to find out what had happened. She ran around the narrow perimeter, blinking snowflakes out of her eyes. On the second turn, **[Improved Assess 4]** responded.

Name: Revenant Blight [1]

Type: Formless

Power level: 17

Terrain: any; thrives in warm, humid environments

Attack(s): special

Immune to: mind control spells and skills

Resistant to: bladed weapon damage, piercing weapon damage

Vulnerable to: elemental fire damage, elemental cold damage

Special attacks: paralysis, dominate

Don't waste time, Aderyn. You have a bigger problem.

Immediately, another message appeared.

Name: Tempest Moth

Type: Unknown

Power level: 26

Terrain: Mountains, plains, oceans

Attack(s): bludgeoning damage, special

Immune to: none

Resistant to: weapons damage, elemental magic damage

Vulnerable to: none

Special attacks: cyclonic burst, typhoon, wailing wind, elemental air damage

The tempest moth doesn't care about the affairs of humans or any other living creature, monstrous or not. Its enormous wings generate a permanent storm system around it, and as it flies on its inscrutable journey, the storm wreaks havoc on the world below. But the tempest moth doesn't do this out of malice. It's just in its nature. And, believe it or not, sometimes the storms it brings leave behind improvements. Yes, more often it's disaster that follows, but the point is that you can't assume a creature is evil based solely on their appearance or actions, even the creatures who sow despair and heartache in their paths.

You're running out of time, Aderyn.

CHAPTER THIRTY-SIX

Aderyn searched the stormy sky for the great shadowy figure and saw nothing. That didn't comfort her. "The tempest moth is coming!" she boomed out with **[Amplify Voice]**. "We have to destroy the revenant blight now, or Taavek is dead!"

She searched her surroundings for the white sheen of fungus coating the walls. The violent winds blew snow in every direction, blinding her regardless of **[Darkvision]**. She flashed on a memory of Owen's story of that army crossing the wintry river in the dark. They had managed it, so—

Aderyn once more Assessed the space in front of her. She didn't read the text that appeared, instead fumbling forward, up the steps slick with snow to the top of the dais. At the second step from the top, her hands came down on an even smoother white surface, bumpy like boiling water frozen in place. She snatched her hands away and scrubbed them off on her trousers. Becoming infected now could be fatal.

"Up here, up here!" she shouted. She scanned the room below, searching for her friends. Moving shapes showed where the giant younglings were. She counted the smaller figures—everyone was there, and it didn't look like Taavek had attacked or hurt anyone. She waved wildly to attract attention and again shouted, "Come up here! The fungus is here!"

Only then did it occur to her to wonder why there weren't any zombies.

She spun around, Assessing the rest of the room, and saw nothing but empty space. The fungus wasn't as big as the others; it covered half the dais, but it looked withered, like it was drawing in on itself from the cold. Beneath it, mostly covered by it, lay a dark form, too big to be human. Aderyn couldn't make out details, but it was clearly a dead giant. Aderyn didn't waste time considering all the things this might mean. She drew her sword and brought it down on the nearest chunk of fungus, shattering it easily.

In the next moment, Isold was beside her, wielding the <Peacemaker's Burden> and smashing it against the dais. More fungus flew. "I see no infected creatures," he said. Then he recoiled from the dead creature at his feet. "What is *that?*"

"It doesn't matter now. Keep attacking the fungus!" Aderyn backed away and returned to the bottom of the dais. Taavek crouched nearby, gripping his head and keening terribly through gritted teeth. Freta, Skalt, and Zalk surrounded him. Zalk held Taavek's iron bar and looked ready to use it on his friend. "Watch out for enemies," Aderyn warned.

"We didn't see anyone here," Freta said. She sounded near tears. "It's too late, isn't it?"

"It's not too late," Aderyn said, willing it to be true.

She ran up the stairs to find everyone hammering away at the fungus, which lay in chunks around them. "I don't understand," she began.

A huge piece of fungus cracked and slid away from where it had adhered to the dais. Owen let out a yell that was partly a hiccup of surprise.

Congratulations! You have defeated [Revenant Blight]. You have earned [33,500 XP]

Aderyn gasped. "That's it! Everybody inside, now!"

She half ran, half bounded down the steps to where Taavek lay. He'd stopped making noise, but his fingers still twined through his hair, tugging on it. "Come on, Taavek," she said, pushing on his shoulder.

"I don't think he can move," Skalt said, his voice almost inaudible over the storm.

"That's not possible." If there was another fungus they'd missed, Aderyn was sure it was over for Taavek. The youngling had already passed his breaking point an hour ago. "Help me get him on his feet."

Skalt and Zalk put their arms around Taavek's shoulders and pulled him to sit up. He was awake, Aderyn saw, his eyes dull and unfocused but clearly conscious, and he stayed upright when they let go of him. But he didn't move any further.

Aderyn shrieked in surprise when someone grabbed her. "The door won't open," Owen said.

"What?" She was still focused on Taavek, and Owen's words made no sense.

"I said, the door won't open. None of them will." Owen turned Aderyn to face him. "Something's wrong. We killed the revenant blight, I'm sure of it, but I don't know what that has to do with the doors."

Aderyn turned an involuntary look on the sky. She still saw no giant insect figure through the blowing snow. "We have to get out of here. The tempest moth is coming."

"Livia's trying to open a hole in the wall," Owen said. "We'll figure it out."

Aderyn followed him to where Livia braced herself against the wall next to the door they'd entered by. Her eyes were closed and she was muttering something beneath her breath. "Almost—"

A flash of blue-white light illuminated the stones, tracing their outlines. Livia jerked her hands away as if they'd been burned. The light flowed swiftly away, pouring through the grooves between stones until all four walls burned with light. Light leaped from the walls to the four braziers, setting them ablaze with blue flames that burned so hotly the snow evaporated from a foot away.

Livia backed away slowly. "It says 'don't,'" she said, stunned.

"What says—Livia, are you all right?" Weston exclaimed.

"I'm fine. It wants something. I don't understand."

"*What* does?" Aderyn shouted.

Livia pointed. "That."

All eyes turned to the top of the dais. The creature of light shone there, pulsing and quivering atop the dead giant. It showed no sign that the storm bothered it.

Zalk rose from where he crouched beside Taavek. "You have to let us go," he said. "We can't survive the monster that's coming."

The creature didn't respond. Zalk walked toward it, one stair step at a time. "We're stonekin, or will be eventually," he said. "I think you understand that. What do you want?" He stopped one step down from the dais and extended a shaking hand.

With a smooth, flowing motion, the creature brushed against Zalk and then moved past him. Zalk shivered, but it looked like a normal reaction to cold and not pain.

Behind her, Isold said, "It's too late for Taavek."

Aderyn jerked around. "What? He's dead?"

"I took a chance that the infection was gone and gave him the <Potion of Life>. It did something, but it can't regenerate missing organs or brain tissue. I think the revenant blight damaged him too badly. His body is alive, but his mind is gone."

"Aderyn," Owen said, "how do we get out of this?"

They'd won, but it didn't matter. Aderyn's numb mind latched onto one thing. "That thing is keeping us here," she said, pointing a shaking finger at the creature that continued to descend the stairs. "We have to kill it."

"Kill what? It has no substance!"

The bluish light circled Freta and passed through Skalt. Owen drew his <Sunsword>. "Stay back," he said, putting himself between the creature and the fallen Taavek. "I made a promise, and I intend to keep it."

The creature paused. Then its body swelled to three times its size, encompassing Owen, Taavek, and half of Aderyn. She felt nothing, not warmth or increased cold, but the light blinded her so she had to cover her eyes with both arms.

The light immediately dwindled. Aderyn risked a glance. The creature centered itself on Taavek, who'd fallen again and whose body jerked in spasms he didn't try to stop. Owen raised his sword. "You sick bastard," he said. "I couldn't save him, but I'll be damned if I let you torture his body."

Taavek sat up.

Owen, in the process of striking with the <Sunsword>, held his blow. Taavek stood, or at least came to his feet; the movement didn't look normal, not the way it did when someone had control of his muscles and used them to stand erect. This looked more as if something had gripped Taavek by the shoulders and pulled him to his feet, not in the puppeteering way of the revenant blight, but like a friend offering a hand to someone who'd fallen.

The snow wasn't blowing as rapidly as before, and Aderyn

could now see clearly the faces of her friends and of the younglings. Taavek's eyes were closed, but she didn't think he was unconscious despite clearly not operating under his own control.

Then Aderyn remembered what the fading storm meant.

Her heart constricted with terror, and she scanned the still-stormy sky, Assessing every second. There. To the north. If she squinted, she could see the massive body.

"We *have* to get off this roof!" she shouted.

"We can't," Owen said, his voice dull. "Besides, look at Taavek."

Aderyn shook her husband by the shoulders. "Owen, snap out of it!"

Beyond him, Taavek drifted up the steps to the dais, following the glowing creature of light. Aderyn's breath sobbed out of her. Why was she the only one who saw the danger?

A voice came from everywhere and nowhere, its words rough and harsh and unintelligible. Aderyn shuddered with fear at the perfect alienness of it. Behind her, Livia said, "Say that again."

This time, it was clear the voice came from the stones surrounding them and beneath their feet. Aderyn didn't know how she could have missed it before, that it was the stones speaking. It still made no sense, but Freta said, "We're not stonekin yet."

"I am," Livia said.

The stones spoke again. "You can't," Livia said. "You can't ask that of them. They're children. It should be me. Take me."

Dread horror filled Aderyn. Livia sounded like she was near breaking, and while Aderyn didn't know what those words had been to bring Livia to that point, she didn't want to see the end result.

Again, the stones spoke, this time at length. It was easier to hear them now that the winds had died to nearly nothing. This time, Skalt said, "I understand. You have to share—you can't have form in our world unless you do. But his mind is gone. He can't agree."

"We can, though," Zalk exclaimed. "It's why we came."

"Stop," Owen said, moving next to Zalk. "It wants to take one of you over. You're too young to make that sacrifice."

"It's not your business," Zalk said. "It was always ours. This wasn't how it was supposed to go. But it's how it ends." He dodged Owen's hand, which couldn't have restrained him in any case, and ran up the steps to throw his arms around Taavek. Freta and Skalt were seconds behind him. The three younglings encircled Taavek as the snow dwindled and then faded away entirely.

Owen swore. Aderyn grabbed his arm. "It's too late," she whispered. "The tempest moth is here." Her words felt empty, meaningless, and as the great gray body descended upon them at the center of the calm, she could think of nothing but how this was, in fact, how it ended.

The four giant younglings clung to each other beneath the tempest moth. Blue-white light outlined their bodies, brilliant and painful to look at, but Aderyn made herself watch. It was the only act of defiance she could manage in the face of destruction.

The light swelled outward from the younglings, cool instead of blinding now. The tempest moth's wings flapped inexorably, pushing back against the light. For a moment, everything was perfectly still, the creature of light balanced against the creature of darkness. Then, with a soft cry that nevertheless shook Aderyn to her core, the tempest moth reared up, beat its wings once, and retreated into the storm.

**Congratulations! You have defeated [Stormwatch Citadel].
You have earned [40,000 XP]**

Congratulations! You have completed the sub-quest [The Tempest Moth].
You have earned [55,000 XP]

Aderyn realized the storm was dying, not the unnatural calm of the eye of the storm, but the natural movement of winds and clouds and snow shifting onward. She released Owen, and the two of them stared at each other with the stunned awareness of two people who have discovered they weren't about to die, after all. "I don't understand," she said. "What just happened?"

She looked at each of her friends in turn. Tears streaked Livia's face. "Those younglings," she said roughly. "That creature demanded one of their lives in exchange—there had to have been another way."

"How do you know that?"

"The stones spoke." Livia swiped a sleeve across her face.

"*You are right and you are wrong,*" someone said. It was the voice of the stones again, but this time Aderyn had no doubt she understood what she'd heard.

Four figures stood atop the dais. Aderyn recognized Skalt, Freta, and Zalk. They looked just as they always did. The fourth figure was Taavek—mostly. A sheen of blue light covered his face and body, twisting his appearance out of familiarity for several seconds before returning him to normal.

"Somebody needs to explain this," Weston said, "because—" His voice cut off as Livia threw her arms around him, burying her face in his chest. "Because anything that affects Livia so deeply worries me."

Taavek, or what had once been Taavek, waved a hand, and the remaining storm clouds vanished, leaving behind a night sky brilliant with stars. "*We never did come up with a real solution,*" he said with the stones' voice. "*You will blame us, I'm sure. But I have to ask, have you never been desperate?*"

"This," Weston said in his deepest voice, "is not an explanation."

"I don't think Taavek is capable of explaining," Zalk said. "He was the Hand, the one who takes action. Speaking is my job." He stepped away from Taavek, smiling fondly at his friend. "And even I don't know the full story. It's been so long we barely remember when giants were creatures of storm as well as stone. We only have fragments, like the saying 'for love of rock and sky,' from that time. But back then, the kings and queens of the Northlands were bound to the land and sky so the tempest moth's flight pattern could be altered. Not kept away entirely, but used to make the lands fertile."

"But the tempest moth altered its pattern a year ago," Jessemia said, "and those kings and queens are long gone. Aren't they?"

Zalk gestured at what was at his feet, now visible as skeletal remains. He didn't look as if the dead giant horrified him. "This was the last king of the Northlands. When the level cap came, and the giants abandoned Stormwatch Citadel, he chose to take a form that would let him continue to control the tempest moth. It made him undying, but not invulnerable. He succumbed to the revenant blight —we don't know where it came from, but it destroyed his body. All that was left was the control magic, and without a mortal host, it was powerless."

"And that left the citadel vulnerable to the revenant blight's spread as well as eliminating the control on the tempest moth," Owen said.

"Right. There had to be a replacement. It's why we came." Zalk smiled at Taavek again. "It was the goal of our quest."

"You mean it really was a sacrifice?" Aderyn exclaimed. "But

Taavek was braindead. He couldn't be... I mean, it doesn't make sense."

"The magic that gave the last king immortality is long forgotten," Freta said, "and maybe even impossible now if we did know it. It's because of the revenant blight and the damage it did that Taavek was taken. The missing parts of him, the ones destroyed by the infection, left a space for our glowing friend to enter. If Taavek hadn't been affected, we would have had to choose one of us. But the revenant blight's infection made the choice obvious."

"*I remember who I was,*" Taavek said abruptly. "*All of who I was. But I remember Taavek, too. Protecting you is what the Hand does. Don't cry over me.*"

"We were willing to make the sacrifice, too," Skalt said. "Trust you to make it all about you." He wiped tears from his eyes.

"*This is better. And now you can live your lives the way the stones wanted for you.*" Taavek's gravelly voice sounded as if the stones were actually speaking.

"That crazy Vorn said three of us would be remembered," Freta said, "but I don't see why it wouldn't be all of us. We all saved the world together."

"*I won't have a name for much longer. It's not important. I didn't do it to be remembered.*" The deep voice became quiet. "*And it's all right to like him, Freta. You never know what the future will bring. Just because the People don't make love matches is no reason for you to fear your feelings.*"

Freta turned scarlet and wouldn't look at Skalt.

Skalt's eyes widened. "Freta?"

"I don't want to talk about it!" Freta exclaimed. She sagged. "It's not like it matters. I know my parents—"

Skalt put a hand on her shoulder. "You have a very strange way of showing affection," he said, "making fun of me all the time."

Freta kept her gaze fixed on her feet. "I thought, if I pretended, it would go away, but—anyway. I like you, Skalt. If I could choose my husband, I'd choose you."

Skalt let out a huge breath. Then he put his arms around Freta and held her close. "Maybe saving the world will change our parents' minds."

Freta hugged him back. "Our king gave us his blessing," she said, sounding amused.

Skalt groaned. "That's just going to give him more of a swelled head, calling him our king."

"Is he, though?" Aderyn felt if she didn't start asking questions, she would burst.

"Yes," the other three younglings said. "But now we know how it works, and this destruction, losing our king, won't happen again," Zalk said.

"*I won't insist you bow*," Taavek said, sounding like himself for once.

"IT FEELS STRANGE, LEAVING HIM ALONE," ADERYN SAID as Owen shut the door to the dais room behind them.

"He has to stay, Aderyn. He's what keeps the tempest moth under control," Zalk said.

"I know, but until ten minutes ago, he was just another youngling. I feel like we're letting down our responsibility to watch over you all." Aderyn laughed self-consciously. "I know. That's ridiculous. Ignore me."

"We appreciate your care," Skalt said. "And it's worse for us, since we have to go home and explain to Oskarl and Kaarina what happened to their son. They'll want to travel here, probably, and they won't believe us when we say Taavek might not remember them when they arrive."

Aderyn's heart ached for Taavek's parents. "They'll understand, I'm sure, but it still hurts, even a loss as strange as this."

"What I don't understand," Weston said, "is how the younglings' actions ended with *us* getting credit for the Tempest Moth quest."

"I nearly forgot!" Aderyn stopped in the middle of the hall and checked her Codex. "The reward was more information about the **[Eye of the Storm]** quest. What I want to know is, if the Northlands have a king again, why doesn't that mean they'll be at peace?"

She focused on the glowing golden dot that enlarged into lines of text.

[Fated One's Destiny: Eye of the Storm]
Bring peace to the Northlands by [see Pursue the Hunters: Reward] and [restoring the king of the giants].

Sub-quest: [Pursue the Hunters]
Rimewolf packs have begun hunting giants throughout the Northlands. Their leader, Bloodmaw, is taking advantage of the destruction caused by the tempest moth to accomplish his goal, which is to drive all giants and humans out of the territory so he can rule as absolute master. Prevent this from happening.
Reward: Additional detail to the primary quest becomes available.

Sub-quest: [The Tempest Moth] COMPLETED

Reward: [100,000 XP] plus any experience gained in the course of completing the quest.

"So I was right," she said. "The giants having a king *is* part of bringing peace to the Northlands."

"Yes, but what about all those humans coming north, wanting to be part of a new human kingdom?" Weston said. "They'll have to clash with the giants, and then so much for peace."

"No idea," Owen replied, "but—does anyone remember what those other two sub-quests were? The invalidated ones? I bet, if we'd taken one of those instead, it would have tackled the problem from the humans' side."

"I'm going to agree with you, because I don't love the idea of us being solely responsible for creating a lasting peace that includes humans and giants," Livia said. "That gives us way too much power, if we can control both groups."

"Or it would drag us into the resolution, and take us away from our goal," Aderyn added. "I think I see what you mean. The **[Eye of the Storm]** quest expects us to provide a boost to one side or the other so that peace is possible. Imagine someone establishing himself as the human king of the Northlands when all those giants' cities didn't have a unifying government? There could never be peace so long as they couldn't agree on treaties and things."

Weston groaned. "But now we have to hunt rimewolves. That could take forever."

"It's just a monster hunt," Owen said. "We've already done the impossible, so how much worse can that be?"

Aderyn led the way down the stairs to the ground floor. "I feel like I ought to chastise you for jinxing us."

"I don't believe in jinxes," Owen said. "Besides, it's not like we're expected to start the hunt tonight. We've earned a rest."

Weston stopped at one of the doors they had bypassed before. "This isn't locked, and Livia looks like she's at her limit, so it's better we leave via the courtyard instead of having her open a passage for us."

Aderyn hadn't looked closely at the courtyard before, having been preoccupied with the bleak despair of the tempest moth. The moonlit view through the door was depressing all by itself, with weeds growing up between the flagstones, some of which were cracked or missing. In full daylight, it would have been worse. "Can we get some distance from Stormwatch Citadel before camping? It's unsettling."

Jessemia walked through the doorway, sniffing the air. Her nose crinkled. "I smell—"

Something big and ice-pale struck her from the side, sending her flying. It happened so fast Aderyn didn't have time to react. Instinct drove her through the doorway and to the left, Assessing as she went.

She didn't need an Assessment. The courtyard was full of pale blue wolves, most of them taller than she was. Jessemia lay in a crumpled heap, unmoving, beneath a heavy paw that pressed down on her in a way no living creature could tolerate. Ice crystals from a freezing breath attack clung to the paving stones around her.

Aderyn met Bloodmaw's gaze. The rimewolf master stared back at her, its implacable eyes marking her as its next target. "Jessemia, no!" Aderyn screamed. She drew her sword and charged.

CHAPTER THIRTY-SEVEN

She threw herself at Bloodmaw, forgetting strategy, forgetting every tactic she'd ever heard of, her whole self focused on Jessemia's still, broken body. Instinctively, she reacted to **[See It Coming]** warning her of the blast of freezing air from Bloodmaw's lungs by dropping and rolling so the attack blew past her, barely touching her hair with its searing cold.

Whiskers charged past her, shrugging off the freezing breath attack, and sank his jaws into Bloodmaw's leg. The rimewolf master shook him off, releasing Jessemia. Whiskers hit the ground, rolled, and bounded back to take up a defensive posture over Jessemia's body.

With another scream of defiance, Aderyn swung at Bloodmaw's leg, cutting deeply into the rimewolf's flesh. Bloodmaw howled, but Aderyn was too far gone in fear and fury to be affected by the sound. She struck again, desperate to get the creature away from Jessemia. It wasn't too late.

She drew her sword back for another blow, and Bloodmaw

pounced, his jaws closing over her shoulder and arm with a force that pinned her sword against her side and ground all her bones against each other. She screamed in agony and wildly, stupidly batted at Bloodmaw's muzzle with her free hand, wriggling desperately to get away. The rimewolf master dragged her into the air, snarling like a dog with a bone. The mad comparison drove Aderyn to hysterical laughter through her tears of pain. A system defeat notice flashed, but she hurt too badly to make sense of it.

With a grunt, Bloodmaw dropped her. Aderyn had just enough awareness to fall properly so she didn't twist an ankle when she landed. The bright light of the <**Sunsword**> filled her vision. "Aderyn, get up," Owen said. "We need to draw Bloodmaw away."

"I agree/*I think he understands us*," Aderyn said with [**Secret Message**].

"I know. Get behind him." Owen held his position, watching Bloodmaw's movements. The monster paced back and forth, watching Owen in return. Aderyn slowly edged away, pretending to be intent on reaching an [**Outflank**] position.

Bloodmaw tensed, his body quivering with the intent to pounce. Aderyn knew a feint when she saw it. In the moment before Bloodmaw turned on her, [**Interchange**] swapped her place with Owen's, and when the rimewolf master lunged at what he thought was a weaker target, Owen's <**Sunsword**> met his attack halfway. This time, the howl was of pain and fury.

Aderyn was already halfway to Jessemia's side. She still had a <**Potion of Life**>, so there was hope. She refused to believe otherwise.

A shrill scream from across the courtyard dragged her attention to where Freta and Skalt backed away from an enormous rimewolf, taller even than they were. Aderyn cast one despairing glance at Jessemia, then focused on Skalt and with greater effort than before used **[Interchange]** to trade places with the youngling. That time, the skill hurt, like something trying to pull her joints out of their sockets, but she ignored the pain and dove in front of Freta, aiming for the blue spots of **[Discern Weakness]** along the greater rimewolf's belly.

The rimewolf let out a yelp as Aurelon's sword scored a deep hit. It backed away, but Aderyn pressed the attack, fear for Freta's safety joining her terror over Jessemia's possible fate. The rimewolf's jaws snapped at Aderyn's head, but she ducked their ghostly outline and rolled to avoid the attack. With a shout of defiance, she thrust her blade deep into the monster's belly and twisted, sending up a gout of purplish blood that froze as it hit the air. The greater rimewolf struck her with one giant paw, its claws scoring a line down the front of her leather coat and scraping along the <**Gossamer Mail**>. It raised another paw to attack, wobbled, and slumped to the ground.

**Congratulations! You have defeated [Greater Rimewolf].
You have earned [27,575 XP]**

"Freta! Go to Skalt and stay together!" Aderyn shouted. She surveyed the courtyard, Assessing for the first time. Bloodmaw, seven greater rimewolves, ten of their lesser cousins. Several ice-blue bodies lay here and there in pools of frozen violet blood, more deaths she'd noticed only in passing. Zalk was backed up against the wall, defended by Isold, who just then let out a terrible howl that sent three rimewolves fleeing out the shattered front door of the citadel. Resistant to **[Cause Fear]** obviously wasn't the same as immune, but she hoped Isold didn't depend on that skill too heavily. The thought of it failing and leaving him defenseless terrified her.

Back near their entrance, the flagstones buckled and rolled, coming together in a roughly man-shaped pile six feet tall. The earth elemental strode inexorably toward Bloodmaw, ignoring the blows of the other rimewolves as it crossed the courtyard. Behind it, Livia tossed aside a potion vial and wiped her lips. She took a familiar solid stance and, in unison with the earth elemental, stomped the ground.

A ripple of force arrowed toward Bloodmaw from two directions, intersecting on the monster with a titanic crash of stone and earth. Bloodmaw staggered and hit the ground. Weston leaped past Owen and clambered up Bloodmaw's shoulder. He spun two knives that burst into flame the moment before he plunged them into Bloodmaw's throat. The monster roared again and swiped at Weston, who wasn't there when the blow landed.

In its moment of distraction, Owen dodged beneath Bloodmaw's front legs and struck a great two-handed blow beneath where the knives had hit. Bloodmaw dropped, crushing Owen beneath his weight, then yelped and rolled away as if stung. Owen got heavily to his feet, relieving Aderyn's mind, and took a moment to regain his balance. Another system defeat notice flashed, and Livia shouted with triumph as *hungry pit* claimed another victim.

Aderyn was already in motion, running to her partner's side, which gave her a perfect view of the greater rimewolf who came out of nowhere to rake Owen with its claws. Owen grunted and dodged the second swipe. His skin looked nearly blue from the constant exposure to the rimewolves' ice aura, but he moved as easily as if he wasn't frozen. Aderyn arrived behind his opponent and slashed at its hindquarters, **[Outflank]** bringing it around to face her just as Owen used its own momentum to slash its throat.

**Congratulations! You have defeated [Greater Rimewolf].
You have earned [27,575 XP]**

Aderyn swiped hair out of her eyes from where her ponytail had come untied. "Bloodmaw's going after the younglings!"

"Coward," Owen snarled. "Let's take him down."

They sped across the courtyard after Bloodmaw, who was intent on the three younglings now kneeling beside Jessemia's body. Zalk had joined Skalt and Freta, and none of the three seemed aware of death bearing down on them. Whiskers, on the other hand, snarled and braced himself against Bloodmaw's approach. The dire otter was tiny by comparison to the great monster, but he showed no signs of fear.

Aderyn focused on Zalk, but when she tried to summon the red cylinder of **[Interchange]**, nothing happened except a pained flutter behind her breastbone. Furious and frightened, she pushed herself harder even than **[Keep Pace]** could manage, and just as Bloodmaw reared up over the three oblivious younglings, Whiskers lunged for his throat and she and Owen attacked him from behind.

Whiskers's jaws fastened on Bloodmaw's throat, tearing a chunk of flesh away. Bloodmaw choked and coughed as if his freezing breath attack had turned back on him. Owen aimed a blow at an earlier wound, driving the <**Sunsword**> deeper. "Get them out of here!" he shouted.

"Go, go! Run away!" Aderyn yelled. The younglings startled, as if they really hadn't been aware of the danger. Zalk picked up Jessemia, and the three of them retreated, though in her final glance at them Aderyn was sure they had no idea where they meant to go. It wasn't as if anywhere was safe. Whiskers dropped to the ground, shook himself, and raced after the younglings with their terrible burden.

Another system defeat message appeared. Aderyn blinked it away and faced Bloodmaw. Purple blood stained his icy-blue fur, and one of his eyes was matted shut, but aside from the heaviness of his breathing, he didn't look on the verge of defeat. Aderyn ignored her momentary despair and raised Aurelon's sword higher. "We won't stop," she warned. Again, she was sure he understood her language.

Bloodmaw's lips curled in a silent snarl. He leaped, and Aderyn dodged and brought her sword down on the back of his neck as he passed. Bloodmaw rolled immediately out of the way of a second strike and kicked out with his hind legs like he was a cat disemboweling a mouse. He caught Owen a glancing blow on his side, knocking him briefly off balance, but Weston rushed past with another of the <**Fire Dancer's Knives**> and laid open the back of Bloodmaw's right rear leg.

Bloodmaw, poised to leap again, collapsed, and Aderyn had to roll away or be pinned beneath his freezing weight. She was so cold she couldn't remember how it felt to be warm. Flexing her fingers, she gripped her sword hilt more securely and circled the rimewolf master. Weston's strike might have crippled Bloodmaw, but Aderyn wasn't stupid enough to assume that made him harmless.

The monster's sides heaved with its breathing, which blew out in great masses of ice crystals that hung suspended in midair as if freezing the moisture in the air solid. Owen circled Bloodmaw as Aderyn did, going in the opposite direction so they ended up facing the giant rimewolf together. Weston approached from the other side, with Livia coming up behind him. Another system defeat notice registered, and Aderyn hoped that meant Isold was watching out for the younglings.

Bloodmaw closed his one good eye. Owen and Aderyn exchanged glances, and Aderyn nodded. Sometimes it didn't take a Warmaster's skills to make a plan.

Aderyn lowered her sword, and Bloodmaw leaped at her, his jaws gaping wide. Owen leaped forward, vaulted onto Bloodmaw's head, and as Weston's knife struck the back of the monster's throat and burst into flame, the <**Sunsword**> impaled Bloodmaw through his remaining good eye, all the way to the hilt.

A gust of freezing air brushed Aderyn's face and left hand as she dodged Bloodmaw's final attack. The monster snarled, a feeble, pathetic sound coming from something so enormous. Another wheeze produced the faintest whiff of cold air, and then the monster sagged in death.

**Congratulations! You have defeated [Bloodmaw].
You have earned [38,500 XP]**

**Congratulations! You have completed the sub-quest [Pursue the Hunters].
You have earned [55,000 XP]**

**Congratulations! You have completed the quest [Fated One's Destiny: Eye of the Storm].
You have earned [100,000 XP]**

Welcome to Level Twenty

Aderyn shivered, and couldn't stop shivering. Owen's arms encircled her. "Aderyn, your health is dropping, and your health bar is ice blue!"

"So is yours. It's just the cold from the freezing breath—"

Memory struck. She cast frantically about for where Skalt and the others had got to and discovered them huddled beside the door they'd entered by, surrounding a fallen form. "No!" She shook off Owen's embrace and ran, staggering and sliding as if the flagstones were covered in ice, to where Jessemia lay.

Jessemia's face was almost pure white and looked astonished. Bloodmaw's freezing breath had caught her by surprise. Whiskers crouched beside her, nudging her chest with his flat head and whimpering. Aderyn dropped to her knees and grabbed Jessemia by the shoulders. It couldn't be too late. "How much health does she have left?" she demanded.

The younglings all stared at her in shock. "We don't know," Freta said. "She's not part of our team now. Her name blinked three times, and then it vanished."

The words were like another icy blow to the chest. "That's not possible," Aderyn insisted. "She's—she's not—"

"Her name is gone," Skalt said. "I can't feel her breath."

Aderyn pressed her frozen cheek to Jessemia's lips. The icy chill numbed her so she couldn't feel anything. She shook Jessemia. "Isold! She needs healing!"

Owen peeled her hands away from Jessemia's shoulders. "Aderyn. Stop. It's too late."

"It is not too late! *Isold!*" Isold's name came out garbled in a choked flood of tears. "Somebody—I have a <**Potion of Life**>, Livia, you can make her drink it, I know—"

"Aderyn," Livia said gently.

Someone gripped her around the waist and moved her roughly to the side. "Aderyn, be ready with the potion," Isold said. "You'll know when." He lifted Jessemia to lie in his lap and clasped both her lifeless hands in his.

"What are you doing?" Owen demanded. "Both of you—"

Isold ignored him. He closed his eyes and began to sing.

In the moment before she heard the music, Aderyn's hopes rose. Then she wanted to slap him. The song wasn't magical, didn't have the powerful energy of **[Inspire Courage]** that could rouse a person to heights of bravery or even the chilling power of

[Cause Fear]. It was just an ordinary love song, one Aderyn had heard him sing a hundred times before. Had heard it recently, she realized—it was the duet he'd sung when they'd all discovered Jessemia's hidden talent for music. The song he and Jessemia had sung together.

The first verse, the man's part, drew to a close, and Aderyn held her breath. She watched Jessemia's dead face, hoping to see her friend draw breath to continue the song. In one shaking hand she held the <**Potion of Life**>, uncorked, ready for whatever came next.

The man's part ended. Jessemia still lay lifeless in Isold's lap, the terrible astonished expression unchanged. Aderyn drew a shuddering breath. Before she could speak, Isold again opened his mouth to sing.

What emerged was Jessemia's voice.

It was faint, not full-bodied as it had been that day, but it was clearly her voice, carrying the bright melody so inappropriate to this frozen night. Isold's lips moved, and Jessemia sang, her words teasing the young man with her love for him.

As the woman's part drew near to the chorus, Aderyn again waited, poised on the brink of possibility. It didn't surprise her when Isold's voice joined Jessemia's for the chorus, his marvelous tenor twining with her increasingly vibrant soprano in a harmony that brought Aderyn to tears with its beauty. Still Jessemia remained motionless.

Jessemia's voice fell silent as Isold began the second verse. Aderyn risked a glance at him. He looked weary, deep lines drawn down from the sides of his mouth and carved at the corners of his eyes, the cast of his skin yellowish in the moonlight. His voice still sounded melodic, but was it not as powerful as it had been?

Aderyn gripped the potion bulb more tightly. Surely, at any

moment, Jessemia would draw breath, or cough, or do something —Isold had said Aderyn would know when the moment was right, and Isold would never lie to her. Least of all about something like this.

Jessemia opened her eyes. In perfect silence, she wrenched almost out of Isold's grasp and convulsed on the flagstones.

Only [See It Coming] gave Aderyn warning of Jessemia's knee connecting with the hand that held the potion vial. She jerked it away before Jessemia could knock it out of her grasp. Owen and Weston flung themselves across Jessemia to still her. Isold, still gripping Jessemia's hands, never stopped singing.

"Livia, hold her head!" Aderyn gasped.

Jessemia's body continued to writhe, but her head became unnaturally still. Aderyn dove on her, gripped her jaw, and poured the <**Potion of Life**> down her dead friend's throat.

Brilliant green light exploded like a star igniting in Jessemia's throat. The light pulsed and quivered and spread throughout her body, outlining blood vessels and nerves and muscles and finally illuminating her skin so she looked like a creature of pure light. Aderyn, panting with exertion, sagged across Jessemia's body as Jessemia drew breath and let it out in a bright stream of green.

Aderyn became aware Isold had stopped singing. She gently pushed herself away from Jessemia and burst into tears when she discovered Jessemia staring at her uncomprehendingly. Uncomprehending, but alive.

"What in the *hell* was that?" Owen breathed. "Isold, you brought her back from the dead!"

Isold released Jessemia and put his hands over his face, rubbing his temples. "It was—what is it you say?—nothing short of a miracle that we achieved level twenty when we did. The [Song of Exchange] became available to me at that moment. Otherwise..."

He lowered his hands, and Aderyn gasped. He didn't just look weary, he looked *old*, his skin sallow and inelastic, his red-brown hair mostly white, his hands shaking. "Exchange," she said. "Exchange for what?"

"Isold, what happened to your health?" Livia exclaimed. "It's practically gone!"

Aderyn checked the team roster. Isold's health had dropped to nearly nothing, but she knew immediately that wasn't what had horrified Livia. "Your maximum health is three-quarters of what it should be. Isold!"

"Life comes at a price, Aderyn." Isold examined the backs of his hands, which were deeply wrinkled with prominent veins. "I don't feel ill. Just tired."

"Was I dead?" Jessemia asked. "I don't remember dying. Just a lot of noise, thousands of voices all crying out to me." She sat up, her hand on Whiskers's head, her gaze fixed on Isold. "Then I heard your song, and I followed it. It seemed the only real thing in the world, and I couldn't help but sing along. Isold, what did you —" Her eyes narrowed, and she snatched up his hand, examining it the way he had a moment before. "*What did you do to yourself?*"

Isold met her eyes. "I don't think the **[Song of Exchange]** is meant for that purpose. It's supposed to trade straight across, health for health. I took a chance—"

"You nearly killed yourself! What were you thinking?"

"I was thinking," Isold said, "I could not bear living if I let you go without a fight."

Jessemia froze. Isold removed his hand gently from hers. "Dramatic, I know," he said. "I have always been terrible at romantic talk."

"You never needed talk before," Jessemia said, her voice faint. She seemed completely unaware that anyone else was listening. "Why didn't you—"

"Because you left." Isold's voice shook. "We shared the most extraordinary experience I've ever had, and I would have given anything for it to go on forever. And you just walked out like it was nothing."

"Like it was nothing?" Jessemia sounded bewildered. "But you—I thought it was what you wanted. One night. That's all."

"I never said that! How could you not know how I felt? It should have been the beginning—"

"The beginning of what? You were leaving in the morning!" Jessemia shouted. "How could that have led to anything but heartache for both of us? You expected me to read your mind?"

Isold opened his mouth to say something, and Jessemia over-rode him, her voice shaking with fury. "You couldn't have wanted a beginning all that much, Isold. When I found out I was coming with you, I thought we had a chance, but you delivered that... that *horrid* little speech about us being professionals, and not letting personal entanglements get in the way of our friendship, and I have never felt so rejected. If that's what you call love—"

"Jessemia—" Isold looked as if she'd slapped him. "You left. I thought you didn't care. I did what I thought you wanted."

Tears trickled down Jessemia's cheeks she didn't wipe away. She laughed, a bitter, despairing sound. "Why didn't you ask me to stay, if you were so blown away by the experience? Too proud to humble yourself before someone you thought rejected you?"

"I wasn't going to push for something you clearly weren't interested in," Isold snapped.

Jessemia laughed again, but this time it was a choked sound as her tears fell faster. "And the night I tried to seduce you, how did you explain that away?"

Aderyn drew in an incautious breath of surprise, but neither Jessemia nor Isold noticed anything outside themselves.

Isold's jaw tightened. "You didn't really want that. Want me."

"You keep saying that!" Jessemia shouted. "You never once

asked how I felt. You just went on pushing me away, over and over again, telling me without words that I wasn't worth your time." Words poured out of her like she'd dammed them up for weeks.

"You don't know anything," Isold said. "I wanted you, but I knew you—" He bowed his head. "I believed you didn't feel the same. I thought you were toying with me, and I had to protect myself."

Jessemia stared at him in silence. When it was clear Isold was done speaking, she said, her words clipped and harsh, "I was right. You were too proud to talk to me. I've gone all this time believing I really was as worthless as I used to be, because the man I love—" Her words dissolved into sobs. "And now you nearly kill yourself to save me, and I don't know what to think anymore. I almost wish you'd left me dead."

"Jessemia!" Aderyn couldn't help herself. She put her arms around Jessemia and hugged her. "Don't say that!"

Jessemia clutched at her arms, not quite returning her embrace, and wept.

Isold raised his head. Aderyn glared at him, but he didn't focus on her; he had the thousand-yard stare of someone seeing a vista of horrors. In the face of his clear despair, her desire to yell at him faded. "I don't know how this all fell apart so completely," Isold murmured. "I was so sure I understood. And I was so wrong."

Jessemia drew in a ragged breath and wiped her eyes. She didn't look at Isold.

Aderyn's heart ached for both of them. She'd never been so keenly aware of a disaster she had no power to fix. "Isold," she began, but couldn't think how to continue.

Freta cleared her throat. "Sorry, maybe this is wrong, but I don't understand. Do you love each other, or not?"

That drew Isold and Jessemia's attention. Isold still looked ravaged. Jessemia pressed a hand to her lips.

"Because, if you do, then the rest of it doesn't matter," Freta went on. "I like—no. I love Skalt. And there's a good chance my parents will tell me we can't marry. But you don't have anything stopping you, do you? Nothing but a lot of misunderstood words." She ducked her head. "Sorry. That was probably not my business. I just think it would be pretty amazing to be with the one you love."

Isold focused on Jessemia. He looked older even than before, with lines creasing his forehead and marking the corners of his eyes. Again, he showed no awareness of his friends watching this exchange. "It would be," he agreed. "But I've been such a fool. Jessemia, I don't think there's any apology sufficient for what I've done."

Aderyn released Jessemia, who watched Isold warily. "No. I don't know if there is."

"I wish—" Isold pinched his lips shut for a moment. Then he said, "I love you. I wished so much that you loved me, too, and that meant—no, please, let me finish," he said as Jessemia started to protest. "Please, give me that much, and I swear I won't ask anything more from you."

Jessemia subsided. Her face was as still and almost as pale as it had been when she was dead.

"I wished I dared tell you how I felt," Isold continued, "but I was afraid—no. You were right. I was too proud to face the possibility of rejection, the one rejection that would truly break my heart. I did everything you accused me of. You opened your heart to me and I turned you down, over and over again. I don't deserve your forgiveness, but I wish—oh, how I wish you might give me a second chance."

Jessemia's lips trembled. "And when you break my heart again?"

Isold's lips quirked in a half-smile. "I wish I could promise, never again, but in the future I want to share with you, I'm sure there will be other heartaches. I can only promise that I will never again assume I know your heart better than you do."

Tears spilled over Jessemia's cheeks. "That was the right answer," she said, and threw herself into his arms.

Chapter Thirty-Eight

They left Stormwatch Citadel and its ruined city behind, retreating all the way to the river before Owen said, "We can camp here. And almost everyone needs healing."

"I hope the <**Healing Stone**> can do something about that freezing aura," Isold said. He gestured to Aderyn to sit. "We should have done this first. You are nearing the limit of what you can bear."

"I just feel cold," Aderyn said between chattering teeth.

"Well, that feeling is gradually lowering your health." Isold wielded the stone over her injured shoulder and side.

"We'll get firewood," Skalt said. "The little fire the <**Soldier's Friend**> makes isn't enough to warm everyone. We need a bonfire." He and Freta and Zalk hurried into the darkness, trailed by a handful of *orbs of light* hastily created by Livia.

"I'll go with Whiskers to catch fish. I'm starving." Jessemia went the other direction, toward the river, with Whiskers loping along beside her.

Livia swore under her breath and sent more lights flying after

Jessemia and the dire otter. "People keep running away. Give me a second to set up camp, and I can at least start water boiling for tea." She hesitated. "Um. How many tents?"

Isold looked uncharacteristically uncomfortable. "Three. No, four. I feel I should not make assumptions, even now."

Aderyn listened to her instincts. "If she comes back and sees four tents, she'll assume the worst, Isold."

Isold's weary, lined face looked suddenly younger with hope. "Do you think so?"

"I'm certain of it."

"Then, three." He smiled, a joyful expression that again made him look thirty years younger. "What a marvelous idea."

"I should hope so," Owen said. "I think my ribs are cracked, Isold. I took Bloodmaw's full weight for about three seconds, before I extended the <**Sunsword**> blade into his belly."

"I'm sorry, I was distracted."

With a fanfare of trumpets and a whirl of frenetic activity, three elegant white tents appeared, surrounding a cheerful little fire. Aderyn sank to her knees beside it and dug through the <**Knapsack of Plenty**> for the kettle. Handing it to Livia, she said, "I think Skalt was right about needing a bonfire. I can barely feel the warmth of this small fire."

"Stay close to it anyway. Your health recovery is only just keeping pace with the cold damage." Livia filled the kettle and set it to boil.

Owen joined her beside the fire. His skin didn't have that bluish cast anymore, but that might have been the firelight. He put his arms around Aderyn. "You can warm me up."

"Likewise."

They huddled together until a crash of wood rattling against wood startled them both to their feet. A short distance away, Zalk dropped another armload of branches atop the pile Skalt had made. No, not branches, but uprooted saplings with thin traceries of roots waving in the air. The three giants set to sorting the wood into piles, handing Freta the shortest ones to arrange in a lopsided cone, leaning against each other like a round tent. She gradually built up the cone until it was as tall as she.

At some point in the fire-building process, Skalt disappeared into the darkness with an empty sack and returned with it bulging with pine needles. He packed the needles in among the shortest pieces of wood, and Freta sparked a tiny flame with steel on stone that made the needles burn. Gradually, the fire spread until the cone blazed with light and heat.

Aderyn drifted toward the pyre as if drawn there by an invisible string. Finally, she felt warm. She reminded herself she shouldn't step into the fire and instead held her hands out to its heat, rejoicing in how flexible they felt. "This is the first time I've wished we had a Flamecrafter with us. Not seriously, you know, but still." She checked her own health bar and was relieved to see it had gone back to its usual cheery blue instead of the icy pale blue-white of frost.

"We do all right without one, but traveling in the north makes the idea appealing," Owen agreed. He put an arm around her waist, not pulling her as close as when they'd both been freezing.

Weston and Livia joined them, with Isold following, and the team stood together watching the bonfire burn. Aderyn noticed Skalt and Freta were holding hands. She remembered what Freta had said about love. What kind of future could the two younglings look forward to? She imagined herself in love with Owen and married to someone else. That could only end in tragedy.

She didn't know how long they all stood there, but eventually Zalk said, "Where is Jessemia?"

That sent a jolt of fear through Aderyn. She stepped away

from Owen and stared into the darkness, wishing the fire hadn't ruined her [**Darkvision**]. "She's been gone a while, hasn't she?" The thought of something else happening to Jessemia made the icy cold feeling return.

"I see her. She's at the river still," Weston said. "It's fine. Nobody panic."

"You mean because we're only due one miracle?" Owen said. He put a hand on Isold's shoulder. "Is that lower health permanent?"

"The lower maximum health, yes," Isold said. "In the sense that it will not recover naturally the way one's health reserves refill over time. I am genuinely older than I was, possibly as much as forty or fifty years older. But as it is possible to improve one's maximum through healthy living and exercise, I believe I can restore some of it in the coming weeks and months. Since all of us benefit from each other having the greatest health reserve possible, I have incentive."

"What about... you know. The, um, wrinkles," Aderyn asked.

Isold laughed. "I have no idea. I—actually, may I borrow your mirror, Livia? Thank you." He studied his face in the mirror, his expression placid. "That's better than I imagined. I may be much older, but I'm still myself. If my appearance isn't what it was, my vanity will just have to endure. And it helps that my love seems to care nothing for the change."

"She wouldn't. How awful, to spurn you for something that happened to you on her behalf," Livia said.

"I'm so glad you worked things out," Aderyn added, hugging him.

Isold returned her embrace. "I consider it another miracle that my pride and stupidity didn't cost me more than a few weeks' heartache. And was something Jessemia was willing to forgive. It will be a while before I stop imagining the pain I caused her."

"Talking things out is the best option," Livia said. "You people, bottling up your feelings. It's why I'm emotionally the healthiest of all of us. I don't believe in keeping secrets."

"Which is why you have always been open about your dancing abilities," Weston said, straight-faced.

Livia elbowed him lightly in the ribs. "I don't know what you're talking about."

"Why is everyone—oh, that feels wonderful," Jessemia said as she approached. She dangled a string of fat, silvery fish in one hand. "I understand now why you all came over here. But it's too big a fire to cook by."

"Then let us return to the other, and set about making a feast," Isold said. His expression softened as he looked at Jessemia. "We have so much to celebrate."

Jessemia wrapped her arms around his waist and kissed him. "We really do."

DESPITE ISOLD'S WORDS, THEIR DINNER WASN'T NOISY or excited. Aderyn's weariness was tempered by deep satisfaction. They'd won. It hadn't been a victory without price, as she was reminded every time she saw Isold's prematurely aged face, or when she became aware of only three giant younglings instead of four. But it had still been a victory.

She watched the younglings closely. They, too, were quiet, but from what little she heard of their conversation, they weren't despondent, just as weary as she was. On a whim, she said, "Did you receive quest completion notices?"

Zalk nodded. "The system tells us we've succeeded and can

return to the quest-giver to report. Then there's a ceremony to make us adults, and after that, the system gives us a class."

"That's when we get to find out what our skills are," Freta said. "Those are better than levels. We work hard at learning things because everybody wants to start adulthood with high skill ranks."

"I'm nervous about getting a class," Skalt said. "I'm afraid I'll be a Farmer because Pa is a Gleaner and that will benefit our herb farm. Doesn't it seem like the system puts those two together, because they're a good match?"

"It's not like you'll go on living with your pa, Skalt," Freta said. She blushed and ducked her head. "You'll be an adult and ready to marry soon."

"Let's not worry about that, sweetheart," Skalt said gently. "We don't know what will happen."

"My parents don't like your father. They say he went dark after Sifa died, and you'll be the same. But it's not true!" Freta wiped tears from her eyes and leaned into Skalt's embrace. "I want them to see you for who you are. Maybe this quest will show them."

"I hope so. Still. There's nothing we can do about it now, so let's just enjoy what we have, all right?" Skalt kissed the side of her head and hugged her closer.

"*I* think the system will make you a Healer, since you're good at herbcraft," Zalk said. "So you have nothing to worry about."

"It's so strange," Aderyn said, drawing their attention back to her. "I'm constantly discovering ways in which the People are like humans. We worry about what classes we'll get, too, because we don't get a choice, either. I hadn't even heard of Warmaster until the system made me one."

"And I thought I'd be a Stalwart because it's what my father is," Weston said. "And Isold wanted to be a Spiritsmith, not a Herald."

"I wish we could choose our classes," Skalt said. "But maybe it's like choosing our spouses, and we wouldn't make good choices if it was up to us. Maybe the system knows what will make us happiest."

"Or maybe we don't need to be guided that closely," Livia said. "You and Freta would probably do all right united, even if it is a love match. And people—I mean humans and giants both—we do stupid things, and make poor choices, but somehow we survive. I don't think it's that odd to imagine choosing your own class."

"That's true, but then look at me," Aderyn said. "Like I said, I didn't know Warmaster existed, and I certainly wouldn't have chosen it, but now I can't imagine being anything else. And a level twenty Warmaster, well, that's even more unimaginable. So there's another way to look at it, which is that we could probably choose well for ourselves, but the system comes up with possibilities we wouldn't have thought of."

"Level twenty reminds me that I haven't looked at my Codex since we reached it," Owen said. "Which says something about the nature of what's kept us from doing that."

Silence broken only by the crackling of the fire fell over the camp. Aderyn brought up her Codex and whispered, "Advancement."

Name: Aderyn
∞ Jacob Owen Lindberg
Level: 20
Class: Warmaster
Skills: **Bluff (20), Climb (16), Conversation (18), Intimidate (14), Sense Truth (22), Survival (13), Swim (3), Knowledge: Monsters (21), Knowledge: World Lore (13), Knowledge: Demons (2), Unite**
Class Skills: **Improved Assess 4 (35), Awareness (24),**

Knowledge: Geography (20), Spot (20), Discern Weakness (34), Dodge (21), Improvised Distraction (20), Outflank (29), Draw Fire (17), Keep Pace (27), Amplify Voice (25), See It Coming (31), Basic Weapon Proficiency (Swords) (18), Read Body Language (21), Basic Map Access (10), Compel (15), Spot Weakness (12), Secret Message (8), Bonded Mind (16), Sense Ambush (10), Reposition (9), Truesight (7), Darkvision (8), Interchange (2), Flash (0)

The usual excitement at receiving a new skill thrilled through her. She Assessed **[Flash]**.

> **You'll like this one, Aderyn, but the explanation is complicated. [Flash] takes you out of time for three seconds, during which it will seem like the world around you is frozen and you're the only one capable of moving. To them, you'll appear to blink in and out in an instant. You make it work by snapping your fingers three times sharply—the snap has to be audible—but you may discover, in time, faster ways to activate it.**
>
> **Within [Flash], you can do anything you ordinarily can, including use your skills or attack an enemy, though an attack won't have any effect until the three seconds are up.**
>
> **Increased ranks in [Flash] increase its duration to a maximum of seven seconds. That may not seem like much, but a second is longer than you think.**

"Wow," Aderyn breathed. "I hoped for a skill like this, but I didn't imagine it really existed. I can't wait to try it out." She got to her feet. "In fact, I'm going to try it out now."

The others watched her expectantly. "Well, what does it do?" Jessemia asked.

Aderyn snapped the fingers of her right hand three times. All the color leached from the world, leaving it a monochromatic blue the same color as her health bar. Everyone was still staring at her, but now they were frozen, Owen's mouth opening to say something, the kettle about to boil over above a now invisible fire, the half a fish Whiskers had just tossed into the air hanging suspended at the apogee of its arc.

Aderyn snatched the kettle off the spit and set it on the ground. It should have felt hot, maybe too hot to touch, but instead the handle was chilly. Urgency, the sense of using up her three seconds, propelled her to move fast. She took the empty plate out of Owen's hand and hurried around the fire to stand between Isold and Zalk. Then she stopped, breathing heavily. After two breaths, color rushed back into her surroundings, and Owen said, "You—where did you go?"

"Teleportation!" Livia said. "And without the noise of *transport*."

"Where's my plate?" Owen said.

Aderyn waggled the plate at him. "It's much better than teleportation. It's like being able to stop time for a few seconds. But I think it's something we'll need to practice, because it's my enemies I want to startle, not my friends." She returned to her seat.

"Well, we already know Isold wins the most amazing new skill award," Owen said, "but I want to know what **[Dominating Strike]** does, Aderyn."

"Oh, wow," Aderyn said after Assessing the skill. "It gives you a chance to knock an enemy back when you connect with your sword. Not like **[Overrun]**, but literally slam them backward off their feet. And the distance increases with your ranks. That could be amazing!"

"I love the sound of that." Owen rested his hand on the hilt of the inactive **[Sunsword]**.

"Mine, for once, requires no explanation," Weston said. His

body quivered, and then it looked to Aderyn like he was surrounded by a heavy, distorting field of heat haze. Everyone else gasped.

"[Invisibility]," Jessemia said. "Oh, I hope that's something I get at level twenty as well!"

"Likely, since we're both rogue types," Weston said. The heat haze vanished. Weston unfastened the <Cloak of Mists> from around his neck and handed it to Jessemia with a bow. "And, one rogue to another, you may have this with my blessing."

Jessemia giggled. "Thank you, good sir," she said with equally exaggerated formality.

"I'm not sure I'm ready for this skill," Livia said. She clasped her hands in front of her and stared at them, her brow furrowed. "[Stone Shape] transforms me into a creature made of stone. Like my arm, only all of me. It gives me all the qualities of the stone I choose, as well as some related immunities. It's fantastic."

"But you're worried," Weston said. "It's not a permanent transformation, right?"

"It's temporary. But I could see myself getting used to it." Livia looked up from her hands. "I joke about how much I love being surrounded by my element, but that's not entirely joking. It's like a mother's embrace, and maybe because my own mother isn't all that maternal, it gives me something I lacked all the time I was growing up. Every time I use [Pass Through Stone], there's a tiny part of me that thinks, what if I didn't go back? And the feeling has grown stronger as my skills have."

She hugged Weston, adding, "Don't look like that, dearest. You are more important to me than magic. It's like going to a dress shop to try on clothes you have no intention of buying, just to see how it feels. But after dealing with Kanan, and nearly losing myself, I don't take my self-control for granted anymore. I hope that makes sense."

"I think so," Aderyn said. "You mean you won't disregard your feeling that you should be vigilant against your weaknesses."

"Vigilant. Yes. That's the word." Livia released Weston and clasped his hand. "So, I'm not ready to transform. Not yet. Plus, I have to have a sample of the stone if it's one I'm not familiar with. Right now, I can only transform to granite, and that's thanks to my arm."

Weston put his other arm around her waist. "I'm glad you keep coming back to me. That's all."

CHAPTER THIRTY-NINE

No one spoke for several seconds. Aderyn, contemplating whether there was anything she might be tempted to abandon Owen for, finally said, "With everything that's happened, death and healing and leveling, I forgot we completed several quests. I know it said we completed the **[Eye of the Storm]** quest, but I want to know what part of it **[Pursue the Hunters]** was."

The silence became the tension of five people all reading the Codex.

[Fated One's Destiny: Eye of the Storm]
Bring peace to the Northlands by [eliminating the threat Bloodmaw poses to all non-monstrous races] and [restoring the king of the giants].
Reward: [100,000 XP] plus any experience gained in the course of completing the quest.

"That's not very informational," Livia said. "And shouldn't there be a new **[Fated One's Destiny]** quest?"

Aderyn re-read the entire quest chain. "I don't understand. The quests have always been offered to us automatically before. This can't be the end."

"Maybe it's not actually over until we bring the younglings back to Jasperton," Livia suggested.

"We wouldn't have gotten experience for **[Eye of the Storm]** if that were the case," Isold pointed out. "We must be missing something."

On a whim, Aderyn Assessed the first quest in the quest chain, the one that simply said **[Fated One's Destiny]**. The system didn't respond. Disappointed, she was about to dismiss the Codex when an idea occurred to her. She had marked **[Eye of the Storm]** as their primary quest back before they left Finion's Gate, and now that it was complete, there was no primary quest marked. She selected **[Fated One's Destiny]** and, when prompted to set it as primary, selected Y.

New letters scrolled across her vision, so fast she couldn't read them. "Slow down!" she exclaimed.

"Aderyn? Is something wrong?" Owen asked.

She shook her head. "Something changed when I made **[Fated One's Destiny]** my primary quest. Do that, and take a look." She skimmed back through the wall of text.

[Fated One's Destiny]
[Discover the Path] COMPLETE
[The Great Old One] COMPLETE
[Fire and Ash] COMPLETE
[Crush the Horde] COMPLETE
[Eye of the Storm] COMPLETE

**A new quest is available: [Enter Winterforge]
Accept? Y / N**

"Winterforge," Aderyn gasped. "But that's what the fake Fated Ones were after!"

"That makes no sense," Owen said. "There's no description, no more information. And yet it looks like 'enter Winterforge' is the end of the quest chain. Enter Winterforge and... what?"

"I've got a bad feeling about this," Weston said. "Fake Fated Ones have supposedly been getting visions directing them to Winterforge, and now the system is steering us that way as well. Doesn't that seem fishy to you?"

"I'm not sure I follow," Livia said.

"What's the source of those visions?" Weston said. "Because, call me suspicious, but sending the fakers to the quest location we just got looks a lot like something or someone wants to interfere with the true Fated One's quest."

The idea sent chills over Aderyn's skin. "But that—" She stopped. Had she told everyone about the system's avowal that it had never spoken to Suveer, and the implications of that silence?

"But, what?" Owen said.

Aderyn glanced at the giant younglings, who were listening with interest, and decided the time for secrecy was over. "The system isn't just chatty when I Assess things. It, um, talks to me at other times. Answers my questions, if it feels like it."

"Aderyn, why didn't you say anything before?" Owen drew back from her slightly, enough to tell her that her not having shared this important development with him wounded him. A sick, cold feeling of having chosen wrong built in the pit of her stomach. She ignored it. Maybe she'd chosen wrongly, but that didn't mean she couldn't choose better now.

"I wasn't keeping secrets, not the way you believe," she said. "At first, I wasn't sure it wasn't my imagination. Then it felt private, something I didn't want to share with anyone. And then it got to where every time it happened, some outsider was present and I couldn't reveal what I knew. You think it's bad Owen being—"

Isold coughed loudly and surreptitiously jerked his head in Freta's direction.

Aderyn blushed. "Right. I mean, either people would think I was crazy for believing the system talks to me, or they'd think I was a tool they could use. So it's just bad luck that I didn't reveal this sooner."

"You're not afraid of what we'll say?" Zalk said. "I've never heard of anything like this. Maybe you *are* crazy."

"Zalk!" Skalt slapped Zalk lightly across the back of his head.

"All right! I'm sorry! I guess I mean I understand why people would call you crazy. You must trust us more than I realized if you're willing to let us hear this." Zalk rubbed his head.

"I do," Aderyn said. "Anyway, that's all beside the point. What matters is the thing Weston said about someone interfering in our quest. Before he died, Suveer told me the system talked to him, too, but what he revealed didn't sound anything like the, um, personality I've come to know. And when I asked the system about it, the system said it had never spoken to Suveer."

Silence followed her last words, filled only by the crackling of the fire. It gave her words the feeling of some dire portent of evil. Finally, Owen sat forward and poked the fire into greater life with a long stick whose end he let burn. "You mean," he said, "there's some other entity out there that can communicate the way the system does."

"That's what I fear," Aderyn said. "I can't think of another explanation. Suveer wasn't the type to make something like that up. Worse, this entity lied to Suveer about me, like it wanted us separated the way Ruan did. Whatever or whoever it is, I'm certain it's in opposition to me. To us."

"That's terrifying," Jessemia said. "What if it has the same power the system does?"

That hadn't occurred to Aderyn. The sick, cold feeling redoubled. "Is that possible?"

"Unlikely," Owen said. "Think of all the things the system could do to screw with us. If this thing, or creature, is malicious and has the system's power, it would have acted against us directly already."

"I think we're missing the key point," Isold said. "You brought this up, Aderyn, because you suspect this entity is behind the visions the fake Fated Ones have received, is that right?"

Aderyn blinked. "Yes. I got distracted, sorry, but that's what occurred to me when Weston brought up the idea of something interfering with our quest. It seems like too much coincidence for there to be something malicious that can communicate like the system *and* for there to be a completely different something that also happens to be sending visions about the same dungeon we've just been directed to."

"But what can we do about it?" Livia exclaimed. "It's not like it's a monster we can fight. What did the system tell you about it, Aderyn?"

"It wouldn't say anything more. *Couldn't* say more, I think. It mentions rules sometimes, rules it has to obey, and this sounded like one of them."

"How can the system have to obey rules?" Jessemia said. "Wouldn't that make it not all-powerful?"

"Remember Sorrowvale," Isold said. "The system apparently wanted it destroyed, but it couldn't take action for itself. It needed us to act for it. That, to me, suggests a rule that the system can't eliminate parts of itself, as dungeons are aspects of the system. Even if those parts go bad."

"All right, that makes sense, but this sounds like the rules force it to keep secrets," Jessemia persisted. "And that could be dangerous to us."

"I admit it worried me," Aderyn said, "but now I'm not sure. It sort of proves the system is on our side, if it's willing to talk to me. I've never heard of that happening, ever. And I think it tells me as much as it's capable of, so at least it's not being deliberately deceptive."

"Okay," Owen said. "Okay. So the mystery is deeper now. I don't think we have any option but to accept the Winterforge quest and see where it takes us. Maybe that means those fakers will try to interfere with us, and maybe there *is* a malign entity out there with mysterious plans for us, but we don't know enough to deal with either of those things yet." He gestured as if selecting Y.

Aderyn touched the glowing Y and then repeated the gesture when offered the choice to set **[Enter Winterforge]** as her primary quest. "Let's see if Jessemia can tell us where it is."

"Fair." Owen straightened. "Issue quest. Guide our team to Winterforge."

Everyone turned to Jessemia. Her eyes were focused on invisible lines of text. "No luck. It says 'must have completed all quests in the **[Fated One's Destiny]** quest chain to accept.' I guess the system doesn't want to make things easy, now that you're nearly at the end."

"I had a feeling something like that would happen, so I'm not disappointed."

"What about the **<Wayfinder>**?" Aderyn exclaimed. "Grandfather said it works over long distances. It couldn't hurt to try." She dug out the orb as she spoke and clutched it in both hands. Closing her eyes, she inhaled deeply and let out her breath in a long, calming stream. She made herself focus on her heart's desire, refusing to think about how she knew nothing about the dungeon. The name would have to suffice.

A stinging pain like being stabbed with a darning needle shot through both palms. She cried out and dropped the <**Wayfinder**>, which bounced once and rolled a short distance away, unharmed. Shaking, she extended her hands. Blood coursed down both palms from puncture wounds in the fleshy base of her thumbs, and when she turned her hands over, two more tiny wounds bled freely.

The others all gasped. Isold whipped out the <**Wand of Healing**> and passed it over her hands. The green light that clung to the wounds didn't feel as soothing as it usually did, but the wounds closed up, and Aderyn washed her hands with water from her waterskin. "I guess not," she said, still shakily.

"Sounds like nothing wants this journey to be quick or direct." Owen stretched. "And now I'm ready for this long-ass day to be over. Livia, will you take us all back to Jasperton in the morning? That's not too much, is it?"

"We're going back immediately?" Freta exclaimed. "But... I was hoping for more time."

Silence fell once more, an awkward, terrible silence. Finally, Aderyn said, "I understand. You want two weeks because you're afraid it's all you and Skalt will ever have. But trust me when I tell you that those two weeks will make saying goodbye at the end so much more painful. It's better to face your future quickly than to put it off and pretend it isn't approaching."

Skalt sighed. "She's right, Freta. We have to—"

"*Don't* be reasonable, Skalt. Please. I want—" Freta squeezed her eyes tight shut for a moment. "All right. I can deal with this now. Tomorrow, we'll know one way or another."

Aderyn considered saying more. It was possible Freta's parents and Jorm might overcome their differences. It was also possible they didn't have other matches planned for their children already, and Freta and Skalt didn't have anything to worry about. But looking at the two of them, holding hands like they feared being torn apart already, she couldn't summon up any optimism for their chances.

World door opened just yards from Jasperton's city wall, and Aderyn stepped through gracefully. Maybe she'd finally mastered the knack. She stepped aside and surveyed the land, watching the distant farmers going about their business, and ended by Assessing Jasperton.

Name: Jasperton

Status: Town

Government: Elected dyad

Civilization level: 10

Resources: Healer x3, Plover x2, Wayseer x5; Level 10 crafters; Level 12 hospitality; Level 11 food supply

Jasperton represents a typical Northlander settlement of the People. Its elected rulers, Oskarl and Ragna, have a reputation for fairness and honesty that stands the town in good stead whenever it's time for them to deal with other towns. You'll notice their civilization level and hospitality are much higher than a typical human town of the same size. Giants pride themselves on their peaceful interactions with strangers and offer hospitality on levels unknown to the average human. Of course, if those strangers are violent or untrustworthy, Jasperton's citizens won't consider themselves bound by custom not to respond in kind.

You've met several of the People in Jasperton, so I won't say more except to remind you that the agreement of the mead-hall is reciprocal. If you can help them, you should. If you can help your youngling friends, even better.

"I think we need to intervene for Skalt and Freta," she said to Owen, who now came up beside her.

"Intervene, how?"

"I'm not sure. Maybe point out how successful our marriage has been, and Livia and Weston's? Encourage them to think of what will happen if Skalt and Freta end up married to other people when they have these feelings about each other?" Aderyn shrugged. "The system pointed out that we agreed to be honorable to the giants just as they're honorable to us, so it's about more than not attacking. I think."

"I'll take your instincts over someone else's certainties any day. *My* instinct is not to get in the way of other people's cultural practices, but my world's rules aren't the same as yours. Besides, I want Freta and Skalt to have a happy ending."

"Me too."

They waited as the others arrived. The farmers working around the fields—they couldn't be tending crops, could they, not this late in the season—didn't show any interest in them despite the dramatic appearance and reappearance of the *world door* oval. Eventually, Livia stepped through the final *world door* and it collapsed behind her. Owen said, "Well, younglings. We won't be able to call you that much longer, huh? What happens now?"

"We have to speak to Oskarl and Ragna." Zalk looked unusually pale, like he might be coming down with some illness. Aderyn was about to ask if he felt well when he said, "Oskarl's going to know immediately that we lost Taavek. I wish there was a better way to tell him."

"Perhaps we could go ahead of you to break the news," Isold

suggested. "Or at least to direct him to wait for you at the mead-hall, so his reaction can be private."

Zalk relaxed. "Would you? I was afraid maybe that was cowardly."

"It's not cowardly to want to spare someone heartache if you can," Aderyn said.

"The news really should come from us, but you're right, it's better if he doesn't see us in the middle of town," Skalt said.

"Why don't the rest of you go, and I'll stay here," Aderyn said. "That way, Owen can tell me with **[Bonded Mind]** when we should come, and no one has to play message runner."

She watched her friends walk away and said, "How nervous are you?"

"Surprisingly, not at all," Skalt said. "Considering that we've had the most dramatic adulthood quest anyone's ever thought of. I wish I had siblings I could boast to. That's more fun than boasting to friends."

"There's nothing left for us to do but report," Zalk said. "Everything else is up to the system now. And Oskarl and Ragna."

Freta said nothing. Aderyn didn't push.

They waited for about half an hour before Owen's voice echoed in Aderyn's ear: *Come to the mead-hall now. Oskarl and Ragna are here.*

Coming.

"It's time," she told the younglings.

As they approached the town, the noise of people talking and laughing and arguing over prices gradually rose until Aderyn couldn't believe they hadn't heard it before. They passed through the gate, with Zalk in the lead and Aderyn trailing behind, walking fast to keep up. The younglings might not have been nervous, but they walked as rapidly as if they were in a hurry to get some difficult business over with.

Gradually, conversations stopped until almost everyone on the street, from shoppers to stall merchants, was staring in silence at the three younglings. Aderyn knew the moment someone put it together that Taavek wasn't with them, because the noise picked up again, this time quiet murmurings as if no one wanted to ask for details but everyone wanted to gossip. Now *she* walked faster, nearly running. It wasn't fair for everyone else to find out something had happened to Taavek before his own father did.

Zalk led their group down the road to the windowless mead-hall and knocked boldly on the closed doors. Almost immediately, the doors swung open, and two elderly giants, one of them Durg, bowed low as if to a king. Neither of them looked up, and Aderyn thought they hadn't noticed the missing youngling. She followed Freta closely and blinked at the dimness as the elderly giants closed the doors.

By the time her eyes adjusted, Zalk, Skalt, and Freta had advanced into the room. The strange fire in the round fireplace burned low, barely radiating heat, and the room felt colder than outdoors, as if the windowless walls held in cold rather than warmth. Oskarl stood to the right of the fireplace and Ragna stood to the left. Aderyn, seeing her friends gathered to one side of the room, hurried to join them.

Oskarl and Ragna showed no interest in the humans despite Aderyn's furtive movement. Aderyn, for her part, watched Oskarl closely. It took a couple of seconds for him to realize what it meant that Taavek wasn't there. In a voice that shook with emotion, he said, "What happened to—"

"Younglings, you have returned from your quest," Ragna said, overriding him with a quelling look, but her voice shook as well. "Did you succeed?"

"We did," Zalk said, "and Taavek—"

"We must hear from each of you," Ragna said. "Tiller to Tiller, Trapper to—" She swallowed. "Tiller to Tiller. Speak."

"I succeeded at my quest," Freta said in a small voice.

"I succeeded at my quest," Skalt said.

Zalk pinched his lips tight together for a moment before saying, "I succeeded at my quest."

"There were four of you," Oskarl burst out. "What of the fourth?" It sounded like a formal statement, part of the ritual, but Aderyn remembered what the younglings had said about no one questing together and was sure this was a father's grief instead.

The three exchanged glances. Zalk stepped forward. "Taavek completed his quest. It's a long story. He's alive, Oskarl, but he can't come home."

Oskarl didn't relax. His heavy breathing was audible even to Aderyn, who lacked Weston and Jessemia's keen ears. "Alive."

"Oskarl. Focus." Ragna's voice still trembled, and her eyes were red with unshed tears. "Youngling Zalk. Youngling Freta. Youngling Skalt. As elected leader of the Tillers, I welcome you home as successful questers. Prepare for your adulthood investment."

She waved at the humans. "What follows is private. You may return later for the feast. And—forgive me—I will withhold our thanks until we know what happened that Taavek can't return." She gestured again, pointing at the door in clear dismissal.

Owen grimaced, but he led the way out of the mead-hall. When the doors were shut behind him, he said, "I understand, but it still feels like a slap, given that Taavek's fate had nothing to do with us. And we kept him alive until then. I mean, yeah, he's not dead, but he might as well be."

"Where do we go now?" Livia asked. "Does anyone know how long this investment thing takes? It's a nice day, but I don't want to stand around outside for hours."

Aderyn saw a giant waving at them in the distance. Her heart sank. "It's Kaarina," she said. "Standing around outside might be the easier option."

"She has to know sometime," Owen said. "Let's get it over with."

Kaarina hurried toward them, cheerfully smiling in a way that made Aderyn feel even worse. "You're back! Then Taavek and the others succeeded. I'm so glad. You were gone days longer than most younglings spend on their quests. I'd started to worry."

"We need to talk to you," Owen said. "Can we go somewhere private?"

THEY ALL ENDED UP IN KAARINA'S KITCHEN, SITTING ON stools big enough to fit two humans each. Kaarina stared blindly into the hearth. "He might as well be dead," she said.

"Don't think like that," Aderyn said.

"It's true, isn't it?" Kaarina rounded on her. "Don't pretend he's going to have a normal life. I can barely comprehend what you tell me, but I understand he's not fully of the People anymore. He'll never gain a class or marry or have children."

"In a sense, he is the most fully of the People of any of you," Isold said. "It's how he can control the tempest moth, by being one with rock and sky."

"But—"

"Look," Owen said, "I won't tell you how to feel. Those losses are true and painful. But another truth is that Taavek gave his life to spare his friends. He wants that sacrifice to matter. I hope eventually that will give you comfort."

"I can take you to see him," Livia said, "tomorrow, if you

want. I'm not sure it will help, because Taavek said the transformation mingled him with all the others who'd ruled the Northlands and he wasn't sure how long he'd remember being Taavek. It might be more painful than if you just remember him as he was. It's your decision."

Kaarina focused on her. "You would do that?"

"Someone has to go back. There's a Remembering Room there twice the size of the mead-hall," Livia replied. "But I want you to find peace, whatever that looks like."

Kaarina nodded, slowly. "Oskarl and I will talk. I don't know what he'll say. But... thank you."

The back door opened, and Oskarl entered. He looked as old as Isold had at the end of the [Song of Exchange]. "They told you," he said. "Good. I didn't think I could bear to break the news."

Kaarina hugged him. "It's not the end," she whispered.

Oskarl nodded. "You can all return to the mead-hall now," he said. "The adulthood investiture is over, the children—" He let out a laugh that sounded ghastly. "The returned questers have received their classes, and everyone is preparing for the feast now. You have my permission to wait there, if you want to join us tonight."

"If you're sure we're welcome," Owen said. "I can see how we might be a painful reminder. We don't want to make things worse."

"We would not be the People if we denied hospitality to those we owe much to. Zalk explained how you kept Taavek alive after that monster infected him. He would be truly dead now if not for you." Oskarl's eyes brimmed with tears. "You are welcome. But for now, I'd like you to leave our family to our grief."

"Of course," Owen said. "Thank you. And we're sorry, again."

Outside, Aderyn said, "I feel so horribly guilty."

"We did the best we could," Livia said. "*You* saved Skalt and Freta's lives when Bloodmaw went after them, so you could dwell on that instead."

That did make Aderyn feel better. "Maybe we can talk to the —I mean, to Zalk and Freta and Skalt. I'm curious about their classes."

To her surprise, the three former younglings stood outside the mead-hall as if they were waiting for their human friends. Aderyn started to Assess them, then changed her mind. It would be more meaningful if they revealed their classes themselves.

"Well?" Owen said when they drew near enough for speech.

Zalk and Skalt laughed, a little self-consciously, Aderyn thought. "I expected to feel different, becoming an adult," Zalk said. "I still feel like a kid, like I don't know what I'm doing."

"Our birthdays are less than a month away," Skalt said. "Maybe it won't feel so strange then. But you're right, adulthood at age eight seems weird."

"Come on, tell us about your classes," Jessemia urged. "We're all dying to know."

"Baker," Zalk said. "I never thought about doing that. I've never cooked anything in my life. But it's exciting, you know? Like there's a part of me waiting to be revealed."

"I thought I would be a Farmer or a Herder, like my parents," Freta said. "But I always secretly wanted to be a Wayseer, and that's what the system chose for me!" She looked happier than she had all day.

"What's a Wayseer?" Aderyn asked.

Freta pointed at Jessemia. "It's like Pathseer, only without fighting skills. I can locate things, and navigate by the stars, and I have a system map, even!"

"That's so exciting!" Jessemia exclaimed. "We should compare skills. Maybe we can learn from each other."

"Skalt?" Isold said.

Skalt's eyes reddened with tears. "It made me a Scribbler," he said. "I'm doing what Mam used to. It—" The rest of his sentence came out choked. Freta put her arms around him as he wept.

"Skalt, that's beautiful," Aderyn said.

Skalt nodded and wiped his eyes. "Pa's going to hate it. He hates every reminder of her. But it doesn't matter. I'm moving out tonight."

"Where will you go?" Freta asked.

"I don't know. Somewhere. But I won't live under his roof any more. He's so angry, all the time, and I never know—I mean, he's never raised a fist to me, but maybe it's just a matter of time." Skalt's words rang with conviction.

"If we can help," Owen began.

"You can't. Sorry to be abrupt, but it's nothing anybody but me can fix." Skalt smiled. "I should have realized that a long time ago. I just wish tonight was now. I want this over with."

"That's true of a lot of things," Freta said.

CHAPTER FORTY

The mead-hall was packed even fuller than the last time they'd been there for a celebration. This time, the giants danced, riotous dances with much gesturing and stomping of feet. Aderyn had tried to join in and immediately had to run to avoid being tripped over or stepped on. Now she sat with Owen and watched the cavorting giants in their colorful celebration clothes. "And I thought our parties were wild," she said.

"You've never seen a rave. I hear those make this look tame."

"I choose to pretend you didn't make a nonsense reference." She rested her head on his shoulder. "I finally feel like the quest is over. This part of it, anyway. It's like I've been tense for weeks, and now I can lay that burden down."

"We haven't started searching for Winterforge, sweetheart. It's a little early to relax."

"Nevertheless. It's a moment of peace."

Owen nudged her. "That moment is over. Look."

The dance had ended, and the dancers were moving around

the room in the manner of people ready for a different activity. But Aderyn saw immediately what Owen meant. Freta, with two taller giants in tow, was approaching them. Freta wore the determined look of someone getting ready to jump off a cliff into a pool she wasn't sure was full.

Owen and Aderyn sat up as Freta came to a stop in front of them. "These are my parents, Ulla and Bron. Mam, Pa, I want to introduce the humans Owen and Aderyn. They're married to each other," Freta said all in a rush. "Owen and Aderyn, will you tell my parents how you became betrothed?"

Aderyn understood what Freta was getting at. "Human parents don't arrange their children's marriages," she said. "We get to know one another, and fall in love, and if we decide we're suited, we unite with the system's blessing. The same as the People, I imagine."

Ulla and Bron nodded politely, but Aderyn could tell they were mystified about what the point of this conversation was.

"I think what Freta wants us to share with you," Owen said, "is that our marriages are happy and solid despite our doing things differently than the People do. My parents, and Aderyn's parents, raised families and shared joy and heartbreak, and Aderyn and I plan to do the same."

"I hope you're not suggesting that it's a superior way to ours," Bron said gruffly.

"No. Not superior. Different. And in a way that produces the same results." Owen clasped Aderyn's hand.

"I wanted them to tell you so you'd believe a love match can be as good as an arranged one," Freta said. Her hands were trembling, but her voice was strong. "Because I'm in love, and I don't want to marry anyone but him. And I want your blessing."

"Who—you mean, Zalk? He's a decent boy, true, but you're too alike to be a good match."

Freta shook her head. "He's not the one. But the one I'm talking about is, is, I know you don't think highly of him—"

Bron's heavily lowering brow puckered over his eyes. "Oh, thunderation, you're talking about Skalt, aren't you? I knew we should have made Oskarl send you away separately!"

"He's not a bad person, and it's not his fault who his father is," Freta exclaimed. "He loves me, too, and I think we will make a good match—"

"You can't know that. You're a child. Children should listen to their elders."

"She's not a child, Bron," Ulla said. "Freta, I know you think you're in love—"

"Excuse me," Aderyn said. "I'm sorry, I wouldn't intrude except that I wanted to stop you before you do something really foolish."

"Don't call my wife a fool," Bron said.

"I didn't! It's just that you shouldn't tell Freta you know her feelings better than she does. That says *you* think she's still a child and not capable of making her own decisions. It's the sort of thing that leads to Freta and Skalt running away together and you never seeing your daughter again."

Ulla frowned, but said nothing.

"Can I say something more?" Aderyn went on. She didn't wait for Bron to agree. "I've watched Freta and Skalt for a while now, and I think they're deeply attached to each other. But I could be wrong. Maybe they're wrong, too, and in a year they'll have fallen out of love with each other. But they're really young still, adults or not, and they don't have to marry immediately. That means you have time to watch them, too. See if it's a match you can approve of."

"I'm never going to approve," Bron said. "Skalt is shiftless and he's got an angry wastrel for a father. That's not a life I want for my daughter."

"He is not!" Freta shouted in a voice that brought the room to stillness. "It's not his fault Jorm hates everyone! You're not being fair!"

Someone arose from a corner where he had been the only one not dancing. "You want to take this outside, Bron?" Jorm growled. "I won't put up with being insulted."

Skalt emerged from the crowd and approached his father. "Pa, don't."

"Shut up. This doesn't concern you, Skalt."

"It does so!" Skalt exclaimed. "You're going to ruin my chance for happiness by proving you're the horrible person everyone thinks you are, all because Mam—"

"You don't know anything about it," Jorm said. "She made me a better person. I lost her."

"I lost her, too," Skalt said.

Jorm focused on Skalt for the first time. "You think that makes it better? Like we're sharing grief?"

"It should!" Skalt shouted. "Us coming together, not you falling into some dark pit and lashing out at everyone like you're a wounded animal instead of a man! You think she'd be happy if she could see you now?"

Jorm bore down on Skalt, raising one meaty fist. "Don't you dare tell me what she wanted!"

Skalt didn't move. He stared up at his father fearlessly. "Hit me, and you really will betray her memory."

Jorm froze. His heavy breathing shook his whole body. Gradually, he lowered his fist. "By rock and sky," he whispered. "You looked just like her, just then."

"I know that makes it harder," Skalt said. "But we can't go on like this. Mam's gone. We aren't. If you can't come to terms with that, I'm moving out tonight. I'm tired of everyone thinking I'm just like you, letting the farm go to ruin because I'm shiftless. I want to prove I'm worthy of Freta. And that can't happen if I'm marked by your actions."

The murmur that went up when Skalt mentioned Freta nearly drowned out Jorm's reply. "It's too late for me."

"No, it's not," Skalt said. He raised his voice over the noise of the crowd. "And it's not all your fault. Nobody gave you compassion in your grief. You People—you all looked for reasons to avoid him, didn't you, because he's short-tempered and doesn't have many friends, when you would have circled round anyone else."

His eye fell on Oskarl. "Oskarl, you lost your first wife young. Didn't it occur to you how Pa must have felt? Why didn't any of you reach out to him? To us? Pa made his choices, but you sure did your best to make the wrong choices the easy ones."

"I don't need charity from anyone, boy," Jorm said. His voice trembled.

"I'm not a boy," Skalt said. "And you do. We all do. It's what makes us strong."

He addressed Ulla and Bron. "I know we're too young to marry, whether for a love match or for an arranged one. I haven't always been admirable, but I hope you'll give me the chance to prove I'm not that boy anymore. Then maybe in a year or two, you'll decide it's the right match, after all."

He looked at Freta, who was silently weeping, and reached out a hand to her. "Is that something you can live with, sweetheart? Because I'd wait a dozen years if it meant marrying you in the end."

Freta smiled through her tears and took his hand. "It's more than enough."

Skalt squeezed her hand once and released her. To Ulla and Bron, he said, "I promise to behave honorably. No sneaking around to be with Freta behind your backs. But I'm not going to conceal my feelings, even though it's not what the People do."

"No, it isn't," Ulla said. "But—" She cast a quick glance at Owen and Aderyn. "Maybe it's not such a strange idea."

"Don't think we won't be watching you," Bron said. "I won't match my daughter with a layabout."

"I count on you watching," Skalt said. "Zalk, can I take you up on your offer of shelter tonight?"

"You don't have to do that," Jorm said. His deep voice sounded raw, like he'd screamed at Skalt instead of speaking. "I don't want you to leave."

For the first time, Skalt looked uncertain. "You're just saying that so you don't have to be the wastrel whose own son cast him aside."

"I'm sure that's how it looks." Jorm sounded so defeated Aderyn's heart went out to him. "You and me, boy—I mean, Skalt. We've not lived the way we should, and I'm responsible for that. You were right. Sifa was gone, and I thought that meant I had nothing left. I never thought of what it meant for your future, me sinking into my sorrow. I'm sorry, son." He extended his hand to Skalt.

Skalt looked at the hand his father offered him like he wasn't sure it wasn't going to turn into a fist. In the silence, Oskarl spoke. "I'm sorry, too, Jorm. Skalt is right—we weren't compassionate. You both should have had our support."

Still, Skalt hesitated. Jorm, his head bowed low, didn't move, but his hand trembled. Aderyn silently urged Skalt to choose without knowing which choice she wanted for him.

Skalt breathed out deeply. He took his father's hand and squeezed it. "We can start again," he said. "I know it's not too late for us, if we can admit our failures."

"I'm ornery and short-tempered," Jorm said. "I don't know if I can. I'll probably make a mess of things again."

"We'll deal with it. Together." Skalt put his arms around his father's shoulders.

Oskarl cleared his throat. "We dance for new beginnings, when a child becomes an adult, but there's more than one kind of beginning. Jorm, will you join me?"

Jorm's head snapped up. "What, me? You know I'm not graceful."

"It doesn't matter. Dance together with me, and let's make another new start."

The floor cleared, all the adults moving to the edges except Oskarl. Aderyn watched, mystified, as the musicians with flute and bell and those fat-bellied stringed instruments struck up a different song. The slow beat had nothing in common with the bright, frenetic music the dancers had leaped and spun to. It throbbed through Aderyn like the heartbeat of some ancient creature that lived deep in the snow-covered forest, or something that loped endlessly across the northern plains, running forever without tiring.

The giants began tapping their feet to the rhythm, though their size made the taps sound more like thumps. Oskarl crossed his arms over his chest and stepped wide, his leg describing a semicircle before he set his foot down inches from where it had started. He kept doing this, going from one foot to the other, faster and faster until he was hopping and kicking out with each step. His whole attention was focused on Jorm, who continued to watch him with astonishment.

Just as Aderyn was sure Jorm would break and run out of the mead-hall, the giant stepped forward, crossing his arms as Oskarl had done and beginning the same slow movements. Where Oskarl was lithe and graceful, Jorm's steps were ponderous, and he didn't quite match the music's rhythm. But as his dancing sped up, his awkwardness fell away, and soon the two giants, one dark-haired, the other blond, were dancing in unison.

The music didn't change, but in unspoken accord Jorm and Oskarl unfolded their arms and clasped and released one another's hands in a complicated pattern, high and low and across bodies as their legs moved to a different pattern. It reminded Aderyn of her childhood, of games played by clapping hands faster and faster until one person missed the beat and everyone dissolved into laughter. This, though—she couldn't imagine Oskarl or Jorm missing. It felt more like ritual than dance.

Oskarl spun, one entire revolution, and returned to his position to clap hands without missing a beat. A second later, Jorm did the same. Neither of them looked dizzy, or tired, or even overwhelmed by the volume of the music and the thunderous stomping of everyone around them. Aderyn's head ached from the thumping, but she couldn't imagine excusing herself. She was no giant, she had no idea what it all meant, but she could feel the importance of the dance in her bones.

The music sped up until the notes came impossibly fast, and Oskarl and Jorm matched their speed. Just as Aderyn thought she would explode from the pressure, the musicians hit one last powerful chord, the watching giants slammed their feet against the floor one final time, and Jorm and Oskarl stopped at that instant. Their hands were clasped as if they meant to arm wrestle one another.

No one moved. Both Jorm and Oskarl were breathing heavily, but they held that wrestling pose for several seconds. Then Jorm said, "I accept your generosity," and Oskarl replied, "I accept your gift," and the two men separated. Cheering rose up from the crowd, which surged to encompass the pair. For the first time since Aderyn had met him, Jorm smiled.

"Do you suppose we'll ever understand what that meant?" Owen said over the noise of the cheering.

"Probably not. We can ask, but it felt like something you have to be born a giant to really get." Aderyn rested her head on Owen's shoulder. "I'm honored to have witnessed it. Giants, Owen! It's just hit me what that means to us. To all humans, I mean."

"Challenges and clashes," Owen said, "but since you're you, I'm sure you meant opportunities and happiness."

"You know me so well," Aderyn replied, kissing him.

SHE AND OWEN AGAIN SLEPT IN OSKARL AND KAARINA'S house. Aderyn hadn't wanted to impose on them in their grief, but she understood giant culture enough not to protest when they offered. In the morning, Livia would take the two giants to Stormwatch Citadel to see Taavek and decide what to do about the Remembering Room. Aderyn hoped the journey would bring them peace.

She lay wakeful in the enormous bed after Owen fell asleep. For once, **[Darkvision]** wasn't a blessing, because the size of the room and the daughters' toys and belongings were clear as day and gave her something to look at that distracted her from sleeping. Finally, she closed her eyes and told herself she was going to fall asleep.

Half an hour later, she gave it up as a lost cause. She dressed, put her boots and coat on, and left the house. The moon, waning toward its half, still gave plenty of light, especially as it reflected off the snow still clinging to the steep roofs after the last storm. Whatever time it was, it was late enough that few windows were lit, though the ones that were glowed softly through the thin stone. The light looked more like sunrise than candles or lanterns.

She reached the gate and stood for a moment looking out over the farms. Only the nearest were visible even to her enhanced vision. None of them were lit. She could easily imagine herself the last living person in the world, a fancy she entertained for about three seconds until it became frightening.

On a whim, she opened her Codex and reviewed the [Fated One's Destiny] quest. She skimmed past the list of completed quests and focused on the final line: [Enter Winterforge]. The two words no longer filled her with dread. True, they might mean anything, but rather than intimidating her, they filled her with confidence. She wasn't going to become overconfident, of course, but there was no reason to think the quest was impossible.

Nothing I give you is impossible, Aderyn. But you might wish it was.

Aderyn startled. "What do you mean? Why would I want an impossible quest?"

Success means change. Change can destroy. Consider what you're willing to give up. You don't have any idea what will be asked of you soon.

"We went into this because we want to answer the question of what the Fated One is supposed to do, and then decide if we want to do it. Was that wrong?"

Sometimes knowledge has action bound up in it. Once you know a thing, you may have no choice but to do it. Soon all

you'll be able to do is move forward. If you're not sure, back out now.

"You can't possibly want us to stop?"

I want you to make your own choices, not have them made for you.

There was no voice behind the silver letters, but Aderyn felt the intensity of the words regardless. "We've come too far to stop now."

That's never true. But I get your meaning. In that case, I can offer you two pieces of advice before running up against what I can't say. One is to remember that as strong as you are together, none of you are weak when you're apart.

No more words appeared. Aderyn, concerned, asked, "What's the second?"

Beware Winterforge.

"Beware Winterforge? But—that's the quest you gave us!"
No response came. Aderyn felt cold despite her wonderful coat. Seeing *those* two words written out terrified her. How could the system give them a quest and then turn around and warn her against it? It suggested something else waited for them at the conclusion of that quest. Something they might have trouble facing.

She tilted her head back and stared at the clear night sky. The stars blazed brilliantly bright to the west and faded the closer they were to the moon. That seemed portentous, a warning about not seeing things clearly when you were too close to them. How close were she and her friends to Winterforge, and what danger did it pose them?

The stars gave her no answers. Shivering, she drew her coat close around her and headed back to Oskarl's house. Tomorrow was soon enough to worry about the future. The system was right: they were strong together, and they would stay that way.

But she couldn't help thinking about what might tear them apart.

Appendix: Character Sheets

NOTE: These character sheets represent the status of the companions at the end of the book, which means it reveals everything the companions learn about their skills throughout the story. If you haven't finished the book, don't read this unless you don't mind spoilers!

Name: Aderyn
∞ **Jacob Owen Lindberg**
Level: 20
Class: Warmaster
<u>Skills</u>: **Bluff (20), Climb (16), Conversation (18), Intimidate (14), Sense Truth (22), Survival (13), Swim (3), Knowledge: Monsters (21), Knowledge: World Lore (13), Knowledge: Demons (2), Unite**

<u>Class Skills</u>: **Improved Assess 4 (35), Awareness (24), Knowledge: Geography (20), Spot (20), *Discern Weakness (34)*, Dodge (21), Improvised Distraction (20), *Outflank (29)*, Draw Fire (17), *Keep Pace (27)*, Amplify Voice (25), See It Coming (31), Basic Weapon Proficiency (Swords) (18),**

Read Body Language (21), Basic Map Access (10), Compel (15), Spot Weakness (12), Secret Message (8), *Bonded Mind (16)*, Sense Ambush (10), Reposition (9), Truesight (7), Darkvision (8), Interchange (2), Flash (1)

Italics are paired skills with partner

Name: Jacob Owen Lindberg

∞ Aderyn

Class: Swordsworn

Level: 20

<u>Skills</u>: Assess (16), Awareness (20), Climb (15), Conversation (18), Sense Truth (17), Spot (17), Survival (12), Swim (13), Knowledge: Demons (2), Unite

<u>Class Skills</u>: Superior Weapon Proficiency (35), Advanced Armor Proficiency (29), Knowledge: Monsters (18), *Exploit Weakness* (34), Dodge (23), Parry (23), Improved Bluff (20), *Outflank* (29), Trip (11), *Keep Pace* (27), Disarm (14), Intimidate (20), Charge (14), Two-Weapon Fighting (19), *Read Body Language* (21), Basic Map Access (10), Overrun (13), Shatter Confidence (8), *Bonded Mind* (16), Weapon Mastery (longsword), Anatomist (12), Combat Momentum (8), Crippling Strike (4), Whirlwind Attack (2), Dominating Strike (0)

Italics are paired skills with Warmaster

Name: Weston

∞ Livia

Class: Moonlighter

Level: 20

<u>Skills</u>: Assess (18), Climb (18), Conversation (16), Intimidate (16), Survival (12), Swim (6), Knowledge: Social (17), Knowledge: Demons (2), Unite

 Class Skills: Pick Locks (23), **Advanced Sneak Attack** (22), **Superior Weapons Proficiency (18), Advanced Armor Proficiency (18), Improved Detect Traps (24), Disable Traps (22), Improved Spot (27), Awareness (20), Dodge (21), Stealth (27), Improved Bluff (20), Dirty Fighting (15), To the Heart (25), Hide (14), Improved Thrown Weapons Proficiency (20), Disguise (6), Hide in Plain Sight (10), Improved Evasion (13), Basic Map Access (10), Escape Artist (8), Unarmed Combat (5), Improvised Weapon (6), Glibness (5), Improved Sense Truth (19), Coup de Grace (5), Slippery (1), Invisibility (1)**

Name: Isold
  Class: Herald
  Level: 20
  Skills: Assess (16), Awareness (20), **Bluff** (15), Climb (9), Conversation (13), Intimidate (10), Sense Truth (22), Spot (20), Survival (11), Swim (5), Knowledge: Demons (3)
  Class Skills: Perform (singing) (28); Knowledge: Magic (19); Knowledge: Monsters (21); Knowledge: History (20); Knowledge: Social (15); Knowledge: World Lore (19); Identify Magic Items (22); **Charm** (23); Distraction (16); Improved Map Access (20); Inspire Courage (20); Fascination (17); Persuasion (15); Perform (drum) (17); Suggestion (17); Resist Magic (13); Shout (9); **Hypnotize** (16); Find Object (10); Coercion (9); Break Enchantment (11); Perform (flute) (8); Cause Fear (9); Sleep, Mass (8); Mimic (2); Compulsion (4); Greater Shout (1); Song of Exchange (1)

  Name: Livia
  ∞ Weston
  Class: Earthbreaker

Level: 20

Skills: Assess (11), Awareness (13), Bluff (11), Climb (6), Conversation (14), Intimidate (20), Sense Truth (15), Spot (16), Survival (11), Swim (6), Knowledge: Demons (2), Unite

Elemental Powers: Earth, stone, acid

Class Skills: Knowledge: Magic (25), Matchless Elemental Blast (earth spray, shower of small stones, rain of large stones, stone sphere shrapnel, burning rocks) (22), Earth to Mud/Mud to Earth (14), Mage Armor (shifting stone slabs) (18), Excavate (14), Summon Elemental Hammer (11), Basic Map Access (10), Tremorsense (13), Sculpt Earth/Stone (13), Speak With Stone (8), Pass Through Stone (8), Counterspell (4), Earthquake (3), Stone Shape (0)

Spell List

0-level spells: Daze; Drench; Light; Telekinesis, minor; Mending; Freezing Ray, minor; Root, Spark

1st Level spells

Air Bubble; Break; Force Shield; Grease; Heat Metal (slow); Loose Bonds; Mudball; Sunder Weapon; Thunder Punch

2nd Level spells

Create Pit; Dust Cloud; Earth's Endurance; Thunderstomp; Mirror Image; Mud Minion; Improved Mending; Protection from Fire, Mass (big earth dome); Skip

3rd Level spells

Iron Spike Attack; Thunderstomp, Greater (directed); Clairvoyance; Dispel Magic; Immobilize; Telekinesis, Greater; Daylight

4th Level spells

Stone Ladder; Stone Sphere; Transport, Minor; Invisibility (self); Earth Glide; Stone Fist; Daze, Mass

5th Level spells

Hungry Pit; Dismissal of Demons; Scry; Lighten Object; Darkvision; Passwall; Burrow

6th Level spells

Move Earth, Major; Stoneskin, Mass; Invisibility, Mass; Dispel Magic, Greater; Truthspeak

7th Level spells

Immobilize, Greater; Sunburst; Reverse Gravity (localized); Summon large earth elemental; Greater Scry

8th Level Spells

World Door; Greater Polymorph; Launch; Iron Body; Crystal Wall

AND NOW A SPECIAL MESSAGE...

Did you enjoy this book? Want more LitRPG adventure goodness? Then the LitRPG Books Facebook group is for you! Find new recommendations, connect with fellow readers, and more!

About the Author

In addition to the Warmaster series, Melissa McShane is the author of many fantasy novels, including the novels of Tremontane, the first of which is *Servant of the Crown;* The Extraordinaries series, beginning with *Burning Bright;* and *The Book of Secrets,* first book in The Last Oracle series.

While her home remains in the mountains out West, she currently lives in Kerala, India, with her husband and two rambunctious Persian cats who believe they own the house. She wrote reviews and critical essays for many years before turning to fiction, which is much more fun than anyone ought to be allowed to have.

You can visit her at her website
www.melissamcshanewrites.com
for more information on other books and upcoming releases.

To subscribe to her newsletter, which is published monthly, visit **www.melissamcshanewrites.com/contact-me-2/join-my-mailing-list**

ALSO BY MELISSA MCSHANE

Champion of the Crown

Ally of the Crown

Stranger to the Crown

Scholar of the Crown

Servant of the Crown

Exile of the Crown

Rider of the Crown

Agent of the Crown

Voyager of the Crown

Tales of the Crown

COMPANY OF STRANGERS

Company of Strangers

Stone of Inheritance

Mortal Rites

Shifting Loyalties

Sands of Memory

Call of Wizardry

THE DRAGONS OF MOTHER STONE

Spark the Fire

Faith in Flames

Ember in Shadow

Skies Will Burn

THE CONVERGENCE TRILOGY

The Summoned Mage